THE OPAL DRAGON

James. A. Calderwood

For Glenys

IBSN NO 9781503219526

Chapter 1

The Philippines

Ali had been following the old silver merchant for three weeks to try to work out a pattern to his coming and goings from his shop to his home in the early evening. He had found that the merchant varied the route taken to his home during the weekdays but on Saturday nights when he had to carry the large kit-bag with the week's takings he would take the most direct route to his house. There was a dark deserted part of the trip in a small lane going past unused old warehouses. The broken windows gaped out from the crumbling walls behind the toothy bars.

The cobbled laneway leading down this lane was too narrow for a car to fit. The only traffic could be the push carts and bicycle rickshaw type of vehicles. Trash lay strewn over the cobblestones and heaped against the dirty walls. The fetid air was clinging to the walls and all who passed by.

There was a doorway set into a wall just around the corner of this dingy alley-way. Ali who had been following the merchant had run down the parallel alley way and crossed into the alley and hid himself in the dark doorway,

The steps of the old merchant could be heard hurriedly walking his way toward the hiding place. He was ready to spring out. The merchant quickly passed by not seeing the hiding lad.

With a flying leap Ali launched himself out of the doorway and using his shoulder hit the old man in the middle of the back, the old man tumbled forward using the bag to break his fall. Ali grabbed onto the handle of the kit-bag after the old man toppled to the ground. He tried to pull the bag out of the old man's grasp, to no avail; the old man had a strong grip on the handle. The old man started to scream, "Help, thief, help me I am being robbed."

The old man grasped Ali's other arm and started to pull himself up, his grip was surprisingly powerful; the old man swore at Ali as he struggled to retain his feet, Ali felt that the surprise attack was starting to be turned in the favour of the old man. He was in trouble, he let the handle of the bag go, and then with difficulty, reached into his pocket and grabbed the handle of the flick knife he always carried, as he took it out of his pocket, he pressed the release of the knife blade, the blade shot out of the handle, he felt the click as the blade fully opened. He pushed the knife blade into the old man's chest. The old trader let go of Ali's arm and the bag and grasped at the knife in his chest, he let out a loud scream.

After a short while Ali heard the noise of people yelling in the distance, he grabbed the large bag and ran as fast as he could away from the sound of the mob. He could hear the mob stop at the old man, then talk to him then start to run toward where Ali had left the scene of the crime. As he fled, he knew the area he was travelling very well, as he had lived in this part of town all of his nineteen years and had played through these alleys with other children from when he was a child.

Ali's mother Zeena was a local prostitute, He survived by working the markets, pilfering from any unsuspecting stall holder and being a pimp for his mother. The robbery of the trader was the first try at a real robbery.

The rowdy mob noise had abated as he turned the corner for home; Ali could not hear the yelling of the mob now. He was extremely exhausted from running and carrying the heavy kit-bag, when searching in his pocket, he could not find the door key.

He banged on the door of a crumbling old building, he banged again. Finally, the door opened and a woman in a torn blue silk dressing gown, she scowled, then said "I told you not to come home early tonight, I have a customer, where is your key?" Ali was puffing from the effort of running with the bag, "I am in trouble, I have lost my key, let me inside," Zeena stepped back and Ali ran past her carrying the heavy bag. "What have you got there?", she yelled after him as he fled, Ali turned back, "You will find out soon."

He went to his small room and turned on the dim light. He lifted the case onto his bed, and then tried to open it by twisting and pulling but the lock was surprisingly strong, he left the case and went to the cooking room and selected a pointy knife from a drawer in a cupboard. As he walked back to his room, he could hear Zeena urging her lover to have more sex. She was desperate to keep the waning numbers of customers which visited her.   After some effort with the knife the lock snapped open, Ali tipped the contents of the case out onto his bed, there were six small gold bars and fifteen silver ingots, and some finished jewellery with gemstones set in them and a large lot of bank notes. The wads of money were thick; Ali started to count a wad of US dollars. There were five thousand dollars, after thinking for a short time he counted out a thousand to give to Zeena to help with the finances as she was having a hard time coping.

In her younger days Zeena had been a very beautiful woman and commanded high prices for her services. Childbirth, drugs and now being nearly fifty years old had taken their toll. Her quality clients and generous payments had diminished considerably.   There had been some clients who were very violent. Although he was small in stature Ali had tried to help Zeena, when he had been in another part of the house. He would come to help when he heard the yelling and abuse, and had been assaulted by some of these men on many occasions.

   He picked up the kit bag and carried it to the door of the house. He then opened the door, careful not to make a sound put the heavy bag down, then stepped out into the street and looked each way along the dimly lit street. When he was sure he would not be seen, he pulled the bag from the doorway, then slipped out of the house, then took the kitbag and headed for the Wharf area. He had a special old deserted warehouse in which he used to hide some of the spoils of his small pilfering.

The quarter moon was enough for him to see as he quickly ran through the dim streets. He was barked at by a very large dog as he passed a fenced in area. The dog hit the fence with force, rattling his resolve. Finally, the door with the roofing iron sheets screwed to it to keep out vandals was in front of him.

With some effort Ali pulled one corner of the iron aside, some of the screws had pulled out of the rotting wood of the door; he then slipped the kit-bag inside the gap, he then followed it through the hole. There was just enough moon-light filtering through the broken windows behind the steel bars to navigate to the fallen down inside wall. He pulled a pile of bricks away to reveal a deep niche in the solid part of the wall, he pushed the bag inside then built a dry wall across the entrance to the niche with some of the old bricks, then scattered the rest of the bricks to look as if they had fallen down. Ali pushed the screws back into the holes in the door to make the entrance at least look impenetrable.

Three times Ali banged on the door before Zeena opened it "Where have you been?" "I will tell you later," "Are you in trouble?" Ali slipped past Zeena and headed for his room "A little bit, I will tell you in the
morning, I am very tired." Evidently Zeena's customer had left by now. Zeena had second thoughts about confronting Ali; she then turned toward her bedroom.

Ali rose from his small bed and washed his hands and face in the basin on the box which was used for furniture in the corner of his room, after drying himself on some rags he walked out to the eating area. It was still quite early in the morning. Zeena was heating some food on the Primus stove on top of the cupboard. He pulled out a wooden chair, which made a squealing sound; he sat down to the rickety wooden table. A loaf of bread and a quarter of some cheese was on the table, he broke of a piece of bread from the loaf on the table, then cut a piece of cheese and folded the cheese in to the bread,

When he finished eating the food he then reached into his pocket and took something round out, Ali walked over to Zeena, who was watching the Primus stove, he then handed her the roll of a thousand dollars. She counted the money. "There is a thousand dollars in here," she said with an amazed look on her face. "I have a lot more than that in the bag, and gold, silver and jewellery." Ali told Zeena about the robbery and how he was nearly caught by the old man and the mob." "I have not looked after you all of these nineteen years to have you be killed by a mob, or have you put into jail. Bad things happen to young men like you when they are in jail, things you would not want to think about." Ali was touched by this conversation as Zeena had always cursed him for losing her good looks and being in the way. Zeena put her arm around Ali's shoulder and gave him a hug; he was very touched by the hug as he had always felt he really was in the way." Is the bag and money safe? " Ali assured her that the bag was hidden very well in a safe place.

Not long after he had left, Zeena had a knock on the door; she opened the door to see a police officer standing on the doorstep. "Was your son Ali out on the street last night?" "No he was home with me all night". The policeman sneered and showed a look of disbelief. "Are you sure "Zeena then glared at him. "I have a witness". Zeena stepped back into the doorway further "Who was it, what is his name"? ''I cannot tell you that, he is a town official and I do not want his wife to find that he was here. I would be in big trouble". The policeman grunted in disbelief and shrugged his shoulders, "I will be back again", he said in a nasty tone, he then turned and left. He stopped at another house down the street and asked the same questions about the people's son.

There was a good crowd at the market; Ali met some of his friends. This was their favourite meeting ground. Youssef asked where he had been lately, "I have been checking a new market on the other side of the town, I have been busy and have found some easy pickings".

"Someone found some easy pickings when they stabbed the old silver merchant last night. People in the market are saying that the robber got a hundred thousand dollars in gold, silver and cash", said Youssef. "Where did this happen "asked Ali, to make sure he was not implicated in any way. "It was in the dark alley by the old ware-house near his home. There is still blood on the ground. Do you want to come and see"? "No thanks. What happened to the merchant?" "I have heard he is OK. The police have the knife. They will have the robber's fingerprints". Ali changed the subject of the conversation, pointing out one of the new pretty girls working in the stall nearby. He then bid goodbye to his friend and left for home. He had found that the silver merchant had not died. He felt a wave of relief at this news.

"The police have been here looking for you Ali". He was taken aback at this news. "I am worried that the police have got my knife and could get my fingerprints. I have also lost my house key. If that was found at the scene of the robbery, the police may be able to match it to our door."   Zeena thought for a few seconds, "I think you should leave town and go to see my sister in the mountains, I have heard her husband has died and she is living alone." Ali thought for a while, he then agreed to this plan as he did not want to be caught by the police. Evidently the old man had recognised him from the market.

Zeena went to the cupboard and found a piece of paper and pencil, and then wrote the name of the small village her sister Sasha lived in on it; she described to Ali how to get to this village.

The village was where Zeena had grown lived when she was a child.

This suited Ali, he agreed that it would be a good idea to leave town for a while until things died down. He went to his room and packed his clothes then put them into a Hessian bag, then tied the top with some twine. Zeena handed Ali one hundred dollars out of the money Ali had given her.

As Ali was ready to leave Zeena gave him a kiss on the lips and a big hug, she had tears forming in the corner of her eyes." You make sure you look after yourself, I will miss you." Ali was very touched by this showing of love by Zeena and was a bit teary as he left to walk to the bus depot.

There seemed to be a lot of police checking in the markets, he tried to keep from open areas where he may have been spotted. Ali walked around the edge of the market and found his way to the bus depot from a small side laneway.

Being in the open bus depot worried Ali as he waited in line to purchase a ticket for the bus. He was worried every time a policeman walked by. He tried to make himself inconspicuous as he waited for the time to board the bus by being in a darkened corner reading a magazine from the old book rack.

Finally the driver called for passengers to board the old bus that would pass through the village where Zeena's sister Sasha lived.

The old Ford bus was full of people and animals. There were old men, women, babies, small snotty nosed children, some chickens in cages and two goats at the rear of the bus. The roof of the bus was loaded with freight in bags and boxes. The animal smell in the bus was not nice, but the smell of the tobacco some of the passengers were smoking was revolting. It smelled like burning dog manure.

The old bus wound its way around the edges of the steep passes in the mountain, with thick tall trees, and jungle, then crossing flimsy narrow bridges with steep drops beneath. Some of the road surface was uneven; the old bus would sway from side to side as it traversed the poorly repaired roadway, shaking the passengers violently from side to side, with the high load of freight tied on top of the bus, Ali was worried that the old bus may tip over and roll down to the bottom of one of the steep gorges.

When travelling downhill toward some of the streams or rivers the brakes would squeal in protest. The bus stopped at every small town and village. People and animals alighted, more got on.

There was even a large pig as a passenger. This pig did not like the idea of climbing into the crowded bus, but finally succumbed to the pushing and shoving to get her on the bus, she was restrained in the rear of the bus by a flimsy wooden gate made from sticks tied together with twine. This was tied to the rear of the seats.

As the bus climbed higher into the mountains the air got cooler. The smelly pig left the bus after two more stops. People in the bus gave her a wide berth as she did not seem to be very happy after her trip. She was frothing at the mouth and trying to snap at the people.

Finally, the bus pulled into the small village where Sasha lived. The small village had a square for the market and an assortment of dilapidated crumbling houses around it, and the same style of old houses led off the square into narrow lane ways. An impressive Catholic church took up a large area on one corner of the square. This church was built of dressed square stone blocks and had a tall steeple with a large bell. The church looked very old.

The bus pulled up near to the front of the church. Ali and three other people alighted from the bus. Some freight was taken off the roof by the driver and one of the alighting passengers. The driver resumed his seat then started the motor. Blue smoke poured from the exhaust pipe as the motor revved up, the old bus grated its gears as it drove slowly off along the wide street which led to the road, heading toward the next village. The worn gears whined as the bus picked up speed. The smell of the tobacco clung to Ali's clothes and skin. The clean mountain air was a relief from the stench of the bus.

He was unsure as to whether Sasha still lived in the village; he walked along the road and found a small shop. As he entered an old stooped man came from the rear section of the shop and enquired as to whether he could help him. Ali asked about Sasha. The old man knew Sasha and described how to get to her plot of land and house, "The poor lady is very lonely where she lives by herself. She does not come to the village very often since her husband has died." He pulled a small piece of paper off the roll on the shop counter and drew a small map to show Ali the way to the house. Ali thanked the man and left for the trip ahead carrying the bag of clothes over his shoulder.

He headed out along the road the bus had taken then turned onto a narrow track leading toward a small river. There were small plots of land with thatched roof houses, palm trees and a few animals. After walking two kilometers Ali crossed the small river on a rickety bridge. There were small rice paddies near to this river. Some paddies had animals and people working in them. The road had ruts carved into the surface from the thin wheels of the wooden carts which were towed by a buffalo in a yoke. Two of these carts had passed by, going toward the village with produce for the market.

The woman was stooped over hoeing a field near the small raised timber house with a thatched roof. Ali walked over to her. As she looked up, he noticed a tired look on her once pretty face. Her hands were calloused from the hard-daily toil. She looked at Ali with a hint of suspicion. "What do you want? I have nothing for beggars, I am very poor". She started to turn back to her work. Ali turned toward her to show his features, "I am Zeena's son", the woman looked closely at him," I can see her in your eyes. Is your mother dead?"

He assured her that Zeena was not dead and was well. Sasha sighed and dropped her shoulders, "Your mother got into a bad business. Has she changed her ways?". "No, she has not and as her looks have faded, she has been finding life hard". "We all have a hard life boy; I only grow enough food to feed myself. I hope you are not looking to live here. I have no money".

Upon hearing this, Ali reached into his pocket and took out the money and peeled off twenty dollars, and handed it to Sasha, she took the money. "Are you in trouble boy?" "Yes, one of my mother's lovers was beating her and I hit him with a chair. He has threatened to castrate me if he catches me" Ali lied. "Nothing seems to have changed with your mother then. Trouble, followed again by more trouble."

Sasha looked at the money and then thought for a minute, "I could buy a goat with this money and have milk and be able to sell cheese". Sasha stood the hoe next to a rock then walked toward the house. "Come boy and have some food". As he entered the small house, He noticed that the furnishing was very sparse, but scrubbed clean. Sasha showed Ali where to put his bag of clothes in a tiny room with a thin mattress on the floor.

The house had the aroma of something exotic, the spicy smell of food which had been cooked. A hint of curry and spices filled the air of the small house.

Sasha lit a small fire in the hob then after fanning the flames to catch the tinder on fire, placed a pot on the flames to heat the contents. The smoke from the fire mixed with the aromas of the food as the food warmed. She collected two bowls from a cupboard on which there was a large bowl for washing, using a large wooden spoon she ladled some food into the bowls, "I was not expecting company. I very rarely ever see another person here in my house. You are lucky there was enough food" she grumbled. The food was a mixture of rice and vegetables. It was flavored with curry and other herbs and was delicious to eat.

The song of the birds in the trees near to the house woke Ali early in the morning, for a moment he did not know where he was. The bird's song was different from the din of the town. During the night he had thought a lot about his first impressions of Sasha. She had seemed to be very grumpy at the idea of having a new house guest.

Sasha greeted Ali as he stepped into the eating area. The last of the food in the pot was served up for the morning meal. Sasha smiled at Ali. "I have been by myself so long that I have forgotten what it is like to have another person to care for and to have a conversation with. I thought about this last night. I think it will be a good change for me." He felt relieved at this conversation. "What are we going to be doing today?" Sasha looked kindly at Ali." I am digging a plot to plant some yams".

Ali went with Sasha to the small plot of land she was hoeing and helped her by pulling up some tall weeds. The yams had then been sowed into the warm moist earth. Sasha had shown Ali how to plant the yams.

That evening he found that Sasha was indeed a very good cook with the herbs she grew on the small plot of land. Ali complemented Sasha as to the tasty food which she cooked. She was pleased with the compliment. "I have tried to keep up my cooking skills, even though I have been living in the house by myself".

Sasha also had a small rice paddy about a half mile away near the river bridge. The next morning, she took him to the river and showed Ali the very small plot of rice growing in the paddy. Ali carried two buckets on a yoke around his shoulders for water for the house. Sasha rolled up her dress and walked into the muddy water and started to pull the tall weeds growing between the small rice plants. Ali put down the buckets and removed the yoke; he then stepped into the soft mud under the water and under her instruction, started to help. After a half hour, he looked down at his legs and saw three slimy leeches attached to his lower legs.

He jumped out of the water onto the bank of the paddy; he had never seen a thing as revolting as the slimy blood sucking creatures, Sasha also stepped out. She also had some leeches feeding on her legs.

She laughed, "These leeches are like a lot of people I have met. They will suck the blood out of you at every chance they get ", with a deft movement she removed her and Ali's leeches by sliding her fingernail up toward the leeches mouth to break the suction which held it on. She then tossed them onto the dry hot bank of the paddy. The leeches writhed in anger at being taken from the food source. Sasha and Ali's legs bled for a while. After the bleeding stopped they went back to work.

The sun was just starting to show a red glow in the clouds when they left the rice paddy, they had finished the chore. As Ali carried the two buckets of water, Sasha said "When we come back here tomorrow, I will bring us a fishing pole to show you how to catch the fish in the river. The fish like to eat the leeches.

The next day Sasha took the fishing rod with a line and hook attached to the thin end of the cane pole. 'I think, now I should show you how to catch the fish in the river." As they walked to the river Sasha hummed a tune. She was evidently happy at having company. The leeches were saved in a small jar with a lid, they evidently were not happy at being in the jar as they writhed around in anger. Later in the day when the work of tending the rice paddy was ended, she asked Ali to pick up the fishing pole and leeches. They walked to the small stream.

A large tree stood on the bank of the small slowly meandering stream, the roots of the tree protruded over the water which was two meters below. The shade of the tree kept the hot sun off their backs.

Ali looked into the murky water and noticed the flash of the silver fish as the chased their prey. They both nestled in a comfortable spot on the web of roots, Sasha took the hook on the end of the twine then removed one of the leeches from the jar, then threaded the wriggling creature onto the sharp hook, the leech did not appreciate this very much. The hook was lowered into the water. In a short time, the pole jerked sharply, Sasha lifted it out of the water with a silver fish of about twenty centimeters long wriggling frantically on the hook.

The fish was laid on the bank behind them and covered with some grass to keep the sun off. Sasha handed the pole to Ali. He did not like the feel of the leech very much, but persevered and threaded it to the fishhook ready to fish. He lowered it to the water, and then almost dropped the pole when the next fish was hooked. Sasha laughed as Ali pulled the fish up. He felt a sense of excitement as the pole was swung up and the fish landed. He caught another five fish.

Sasha took some twine from her pocket and tied this through the fish's gills to make it easy to carry them home.

When they arrived, Sasha found a large bowl, and then half filled it with water. She showed Ali how to scrape the scales off the fish and then how to cut the fillets off the bones of the fish. 'You have left too much meat on the bones' she admonished him. He tried harder on the next fish and was rewarded with a hug. "good boy, you are a quick learner'. Four fillets were saved for the evening meal. The other eight fillets had string tied to the tail and then hung on a piece of string to dry in the afternoon sun.   After Sasha had shown him how to catch the fish, and to fill the two buckets with water for the house and washing, Ali would walk to the river and catch tasty silver fish with the thin bamboo pole with the length of line attached to the thin end. He would catch the crickets, leeches and other insects to attach to the hook for bait to lure the unsuspecting fish onto the shiny hook. The fish would make a nice meal to help with the diet. He would carry them home with the yoke over his shoulders with the two water buckets. The dried fillets lasted a long time before they had to be used.

Some days Ali would share the bank of the river with one or two of the neighbors. He would talk to them and found out a lot of what concerned the poor people living in the mountains. The people laughed a lot and were resigned to their lifestyle as they did not know of any other.   Sometimes these people used a cast net to catch the fish in the shallow waters. Ali would talk to the people as they fished. He was interested in their views on life.

One day when talking to some people Ali noticed a pretty girl of about his age looking intently at him. She was evidently with her father and mother and was helping to catch the fish. Ali had moved closer and had begun to talk to her. Merci was her name

The meetings with Merci started to take on a regular occurrence. Merci would come to the river alone on certain days to catch some fish. Ali worked out when she would be at the river and looked forward to the times they sat and talked, while waiting for the fish to take the hook.

The problems of the world with Zeena seemed far away. The people in the village seemed content with the lifestyle which they had inherited from their parents. The church was involved into a large part of their lives; the priest was their confessor and adviser.

Ali spent a lot of time talking about the people's outlook on life. After he had taken some produce to the market he would sit with the men and talk, He would talk of the drugs and crime in the large town where he and Zeena lived.

There was no crime in the village or surrounding area, nearly all of the people were as poor as Sasha. There was an unwritten law about taking from some other person without asking. When one of the people were in trouble or sick the others always helped, whether it was repairing houses or delivering babies.

When Sasha went with Ali to the market one day, she spent some time looking at a lot of the goats which were for sale; after a lot of time inspecting the goats, and then a lengthy barter with the owner, she bought herself a nanny goat in milk. The goat was led home with a piece of light dog chain Ali had bought. The chain was hooked to the wide heavy collar. This was to be used to tether the goat near a weedy patch of the plot which needed to be cleaned up ready to hoe. The goat had a plastic drum with the lid chopped off for her water.

Sasha grew to like the goat, Missy was her name. She talked to her as she squeezed the milk from her teats into a bowl every morning and night, some of the milk was used in the food preparation but most was let stand to make a tasty cheese.

As she squeezed the milk out, Ali would tease her about the conversations she had with the goat. Sasha would laugh when he did this. Her laughter was like the tinkling sound of water as it trickled down through the rocks in a small steam.

One morning Missy was acting cantankerous. Sasha told Ali that she was in season and looking for a mate. There would be a further chance of more income if the goat were to have a kid.

Sasha asked Ai to take Missy for a trip along the road to be mated with a Billy goat. She described where a man with a herd of goats lived.

Ali took Missy for a walk to the third house along the road to where the goat herd lived. The people who lived on the small plot of land had a small herd of goats. An old man was tending to the goats, while the rest of the family were in the fields working. He was filling the water troughs and carrying feed. Ali introduced himself and then asked if the old man would not mind if he were to let Missy be with the Billy goat for the day. The old man laughed and agreed. "I will have to ask the Billy goat first". He cackled with laughter again. Ali reached into the home-made bamboo leaf basket and took out a special treat which Sasha had cooked for a trade for the Billy goat service. The old man smiled, "Ah this is Sasha's special food. I have eaten this before. My goat and I thank you."

The smelly Billy goat was standing on his hind legs at the fences niffing the air. He could smell that Missy was in season. He rolled his lips back showing his dirty yellow teeth and let out a noisy bleat. Missy seemed to be impressed by this show and bleated back. Ali led her through the gate into the Billy goat's yard. He was very careful not to turn his back on this cranky goat. Sasha had warned him about getting bunted by the Billy.

Ali stood back and watched as the Billy went through his routine. He first started to hit Missy on the rump with one of his front legs, Missy hunched up to pee, The Billy then stuck his nose into the running stream of urine. He then let out a very loud bleat, rolled his lips back again, and then mounted Missy, after a bit of jabbing in the wrong area the Billy found the home spot and drove his weapon home. He lurched back and forward a few times, bleating loudly as he completed his task. He then slid off, looking quite exhausted.

The old man was standing next to Ali, "I think him like that one ok." He cackled with laughter. Ali offered to take Missy out of the pen. "No, you leave her in the pen for a while more. He will get it up a few more times yet. You have to make sure he got the job done right." He cackled with the laughter again. The Billy goat started to get the routine going again and reared up and mated Missy again. Ali and the old man went to sit in the shade.   Both Ali and the old man had eaten the food which Sasha had sent. The Billy had mounted Missy four times in two hours and was standing on the other side of the pen. He was sweating profusely from all of the hard work, this sweating made him smell even worse than normal "I think he a bit too tired to have some more now. I do not think he would have the energy to bunt you now. You can take the nanny out now. I think she full up".   Ali hooked the chain back to Missies collar and led her from the pen. The Billy did not seem to care; He had had his wicked way with her and was not interested anymore· Missy did not bother to look back. S*o much* for *love in the goat world*, Ali thought

Missy was not too energetic on the trip back home. Ali had to stop to give her a breather on two occasions.

The rural life agreed with Ali. During the day he was enjoying tilling the fields to remove the weeds, planting seeds for the melons and other crops. He did not mind even when he was standing in the water of the paddy fields weeding and tending the small rice crop. Then have to pull the blood sucking leeches off his legs during the day. The leeches were very handy to use to catch some fish for the cooking pot.

As he passed by, Ali would stop and talk to the goat as Sasha did. Missy liked being scratched between the horns, where there was dandruff like substance which she had trouble reaching when she scratched herself with her hoof or rubbing herself against a tree.

A real bond had developed between Sasha and Ali, the bond was more of a mother and son bond than Ali had ever experienced before in his life. He and Sasha used to spend long hours talking of their lives and other daily problems as they toiled together side by side in the fields or were sitting at the table for a meal, before going to their beds Sasha would give Ali a kiss on the lips.

Sasha had also been able to save some money from the sales of cheese and farming products. Ali was very content with his life. He called to visit Merci when he carried produce to the village to sell.

Her father was working in the village repairing houses. His payment was more in the form of trade for food or other necessities than money. Ali spent a lot of time talking to her and her family about the bad times in the other life, before meeting them. He would take some of the produce which was going to the market to give her family. Ali would stay and eat with the family before travelling home from the market. Ali and Merci would go outside of the house and talk for hours after the meal.

One evening Ali and Merci had walked hand in hand out of the village to an old tumble down shed. They had opened the door then sat facing and kissed each other. Ali gently reached out and drew Merci toward him. He loosened the top of the clothes and reached gently for her breast. Merci let out a soft moan and clung tighter to him. She reached down between Ali's legs and felt his manhood. It was throbbing with desire. Merci parted the folds of the sarong and lay back, gently pulling him with her. She parted her legs. Ali was trembling as he pulled his trousers down. He moved close between Merci's legs, She reached between them and guided Ali inside her. At this moment Ali thought he was going to stop breathing. He had never been with a girl before. As he moved and the excitement was almost at its peak Merci would slow him. "I want this to last a long time Ali, Just think of something else so we can start again". The lovemaking went on for about an hour. When they both climaxed Ali thought he was going to explode. He had never felt such a sensation in his life before. It was if fireworks were exploding in his head. As they walked back to the village Ali had a job to walk, a quick thought crossed his mind. He now knew why the old goat had problems after doing this job.

The weeks turned into months as Ali worked in the fields with Sasha. The small rice crop had been cut and threshed for the grain with a leather flap on the end of a pole. The grain was then winnowed in the wind by tossing it into the air and having the chaff blown off by the wind. The rice grain was stored in large plastic drums with lids screwed tightly to the top. Missy would muzzle through the chaff to seek out any missed grains.

Ali felt as if he could stay in the mountains and become a part of the village life. The problems of money and the crime in the city felt so far away. He was really enjoying the simple way of life without the hassles of the dirty city. He would walk to the village three times a week and meet with Merci, then travel to the love nest and slowly make love. The long trip home always took a lot of effort.

In the mountains behind the village there were a band of rebels who preyed upon some of the larger towns for food. These people were a bad lot, as they had no regard for any but themselves. These people would arrive in a town and shoot at all people they could see and then loot rape and steal. The people in the village were not worried about these rebels as the area was so poor. They thought the rebels would not bother them for their meagre produce.

Nine months had passed since Ali had escaped the city; he was really content with his lot now. He had a new caring auntie, who was like a mother to him, and also a nice loving pretty girl called Merci.
Ali was travelling to town with a yoke over his shoulders and two heavy baskets of produce for sale. He had just walked into the market, and was thinking about the meeting with Merci, when the gunfire broke out. The rebels were attacking the marketplace. People were running and screaming, some fell when hit by bullets trying to escape, some people lay writhing on the ground. Ali dropped the yoke and baskets, then ran through the village ducking and weaving as he went. He ran back toward Sasha's house.

In the distance Ali could see a haze of smoke hovering near to Sasha's house. He ran as fast as he could. He felt relief when he noticed the smoke was coming from the next house along the road.
He entered the house to find his beloved auntie Sasha lying in a pool of blood. She had been stabbed in the chest. He clothes had been torn off her. She had evidently been raped before being stabbed. Ali cradled the dying Sasha in his arms and told her quietly that he loved her as she slipped away. He felt a terrible sense of loss and rage.

Out from the rear of the house Ali heard a noise. He peeped around the rear doorway and saw a young lad about his age butchering Sasha's goat Missy. A red wave of rage engulfed Ali; he crept to the cooking area and found a long pointy knife. He sneaked back to the door, then launched himself at Sasha's murderer, stabbing the long knife into his back.

The lad swung the knife he had been using to butcher the goat and slashed Ali's cheek from jaw to ear; a large flap of skin was cut and hung loose bleeding profusely. The rebel started to tremor and kick as the blood flowed from his heart. Ali felt no remorse, and felt like stabbing the rebel over and over for the murder of his dear Sasha and Missy. Ali waited for the lad to die; he pulled the now dead rebel away from the house, so he was not near to Sasha as she lay dead. The sight of Missy gutted and cut up was also a very distressing sight for Ali to comprehend.

Ali returned to the house, he stooped and kissed Sasha on the cheek. Blood pulsed from the huge cut on his face and landed on Sasha's calm lifeless face. Ali found a rag and wiped it off, he then bound the cheek wound up with the same rag, He tied the ends to keep the wound tight, and then walked from the room onto the road, then headed back to the village. He realised that if he did not get help he would probably bleed to death.   Tears from his crying stung the wound on his face as he staggered along. The blood from the large wound seeped out from the bandage and covered his clothes. He had to stop a few times to get his breath. Finally he headed into the market, where people were talking and working on the wounded.

There were makeshift pallets on the ground with the dead and wounded on them. A man came to Ali and led him to some women who were cleaning some of the wounded people. A lady took the bandage off Ali's face the called to a man to look at Ali's cut face, after a few seconds the man went to a table and got a needle and some cotton, he proceeded to sew the gash on Ali's face back together.

The sewing really hurt, Ali realised that this would have to be done. Finally the pain lessened as the man packed up to attend another. Ali's face was throbbing. He had a splitting headache. One of the women came to him and gave him a glass of bitter liquid to drink, Ali quickly dozed off.

The sun was high in the sky; it was about noon when Ali finally woke. His face was still throbbing and he felt dizzy. He forced himself to rise, and then he staggered to the door of the strange house. A woman stepped in his way and tried to stop him. Ali gestured toward Sasha's house then made a gesture of shooting a pistol at his head. The woman understood and stepped aside to let Ali past.

The trip to Sasha's house took a lot of effort, he had to rest on a few occasions, finally he arrived. Sasha was laying on the blanket her dead brown eyes staring at the roof, flies buzzed around her body Ali went to the cupboard and took a clean cloth and gently laid this over Sasha's face to keep the flies off her.

He then went out and found a pick and spade, then set about digging a grave for his lovely caring aunt. Tears coursed out of his eyes then ran over the throbbing cheek, this just made his grief worse.

Ali had dug a grave for Sasha about a meter deep; he walked into the fields and picked a large armful of wild flowers. These flowers had usually been a chore to keep hoed out of the crops. Ali entered the house and got a clean blanket off Sasha's bed then laid her with great gentleness upon it. He placed the flowers each side of her peaceful face then folded the sides over her, finally covering her gentle brown eyes, he carefully picked her body up and carried her to the graveside.

As he stood in the hole and gently lifted Sasha's body into the grave, He let out a moan and started to shudder with grief. He arranged her body then climbed over her out of the grave. Filling the hole was a very hard thing to do; finally Ali got one of Sasha's favourite pots and placed this at the head of her grave. He packed his few clothes and the money which was hidden in the house, then stepped down from the floor to the ground.

Before he left for the village, he looked across the field to where the terrorist's body was and noticed the big birds of prey sitting on him and pecking at his body. This gave Ali some solace in that they were having their way with the murderer.

The young girl's parents asked Ali to stay with them. They were devastated. Merci had been raped and murdered by the terrorists. Ali cried at the other loss. The sobbing really hurt the stiches in his face declined as he did not want to be in the village after the trauma of losing two the nicest persons he had ever known. He had to answer in sign language by gesturing with his hands as the swelling in his face made it impossible to speak. He agreed to stay while he waited the two days for the bus to arrive to take him back to the city. Ali could not bear to return to Sasha's house and be there with her lying under the ground behind the house.

The trip down the mountain was a lot scarier than the up trip. The driver would shift the gears to neutral and let the bus coast down the steep slopes to save petrol. The brakes would squeal in protest as they neared a bridge or met another vehicle. The tobacco smell was still the same from the people smoking the home- made cigarettes. Dust from the dry dirt road filled the cabin of the bus.

When Ali had finally arrived and walked through the market on the way to his home from the bus, he had seen some of his friends in the market-place. Youssef walked straight past Ali without recognising him; Youssef had not recognised him because of the grossly swollen face. Ali had not tried to communicate with him or any other of these lads as he thought it would be an advantage to remain anonymous.

After knocking on the door of his house three times, Zeena opened the door; she looked at Ali and asked him what he wanted. He suddenly realised that she did not recognise him. Ali still could not speak so he undid the sack of clothes and showed her the shirt she had recently bought. Zeena then realised who he was. She let him inside then hugged him and cried.

After entering the house, Ali went and got a pencil and paper and wrote down what had happened to Sasha. Then wrote of how he had slain her murderer. Sasha was Zeena's only relative. She sobbed softly for some time.

Zeena told Ali that the police had been around two more times looking for him. There had been no mention of a key being found, so that had evidently been lost during Ali's running home with the

Kit-bag. This news really worried Ali; he was almost unrecognisable due to the large scar. He did not want one of his acquaintances to recognise him and to start talking to the wrong person to have the police on his trail again.

Late in the night Ali set out in the dim moonlight to the warehouse and retrieved the Kit- Bag full of the precious metal and money. He was careful not to be seen. He stashed the bag in his room.

In the morning Ali showed Zeena the contents of the kit-bag. The money was sorted into piles of the same currency with a rough count being done on each pile.

After thinking and talking to Ali for a while, Zeena told him of an Indian metal trader she knew in a far part of town, who may buy some of the silver and gold. Zeena told Ali to keep his eye on this man as he was very violent.

He left to go to the market to purchase some food, when he was there at the market; Ali purchased some better clothes and some new sandals. His old friends still did not recognise him, Ali left it so. He was going to take a third of the silver and gold to see if he could sell it.

After walking and searching for a few minutes Ali found a lad on an auto rickshaw and with difficulty talking because of his swollen face, asked him to take him to the Indian jewellery store. The lad could not understand the mumbled conversation. He gave directions Zeena had written on a piece of paper to the auto rickshaw driver to the premises of the dealer.

The Jewellery shop was large and painted bright red. It had heavy steel bars on the windows and doors. Ali walked in and noticed a lot of customers and five working girls. With difficulty, Ali asked one of the girls if he could speak to Mr. Kahn about selling some gold. The girl walked off and came back with a greasy dark-skinned ugly man with a pock marked face, he had a turban on his head, and there was a thick gold chain around his neck. and a very large diamond ring on his finger.

The man ushered Ali to his office. "Sit down boy, what have you in the bag for me" Ali mumbled slowly with effort, from the swelling of his face "My father was killed in a robbery of his shop. I was attacked by the robbers, they cut my face. I was able to save some of the gold and silver and run away. I have the gold and silver my father was using in the shop to make jewellery. We are now very poor and need the money for food." he tipped the gold and silver bars out on the desk top.

A gleam of greed crossed the Indian's eyes as he perused the pile of precious metal. The Indian weighed the metal and offered a price. "My mother told me this was worth a lot more than you are offering. The greasy man leaned back. "How do I not know if this is stolen". He smirked showing a large gold tooth. "This is my price. Take it or leave. Ali reached for the pile of gold and silver and picked it up; he then moved to get up. The greasy man said. " Wait, I may have made a mistake with the weights" he reweighed the metal and offered nearly twice the amount. Ali agreed to the sale. The man pushed his chair back on its rollers then got a key ring full of keys out of his pocket. He found a well-worn small key and unlocked one of the desk drawers. He took some rolls of cash from the drawer of the desk. He then paid Ali, laying each note to be counted. Ali took the one thousand five hundred US dollars, then handed the silver and gold across.

On the way home Ali shuddered at the thought of this gross ugly man being with his mother. Her life must be hard to have to let a man like the ugly Indian have his way with her.

During the Afternoon Zeena and Ali totaled up the notes and then added the gold and silver price sold that day, then the worth of the gold and silver left. The figure was thirty-five thousand dollars; the jewellery would almost make the figure forty thousand. "Why don't we leave this town and get a new life "suggested Zeena, "We could go to Manilla, I may be able to get a proper job. I am tired of being used and beaten by the dirty violent men." Ali was extremely pleased with the idea of losing the shackles of this town, which now had the police problem looming over his head.

Three days later they had disposed of their meagre possessions and were ready to go on the ferry to Manilla. Both Ali and Zeena had spent a small amount of the money to buy some new clothes. Instead of the hessian bags they both had suitcases and the kit-bag from the robbery. The money was in a money belt around both Ali and Zeena's waist, and gold and silver bars were secreted into the lining of Zeena's new large hand bag. Zeena looked ten years younger at the prospects of leaving her old trade.

They carried their possessions down to the bus depot in the market and booked seats to travel to the seaside town where a ferry would take them to Manilla.

During the bus trip Zeena told Ali that a huge load was being lifted from her shoulders by leaving town. She was pleased to be able to change her status in life from one of the local whores to a normal person. The prostitutes lot was not a good one, most of the local men were keen to use her; none would recognise her when she was not at work. Most of the local wives were suspicious about who her clients may have been. *Were their husbands going to visit her on the sly*? : "I should have gone and seen some of the women in the street who have always avoided me and told them what bad lovers their husbands were". She laughed at the thought.

The bus crested a ridge when heading for the coast. The wide vista of the ocean stretched before their eyes. The enormity of the blue expanse with the smaller dotted islands was far different in reality from the pictures in the magazines they had seen.

The bus crawled through the outskirts of the coastal town toward the sea. This town was of a much better standard than the smaller inland town in which they had spent all of their lives. Even in the poorer areas the houses looked cleaner and had been painted. Multi storied buildings thrust out of the down town area near to the sea. There was an air of prosperity in this town.

The bus finally stopped at the ferry terminal. There were evidently a lot of tourists walking around the streets. These were evident from the clothes, cameras and other regalia they carried.

The ferry did not leave for two hours for Manilla. Ali and Zeena spent most of the time just watching the procession of different people walking around the wharf area. "Look at that man with the funny hat" Ali pointed to a skinny man in shorts and a bright Hawaiian shirt in the distance. Zeena noticed some of the women tourists; they were wearing very strange clothes.

Chapter two

The Kimba three-year drought

The coppery Australian sun shone down on the dusty paddock. A cold breeze pushed the thin dust before it as it blew lazily across the barren landscape. Patches of ice still lay on the ground, left over from the previous night's frost—a typical day in a drought. John was just leaving the house with his son Tony when Helen called, 'Stop, John, you are wanted on the phone. It's the bank.' John's shoulders dropped as he turned back to the kitchen. Tony followed with a look of gloom. He pulled out one of the kitchen chairs from the table and sat down.   This phone call was not unexpected as the bank overdraft was getting out of hand. The high interest rates and the bad season on the farm surely did not help. John answered the phone and spoke briefly to the teller and made an appointment to see the manager. 'The bank. 10.30. Tuesday,' said John. 'Did you speak to the manager? ''No, only Debbie.' Debbie was the teller in the small bank. 'Well, that's that, I suppose. Where can we get some extra money?' John was evidently upset as he left with Tony following him. Bloody Lizard! John thought. He had no love for the manager of the local bank and referred to him as the Lizard. Most of the previous managers in the bank had joined in with local community events and played some sort of sport. This man had no friends or even acquaintances in the district. His wife did have a couple of friends in the school council.

John and Tony got into the battered farm's four-wheel drive utility and drove it to the grain silo, where a full bin of oats on a trailer waited. Tony alighted and hooked the bin to the utility and got in. John drove off to feed the sheep. It was halfway along the lane before John spoke. He had evidently been doing a lot of thinking. I wish we didn't have this blasted bank problem. Where in God's name are we going to get any money to pay the bank?

The old four-wheel drive stopped halfway along the lane way whilst Tony opened the wire gate. John then drove out of the lane way into the adjoining paddock next to the lane .

Behind it in the dusty paddock, a mob of skinny sheep ran back and forth, trying to eat as much of the oats which had been let out in a trail behind the bin. The occasional sheep would have an altercation with its neighbor, and a bunting match would ensue. Both sheep would back off and charge each other head first. They would meet together with a sickening thud as their heads banged together. They would back up and charge again until one sheep gave in and turned away. This sheep usually got a bunt in the ribs or the bum to send it on its way.

A few of the greedier sheep followed the trailer to the open gate, hoping for an extra feed of the precious oats. One of the sheep ran past the ute and on to the lane way.

Tony was just getting out shutting the gate as they left the paddock, when a sheep veered past him. 'Here, Laddie, fetch him back,' he said softly to the sheepdog sitting on the tray of the ute. The black-and-white Border collie jumped out of the ute tray and ran up the lane way, passing the sheep, heading the escapee off, ran after the escapee, and then turned the runaway back down the lane towards the gate. Tony ran out into the lane to direct the sheep back into the paddock. Laddie trotted back to the ute and then walked over, puffing lightly, and muzzled at Tony's hand. Tony crouched down and patted Laddie's faithful head. 'Good boy,' he crooned to the dog.

Tony shut the wire gate and got into the ute. Laddie jumped up on to the tray. 'Well, it looks as if it's going to be another prick of a day. It would not surprise me if the damned wind sprung up and started to blow from the north and start a dust storm,' grunted John, as he let the clutch out, and the ute rattled on its way. 'There's lots of other places I'd rather be at the present time than trying to farm in this dust bowl'.

They drove along the laneway back towards the homestead, which shimmered in the distance against the cloudless sky. Dust billowed out from behind the ute. Usually this time of the year, the potholes in the lane were full of water.

A group of crows took it in turns to pick at a dead sheep in the paddock. The crows flew off a short distance and sat in a small mallee tree, which was growing out of a stone heap. 'Bloody bastards. They are the only ones who will do any good out of this farm this year,' growled John. 'Remind me to put the rifle in the ute cab. At least, some of the bludgers might have to pay.' The crows were a bad enemy in times of drought because they picked the eyes out of any poor hapless sheep which could not get to their feet in the morning and join the mob. The only thing to do then was to cut the sheep's throat to put it out of its misery.

John stopped by one of the wheat paddocks. Both the men got out of the ute and climbed through the fence to look at the water-stressed wheat. The plants were stunted and were quickly day by day, turning blue. A few small area of crop on the stony rises had already turned brown and died Tony dug out some plants, and then dug down into the sandy soil, looking for any sign of moisture. He let the dry soil run through his fingers and blew away in the breeze. 'Dry as a bloody lime burner's boot.' The men walked further out into the crop. The story was the same. The soil was extremely dry. The crop must be living on the memory of the earlier thunder storms after which it had been sown. 'Well, let's go. We aren't doing much good here. It must be getting close to smoko time.' The men walked back to the Toyota and drove off towards the house, which shimmered in the distance at the end of the lane way.

There was a cattle grid in the road with an old worn-out tractor tyre on each side to stop the stock from passing the barrier. Next to the grid was a large wire gate, which could be opened to allow farm machinery and livestock into the house and shed yard. The grid was just before the house. The ute rumbled over this and then entered a small bare area, which was surrounded by a house on one side, then a large implement shed, and a hay shed, which by now was nearly empty. Most of the hay that was left in the shed was poor-quality hay, which had been rained on soon after it had been baled some years before and had gone mouldy. There were a large assortment of grain silos for seed grain and stock feed. A small shearing shed which was raised off the ground on piles. this allowed the sheep manure and urine to drop through the grating on the floor There was a small, oil-cum-chemical shed with diesel and petrol tanks next to it. A large scrap heap of old, definitely dead pieces of machinery was heaped up behind the implement shed.

John pulled up outside the double car shed behind the house. They got out and walked through the gate along the concrete path towards the veranda. The washing machine could be heard thumping away in the laundry at the back of the shed. Rows of newly washed clothes swung in the light breeze on the rotary clothes hoist a short distance from the laundry.

The house was a mismatch of materials surrounded by an iron fence. The front section of the house was built out of the local limestone, whilst the rear was corrugated roofing iron, which was laid on horizontally. The whole lot was covered by a bungalow roof and a wide veranda. The poor house was desperately in need of a good coat of paint. The old paint was peeling off in places, leaving the remnants of the old, previous paint colours showing through. Looking at the paint brought back memories of the previous colours used in the past painting exercises.

In the front of the house, there was a series of garden beds marked out with the local limestone used as borders. A few straggly flowers struggled to survive the dry in the garden. These were mainly daisies and a rockery of succulents, which seemed as if they could almost live without water. At the rear of the house though, there was a vegetable garden. It was watered by the washing and shower water, which was directed on to the different beds by a thick hose led from the sink and shower drain. The flower garden, in better times, had been Helen's hobby, but as money was very tight, the water had to be saved for the necessities, such as the livestock, and the used shower water was for the vegetable patch. As they walked past the vegetable garden, John bent down and pulled a few weeds out from between the rows of vegies. They took their dirty boots off, then opened the rear fly screen door of the house, and then walked into the kitchen. Laddie the dog, had followed them into the veranda and settled himself close to the door on an old grain bag, which was his bed.

Helen looked up from the timber table on which she had some bread dough rolled out. She brushed a strand of blonde hair out of her eyes with a flour-covered hand. Some of the flour stuck to the side of her face, leaving a white mark. 'Smoko time already. Don't just stand there. Shut the door, Tony. The flies are getting in!' Tony quickly shut the door to keep the small sticky bush flies out of the house. 'How time flies when you are having fun,' said Helen as the two men sat down at the table.

Helen got three mugs out of the kitchen dresser and put coffee and sugar in them. She then put them on the table, then walked over to the large slow combustion stove, got the kettle which had been simmering on the side of the hot plate, and filled the mugs with hot water. 'What are things like out in the paddock?' she asked, with a worried look on her face, as she topped the mugs up with milk from a small jug.

'The crops look as if they can only last another week or two before they die, and there were two more dead sheep. The bloody crows got to them.'

Helen shook her head. What are we going to do about the bank? She had not asked John before because he was a deep thinker and would have spent some time remonstrating. To wait was the best way with John. Helen knew that he and Tony would have discussed this in John's own time.

John pushed his chair back from the table. It made a screeching sound as the legs dragged over the linoleum. In the silence which ensued, the tick-tock of the old Ansonia mantle clock, which sat on the smoky mantelpiece above the combustion stove, was the only noise in the kitchen. As if to break the silence, the old clock cranked up and started to chime its brassy clang. The ten chimes seemed to bring John and the others back to the real matters at hand.

John let out a sigh. 'Urgh! Well, I was expecting that. We've had nearly no income for the last three years, thanks to this bloody drought.' John sat down at the table and sipped his coffee, evidently deep in thought. 'What did the miserable little prick have to say for himself? Going to give us a few thousand out of the goodness of his heart I suppose,' he stated sarcastically

John had been worried about the bank loan for some time. He had tried to get some off-farm work, but all farmers in the district had tightened their belts financially because of the droughts. The phone call from the Lizard had been expected for some time.

John and Helen had bought the farm cheaply some twenty years before.

John had been share farming and shearing in the district since his teens. John had a reputation as a tough football player. He, as a lot of other country lads did, liked a drink at the local Hotel after working hard at shearing sheep. This had got John into trouble with the local police man on quite a few occasions. He had a loud mouth when he had been drinking and was inclined to give any opposition to his ideas a punch in their nose. On the football field, many an opponent left the field with a black eye when standing against him. In all fairness, John copped his fair share back. He was always told by his mother he had the bad temper of his Irish grandfather who had come out to Australia as a lad in the early nineteen hundreds.

John had amassed a small amount of cash for the deposit on the farm from his share farming and shearing. They bought the farm two years after he had married Helen.

Helen's grandfather and grandmother had come to the district from the Barossa Valley in the 1920s as a young married couple and had amassed a large holding of land. Her father was from tough German stock and definitely was not afraid of work. The 1930 depression had cost the grandparents most of the land, leaving them with just enough land to survive. Helens father was the eldest son. Big Herman was his nick name. His wife was Helga. He was ready to help all and sundry in the district. The family had ten children. Helen was the youngest. Big Herman was far from impressed when Helen had started to keep company with John. He had no time for the Irish and wanted Helen to marry one of the local German boys from the Lutheran church. He would say "That Bog Irish you are seeing will cause you nothing but trouble with his fighting and drinking." Helens mother would sit back and nod her head in assent but would say nothing.

The crunch time came when Helen became pregnant. John had been terrified when he and Helen had to go and tell Herman and his wife. Big Herman's face had changed colour to a plum red colour and the veins were prominent in his neck. "I should have put the burdizzo's on you when you first came around you mongrel." John had seen the bloodless castrators being used and had always thought that he would not like the experience of having them used on him. Helga stepped between Herman and John. "For once Herman in my life I will tell you to shut up and think about Helen. I have put up with being bullied by you all of these years. You are not going to do this to Helen". Herman was taken aback from Helga's remonstration and slumped down," Do you love this man?" "Of course, I do" "Ja then I suppose you should get married". He shook Johns hand with a look of sufferance. John had the feeling that Herman's huge calloused hand was going to crush his to pulp. "If you do not give up the boozing in the pub and fighting, I will fight you myself. I could flatten you with one of these -hands tied behind my back". John had no doubt that he could; He was still built like Panzer Tank.

"You will be married in the Lutheran Church. I do not want your children growing up as Catholics. We came to Australia one hundred years ago to escape what the Catholics were doing to the people. John quickly agreed to them about getting married in the Lutheran church.

The wedding had been set for a month later.

The church was filled with the local German descent families who lived and worshipped in the district. Herman and John had buried the hatchet and had become good friends.

John and Helen's farm was only partly cleared when they purchased it. They had put very long hours in dusty hard conditions, chaining and ploughing the new land each year, spending many weeks picking stumps and stones by hand to bring the land into production. A lot of the farm income during the good years was ploughed back into the property to improve the land and build fences.

When the children were born, they had spent a fair amount of their time, being pushed around the dusty paddocks in a pram or stroller as Helen toiled in the paddocks.

John had kept his shearing round to help with the finances. Eventually, Tony had joined him, after leaving school. The other two children had gone out of the district. David had an apprenticeship in Adelaide, whilst Emma worked at a supermarket at Whyalla.

Through hard work and persistence, the farming venture had started to pay off. They had been able to upgrade their old, worn-out plant with a reasonable second-hand assortment of implements. John had gone to a government auction a few years previously and had purchased an old Caterpillar D7 bulldozer. This had been invaluable in digging some large dams for water for the livestock, prior to the reticulated piped water being laid to the farm, and, finally, in clearing the last of the large stumps and stones from the land. This old dozer was John's pride and joy, mainly for the hard work it had saved them in finishing the clearing work on the farm.

A few years back, the farm was made more viable with the reticulated water being connected. This permanent water had allowed them to run more sheep, as they were not solely reliant on the dam water. The dams had dried up during the last summer and were still dry as there had been no decent rains, causing water run off to fill them. This would have meant that they would have had to sell all of their livestock prior to having the reticulated water being laid on. There was only rain water in the house and shed tanks for their use.

The last three years had been a nightmare. Three years ago, they had only received half of their annual rainfall. Consequently, their crop and wool yields were cut by about half. This had happened before, and as they lived in a marginal area, they were used to such events. The next year had been worse with them, only reaping enough grain for seed, having to cut the remaining flock by another half, and selling the excess sheep for almost nothing as there was no demand for skinny sheep because of the drought.

John had borrowed carry-on finance, but the factors of the bad season and the drastically rising interest rates had compounded, leaving them in a bad situation. As was usual in a drought situation, the land values had dropped very low as there would be no local buyers looking to buy a property in the middle of a drought.

To make matters worse, there were only about a third of the sheep left in the district, and most farmers were shearing their own sheep to save on costs.

John had been talking to a few neighbors who had informed him that the bank was getting tough and threatening to start selling some farmers' land up to recover costs.

The men rose from the table and then walked out into the cold sunshine. 'What do you think we should do about the dead sheep lying around?' Up until now there had only been a few, but as the feed situation worsened, both men could see the situation worsening. John felt a sense of guilt over the plight of the poor skinny sheep.   John got into the ute and drove it over to the large silo which contained the precious oats they were feeding. Tony had walked over in anticipation of having to unhitch the grain feeder. He unhitched the trailer and left the bin and trailer sitting under the grain auger ready for the next load of precious oats. John walked over to the silo and tapped at the wall of the silo, trying to tell from the noise on the iron as to where the level of the oats had descended to.

Tony had been pondering John's conversation about the dead sheep. 'Why don't we get the dozer going and dig a trench for the dead sheep? At least, it will keep the flies down and make us feel a bit better if we don't have to see them when we drive out in the paddock. I feel as if it's my fault that they are dying.' They both agreed the sheep could be buried to keep the crows and foxes away. Tony walked over to the large skillion-roofed shed, which held most of the farming plant. John slid in to the worn seat of the ute, drove it over to the shed, and parked in front of the old Caterpillar D7. He turned the rattling diesel motor off. 'Get the battery out of the Chamberlain tractor, whilst I check the oil and water in the dozer'. Tony climbed up and undid the tractor's bonnet and started to remove the battery. Laddie noticed that John was checking the dozer. This was usually a good source of sport, as, like the header, it was usually the home of some mice.

The battery was carried over and put it into the battery box on the dozer. 'I'll go and let the pup go, may as well let him have a bit of fun too.' he walked off around the corner and unleashed the young sheepdog from its running lead from the kennel, which was under a mallee tree behind the shed. The dog was pleased to be set free and jumped at Tony, licking his hands, and then ran back and forth, yipping. 'Calm down you silly young bugger.' laughed Tony.

The D7 had not been started for two years. John filled the petrol tank for the pilot motor from a plastic can, then turned the petrol on, and then turned the starter key. The petrol-starting motor spluttered to life, shooting loose black soot out of the small exhaust poking out of the bonnet. It settled down to a steady roar. John pulled the hand clutch on the side of the motor in and started the main motor, turning with the compression lift on. He watched the oil pressure gauge. When the oil pressure rose, he dropped the compression lift and pulled the throttle out. The big motor roared to life, tossing more loose soot towards the shed rafters. John then released the hand clutch of the pilot motor and then turned the petrol tap off. Finally, he turned the key to the off position, and the roaring pilot motor stopped. The big diesel idled steadily, its turbocharger making a whistling noise.

The dogs, who had been quivering in anticipation, jumped on the first hapless mouse which ran from its dozer fortress. John climbed up on to the machine and sat in the seat. He opened the throttle, pulled the gearshift lever, and then drove the dozer out of the shed. The dogs were dispatching almost every mouse which ran out with a quick nip to the back of the head. The occasional one had the good fortune to escape and climb up under the truck, header or the tractor.

Tony walked over and opened the gate in the fence by the shed so John could drive over next to a stone heap in the paddock and dig the grave He then started the ute and drove over, then pulled a bale of hay from the hay shed, and tossed it on to the tray of the ute. He took it to a small mob of sheep which had been put into a holding paddock by the shearing shed.
This was the hospital paddock where any sheep which had gone down were brought to be cared for. There were around twenty sheep in this small paddock, which was usually used for a holding paddock at shearing time, either for the woolly sheep waiting for their turn in the shearing shed or for the freshly shorn sheep waiting to be let out into the paddock at the end of the day.

John stopped about two hundred meters from the sheds next to a large heap of limestone, which both he and Helen had picked off the farming land when they had first bought the farm. These rocks had been thrown into the tray of an old tip dray, which had been converted to be pulled by a tractor.

The heavy dozer had rattled the accumulation of dust and mouse nests from under the tracks on the way. The dozer tracks were rusty and squealed in protest when John turned a corner. John lined the machine up, then dropped the heavy rippers into the stony ground, and drove forward. The extra effort caused the exhaust manifold to get hotter. The smell of cooking mouse manure and urine was overpowering. Finally, after a couple of rips, the smell started to abate.

John had scooped a hole about five meters long and two meters deep, the width of the blade. There was not a sign of moisture even at this depth. This was the legacy of the three dry years. The usual subsoil moisture, which helped the crops to grow in a normal drought, was all but gone, a bit like the money in the bank account. John thought as he turned the machine on its axis and then drove the dozer back to the shed.

John was not looking forward to the trip to town. Helen carefully packed the eggs into the baskets, placing a sheet of newspaper between each layer to make sure that none broke on the trip to town on the rough dirt road. To have eggs break and leak on to the floor of the car was not a good idea as the smell was almost impossible to remove, as they had found from a previous occasion. These eggs were used in part to swap for some of the groceries. These were the basics such as flour, sugar, soap powder, and other items of daily use. John butchered their own sheep, and Helen had a pretty little jersey cow, which she milked daily for their milk and butter. The cow was housed in a small paddock adjoining the house yard. During the night, the cow's calf was allowed to drink from her. It was shut away during the day so the cow could be milked at night.

All three were very on edge all the way to Kimba. They were definitely not looking forward to the meeting with the Lizard. They had all talked long into the night about the problem they had in the previous evening, but they could not come up with any answers. The machinery was certainly not worth a lot of money, and owing to the drought, it would only bring half of its value.

After going to bed, John and Helen had cuddled for a while. This had helped to take their minds off the daily problems. They had talked well into the night between themselves, being too keyed up to sleep.

Selling the farming machinery was not really an option, as if they could survive this year. It would be needed the next year. There were definitely no luxuries. They were living on the bare minimum.

They approached the small town. The large concrete grain silos were the most prominent structure on the skyline. The silos would hardly be used this year, which would be another detrimental blow to the town as a lot of the town's people relied on this seasonal work for a living.

John drove through the nearly deserted streets, turned the car into the curb, and stopped in front of the small bank building. They got out of the car and walked inside. The young girl Debbie the teller, asked them to take a seat as Mr. Wilson was busy and would be with them in about ten minutes.

A heated discussion was taking place in the manager's office. After half an hour, a red-faced man walked out. 'Bloody little turd,' he said almost inaudibly. He turned to John and grimaced. 'G'day, John, bloody hard times. I hope you do a bit better than I did with the little shit. He threatened to sell me up.' The man stormed out through the bank door, muttering to himself. Debbie walked into the manager's office with a sheaf of papers in a folder. 'Mr. Wilson will see you now.' She went back to working behind the counter.

They walked into the office. The Lizard was shuffling the papers on his desk. He rose and shook John's and Helen's hands. He omitted to acknowledge Tony. John always thought that his hand felt like a cold dead fish, soft and slimy. 'Ah, Mr. and Mrs. Nickols.' the lizard smirked at the prospect of being able to put the screws into John. "Take a seat, please whilst I sort some of these papers.' The manager had a superior smile on his face. He sat back down on his chair, then leaned back, and surveyed the trio sitting in front of him. He folded his hairy hands over his stomach and peered over the top of his bifocal glasses.

The name Lizard was almost true to label. The man had a thin, pinched-in face, which always seemed to be in need of a shave. He wore thin steel-rimmed glasses, which covered the small beady eyes, which seemed to be darting back and forth around the room. 'Looking for flies to eat,' John had always joked. His lips were just like a pencil line on his face. He was almost completely bald, having just a thin ring of black hair around the sides of his head, a very unattractive man. His voice had a nasal squeak to it. The Lizard leaned towards the desk again. 'We seem to have a large problem at the moment regarding your overdraft. What do you expect to do about it?' squeaked the Lizard. He shuffled through the papers some more. He then looked up and stared at John with the reptilian eyes.

'I think that you should know our position better than most. We have tried almost everything. What would you suggest?' said John, his face getting red from the effort to contain himself. 'It's not for me to suggest anything at the moment. This is your problem.'

John leaned forward. 'I beg to differ. This is also the bank's problem. If you rotten cows had not raised the interest rates to nearly 20 per cent, thanks to the new inept Prime Minister Paul Keating's recession we had to have, most of us would not be in this mess.

You did not even have the good sense to keep the extra money you earned. Your bloody bank nearly broke the state's finances because of the airy-fairy investments it made.' The Lizard took offence at these remarks; he sneered sarcastically and then sat upright and informed them that if there was not a reduction to the overdraft in the next month, there would be actions taken by the bank to recoup moneys owed to it.

The discussion became more heated with both Tony and Helen having their say. This was unusual for Helen as she was not usually the type to become belligerent.

The meeting ended as the previous one evidently had, with a lot of yelling and nothing resolved. The Nickols' walked out. John, as the previous man, muttered under his breath, then stopped, and greeted the next customers waiting. 'Hi, Fred, hope you have better luck with the little arsehole than we did.' He was still muttering as he walked out through the door. 'I reckon the little prick gets off on stirring everyone up. Pity help his bloody wife if he is that big an arsehole at home,' Tony added as they got into the old car and then reversed back into the near deserted street.

They were still stirred up when they stopped out in front of the local supermarket where Helen was going to swap the eggs. Under normal conditions, they would have had a counter meal at the hotel and a couple of beers with the local patrons of the hotel before travelling home. The hotel trade had dropped off drastically since the drought had taken hold on the district. John and Tony walked over to the stock and station agents, Elders. John was interested in what had been happening to some of the other farmers in the district.

Tony's interests were more in the pretty girl who served behind the counter. The news was not good. The Lizard had woven his ways throughout the district. Most farmers were upset. 'Billy Franklin offered to punch his nose for him. Bloody lucky for him, he didn't. He's a real scrapper when he gets going. The manager was going to get the Police on to him. 'I think the boy fancies your counter staff,' John joked to the stock agent. They both had a laugh. Tony was trying really hard to make a good impression. 'You've kept the poor young bugger out in the bush too long. He looks as if he is egg-bound,' said the manager laughing. The only news that John had found out was bad. There was not any money around to buy farms. No one in their right mind was going to borrow money at the exorbitant interest rates to buy a farm in the middle of a drought. It was a buyer's market if they were silly enough.

'Come on, Tony, we had better go and get mum and shoot through.' Tony reluctantly left the pretty girl.

'Stuff the bloody droughts and farming,' he mumbled as he walked out the door, reluctant to leave the pretty girl.   As they drove back to the farm, John was deep in thought. He was trying hard to take his mind off the problems with the bank. 'I reckon that if we could control those bloody crows, we might have a bit better chance of bringing a few of the weaker sheep home to the hospital paddock. I think we ought to build a crow trap when we get home.' Tony had never heard of a crow trap and asked a lot of questions during the trip home. At least, it took their minds off the real problem, the bank, and the lack of money. 'I think you are trying to pull my leg. Those crows are that cunning that all you have to do is pick up the gun in the workshop and they're gone before you poke it out of the door. Those mongrels have sixth sense. I've walked out of the shed with a broom and pointed it at the tree with the crows in it, and they just laughed at me. But the minute you pick up a gun, that's different. They fly away before you can poke a bullet into its breech.'

'Well, have it your way, but most of the cunning animals or birds have a foible. It is usually greed.'

John carried the scant groceries into the house, whilst Helen pushed the kettle further on to the hot plate of the stove so it would boil for a coffee. Tony got some cold roast mutton, bread, and chutney out to prepare some late lunch. The mutton was lean and stringy as there were no decent fat sheep on the farm to slaughter for food.

After lunch, John and Tony drove to the back of the machinery shed to get ready for the crows.

They loaded some old rusty wire netting and some fence droppers on to the ute and set out down the lane to the dead sheep near the lane way, which the crows had been hanging around. Tony opened the gate, and John drove the short distance over to the dead sheep. The crows flew off, cawing in protest at the disturbance of their feast.

Tony threw the fencing materials off the tray of the ute, whilst John selected six of the straightest used steel fence droppers.

John hammered six fence droppers into the ground with the light sledge hammer to form a circle three meters across around the dead sheep. The crows sat in the mallee trees and still cawed their disapproval at having their feast interrupted. They watched the proceedings with much interest. 'Never mind, boys, you can have all you like soon. Just wait for a while,' John chuckled. Getting some sort of revenge against such cruel birds as the crows was going to be sweet justice.

Tony pulled the netting tight around the circle and tied the ends. 'Ow, I always do that with this blasted stuff.' Tony had pushed one of the sharp recently cut netting ends into his finger, up under his finger nail. He gave it a quick pull to get it out; bright red blood squirted out of the puncture. Tony reached into his trouser pocket and got his handkerchief, which he wrapped around his finger, and went on working. John pulled a couple of pieces of netting over the top, then twirled the edges together, and then cut a hole the size of a small hat brim into the middle of the top. 'They're all finished. Let's drive off a bit and see what happens.'

They drove back down the lane for about 150 meters and waited. 'I still reckon that this is all bullshit,' chided Tony as they sat and watched. After about five minutes, one of the hungrier crows flew down and sat on top of the trap. He walked around on the netting, protesting loudly. He cocked his head from side to side as he studied the trap. He was soon followed by more of his mates.

One of the gamer crows was not going to be done out of a meal by this cage with a hole in the top. He had worked out that he could drop down inside quite easily. Crows were notorious for finding their way into the fowl run and stealing eggs if there was a hole in the netting.

The crow dropped down and started to feed. He was soon followed by some more. 'Now this is the funny part. The greedy bludgers can drop through the hole with their wings shut but cannot fly out with their wings open. See.' One of the crows had eaten enough and had tried to fly out and could not manage it. It flapped its wings against the sides of the trap as it tried to escape. Still more crows landed on the trap and upon seeing so many inside, must have thought that they were missing out on something really good. They too jumped down and feasted off the dead sheep. 'Right, let's go. We'll clean it out tomorrow morning. You can give mum a hand and milk Daisy when you get home. She is still pretty upset today after the bloody visit to the Lizard.'

Tony had just finished separating the milk in the laundry to get thick farm cream and was cleaning the cream separator, which was always a bit of a chore as there were lots of pieces to wash and dry. He was just walking out of the iron laundry at the back of the shed with the skimmed milk for the four small pigs, which they were fattening up to eat, when an old Land Cruiser rattled over the cattle grid and pulled up at the back fence.

The door of the ute swung open. 'Cripes, things must be bloody bad on this farm if you have to eat bloody crows.' One of the men yelled as he half-fell and got out of the ute. The other man climbed out of his side with effort. The two men were as skinny as rakes, and their skin was weather-beaten and lined. Their skin was burnt by the sun so much that they were both nearly black.

The Kelly boys, Bert and Harry, were two bachelor brothers who lived two farms up the road. 'Put the milk down and give us a hand.' Bert handed Tony a carton of beer. 'I got this bottle for your mum.' He showed Tony a bottle of Irish cream, Helen's favourite. Helen and John came out to see what the noise was all about. 'I have something for you, M'lady.' Bert gave a mock bow as he handed Helen the small bottle of Irish cream. 'Come in and take a seat,' offered Helen. 'Oy, Tony, bring the booze. Don't try to sneak off with it,' joked Harry. Tony carried the beer inside and then walked back out to finish the job of feeding the milk to the little pigs.

Harry and Bert were evidently a bit worse for wear already. Tony gratefully accepted the cold beer which was thrust into his hand as he walked through the door with the bowl of cream. 'We've come to celebrate with our friends. We have just got rid of the debt at the bank. You should have seen the look on the rotten Lizard bastard's face when we paid him off with new hundred-dollar bills. Here, have another beer.' More beers were handed around.

'What have you guys been doing? Growing whoopee weed?' asked John. 'Nah, this is better than that. This is legal. We've been to Coober Pedy and found some opal, sixty thousand bucks worth. You should have seen the Lizard when we put the forty thousand dollars on his desk. He almost smiled. We told him we had just reaped out marijuana crop.' Bert had another drink from the beer can. 'He said he was not worried as to where the money had come from. We'll probably have the local cop out to check us over. I wouldn't put anything past that devious little prick.' 'You're going to stay for a meal?' asked Helen. 'Nah, we had better get going soon. We have got some stew on the side of the stove ready to warm up for tea. Thanks anyway Helen.' This was a bit of a game by now, the Kelly's always stayed. 'Hey Tony, how about going out and getting the other carton of beer out of the Toyota. Some rotten cows have drunk all of this one.' Tony went out to fetch the beer. Helen busied herself and took a frying pan from the cupboard, then put the frying pan on the stove, put some oil in it, and started to cook chops and eggs.

Harry and Bert hoed into the meal. 'Skinny chops I'm afraid.' 'Nah, it's better than our stew. This one didn't turn out too good. Harry and Bert were famous for their four-day stews; they usually had everything in them. The meat was cut up with a blunt meat cleaver, so there was a large amount of bone splinters as an extra barrier to anyone foolish enough to try one. The four days entailed. Day one, the stew was barely cooked; day two, the vegies were just getting soft; day three, there was a green mold starting to grow around the edge of the pot; and day four, the two mangy dogs usually got the rest.

'I reckon you would have a new strain of penicillin in that pot of stew if anyone was game to test it,' joked Helen as she served more chops and eggs.

The discussion became more serious as the night progressed. John told the men about his run-in with the Lizard. 'Why don't you come up to Coober Pedy with us? There's plenty of unpegged ground around where we are working.'

The Kelly's had gone to Coober Pedy some ten years before when things on the farm were not too financial and had found around twenty thousand dollars then. 'The funny thing is that the place where we are working is next to the spot we got the opal before. All the miners reckon it's a dead area and there is no opal there. There's heaps of room if you and Tony want to have a go.' Bert and Harry had gone up the previous time with a home-made windlass and an assortment of picks and shovels off the farm. They had dug a few shafts by hand, down to around twenty-five feet. They were about ready to come home as they had not found anything, when they had bottomed out on to a seam of opal. They had sold the opal and returned home to Kimba. There had been stories a few years ago around town as to how they had found a half a million dollars. These stories always seemed to abound when someone tried something new.

Helen was the one to suggest that the men give mining a try. The prospects of anyone getting any other income seemed almost impossible at the present time.

'We're going back to have another go at the mining in two weeks' time,' said Harry. 'You'll be very welcome to come up with us and have a look.' Tony and John decided to give the opals a try and agreed to go with them to have a look. The Kelly's had one advantage over John and Tony. They had sold all of their sheep the year before. 'Don't worry about them,' Helen reassured them. 'I can look after the sheep for about ten days. It would do you both good to get out of the farm for a while.'

The two weeks seemed to take a long time to pass. Both John and Tony were getting quite excited at the prospect of the new adventure. The number of crows had diminished considerably. They had caught over two hundred in the last two weeks. Occasionally, a new dead sheep was substituted for the previous one. Occasionally, a couple of the hapless crows were hung on the fence of the chicken run to frighten off their mates. Crows were notorious egg stealers.

The morning after the Kelly's had left had been quite a fiasco where the crows were concerned. John had the bright idea as to get the crows out of the trap. 'All we will need is a long piece of eight-gauge wire with a hook on the end. The same as we use to catch a chicken when we want to eat one.'

There were about thirty crows flopping around in the trap when the men arrived. They got very agitated when the men walked up. John put the heavy wire into the trap from under the edge of the wire netting, which he had lifted slightly. 'I told you it would be easy,' he boasted as he hooked the first struggling crow out. Tony took the crow and hit it on the head with a short piece of wood. The other crows watched this happen. John hooked another and then another. The crows were studying the method of capture. Suddenly they seemed to work out that to be near the thin piece of wire was bad news.

As soon as the wire was poked into the trap, most of the crows would climb up the sides of the netting, making it almost impossible to catch them. Finally, the men honed their skills and emptied the trap. The dead crows were put into a bag ready for the trip to the cemetery, as the hole where the dead sheep were put was called. They discussed taking the BSA air rifle out to shoot the cunning crows the next day.

There had been a few light showers of rain. It was certainly not enough to get excited about, but it did make the crops green up a bit. 'God, I hope we get a bit more in the next few days,' said John at breakfast as he emptied the rain gauge into the measure. 'We had twenty-two points.' He walked over and wrote the figure on to the rainfall chart with the pencil hanging on a piece of string from the nail which held the sheaf of yearly rainfall charts on the back of the kitchen door. These charts also contained information as to when shearing and seeding were completed and what the harvest and wool clips yielded. 'Hell, there are a lot of gaps between each lot of rain on the bloody chart. No wonder things are so dry.'

John sat down at the table to a bowl of cereal. He poured the fresh farm milk on to the breakfast cereal. 'Four days to go. I saw Bert yesterday when you were out checking the sheep, and I was down at the main road, fixing the hole in the fence, which the kangaroos had made. He stopped for a bit of a yarn mainly to see if we had not changed our mind about the trip up north. I reckon they must have given the pub a bit of a go lately. He sure looked skinny.'

Chapter three

Leaving for Manilla

As they stood in the line to purchase the tickets, they noticed that the wind was getting stronger. Finally, the ticket clerk sold them the two tickets to Manilla. They filed up the gang plank of the ferry carrying the bags, then found some seats among the large crowd of people. The cases and bags were stowed under the seats.

The weather was now quite windy; not long after leaving the pier the heavily laden ferry moved out into the rough water, it rocked from side to side and front to back, both took it in turns to visit one of the large buckets near the bathroom to be sea sick. Half way through the voyage the wind dropped out and the waves stopped, the ferry stopped rolling. The queasy tummy feeling started to subside; they had been on this ferry for five hours. It was now dark with a full moon shining on the now still water. This was a very different experience for both of them   When alighting down the gang plank to the pier. The rocking started once more. The pier was now moving. This sensation took some time to go as they both walked from the wharf area into the edge of the city.

A small boarding house with a bright neon light advertising cheap rooms was across the road in front of them. They did not feel very comfortable walking round the dock area at night, Ali and Zeena walked in to the dingy office and booked in for the night. A tired scruffy looking woman told them to follow her up the stairs to the room. The inside of the house smelled musty and also had the odour of food, which had been cooked in the rooms. The room was not clean, but was at least somewhere to get off the streets for the rest of the night,
After a restless start to the night being chewed up by bed bugs, they sprayed the beds with some mosquito spray which was found in the cupboard. This evidently slowed the bugs down, they finally went to sleep.

The weather was beautiful; a light cooling breeze was blowing in the morning as they left the boarding house. Upon entering the street in the daylight they noticed how run down all of the other buildings were. People sat outside on chairs on the footpath, some women were using old pedal sewing machines to make clothes. A group of men sat at a table playing Mah-jongg, some skimpily dressed young girls sat in front of some of the doorways, they bantered all of the men as they walked pas., One of the girls yelled to Ali offering a very cheap full massage. They kept walking.

After leaving the wharf area, with the seedy streets they walked and walked, carrying the heavy luggage. They marveled at the good shops and upper-class tourist Cafes.

When walking along a small street Zeena noticed a To- Let sign in a ground floor flat window of a building. Zeena asked Ali to come in the main door to a clean foyer with stairs and a elevator leading off. She knocked on a door with a sign 'MANAGER'. The door opened and a young man walked out. Zeena asked the man about leasing the flat." Wait while I get the keys, I will show you through the unit". He turned then returned inside. He came back with the keys on a small key-ring. The two bedroom unit was furnished and had an electric stove and refrigerator. A far cry from the dangerous kerosene primus stove and ice box, which had been in the old crumbling house they had left. The man showed them where a small food shop was, about one hundred meters away on a cardboard map of the area which was glued to the back of the entry door. He also pointed out other services nearby. A deal was struck and the lease paid with a bond. The whole deal seemed too easy. The suit cases and kitbag were put into a wardrobe with a blanket over the top of them.

After leaving the new apartment, they went for another long walk to check the scenery out in the section of Manilla away from the wharf area. It was now early evening; Zeena had studied the map of the area where the new apartment was, so they did not get lost in their travels, and making sure they could find the apartment again.

Before returning to the new apartment they went in to a small coffee shop cum restaurant for an evening meal. Near the door taped in the window, was a sign, 'looking for a waitress'. The restaurant was spotlessly clean inside and seemed to have a good lot of tidy diners eating their meals. Zeena asked at the counter about the job, the girl went to get the manager. The friendly man came and looked Zeena over. "Have you ever worked in a diner before" Zeena said "Yes a long time ago, but one never forgets" Zeena lied, the prospect of a permanent job appealed to her. "Ok you have got a job. I will put you on probation with pay for two weeks. If you do OK you will have a permanent job." Zeena was elated.   As they ate their meal Zeena studied the waitress's serving the tables. They talked in a friendly manner to the customers, as they did their work.

Almost every day, Ali worked with the stall holders in the market. He still had the idea of the drug business. He had been watching some of the smaller dealers at work and quickly learned that if one got too far above their station they were usually destined for a swimming lesson at the wharf during the night with some heavy chains tied to their legs.   As the months rolled on, as he worked in the market, making deliveries and helping set up stalls in the morning, Ali would notice that some of the small-time dealers would go missing. The big bosses of the drug cartels would make it known that certain people had been learning to swim. At least three people Ali knew were reputed to having the all night swimming lessons while he had been working at the market.

Working in her new job in the coffee shop diner, Zeena was very happy and was popular with the customers. She had met a nice man who had a very good government job; she was very pleased to have this new chance at life, and looked relaxed. She even joked and laughed on occasions.   While he worked in the market, Ali noticed that one of the head men in the family of the drug syndicates would sit sipping coffee and talking to the Police and district officials. A few days later there would be a member of one of the other families treating these same officials to a sumptuous feast.

The heads of the drug syndicates were the Sanchez, Gomez and Rinaldo families. Emilio Sanchez was by far the most powerful. These men were driven around in large expensive American cars and always had some minders with them; these men carried semi concealed arms as protection. Ali had seen some of the houses these people lived in the best part of the city when out delivering goods for some of the stall holders in the market. Their children were escorted to the best schools by bodyguards in these large cars. He was envious of their money and power.

After helping to clean up at the coffee shop, Zeena was walking home from her work one evening. As she walked past a doorway, an arm shot out and grasped Zeena firmly by the shoulder; Zeena was pulled into the doorway and forced against the door. The greasy Indian jewellery trader faced her. "I have wondered where my favourite woman had gone to; I have seen you working in the coffee shop, I want to have sex with you tonight". Zeena tried to escape but the greasy man held her with a vice like grip. "I do not go with men any more. That part of my life has finished". The man laughed. "If I were to go to the place where you work and shout that I knew you were a poor class harlot, I would bet that you would lose your job". Zeena was extremely frightened. "If you come for one last time, is that what you want" He smirked and showed the large gold tooth. "No I want you when I please, when I am in Manilla on business, and I will not pay. You were the best woman I have ever had". Zeena was frightened. She knew this man would carry out his threat. She told him her address and said to come at nine o'clock in the evening. The man slapped her face and laughed. That is for trying to get away. He then let her go. Zeena ran home crying as she ran.

Ali was sitting at the table eating a piece of cheese on some crusty bread. He had just arrived home, When Zeena burst into the room. Her hair was askew, and she had tears running down her face. She sat down at the table. She felt she would fall down. She related the meeting with the greasy Indian to Ali; she did not know what to do. The prospects moving again did not appeal to her. Her past was catching up with her. This was a real worry. Her new job and the new nice partner were at stake over the greasy Indian problem.

After thinking deeply for a short while Ali devised a plan to get rid of this man for good, he would hide in his wardrobe, and then as this pig of a man was having his way with Zeena he would pull a wire garrote around his neck and choke him. This would save having blood on the floor of the flat to clean up. He would get the cart from the market to remove the man and take him for a swim, the next night.

Ali left the flat and walked to the small corner shop, he purchased a small coil of steel wire and a wooden spoon with a stout handle. Upon returning home Ali cut the handle of the spoon in half with a sharp knife, he then cut a piece of wire from the coil, He cut the wire by working the knife back and forth on the wire then bent the wire repeatedly until it broke. There was plenty of wire to go round the thick greasy neck, the spoon pieces were attached by twirling the wire around the handles, then twitching the ends.

There was a loud banging on the door of the apartment. Zeena carefully opened the door. When the man entered the house, Ali was hiding in the wardrobe; The Indian hit Zeena as she let him in the door. He looked through the house, checking behind doors, and then asking if there was any other person there. Ali had been standing in a heavy coat in the wardrobe and had not been noticed by the Indian, as he had checked inside it. Zeena said they were alone. The man dragged Zeena to the bedroom and demanded she take off her clothes, she removed her clothes then lay on the bed, The Indian wasted no time removing his turban and clothes. He mounted Zeena and penetrated, hurting her as he did so. He was making grunting noises like a pig as he was having his way with her. He slapped her face hard," Move you bitch." he complained Ali sneaked out of the wardrobe and entered the room. He was out of sight of the Indian, as the bed faced toward the doorway. The Indian reared up to change his position when Ali slipped the loop of the garrote around the man's throat, then pulled with all of his might, as he did so he jumped onto the bed then pushed his knee into the man's back to get more leverage. Ali twisted the ends of the wire together, then poked the handle ends under the wire so the man could not undo them. The man was clawing at the wire trying to untie the wire. The man leaped back off Zeena and swung around. His face was swollen and purple. Ali nimbly leaped away from him, Zeena slid off the bed and rolled under the mattress onto the floor. Finally, the Indian crashed to the floor; he writhed around for about a minute and then lay still. Zeena slid out from under the bed and joined Ali to see if the Indian man was dead.

Ali and Zeena dragged the heavy man out of the room into the small kitchen- lounge part. Zeena found an old blanket, and then they rolled the man onto it.

The man was quickly swelling up like a balloon. "Take the wire off Ali or he will not sink when we carry him to the wharf .".Ali un-twirled the wire, when he did so a long gush of stinking air came from gushing from the Indian's nose and mouth. "We should dress him and lay him straight so he will fit on the market cart". Ali went rummaging through the greasy man's clothes to remove all identification and valuables.   The large diamond ring was taken off his finger, it was very tight so Ali wet to the kitchen and returned with some olive oil which he lubricated the man's finger with.   After some hard work the diamond ring was able to be dragged off the dead man's finger. The gold bracelet was taken from his arm, and gold chain from his neck. Zeena found a small suede leather pouch in the man's pocket; she opened the drawstring and tipped the contents on the rug, the contents seemed to be alive with colour as the tumbled out. "Look, Ali, these are diamonds" she counted forty stones which were about the size of a pea.   As he searched Ali found a wallet stuffed with cash. Zeena spat on the man, "thank you, pig I hope you go to rot in hell. I hope the pigs of hades eat you".

When the man was re dressed the blanket was pulled around him and the ends tied with pieces of the wire. Ali also used the man's turban to bind the edges of the blanket by looping it around many times then tying the ends together.

The man would have to wait for the next day to be taken to have his swimming lessons at the deserted part of the wharf the next night.   Ali was going to have to get some heavy weights to make sure the man did not float during his swimming lessons.   Both Zeena and Ali had a fitful night of sleep knowing that the dead man was in their house.

Ali was on a mission. What was he going to use to weigh the body of the Indian down with so it did not float? The Sanchez and Rinaldo have evidently had a large quantity of heavy chain, Ali could not think of a suitable substitute.

As he worked his way through the markets Ali looked through the wares of an old scrap metal merchant's lot, he found four heavy window sash weights. After a bit of bartering with the man Ali bought the weights" What do you need these for boy." asked the old man ." My uncle is restoring an old house and needs these for some new windows he is making ." " You are lucky, these would be very expensive and hard to find" Ali paid for the weights.

The man Ali did some deliveries for had a hand cart with thin large diameter, pump up motor cycle tyres. The cart had drop down sides and was almost two meters long, Ali had dragged this cart with some heavy loads through many places in the area while working with this man . Ali asked if he could borrow the cart that night as he had brought a heavy piece of furniture for his mother. The man thought for a few seconds, "OK, you can borrow the cart Ali as long as you return it when you come to work the next morning".

On his way from the market that evening, Ali towed the empty cart to the scrap metal lot. "I wondered how you were going to get the heavy weight back to your uncle" said the old man as he watched Ali toss the weights into the cart. Ali towed the cart home and arrived just on dark.   He pulled the cart up the doorstep through the door, luckily it just fitted. There was a stink of death in the flat. Zeena was spraying a very strong deodorant in the rooms. The man was rolled into the cart, using a lot of effort to move the heavy body; a plastic sheet had been laid in the cart floor. Ali attached the heavy sash weights to the dead man's legs with the wire. While Ali worked on the man, Zeena had a pail of hot water and a mop. She added some of the strong disinfectant then scrubbed the mess off the floor where the man had been laying. Some of his body fluids had leaked out onto the floor of the kitchen.

Zeena had been preoccupied at work during the day, and had found it hard to concentrate. Her boss had asked her if anything was worrying her. "Just woman's business I should be OK tomorrow".

When Zeena had returned from work Ali had been working on the cart. The cart side was closed then the top was covered with a blanket which was tied down with twine.

Zeena and Ali both pulled the cart to the end of the wharf, travelling by the thin moon and starlight, the top blanket was removed the greasy Indian was emitting some nasty odors after the rough trip to the wharf. The cart was pulled parallel to the edge of the wharf, the side was dropped and the man rolled into the stinking black water. There was a loud splash as the body hit the water. It floated for a short while, much to Zeena's and Ali's alarm. After a shot while the clothes absorbed the water and the heavy weights pulled the man's legs under the water, his body slipped under and out of sight. "I hope you stay standing forever, pig! Have a nice swim with the fishes," said Ali as the black water covered his body.

Zeena had to keep telling herself to keep this man out of her head during her working day. The shop had been very busy; this did not give much time to brood on the murder. She kept convincing herself that there had not been any other way. She was happy now and did not want to be forced to run-away by this man.   Life started to return to normal. Ali's face had lost the swelling and had stopped giving him discomfort. The scar showed prominently from his ear to chin. Each time he looked in a mirror he had memories of the gentle Sasha and Missy on the small property; he missed the simple life with her and the young village girl.

Ali had done a lot of deliveries for a gem merchant in the market. He had gained this man's trust. He had talked to this man when they had met in the market. He talked to this man about buying a gemstone which his mother had been given years ago. The man agreed to have a look at the stone.

It had been three weeks since the greasy Indian incident; Ali took one of the diamonds to this man to find what it might be worth. The man studied the stone for a minute then weighed it. "Hmm this stone is large, one point four carats". He put a price of one thousand five hundred dollars on the stone. "Where did you get this stone, it is a very good quality diamond", he asked, "This is my mothers. She had it given to her many years ago and was going to make a ring with it. She thought it may have been a zircon, as she did not know very much about it back where we came from." "This had probably been stolen then!" "My mother would not have a stolen stone if she knew it had been stolen. Is it really a diamond?" The man assured Ali that it was. "Do you want to sell the stone?" "Mother told me if we were to get a good price to sell". The deal was sealed and the stone taken by the dealer in exchange for the money.

One of the Drug dealing cartels, the Gomez family had tried to take more of the market than their share, a mini drug war started when one of the older sons of the greedy family had his car blow up with him in it. The explosion had been an over kill, the car and the young man's body had been strewn over a large area.

Nearly all of the house windows in some of the close streets had been broken. There were a lot of people working to scrape pieces of the young man and his car off the paving and walls of the adjacent houses.

The market was abuzz with the information. Armed thugs openly patrolled the market trying to collect information as to who had been the bomber. The hit would have been organised by Emilio Sanchez. As the Gomez family had been trying to get some of his territory.

Ali saw this as a time to buy some drugs and to start to set up a very small network of young people he knew used drugs. Three secondary pushers helped Ali distribute the marijuana.

There were a lot of people using marijuana. This trade was the lower end of the market. The real money was in the heroin and other related hard drug trade. The major families tolerated a small amount of opposition to the marijuana trade; to go against all of the small dealers in this trade would have been very hard.

The marijuana trade was quite lucrative for Ali. As he walked through the market he talked to the tourists. He was a good talker, telling them where to go to see different sights and where to go to get a woman for the night. He plied his trade with some of these tourists who were visiting from overseas.

One of the smaller dealers for the drug syndicate was speaking to Ali one day and warned him about being too greedy, "You do not want to learn to swim do you"? This warning rattled Ali. He did not know how to swim, and did not want to be taken to the wharf to find out.

As most of the drug dealer's sons and daughters finally graduated from school. Most of them went into the law, medical and other associated trades. These trades were not as profitable as the drug trade but were legal. The family reputation and money was a very good reference for a good job.

There was a good prospect for deliveries to be made from the market with a van. Ali decided wanted to learn how to drive a car. He searched around for a driving school; he found a school not too far from the market. The young man running the school had an old Ford Prefect car. This car had a habit of jumping when the clutch had been let out too quickly. Ali had signed up with the young man, Rico and took the driving lessons. The leaping Ford was quite a handful to get going without stalling the small motor. He had wanted to own a car for some time, when he finally completed the course with Rico. He obtained his license to drive a car from the local police station. He then purchased a used Morris Minor van from a used car dealer.

The small van had the ability to be able to be driven into some of the smaller laneways. This made it useful to pick up some of the freight too heavy to be moved in the hand carts in some of the steeper parts of the city. The small van was used to ferry the drugs and other freight around to the markets and the wharf area of Manilla. He also drove up into the hills on occasions to purchase marijuana from some growers.

Some of the business in the market used Ali to do the heavy pick up and deliveries; He was using the van to off-load some freight for one of these business's, he noticed a very pretty girl in the office when he had gone to be paid. He did not think that a pretty girl like her would give him a second look. He made some clever remarks and had told some jokes. He had then asked her to have dinner with him one night. He was really only flirting. The girl, Marci said "What about tonight. I am not doing anything ". Ali was amazed and could not get her address quick enough.   The street address was in a better part of town. Ali had polished and cleaned the Morris until he could see his face in the shiny paint. He was tidy with a new haircut and shiny shoes. He looked in a mirror. In his eyes he only saw the ugly scar, not the person behind it.

The scar was one of the reasons Ali worked so hard in the drug business, he had scant regard for his own safety. It was a constant reminder of the simple life with Sasha and the small farm, and Missy the goat.

One problem with Ali's marijuana business was keeping it small enough to not feel the wrath of the major drug lords. Ali kept his prices reasonable. There were still huge profits to be gained in the trade by not ripping the poor customers off too badly.

Ali was just getting the keys to the car when one of the lads he knew in the market banged on the door of his flat, Ali opened the door. "Quick Ali, Emilio Sanchez is sending some men to get you" the lad came in as Ali rushed to get the box of money and the diamonds. He gave the lad the money he had in his pocket. It was about two hundred dollars. He ran to the car and started the motor then zoomed off. A large car came careering around the corner. The lad had run down a narrow alley-way behind the building. Ali followed him in the car. The lad jumped into a doorway as Ali sped past. The lane -way was only used for hand carts to collect the trash and deliver goods. It was very narrow.

The Morris Minor just fitted past the protruding doorsteps. The occasional rubbish bin skidded into doorways, as they skidded along in front of the car. The large car chasing Ali sped into the alley-way to follow.   The car just fitted width wise. The car travelled a short distance; it bounced over two parallel door steps, and then crashed down on the steps lifting the rear wheels off the ground, the wheels spun in mid-air, both the doors of the car were wedged by the walls of the buildings, preventing the hit men from getting out of the car door or windows.

At the end of the alley there was a sharp turn to the right to allow the hand cart to turn into another alley-way. This turn was too tight for the car to turn in to. In front of Ali was a short flight of stone stairs, luckily the same width of the lane way. The Morris Minor bounced to the bottom of the stairs; two terrified people were running in front of the car, they jumped over the side of the steps to let Ali past. He then turned into a square open area with some streets leading out.

When he turned out of the Square Ali headed away from the wharf area. He was extremely shaken up by this experience. If it had not been for the warning Ali would have been getting ready to meet the fish in his swimming lesson. He had no intention of meeting the greasy Indian under the wharf.

Zeena would have to wait to find out his fate as Ali had no intention of going near her work place, as a lot of people knew she was his mother. He definitely did not want her involved with the Sanchez drug syndicate. Emilio Sanchez was an extremely dangerous and vindictive man. He was the man who had ordered the son of the rival drug baron to be blown up a few months before.

In his panic Ali was having trouble working out what he should do. The Drug families were like a giant octopus. They had tentacles reaching far out of Manilla. The large scar on Ali's face was now a huge liability as it was now like a beacon, advertising his identity

Chapter four

Travelling to Coober Pedy

The Toyota had been packed the previous day. There were spare drums of diesel, a plastic jerry-can of water, a large toolbox, blankets, and a large icebox full of food.

The trio walked out of the house to see the sun just coming up over the horizon.

After a teary farewell from Helen and lots of cuddles for both men, John and Tony got into the ute and slammed the rattily doors; the old ute finally drove off, leaving Helen alone. Helen watched as the ute drove the full length of the drive and then turned on to the Kimba road.

When the plume of dust was no longer visible in the early morning sun, Helen walked back into the house. She suddenly felt very lonely. Helen tried to shake the loneliness off by trying to think of the good things which might come from the men's adventure. Her thoughts then centered on the fact that the farm was getting very hard for the men to bear over the last few weeks and the change would do the men good.   Bert and Harry were not waiting at their gate. The gate was typical of the rest of the farm. It had been hit on numerous occasions on the way home from the hotel after the two had over imbibed. The middle of the gate had a large bend in it.

Tony unhooked the gate, which nearly fell over as the top hinge was broken. He carried the gate to an opened position. As there were no livestock on the farm, Tony left the rickety gate open whilst they drove up the driveway to the Kelly's mansion?   The shack in which they lived was not much better than the rickety gate. It was a lean-to on the side of the large implement and shearing shed. One large shed partitioned off into three; a small galvanized iron ablution block stood five meters from the shed.

The dogs usually had free range inside the dwelling. The inside of the shack was furnished with cast-off furniture, which Bert and Harry had bought cheaply at farm clearing sales throughout the district. There was hardly room to move between the boxes which had been bought at the farm auctions and carried inside but had never been unpacked. These boxes were heaped one on top of the other against the walls. There was a strong dog smell in the air. The two dogs were chained in the back of the ute and could be heard barking as the Nickols' drew near. 'Shut up, you mangy buggers,' growled Harry as John pulled in next to them. The dogs wagged their tails. This was usual. When the dogs were growled at, they usually wagged their tails, but when they were spoken to kindly, they cowered off with their tails between their legs. Nice talking and coaxing usually meant that they were being caught for some unpleasant reason—a wash—down with some concoction to kill their fleas or a belting for some wrong doing.

After a couple of minutes of talking, Bert said, 'Follow us. We'll lead the way.' They headed off down the driveway. Bert drove through. Harry got out to shut the gate and then waved John through. The two utes then headed towards Buckleboo, a small town with not much more than a hall, an oval, and a few old houses. Tony knew this area well as he often visited the town to compete in football and cricket matches.

All of the paddocks were brown with only a few tufts of grey green showing on the lighter soil types. Things were worse here. At least, most of their crops were still alive, albeit struggling to do so. There was an air of desolation about the place—so different from four years ago, when record crops were reaped in the district. Dust blew across the red paddocks in the light breeze. Some of the fences along the roadside were already half buried with the red sand, which had blown off the bare paddocks in the strong winds of the last few weeks.

Past Buckleboo, the farming country started to get less. It was a patchwork of cleared farming ground amongst the mallee scrub. Finally, the farming country with its cleared paddocks ended. Then the narrow road went, winding through the large mallee trees, with open-range land between them. This was the start of the station country. The open areas between the trees were covered mainly with salt bush, but, because of the drought, even this hardy plant looked stressed and nearly dead. The few sheep that were seen did look in better condition than the poor ones in the farming country because they had the saltbush and other natural herbage to graze on.

The road was no more than a track graded through the red dirt of the plain. This road was notorious for being un-passable in the rain because the red mud would stick under a car and nearly block the mudguards with it. There was sure no problem with wet weather this year   They followed Bert and Harry at a safe distance to keep out of the red dust, which billowed out from behind their ute.
After about forty kilometers, the mallee finally gave way to the traditional vegetation of the station country, myall, mulga, and saltbush.   Every few kilometers, there was a gate to be opened and then shut behind them. They were lucky as a lot of the gates now had stock grids replacing them. These were built up on to a mound because the traditional grid with a pit under it would fill up with dirt in times of dust storms and flood. Up and over the old utes clattered.

On and on the road wound, occasionally, a small side road led off from the large mailbox—sometimes an old kerosene fridge but mostly an old oil drum bolted to posts. They had the names of the sheep stations painted on them. John had been up into this country some years before, shooting kangaroos for their meat, which was sold as pet food. Even the few kangaroos seen were too skinny for this at present. Also most of the kangaroos had departed, chasing better pasture elsewhere.
John had to fall back further behind the Kellys because of the fine dust which floated in the air for a long way behind them. This was getting through the ute and into their eyes, nose, and throat. 'I know now why the old coots were in such a hurry to go first,' said Tony as he blew his nose to clear the dust out of it.

Occasionally, there was a windmill and tank to have water for the sheep. There were also two large galvanized iron roofs which covered some steel posts next to water tanks. These were to catch the rain water where there was no underground water.

Finally, just before lunch, the small town of Kingoonya came into view. Kingoonya was almost a ghost town now as the Adelaide to Alice Springs road had been re-routed when it was bituminized. There were only the remains of the timber and iron service station, an old pub, a hall, and a few other derelict buildings. Most of the houses had been sold and carried away. The old service station was very interesting as it was surrounded by the carcasses of the unfortunate cars which had broken down on the rough road over the years. It was like a trip back through time to see the old Austin's, Vanguards, Dodges, Chev's, Fords, and Holden's lying derelict in heaps. They then crossed the main east-west railway line, which led to Perth, and then turned towards the new, sealed highway.

Just before turning on to the main road, Bert had stopped and was waiting for them. They pulled in next to them. 'How was the dust?' Laughed Bert, John spat out of the window on to the ground. 'You can have some of it back if you like.'
We'll shout you blokes to a steak for lunch,' yelled Harry. 'Follow us into Glendambo to the pub.' John hesitated No, it's all right. Helen packed some sandwiches. They are in the Esky.' John felt guilty about bludging on someone else for a meal. 'Don't be so bloody stupid. What about all the times that we have eaten at your house?' 'That's different,' said John. 'Ah, bullsdust! You're the only people in the district who feed us old buggers. No one else wants to know us. Follow us.' Bert drove off, and John followed as they turned right, back down the new road to Glendambo, which was only about a kilometer away.

Glendambo consisted of two service stations and a few houses, some of which had been moved from Kingoonya some years before when it was bypassed by the new road.
The large hotel was a copy of a bush-shearing shed. There were a few accommodation units along the side of the main building.
The two ute's pulled in to the parking area in front of the hotel. All four men got out and stretched their legs. Bert let the two dogs go for a run to stretch their legs and relieve themselves, which they did on most of the car tyres outside the hotel. Where they got the extra fluid from for the job was a mystery. The dogs were told to get up in the bus, and they quickly did so. 'Don't you move,'

warned Bert. The dogs made themselves comfortable in amongst the bags of clothes on the ute tray. Bert and Harry walked through the large doors into the bar. They were followed by John and Tony. A few people sat at tables in the large bar, some jackaroos from one of the nearby sheep stations, which was evident from their cowboy hats.

John caught up with Bert at the bar just as he was ordering. 'Righto, matey, we'll have four steaks and eggs and four schooners of beer,' Bert told the waiter. 'Cummin roit up,' said the waiter. 'A bloody pom! What the hell is a pom doing all the way up here?' said Bert in an undertone, as the waiter walked away.

After two more schooners of beer each, the steaks arrived. The men moved from the bar to a table and sat. Bert started to chew. 'Shit! I wish I had my bottom teeth in. This steak is like bloody leather.' They all agreed. They picked at the pieces which were chewable and piled the gristle up on the edge of the plates. At least, the eggs were edible. They mopped the plates with a piece of bread. The waiter walked past.

'What's your meal like?' he asked. Do you get your own meat up here from a station?' asked Bert.

'No, mate, it all cums oop from Adelaide. Why?'

'I thought that this one might have been driven up from down south in a bullock team. I reckon he might have mated a few cows on the way. This is some of the toughest meat I have ever tried to eat.'

'Suit yourself, mate,' the barman said and walked off. 'Bloody old coots!' He could be heard to mutter as he walked back into the kitchen. 'Right, we had better leave. There's not much chance of us being served any more beers. Thanks to Bert,' joked Harry. They all departed. The waiter looked out of the door of the kitchen and was talking to someone as they walked through the door.

What a change to be driving on a sealed road! They were able to drive a lot closer without dust. A few kilometers past Glendambo, a little blush of green grass started to show up on the side of the road. The further the men drove, the greener the surrounding country became. There were beautiful wildflowers, brilliant scarlet Sturt peas, Blue Desert roses, and a carpet of purple and yellow succulents. Dead, road-kill kangaroos, emus, and the occasional sheep lay on or near the side of the road, mostly victims of the large road trains, which travelled the highway at night. After a few more kilometers, the country reverted to its normal brown. The green had evidently been the result of a thunderstorm a few weeks before.

Nature was strange. Kangaroos, many from a long way off, congregated on the new green feed. 'How did they know it had rained so far away?' asked Tony. John had no answer for this as a lot of unusual things like this occurred in the bush. Some of the dead kangaroos were really smelly. The odour took some time to be blown out of the ute.

Most road kill had some crows and a few wedge-tailed eagles feeding on them. This was fairly dangerous as some of the greedier eagles waited until the cars were nearly on them before they took to the air. A bird of this weight and size could easily bust a windscreen if it was hit at speed. A half-dead, wedge-tailed eagle in the front of the ute would not be a very exciting experience. The eagles had extremely sharp beaks and claws.

John was deep in thought. I wish we could fluke a thunderstorm like that back on the farm at the present time. Just think of the change it would make to our poor wilted crops. The road seemed to go on and on. There was not much change in the landscape other than the dry water courses and the low hills, which they climbed and descended. A few small mobs of sheep were seen, as well as some emus and a few kangaroos.

Occasionally, there was a signpost on a dirt track, leading off the main road with the name of the distant sheep station and the distance from the road. Most of the station names were well known by hearsay to the West Coast population.

Finally, there were old car bonnets propped up with fence droppers every few kilometers. Each one had messages like 'Best Opal At The Big Winch', 'Cheap Meals At The Acropolis', and 'Cheap Fuel At Bulls'. All of these signs were hand-painted; some displayed a bit of artistic license, but most looked as if they had been painted in the dark by a blind man with a stick dipped in tar.

In the distance, a cross-shaped structure appeared over the low hills. John could not work out what this might have been. Finally, the cross started to turn. They worked out it was a large wind generator. Further along, there were some small mounds of earth which looked as if they had been pushed up out of the ground by giant ants. Behind these, there was a seemingly endless line of white mounds. The town finally came into view on the right of the main road as they turned around the next corner.

What a dry dusty barren-looking place, thought John as they drove off the main Alice Springs road in towards the town. There was a flat area, leading from the main road to the town. This was covered with stunted shrub-type vegetation. Every second shrub seemed to have at least one plastic shopping bag caught on it which was blowing like pennants in the wind.

The roadside signs were closer together but of a more orderly nature, and most, at least, had been painted by some sort of a sign writer. On the right side of the road, about fifty meters from the road, were some houses. Nearly all these had some sort of machinery outside, tractors, backhoes, old drilling rigs, and an assortment of wrecked cars. Most machinery looked as if it had not been used for many years. There were some clubrooms flying a foreign flag. On the other side of the road was a large, almost new, petrol station. Past this was an imposing building consisting of large, two-storied motel units and then the hotel. John was not surprised to see the Kelly's turn in to the front of the hotel. John pulled in next to them. 'Christ! I think it's beer time,' croaked Harry.

'Let's go in and see if the beer's still all right. It was the other week. Harry got a plastic drum of water and filled a cut-off four-gallon drum with water for the dogs to have a drink. The dogs were pleased to see the water as the last walk and drink had been at Glendambo.

The four walked towards the bar. This was so different than any pub which John or Tony had ever been into before. They passed a small group of people at the door. Their hair was matted together, and their clothes torn and dirty. They had obviously been drinking. The men made sure that they did not step into the group. One of the people asked for some money for a drink. 'I can be pretty friendly when someone buys me a beer,' she slurred. The party skirted the group, not answering the request.

A long bar ran along the rear wall of the room. There was a mob of people inside, some at the bar, some standing at a servery window, betting on the races and others sitting at tables, checking their betting tickets. All were speaking loudly in one or another language.

The people in the bar were an odd-looking lot, a mixture of most of the races on the planet. Bert described them. 'There's meant to be people of fifty different nationalities living here,' Bert said.

'Here, wash the dust out of your throat.' Harry handed out four beers and sat them on the table. 'Bottoms up!' It didn't take long to down the first round of beers.

'I think we should see about getting somewhere to sleep. Some kind of shack or house,' said John. 'Leave it to me,' said Bert, he walked over to the bar and spoke to the barman, 'Do you know of anyone who wants to rent a house around here for a few weeks?' Bert and Harry had rented an old caravan the last time they were in town. The barman thought for a while.

'Go and ask that slippery-looking little guy over.' He pointed to a man sitting with a motley-looking group at a table by the betting window. 'He usually knows if there are any vacant shacks. Silvio is his name.' Bert walked over to the small, stringy, mean-looking man.

'Excuse me, but the barman said that you might know where we could rent a bit of a shack for a few weeks.' The little man looked up from his betting tickets. 'Nah, sorry, mate, I don't know of nothing for rent in town.'

Bert walked back to the table. 'Looks as if we might have to get a room at the pub for the night and have a look around for a shack tomorrow. We should have kept the caravan we had a few weeks ago.' They enjoyed another beer, Silvio walked over to their table. 'Excuse please, but I don't have the house. But my mate over there do.' He beckoned another mean-looking, grey-headed man with a lopsided mouth over to the table. 'This is Tom. A friend of his has a dugout over by the waterworks reserve for rent. You want to have a look?' The men introduced themselves and then bought a round of beers for the four men at the table.

After some small talk, they followed Tom and Silvio out of the hotel. Tom got into an old Ford utility, which had a winch mounted to its tray.

'You follow us,' yelled Silvio as he got in.

The old ute roared out of the car park, nearly collecting another ute which was driving down the main road at just as dangerous a speed. The ute then tore off down through the town at breakneck speed. When through the main shopping area, it veered to the right around a corner and drove off towards a low range of hills; smoke billowed from its exhaust. It was hard for the men to keep up. After that, it then wound its way through some old mine workings. There was an old concrete mixer barrel by the side of the road. They turned right again and then wound up through a small lane way and stopped outside a doorway which led into the side of a hill.

There was a veranda outside the hill, which had been cut away with a bulldozer, leaving a flattened area for a car park. There was a small shed at one end of the veranda, evidently a toilet and a shower. The men climbed out of their utes.

'Here you come inside. Bloody good dugout.' The dust was still settling from the rapid stop. The four men followed them into the dugout. The dogs barked to be let go to no avail.

Tom unlocked the flimsy door. This led to a tunnel of around three meters, leading to the first room, the kitchen. The room was surprisingly large. It had rough walls, still showing the pick marks from when it was hand dug many years ago. The ceiling was domed above their heads. The floor was just the virgin sandstone with a few squares of old carpet scattered around the most used areas.

Silvio turned on an old fridge which started with a jump and whined away in one corner of the room. There were various dressers, a gas stove, and a sink with one tap above it. The old table had an assortment of mismatched chairs. Two other tunnels led from the room. 'This first bedroom.' Tom turned on the light to show two old, piping-framed beds.

A niche had been dug into one of the walls and was covered by a dirty curtain. This was evidently the wardrobe.

The other room was slightly larger with almost the same layout, except for the large safe, which dominated one corner of the room. 'Bloody good safe that one if you find any opals, only one set of keys, we give them to you if you want. A deal was stuck at hundred dollars a week. Harry dealt the twenty-dollar bills out on to the table for two weeks' rent. Tom and Silvio took a long-neck bottle of beer, which they were offered, with them and left, driving in the same manner as they had come.

'Cripes, what a shifty-looking twosome they are! I reckon they would slit your throat for twenty dollars.' 'Well, at least, we have got somewhere for a base. Let's have a look at the bathing facilities.'

Harry walked over to their ute and let the dogs go. The first thing they did was to pee on John's ute tyres. Then they departed for a good empty out, away from their sight, thank goodness. John really did not want to have to step over dog poop around the door of the dugout.

The bathroom consisted of a toilet, which was, at least, not a long drop, and a shower. In the far end of the shed was an old Simpson wringer-type washing machine. There was also a cement wash trough with the drain leading out of the shed wall. The walls of the room were full of nail holes from when the iron had been used on other covering jobs. Sunbeams from the setting sun shone through these, illuminated by the dust in the air, not exactly private. The shower was heated by an old chip heater, which was bolted to the wall. The heater had a drip feed of diesel for its fuel. A can hung from the rafters by a bent piece of wire. This old gallon can had a tap soldered to the bottom of it. This led to a spout of thin copper pipe, which poked through a hole, which had been drilled into the door of the heater. John and Helen had used a similar heater on the farm when they had first bought it.

The shower was lit with a wad of newspaper, and then the water was turned on. The drip feed of the diesel was adjusted back so the diesel dripped slowly into the cylinder. Smoke rings shot out of the hole in the door as the heater roared.

The men went back inside the dugout. They then carried all the provisions and clothes inside. 'You can have a shower,' said Bert. 'I don't think too much water on your skin does you any good.' Tony walked past the twosome with his towel draped over his shoulder. 'You can please yourself, but I reckon I stink.' Bert and Harry offered to go and get a pizza for tea whilst they had their shower.

John had not noticed the closed-in feeling when they had first walked into the dugout, but as they were waiting for the men to come back, he felt as if he wanted to go out into the fresh air outside. The musty smell of the earth certainly did not help. He commented on this to Tony, who did not have the same feeling.

When the men returned with pizza, the feeling seemed to go, and after a few more beers, he forgot about it altogether. John woke about 3 a.m. He felt really clammy. The roof of the dugout seemed to be closing in on him. It was pitch-dark in the dugout, similar to being deep in a cave. John lay for quite some time, unable to sleep, until, finally, he dozed off again.

God, this old bed is uncomfortable. It must have rocks in the mattress. I'm glad I brought my own pillow, thought John, he decided to keep his feelings of being closed in to himself as he knew that the others would only make fun of him. 'Hey, are you two awake?' John woke with a start. The room was as dark as doom. 'What time is it?' 'Nearly eight o'clock,' upon checking a small shaft of light weakly struggled through the small air shaft in the corner of the ceiling. The men had not thought of the lack of windows.

'I think we had better get a small clock radio to wake us in the morning,' said Tony as he sleepily rose from the old bed. They both dressed and walked out into the kitchen, yawning in unison as they walked. 'Hell, that old flock mattress was full of rocks. I had a job to get to sleep, even though I was dog-tired.' 'You young blokes don't know what it is to rough it. When we were young, we only had a chaff bag half filled with chaff to sleep on.' John and Tony had been told this story over and over before. 'Anyone want bacon and eggs for breakfast?' They all agreed. John lit the gas burners on the stove and proceeded to cook the home-cured bacon and farm eggs, whilst Tony watched the toast on top of the gauze toaster on the other gas burner of the stove.

'Hell, that farm-cured bacon tastes good. What do you think?' Harry agreed. They all walked out of the door. Harry locked the flimsy old door after them.

Harry yelled out for the dogs. They came around the hill and walked up to him with a sheepish look on their faces. Both were covered in a smelly green slime. They had found something smelly whilst on patrol at night. 'Ooh, you dirty buggers. Get up in the back.' The dogs effortlessly cleared the side of the ute and wedged their way as far from Harry as they could. Harry could not reach their chains, so he left them loose. John and Tony got into the ute and followed the men out through the town. They then turned on to the main road towards their claim. First, they travelled out of town on the bitumen road towards Alice Springs for about fifteen kilometers. All along the roadside, there was worked ground, mainly the mounds left by blowers. Occasionally, there was a larger mound which had been pushed up by a bulldozer. Old trucks with unusual-looking blower machines on their trays were in small groups next to white mounds of worked sandstone.

The men turned off the main road on to a good dirt road, then followed the Breakaways road for about two kilometers, and then turned left towards a large worked area of ground. Both John and Tony had marveled at the amount of machinery which was visible from the road. There were drills, bulldozers, excavators, and another unusual-looking machine, which were built on to the back of an old truck and looked like a giant bird squatting on the plain. Quite a few of these bird-looking machines were working, spewing a huge amount of white dust up into the still morning air.

Bert wound his way through old workings, bulldozer cuts, and conical heaps, which were seen under the blowers, the bird machines.

The front ute stopped in a large non-worked area about the size of four football ovals. This was surrounded by the high dumps of old bulldozer cuts. There was two small heaps of dirt, one of which had a motorised winch next to it. On the outskirts of the workings were four posts with little pointers on each one. 'Ours is a pretty low-tech, our mining operation. Hardly anyone uses these hoists any more, but we've found a few bucks, and it's reasonably cheap to run.' Harry was busy unloading tools and electrical cable from the ute. 'There's all of this ground around us which has never been worked. No one has even bothered to drill it to look for trace. We could never understand why. I suppose it's like fishing. Someone found some opal elsewhere so everyone shot through to the new area and left this area non-drilled and not-worked.'

Tony and John gave the men a hand to unload the ute and then helped them to lower the three- meter-long sections of ladder down the shaft. Each one of these was hooked together. The top ladder was hooked on to a stout length of water pipe, which crossed an edge of the round hole. Bert turned the petrol on, then pulled the rope, and started the alternator which was on the Ute. The tools on the back of the ute rattled with the vibrations of the motor. The dogs jumped off and started to bark at the engine noise. 'Shut up, you mongrels,' yelled Bert over the noise of the motor. The dogs walked of and dug a shallow hole and then lay together on the ground.

Bert then plugged a lead with a trouble lamplight into the extension cord, making sure, as he did, to tie a knot at the plug so the joint would not come apart. He lowered the lamp carefully down the shaft.

Tony followed Bert down the ladder into the round mineshaft. John also reluctantly followed. The shaft was only around seven meters deep by one point two meters wide. John had a very uneasy feeling as he descended below the level of the ground. The hole, which was just over a meter wide, felt very constricting. He could hear Bert and Tony talking as he wobbled down the ladder. Bert was explaining the different colours of the level which they were following. 'If it's OK by you guys I would rather go back up to the top again,' quavered John nervously. 'Don't be so bloody silly,' retorted Bert with a laugh. 'You'll soon get used to it.'

Tony followed Bert along the narrow drive. Bert was showing him where they had found a bit of opal trace, which was still shining in the wall. Bert shone the light further in front of them 'The stinking rotten mongrel bastards. Look what they have done.' He shone the light on a large pile of dirt, which almost blocked the drive. Even

John, who was nervously waiting under the shaft, edged forward to investigate.

"Some rotten cow has been down our shaft when we were down south and has put some shots in the wall and blown some opal out. There were some thick traces here. We were going to work them next.' Bert shone the light on the heap of dirt and then started to dig into it with his hands. There were small chips of potch and opal gleaming in the light of the electric lamp. 'Cripes, you can't trust anyone. I would like to catch the bugger who has moon-lighted our claim and pinched our opal.'

The men turned, then walked back towards the ladders, and then climbed out of the shaft. John hurried to be first as he did not want to be left until last as the claustrophobia had really got to him. 'Some rotten mongrel has moon-lighted our claim whilst we were away,' yelled Bert over the noise of the alternator. 'I have just noticed a few car tracks around here whilst you were underground. I thought it must have been some aborigines noodling on our dump.'

'Well, I don't suppose that there's much we can do about it except dig the dirt out and start again. It's no use going to the cops. This evidently happened a few weeks ago. It's bloody hard to prove who has been around here. There's always someone checking out your claim when you're not here.'

Before they started back down the shaft again, Bert showed John and Tony around, explaining as to where the run of opal was thought to go. He gestured with his hands to the expanse of good, non-worked ground in front of them. 'I reckon there's plenty of opal just in front of us if you want to peg a claim and give it a try. Opal usually goes in what they call a run. It follows a line, making and breaking opal, then nothing, and then opal again Harry walked back to their ute and rummaged around in the tray for a while. He came over with two thick bronze welding rods, which had been bent at right angles near the ends, and started to walk across the ground with these poked straight out in front of him. Tony and John stood fascinated by this odd display. 'What the hell is he doing?' asked Tony as he watched the rods swing out at right angles to Harry's body as he walked ahead.

'He's divining the slips and slides under the ground, just like divining for water. All of the slips and slides are cracks in the subsurface and usually are damp,' said Bert. 'Here have a go.' Harry handed the rods to Tony. 'Hold the rods as hard as you like, if it's going to work for you. You won't be able to stop them swinging.' Tony took the two welding rods and started to walk. This is all bullshit. I must look like a real dork walking around with these wires, he thought. As he slowly walked, he could feel the wires pulling in his hands. He could not stop them from pulling out at right angles to his body.

'I'll tell you a good test. When you find a slip, go a couple of meters further down and cross it again. Try to find the line in which it is running, and then go well back and walk towards it with your eyes closed. Tony did this and was amazed that every time he crossed the line drawn on the ground, the wires swung out.

'Here you have a try, Dad.' He handed the wires to John who walked back and forward to no avail. 'All a lot of crap if you ask me,' he said after some time without any results. 'It does not work for everyone,' said Harry.

Bert and Harry went back to work, emptying out the moonlighters' mess. They had shown John how to use the Yorke hoist so he could pull the large buckets filled with dirt up from out of the shaft. Tony went on divining the large area which was not inside the pegs and not worked ground.

The Yorke-hoist way of mining entailed a lot of hard work, something which Bert and Harry were accustomed to. Bert filled the buckets, which were sixty-liter oil drums, which had an eight millimeter steel rod handle added. These were pushed into the rocks and sand, and then the dirt was scratched into it with a short - handled, round mouth shovel. Harry pushed each bucket along the floor of the drive on a custom-built, low barrow to the shaft where John had the emptied bucket sitting on the floor of the drive waiting for a full one to be attached to the cable ready to be winched out.

Under the shaft was an opened-out area, so there was room to man oeuvre the buckets on and off the winch cable. The winch was driven by a small petrol motor, which spluttered away noisily. A steel piping pole held the winch. This was guyed with some heavy fencing wire to three substantial pegs. The winch was positioned so the pulley end of its long arm was directly over the shaft. When the bucket was pulled up, it could be swung in an arc so the bucket could be emptied some distance from the shaft, a far cry from, and safer than, the old-hand windlass idea.

The winch itself was controlled by a lever. In the down position, the brake was on. As the lever was lifted, the drum of cable would freewheel, and then as it was lifted higher, the outer part of the drum would come into contact with a small fiber wheel driven by the motor. This would wind the cable up with the drum. It was difficult at first to get the controls into the right position for a start, but John soon got used to it.   After an hour and a half, Harry yelled out for John to turn the motor off. There had been a lot of buckets of dirt pulled out of the shaft. Harry poked his head out of the shaft first. 'The bloody swine have had a field day. They dug in about three meters. You can see the opal trace on the walls where they have been.' He climbed out of the shaft, quickly followed by Bert.
'Shit! I wish I knew who the pricks were who moon-lighted us. I'd ring their bloody necks.' Both men were covered in the sandy dirt from the walls of the drive. Both had been sweating profusely. The sweat was still running out of their pores. The smell of body odour prevailed. 'A bit of booze coming out,' joked John. 'Probably is, but everyone sweats like this when you work underground. There's a lot of humidity down there. Go down again and find out.' 'Bugger you, that's the first and last time I go
underground. I nearly crapped myself.'

Bert went over to the ute and turned the alternator off. The globe in the trouble light on the ground slowly lost its light and faded to nothing as the motor slowed down.

Tony walked over. 'Find anything interesting?' asked Bert. 'I wouldn't have a clue. I have drawn out on the ground a heap of lines where things seem to cross each other, but I don't know what it all means.'
'If we knew that, we would all be millionaires. This wiring a claim is only a guide. There's no rule when it comes to opal. Sometimes you can have everything right—beautiful sandstone, plenty of good slips, and no opal. Other times, it shows up where you would least think it would be. It's easy to put a shot in and blast next to a pocket of opal and ruin it.' They sat down in the dirt and had lunch off Helen's sandwiches she had made for the previous day.

Bert and Harry asked if John and Tony wanted to go to the pub for a meal. The men declined the offer as they felt tired from the trip up the previous day. They knew what a trip to the pub meant to Bert. When he got started on the grog, he was a real pest to try to get to go home. He usually became belligerent and argued when he had too much to drink.   John cooked some bacon and eggs again, and soon after, they both went to bed.

Around 3 a.m., the Kelly's came into the dugout, banging and crashing around and talking loudly. 'Shit! I wish they would shut up. I'm bloody tired.' 'Don't let them hear you, or they will be in here with us. We'll never get back to sleep.' After a while, the noise subsided, and the men got back to sleep.

'We got lost, coming home from the pub last night. You should try and find your way around this place in the dark. We must have done miles, looking for some sign of how to get home. At one occasion, we were driving around in the small settlement just out of town. A couple of men told us to tick off. If it hadn't been for the old concrete mixer barrel down at the corner, we would have had to sleep in the ute. It was really cold.' After a couple of strong black coffees, Bert and Harry started to look a bit more human. 'Want some eggs and bacon?' asked Tony. 'You can stick your food.' Both the men agreed.

'You should go to the Department of Mines and order your tags so you can peg a claim each, if you want to, of course.' Bert poured another coffee. 'Black and strong, just like my women,' he said.

Chapter five

Leaving the Philippines

As he headed out of the Manilla suburbs, Ali then drove into the country. He realised that the Morris Minor was now another beacon showing the Sanchez drug network where he was going.

There was a young man working next to a beat up old nineteen thirty-six ford pickup truck unloading the contents of the tray on to the shelves of a roadside market stall, he was just packing up to leave. Ali stopped the Morris then got out next to the young man. He sidled over and asked. "How would you like to sell your truck? The young man looked Ali and asked "Why would any person want my old truck." "I have a friend who is restoring one of these old trucks and wants some spare parts". "What would you pay." Ali thought for a few seconds." I will give you my car and $50 dollars". The young man looked at the Morris Minor. He listened to the motor running, and then agreed to sell. Ali tossed his box of money and kitbag full of marijuana into the front of the Ford. As he drove off, he saw the young man was telling his friends and making signs that he thought Ali an Idiot.

This was the first of three changes of cars which Ali did that day. The second car was an old Hillman in a sorry state with rusty mudguards and doors. The Ford pickup was left on the edge of a park. Ali had bought the Hillman for more than it was worth. He paid two hundred dollars for this dilapidated car. He had not signed any paper work. He then paid out four hundred dollars for a better car, a Ford Consul. Ali felt he had left a bit more of a headache for those chasing him. These deals had been done some hundred kilometers apart. The last old car had been left around the corner of the dealers he had bought the Ford Consul from, with the keys in the ignition and the windows open. He was hoping some person might like the old Hillman and steal it.

The problem was still the face with the scar.

He was worried about Zeena. Did the Sanchez mob know that she was his mother? A lot of people he had dealings with in the earlier time in Manilla knew this from them living together in the flat.

After thinking hard, Ali wrote a letter addressed to the place Zeena worked. He explained that he was once again in trouble and had nearly met the greasy Indian at the end of the Wharf. Zeena could send a reply to the post office in a town. This town was fifty kilometers away from where he had rented a small flat.   Ali was starting to grow a beard. The whiskers would not grow on the scar, but they would help cover it in time. Ali was doing a few deals with some of the local men with the drugs in the small case full of marijuana trying to cash it in.

A week later he set off for the post office in the nearby town and arrived at office where he had asked Zeena to address the letter to. The post office had just opened for the day. He had blackened the scar on his face where the beard was growing with mascara. The top of the scar had woman's make up blending it in so it did not show so clearly.

There were no cars or people outside the building, Ali walked in and asked if there were a letter for him. The young girl searched through a pile of letters, then found one with his name.

Zeena explained in the letter how the mob had sent one of the thugs to see her. He had caught her on the way home from work. He had dragged her into an alley, and had tried to beat out of her as to where Ali was. Zeena did not know where he was, and had maintained that she did not know. The thug had given her a fortnight to tell him, or she would take his place in the swimming lessons. There was a week left.

This news made Ali extremely angry. He walked the three blocks to where he had parked his car. He was shaking with rage.
No one had followed him during the circuit he had taken to get the car.

He started to drive back to his flat. As he drove the fifty kilometers he was hatching a plan to get even with Emilio Sanchez. He was trying to think something nasty, which would really hurt the man and his drug dealing sons.

Emilio was not very predictable, except for Sunday when he and his wife would go to Church, Emilio was a devout Catholic on

Sundays, and every other day of the week he would work for the other side, Satan, in his dirty dealing.

In the case he needed some insurance Ali had done a small amount of following Emilio and the two other different Syndicate bosses The Gomez and the Rinaldo bosses, in the Morris Minor some months ago, just in case there was a need for retaliation. Ali was very careful not to be seen doing this. The two other syndicate bosses and family took the body guards to church as protection on Sundays. The drivers sat in the car and waited for the families to emerge from church, they then ushered them to the car.

Evidently Emilio was so powerful he thought he had a pact with god, and had immunity from troubles on Sunday. Emilio would drive his car to the church with his wife on Sundays. No bodyguards would follow or accompany them.

Trying to work out a way to save Zeena and get the Sanchez family off his back was a main concern now for Ali. In the Philippines, there was really nowhere to hide from the family. The Sanchez syndicate had growers and agents in all of the islands. This was the Philippine version of the Mafia and just as strong and ruthless.

Slowly Ali devised a plan. He had a machinist in the small town make some road spikes like he had seen in a movie he had been to. Thin pieces of thin steel tubing were cut at a sharp angle on one end, then three other pieces welded to them so one of the tyre spikes would always be sitting up to stake a tyre and quickly let the air out of it. Ali had thirty of the spikes made, some short tube was cut to use as spacers in between the spikes. Ali told the man making the spikes they were a new experiment to be used to harvest coconuts. The idea was to give the large heavy car a puncture on one side so it was virtually impossible to steer. After picking up the spikes and paying for them, Ali went to a fishing shop and purchased a long length of black very heavy fishing line. He threaded the spikes on this fishing line with the spacers in between each one so there was a length of line with the spikes about two meters long, along the twine.

During Ali's research on the Sanchez church visits on Sunday's the route was always along the same for the three-kilometer trip, some of the trip went through parkland, a heavily forested area. This was where Ali had decided to conduct his ambush.   On the Saturday morning Ali bought a suit, shirt, tie and new shoes. As he dressed, he noticed he looked more like a tourist than a market peddler. The beard was blackened and the scar had the make-up treatment.

As he drove through to Manilla, Ali had his wares for the ambush. There were the road spikes on the length of heavy line, two bottles filled with petrol, which had corks in them, cigarette lighter, a heavy hammer and some torn rags.

Almost all of the marijuana had been sold, the rest was left in the flat. The strong box contents were put into a false bottom of a suitcase.   The cache of gold, silver, diamonds, jewellery, plus nearly two hundred thousand dollars in cash was placed on the bottom of the heavy case. A layer of thin plywood was placed over this, and then the lining of the case which had been stripped back was glued carefully over the plywood. Clothes and other effects were placed on the top of this.

After driving around the place where Zeena worked looking for a car one of the mobs may drive, he parked the car in a side street near where Zeena worked. He entered the coffee shop and sat down. There were a few people in the shop, none of the men looked like the heavies in the drug ring. Zeena was serving a table.
He noticed she had some bruises on her arms from the beating by the drug heavies.

Ali waited for her to look his way. He motioned for her to come, in an under the table gesture. Zeena looked a trifle confused but came over to the table. As she arrived, she recognised Ali. She carefully started the normal small talk. Ali spoke quietly as a tourist would. "Get your clothes and things together when you finish work, ready for tomorrow. I will pick you up at two o'clock at your house. If I do not come you will know I have not succeeded. You will probably never see me again, I have a plan." Zeena walked off to get a coffee and cake, as she would for a normal customer.

Ali paid, then drank the coffee and ate the cake then walked out.

Church usually ended at lunch time, most people departed at mid-day. Ali had noticed the Sanchez car travelling to church with Emilio and his wife as the only passengers.

Ali drove into the parklands, he then stopped and reversed back and parked his car in a small offshoot of the road which would usually be used for maintenance vehicles. There was a culvert under this short road, as the edge of the main road had a deep gutter to direct water off the road. The car was partially covered by the lower leaves of the large trees. He paced back on hundred meters from the culvert carrying a bag with the tools for the job. Only three cars passed as he was pacing the distance, he had stepped back into the undergrowth before they had appeared around the corner. Across the other side of the road Ali tied one end of the rope to a stout tree. He measured from the tree to have the distance for the spikes start at the edge of the bitumen surface, the twine which was a dark colour was towed across the road to another tree. The spikes were laid in a straight line in the grassy verge just off the road with a slack length of rope to the tree. Ali walked from the other tree the hundred meters down to nearly where his car was, playing out the twine as he went.

In readiness for the ambush Ali pulled the corks from the two bottles and put the pieces of rag inside ready to light. The hammer was laid next to the bottles; the cigarette lighter was in his pocket. Two other cars passed Ali as he hid behind a bush. The next car was the large black Packard sedan of the Sanchez family. Emilio was driving.

With a lot of effort Ali tugged the rope; it slid around the tree on his side of the road, pulling the spikes onto the road. The big car was travelling at about thirty miles an hour Ali could see the spikes rip into the tyre, they then tore out, and the rope was jerked hard in his hand as the spikes were pulled from the torn tyre. The rear wheel ran over the spikes also.

The front tyre was quickly deflating pulling the car off the road into the gutter. The front wheel hit the high culvert causing Emilio and his wife to rise out of their seats and hit their heads hard on the front windscreen.

The motor had stalled. Ali ran across the road and hit the side window with the heavy hammer caving it in. He lit the rag in the bottle and tossed the bottle against the door sill. The bottle broke and the petrol ran down the inside of the car all over Emilio. Emilio was just regaining consciousness when the petrol and flames engulfed him. He tried in vain to open the door. He was screaming in pain as the fire scorched his face.

Quickly Ali ran around the other side of the car and opened the door and pulled Mrs. Sanchez out and laid her away from the car, he beat the flames on her clothes out. He slammed the door shut and ran for his car.   He carefully drove past the Packard; there was only just enough room for him to get past the car which by now was well alight. Emilio had not been able to get out. The whole exercise had only taken less than a minute. Luckily no other cars had come this way.

As he sped away from the burning Packard, Ali could not explain why he had pulled Mrs. Sanchez from the car. He felt good about saving her. She was not the cause of the problem. Emilio was not going to be any more. Ali took a turn to get off the parkland road and headed for where Zeena lived

The Consul pulled into the front of the flat, Ali tooted the horn in two long blasts. Zeena ran outside carrying a small suitcase. She jumped into the door which Ali had leaned over and opened. There did not seem to be any other cars parked on the side of the street near Zeena's house.

As they drove out of the city Ali was taking care not to speed and be caught by the police. This would be a disaster as a fair amount of the police force was on the Sanchez payroll; finally, they left the outskirts of Manilla.

The car was filled with fuel an hour after leaving Manilla. As the car was being filled, he heard on a radio in the fuel station a police report of a gangland hit. A member of the Sanchez family had been murdered.   "Was that you" asked Zeena. "I could not think of any other way we would ever get out of the clutches of the mob. If I were to leave, they would have killed you", "Where are we going?" "As far away from the Philippines as we can. I have a plan to get some passports forged then get on a boat carrying freight from one of the small ports. Then head for Australia". Ali explained how he had instrumented the plan to get Emilio and the mob off his back.

"I Watched Emilio catch on fire then pulled his wife out of the car. I could see no reason she should pay for his sins".

Four hours of driving took them to a small seaside town in the south of Luzon Island. There was a large wharf area with neat piles of newly cut logs waiting to be loaded onto boats bound for Australia.

Ali found a small boarding house in a reasonable part of the town. The main problem now was to find some person who would print the passport and visa. This meant getting in touch with people tied up with crime again.

No one would recognise him with his beard and makeup. Zeena on the other hand had disappeared; evidently no one had been watching her and her house. This must have been a slipup, as Ali was very worried about being chased by the mob, when he picked her up.

During the night in their room at the boarding house Ali apologized to Zeena for once again ruining her life. "At least I still have one for now. My chances if you had not saved me could have been very slim".

A lot of the logging crews and timber cutters frequented the bars in the town. Ali made a point in getting to know some of these people so he could ask a trusted person about getting on a boat bound for Australia.

Some of the bar patrons attended card games in a ramshackle old building by the wharf. In terms of earning money the hard-working people involved in the timber trade were well paid, when looking what a lot of other workers were earning in the
Philippines.

The gambling was controlled by one man. This man was serving a niche market for the men and had a reputation for being tough but fair. He also had a few girls working in the premises who made some money on the side from the timber working men, Ali made a point of getting to know this man.

Enrico Gonzales was his name. For a Pilipino Enrico was a large framed man. He had a shock of peppered grey hair. Ali had the impression that Enrico could be a good friend, but a very bad enemy. He had an air of toughness and authority about him.

There was an urgency to get out of the Philippines, but there was also the need for the passports and being able to sign on a ship for Australia. Too much haste might make people like Enrico suspicious and liable to start to check on where Ali and Zeena had originated from.

Ali had met Enrico one night in the club and had struck up a conversation with him. Enrico wanted a few jobs done around town and asked Ali if he would like to earn some money. Ali was more inclined to get out of town on a boat but listened to Enrico's proposal.

Some of the people Ali had contacted for Enrico during the day evidently had some connections to the drug and sex trade. They had been open in talking to Ali, as they believed that Ali would not be helping Enrico if he thought him mistrustful.

Ali was invited to have lunch with one of these men, Pepi. As they were having the conversation, the corruption in government in the Philippines subject came up. The conversation turned to the Manila drug families, "Have you heard that old Emilio Sanchez was torched in his car". "No, I did not. When did this happen"? "Four days ago. One of the Gonzales sons is meant to have done the job. It was an elaborate set up to get the old man. The killer used road spikes to send the car in a ditch next to the road then burned the car. I cannot work out why he pulled the old man's wife out of the car though. She evidently, she could vaguely remember being pulled out of the car. They should have let them all burn. Sanchez had one of my cousins tossed in the sea". "What is happening in Manilla now?". "It's like 1930 Chicago, its all-out war, cars with guys with tommy guns shooting up each other. Even the Rinaldo's have got into the act since one of their guys was shot by mistake". The lunch carried on with a different dish.

"Are there any good forgers around town to do documents? I have a crooked brother who is trying to dupe me from my fathers will". "There are a few here who say that they are good. But are as big liars, as they are dishonest. If one of them were to do your will you would lose the lot and probably go to jail". The meal continued Pepi thought for a while. "If you were to go thirty kilometers to a small town to the north, there is an old artist. He would be the best in the Philippines". Pepi wrote the address on a paper napkin on the table. Tell him you know Pepi and Enrico.

The deliveries took another three hours from the lunch with Pepi. When Ali returned to Enrico's establishment the crowd was just beginning to filter in.
Enrico asked Ali to get his mother and bring her for a meal.
Zeena dressed herself up to make a good impression. Ali dressed in his suit and tie. This was an occasion to get to know the family of Enrico.
As they walked into the rowdy establishment, with the girls, music and the noisy crowd, a man asked Ali and Zeena to accompany him to
Enrico, Ali felt a cold wave of fear.

The fear was unsubstantiated as he entered the room and found Enrico, his wife, Children and mother in law. Zeena was ushered to sit with Enrico's wife's mother, a pretty woman with peppered grey in her hair. Ali sat next to Enrico. "I phoned Pepi about a bit of business today after you had left,"" Checking up on me" Said Ali with a smile, "Err well sort of but I had other business to discuss. One cannot be too careful these days.
He spoke highly of you even though he had just met you", "Well that's good; I liked the guy from when I first met him". "Enrico said you wanted some documents copied and altered". This put Ali in a bit of a spot. He looked at Enrico "Actually I want to get two passports for my mother and I. We would like to go to Australia". "You didn't set fire to the old Sanchez guy?" Joked Enrico "I have only just heard of that today. Pepi told me.". "I would not like to be in Manilla at the present times. About twenty of the mob have been killed, some shot, some beaten to death."
" My mother and I were involved in something I would not want to talk about. There are a couple of private eyes chasing us. They must be pretty good as they have nearly caught us a couple of times". Enrico raised his eyebrows, almost asking for a further explanation.

"My mother was married to a really violent man. All of his life he was the wrong side of the law. He had amassed a lot of money. He was beating my mother one day. I thought he was going to kill her; I hit him on the head with a heavy chair. I thought, as there was blood everywhere, I had killed him.

He had a payment from one of his dirty deals in the office with the safe open. Mother and I cleaned out the safe and ran. We have since learned that he regained consciousness and is now looking for us. He is tied up with the mob. We have the money in a bank safe in a town near here". Ali did not want the message of the large lot of cash and the extras being with him.

"Serve the bastard right" said Enrico. "Life never seems to go as we would have planned it." Ali agreed with this comment as his mind slipped back to some momentous occasions. The conversation then drifted to the vicious drug wars in Manilla. "I have heard that it was a thug from the Rinaldo Mob who topped old man Sanchez".

The old artist lived some distance from the town. Driving through the thin road reminded Ali of the way to Sasha's house, as he thought of Sasha and Missy the hint of a tear formed in the corner of Ali's eye as he drove over a similar rickety bridge

The old man lived in a large comfortable house with its own power plant, which was evident from the high wind generator tower at the rear of the complex. Ali and Zeena walked to the door and knocked. A wizened up man opened the door "Yes" he asked, as he studied them as they stood in the doorway. "I have been given your name by Pepi and Enrico. He has recommended you to do some work for us", "How is Enrico, has the scar on his face healed up yet." Ali thought this a bit odd because Enrico did not have a scar. He then realised this was a trick question, "Enrico does not have a scar on his face". The old man laughed in a raucous screechy laugh. "One cannot be too careful these days".

The entrance hall and all of the walls in the house had beautiful painting's hanging or leaning against them. Ali studied some of the work. "You have some very beautiful work here". "Yes you can see I love painting. This allows me to capture the soul of the moment, or person" Ali agreed as he studied the portrait of a young woman, he could see her soul in her eyes. This man was a very good artist. If his forgery was as good it should stand the test.

Zeena and Ali had to sit for some photographs for the identification on the passports. When this was done, they sat and had some tea with the man. "What name do you want to have on this passport?" Ali thought for a while regarding the new name. The fiery car with Emilio Sanchez flashed across his mind. Ali and Zeena Dragon sound's ok for me. "In four days' time I will have your documents ready. This will cost you five hundred dollars US each. Ok, have you got the money to pay?" " Your prices are a bit steep. I will have the cash with me ". "You will see why the prices are high. I do a very good job of everything I do".

They stopped in the small town for lunch following the visit to the artist Ali had driven into a clearing off the thin road and had cleaned out the suitcase bottom and had wrapped the gold, silver, diamonds and money in some black plastic sheeting which had been in the boot of the car. This was taped up with sticky tape then placed in the bank vault of the small town. Ali was given a key to the drawer in the safe. As he slid into the car seat, he slipped the key under a bracket which held the steering wheel. All seemed to be progressing easily. This had happened before. A fly always seemed to get into the soup in all of their previous dealings.

The nightly dinner with Enrico and his family was a regular event. "Are you sure you wouldn't like to stay and help me" Enrico suggested one evening. "Good cunning people like you are hard to find." "No I said the men were looking for us. That husband of Zeena's would have us killed for crossing him. He has had some bumped off for less. His methods of killing are not very nice we have heard. He does it slowly bit by bit. Helps keep the troops honest".

The town wharf area had two ships being loaded with timber for export. The trucks lined up with the large heavy logs on the trailers. The loading was quite time consuming as there was a lot of work in lifting the logs with the heavy cables attached.

One boat, The 'Wandana' had just started loading. It had an Australian flag flying.

As he did not want to make a show of himself Ali wore working clothes. He climbed the gang plank, and then asked a crew member if the captain was available. "He is in the cabin working the books." the man pointed along a passageway. The cabin door was slightly open to help let some of the breeze through. A man was poring over a book, making corrections as he did so.

Ali coughed lightly. The man looked up, their eyes met. "Could I help you". "I am looking for passage to Australia". The lanky blond man pushed his chair back from the desk, then stood up. He offered Ali his hand. They shook hands. "Hi, Peter Fitzgerald. It looks like it is your lucky day we are travelling to Cairns in Queensland with this load". "I am Ali Dragon. When will you be leaving for Australia?" Asked Ali. " It should be in about a weeks' time. That's if this mob do not run out of logs like they did last trip". "What will the cost be "asked Ali "We are a bit understaffed, if you would like to help." He thought for a few seconds. "Can you do a bit of work? Is two hundred dollars OK". "I have my mother with me; she is a good cook. Her uncle has died in Australia and we have to go to Brisbane to hear his will read". "You might be rich, Ok four hundred for the two. Have you got passports"? "Yes, we are getting them now. I will come to the ship and pay in four days' time".

Ali looked back at the 'Wandana' as he left the wharf; the small ship looked well maintained, the crew sounded happy as they joked and laughed as they worked with the logs. This was a gateway to Australia he thought.

Enrico still lamented Ali as to his desire to leave. "We could do some big things together", "yes and I might have my fingers and toes cut off with a bolt cutter before being tossed into the river". Enrico sighed. "There is always some crap which rears its head from our past. I have had my fair share. I have had a couple of family members try to con me into some deals. I very nearly got caught with one of them". "What do you do with family" asked Ali. "That's the problem. If I were to do what I should, my wife and mother-in-law would not be happy".

Ali helped Enrico with some deliveries. He felt that he and Zeena were almost family members, as they sat down for the evening feasts at the club.

Enrico had been following the news of the drug wars in Manilla. The killings had quietened. No one person had been found in the matter of the torching of Emilio Sanchez. The talk still centered on the Gomez family. The Gomez family were short of two close relatives, one son and a brother in law.

The Dragon had certainly burnt a hole in the drug business in the Philippines. Some of the corrupt police had been caught up with, as the government had to try and show they were making some sort of effort to de-fuse the situation.

Ali kept his beard growing; Zeena would give it a slight trim when needed. The mascara and make up was still applied. The focus should have been taken off his case, while the wars continued to be waged in Manilla.

Ali and Zeena drove out into the country to the town near the old artist home.

The small bank was almost deserted as Ali and Zeena walked in. He had the key from next to the steering wheel. The girl called the manager, who took Ali to pick the parcel up.

The trip to the artist's home in the mountains still bought the unusual recollections of Sasha and Misty. The emotions flowed through Ali's brain. He felt privileged to have been able to share a part of his life in such a simple uncomplicated way. He felt a warm glow as he recalled the talks he had with Sasha, also the scratching of Missy's head and talking to her.

The rattle of the timbers of the bridge on the way to the artist's home bought him back to reality.

The artist invited Ali and Zeena to have tea before the payment. Ali asked to see some of the paintings. He selected a painting of a beautiful young girl standing in a rice paddy. The old man picked up the painting and gave it to Zeena. "You say my prices are a bit high. You take the painting to remember me." Zeena refused and offered to pay. "You see that I have many more. This is just a small one, not much loss".

The work on the passports was excellent; every fine detail was to the highest standard. After paying the price, there were more cups of tea as the old artist evidently enjoyed the company.

"I will wrap my painting before you take it to make sure it is not damaged". The artist found some thick brown paper then covered the painting; the parcel was then tied up with string. Ali carried the painting out to the car then placed it on the rear seat for the trip back to Enrico's.

Soon after leaving the artist's home Ali stopped the car just off the thin road and unlocked the boot. He lifted the spare tyre from under the floor and placed the package with the money and jewellery in it. The tyre was then replaced and the floor cover refitted.

The wharf was abuzz with action as the heavy logs were swung on board of the ship. All of the crew seemed to have designated tasks and operated like a well-oiled machine. Peter Fitzgerald was overseeing the operation. Ali introduced Zeena; Peter took her hand in a gesture of greeting. He ushered them to his office. He paid the money and showed Peter the passports. " We should be leaving in two days' time. Keep in touch. I will be around the ship somewhere".

That night as Ali walked into the dining area, he went to Enrico's wife Maria, He offered her the present. Maria carefully opened the parcel; Enrico was looking over her shoulder. "This will take pride of place in my home. I know exactly where I shall place it". "I told you the artist was good" said Enrico as he studied the painting.

The stability of the life with friends was a beautiful sensation for both Ali and Zeena. How different things were away from her old business and the confines of the city.

The city of Tuguegarao appeared over the rise in the road. Ali and Zeena were doing the tourist run. They had driven through the mountains and were thrilled by the tall straight trees which covered the steep hills and valleys. There were the occasional lumber felling gangs working in the distance felling the selected trees for market. They stayed in this town for the night at a tourist village accommodation.

"You and Zeena must have bought me some good luck Ali, as this is the first time in all of the trips to load timber that we have not been delayed by some sort of mishap."

He undid the doors of two adjoining cabins to show where Ali and Zeena were to be sleeping. They were surprised; the rooms were very well fitted out. I thought we may have been given hammocks swinging from the ceiling." Peter laughed at the joke. "We do have quite a few tourists take the voyage at times. This is why we have the accommodation." both of the rooms had a shared bathroom between them.

"We have to wait for high tide to get out of the port. This will be at three PM tomorrow. If you can get your gear on-board by lunch time it would be good".

The bottom of the suitcase was only about two centimeters thick when the money and jewellery was tightly packed. Any loose items such as the finished jewellery had tissue paper wrapped tightly to stop them from rattling or slipping, the gold and silver ingots had a similar treatment. The false floor was stuck down. Finally, the lining of the case was re glued. The inside of the case did not look any different from a normal suitcase. Clothes were packed on top of the false bottom.

Enrico had invited a few friends to farewell Ali and Zeena. As the night progressed, Ali, while talking to Enrico, offered to give the Ford Consul to Maria. Enrico offered to purchase the car. Ali declined, "since we have been in this town you have treated us like one of your family. We have never met people like you in the city before. Just drive us down to the ship tomorrow", Enrico laughed and slapped Ali hard on the back. ''Ok it's a deal''

The whole family was at the wharf to farewell Ali and Zeena. They waited until the ship was pushed from the wharf by the small tug-boat, and then picked up speed, as it headed out of the harbour. Ali and Zeena watched the ever-growing smaller figures return to their cars and leave the wharf. Ali felt a lump in his throat as he thought about how he had made such a good friend in such a short time. Leaving the Philippines for an unknown future also weighed on his mind.

The boat motor set into a steady rhythm, as it pushed the water through its large propeller, heaving a churned up frothy line across the water out to the stern of the ship,
As night fell there was no sign of land, only the refection of the lights of a large town shining into the darkening sky.

The mess on the ship was neat and very clean, Ali and Zeena had dinner with the captain and the first mate,
"Looks like I will have to find you a job tomorrow" said the first mate to Ali. "I really do not care what you have for me as long as I do not have to hang on a rope over the side painting ". "I think we can do a bit better than that, the ship is low in the water now, so we usually paint when she is lightered off".
"I would like to help with the meals if that is possible" asked Zeena. The meal turned to an amicable conversation about life in Australia. How the streets were paved with gold and kangaroos and emus strutted their way down the streets causing accidents with the cars and motorcyclists.

Ali was given a chipping hammer and a pot of orange paint, He joined the crew working their way around the decks looking for blisters in the paint. The blister of rust was chipped back, and then a dab of the orange rust proofing was daubed into the chipped area. When this dried a daub of the ship colour was painted over.
The jobs varied from the chipping to working in the engine room with the large turbines cleaning and oiling. Ali was enjoying the work; He talked to the crew as he worked. These men were from all over the world. One was Greek, two Philippines', one South African engineer, and four Indonesians. These men had travelled all over the world during their working life. They had some very interesting tales to tell.

Ali asked one of the men about the Emu's and Kangaroo's in the cities. "I'm glad you asked me. If you had asked the captain or the mate, they would have had a good laugh. Aussies are all like that trying to trick you. It's just for fun though." Pedro had a bit of a laugh. "We have Komodo Dragons running in our streets biting people. Would they be relatives of yours Ali"? Ali realised the harmlessness of the jokes on the new members of the crew.

The kitchen work agreed with Zeena, as most Philippine women are good cooks. The menu was supplemented with spring rolls and other yummy pastry dishes.

Ali did not discuss the past very much with the crew or the captain and mate. The least said the better; he stuck to the story of the uncle dying.

The warm days and calm weather made each day very enjoyable. The camaraderie with the crew and the nightly discussions with Peter and the mate were very interesting in regards to opportunities in Australia. "I thought that you were only going to see about your uncles will'.

" What would we do if we want to stay and work? We could probably live in uncle's small house in Brisbane". Peter was not too sure about what the protocol was to becoming an Aussie. "My mob came out from Ireland over a hundred years ago. They had just about starved there when the potato crops failed".

The ship passed by some islands as it travelled. Some of these islands had been strategic battlefields during World War 2. These islands had been the last line of defense against the Japanese. Ali was getting a good lesson in Australian history as they had passed these islands. Peter and the crew had seen these islands many times before and knew a lot of the history about the Japanese occupation.

On day nineteen the top of Australia, Cape York was said to be off the starboard side of the ship. This was far too great a distance to see, but this put the ship in Australian waters. There would be six more sailing days to be in Cairns.

The mooring lines were tossed across to the wharf. The wharf crew picked up the light lines then pulled the heavy mooring limes

---

to the bollards. Next job was to swing the gang plank down to the ship to the wharf. Australia looked very different from the Philippines. Not as many people.

Ali and Zeena had to wait until a customs officer boarded the ship and checked their medical history plus looked at their passports, then a quick check of their luggage. After half an hour of signing forms and answering questions they were allowed to leave the ship. The Passports Visas and documents were duly stamped and handed back. Ali was classed as a minor as he was not twenty-one years old yet.

During the voyage both Ali and Zeena had been able to hone their understanding of the English language. Both had learned English as a second language some years before. Peter and the mate had helped a lot.

Chapter six.

Drilling for opal at Coober Pedy

Bert and Harry had driven out to the claim to start working. John and Tony had decided that they had no alternative than to give the opal mining a go to try and relieve their financial dilemma. They had talked about this well into the night. There did not seem any other way to make enough money to get out of the finance problems they were having on the farm.

Tony was prepared to spend the few hundred dollars he had been saving to buy a second-hand utility. He had earned this money from his sheep shearing in the previous years. 'If I lose it, so what? We'll also lose the farm,' he said with a final resignation.

Bert explained what to do about getting a precious stones prospecting permit each. This allowed them to peg a claim each. The size of the claim was either fifty meters square or fifty by one hundred meters for a large claim. The claim was only leased from the Mines Department for a twelve-month period, and of course, a large claim was dearer to lease.

Bert and Harry had gone off to work. They had explained the way to get the tags needed for the men to peg a claim, before they had left.

John and Tony drove through the town towards the Mines Department office, which was next to the new police station. They took their time, as this was the first occasion they had driven through the town at a normal speed, although everyone else seemed to still be in a hurry.

The town seemed very busy. A combination of the obvious mining vehicles and the tourists in their four-wheel drives with caravans moved around the streets. Number plates from all over Australia were displayed on the visiting vehicles. The men turned right before the new service station, left the main street, and then pulled in to the car park in the front of the mine's office building. There were two other vehicles in the park. These were the typical

Coober Pedy miners' vehicles, rough, old, four-wheel drives, complete with the winch on the back and a tray filled with tools of all kinds.

The Mines Department building was a large transportable structure surrounded by a high-chain wire fence with barbed wire on top. The men walked through a small gate and entered the building.

Two groups of people stood at the counter, each speaking in a foreign language. One of each group was trying to act as interpreter for the rest of the group. They were not doing a very good job. Both the groups and the counter staff were getting agitated, gesticulating wildly with their hands as they tried to make the woman realise what they wanted.

The woman reached under the counter and got the appropriate forms and handed the men the forms to be filled out. The woman explained what they had to do.

They filled the forms out and then had to hand their driver's licenses over for identification. Tony took out his wallet and counted out the money and paid for the permits. 'The tags for the claim pegs take three days to come up from Adelaide,' said the pleasant, friendly woman. So this meant the men had three days to spare before they could put the posts in and officially peg the claims.

'We should go for a drive and have a look around the field to try and get an idea of how most other miners were working,' said Tony as they left the Mines Office and walked over to the Toyota ute.

They left the Mines Department. First, they drove west from the town, after crossing the main road, driving between bulldozer dumps on each side of the road. Occasionally, they would stop, get out, and walk down one of the old bulldozer cuts and look at the walls for signs of opal traces. Tony picked up a few pieces of potch from one of the dumps they had stopped at. One piece even had a bar of red colour in it, their first opal.

There was a billowing cloud of dust coming from one of the old dozer dumps. It blew across the road in the light breeze, obscuring the source. After driving slowly through the dust, they could see a large rubber-tyred, four-wheel-drive loader loading an unusual looking machine. The machine seemed to be screening the dirt from the dump, after the dirt was screened. It passed through a small shed, finally coming out the other end and then being carried away by a long conveyor belt.

John and Tony spent some time watching the four-wheeled drive loader dig into the dozer dump, reverse back, turn, and then tip the dirt into a hopper on the end of the machine. The hopper had a heavy screen on top of it, which rolled the large rocks off on to the ground. They had never seen anything like this before and were both intrigued as to what this machine was really doing. The loader stopped, and the operator got out and walked across towards the men. John had a feeling that they may have been on the man's claim, although they had made sure they were outside of any mining pegs.

Harry had warned them about going on to someone's claim without asking.

'G'day, mate, ow're you going? I'm just gunna have a cuppa. Do you want to come over and have a look at the machine?

The loader driver was a farmer from the Ceduna area. He was working with his son, trying to keep the bank off his back as well, for things had not been any good seasonally at Ceduna for some years as well. His name was Charlie.

Charlie banged on the door of the noodling machine. The belts and the rotating screen stopped turning, and the door opened. A lad of about Tony's age poked his head out. 'This is me boy, Josh.' they all introduced each other, then squatted down in the dirt, and had a talk. A diesel motor thumped a short distance away. It drove the alternator which ran the machine.

Greedy banks and droughts were one of the main subjects of discourse. Charlie and Josh were making around two thousand dollars a week. Some weeks, it was a lot more. The best that they had done was to find a pocket which had been missed by the bulldozer checkers. This had been fifteen thousand dollars in one day. 'Do you want to have a look whilst we are working? The more eyes we have, the better our chances of finding something.' The men were interested in finding out what this weird machine was doing. John and Tony followed Josh up the short ladder into the small shed. There was a long conveyor belt running the full length of the shed. Above this was a series of fluorescent lights. These lights had a black tube in each one. Josh asked Tony to climb over the belt so there was more room. He explained where to put the opal when it was picked off the belt. A small bucket was hooked conveniently next to each chair.

Josh pushed the starter buttons for the electric motors and then shut the shed door. The shed was pitch-dark inside. Josh then turned the ultraviolet light on. This cast an eerie dark purple light down on to the belt.

Rocks started to run along the belt. They ranged in size from a baseball down. The rocks glowed a dark purple colour. 'Occasionally, one would shine a dull yellow. Alunite,' Josh explained. Dispersed with and in the rocks were pieces of material which shone a brilliant white as if they had a light inside of them. This was potch or opal. This had to be picked off and went into the bucket. Occasionally, a large piece of shining material would travel down the belt to be picked up.

John and Tony became engrossed with picking the opal out of the rocks. Suddenly after around half an hour, John had the funny feeling that the belt had stopped moving and the chair was travelling next to the belt. It made him feel a little giddy. The feeling finally went away.

After another hour, there was a loud bang on the side of the shed. John nearly jumped through the roof. It gave him such a fright. Josh stopped the belt, turned on a light, and then opened the door. At first, the men could not see from the bright light, but after a short while, their eyes became accustomed to the light.

Let's see what we have got,' said Charlie. Josh reached into the machine and got the three buckets out. He tipped the contents out into a large flat plastic bowl. Josh then pulled a large plastic drum from under the machine and then poured a small amount of water from it in the bowl. This helped to wash the dirt off the opal. The men then started to sort through the material in the bowl in the bright sunlight.

A large portion of the material was discarded and tossed into another bucket. About a third of the material was opal. Every now and then, Josh would lick a special piece which he had found and then hand it to Charlie, who, in turn, would show it to John and Tony. There were a few very nice pieces of opal. These were placed in another bucket. 'We keep the potch and check it again under a large magnifying lamp, just in case there is a bar of colour in it.'

'It's easy to miss some opal when you are doing a dozer cut. Either the checkers don't see it, or the dozer blade skims it off the floor before it is ripped. Sometimes the loss can be around 30 per cent, and seeing some of these claims has produced a few hundred thousand dollars' worth of opal. It's worth looking for.'

'Well, we had better get back to work,' said Charlie as he put the opal back into a small bucket and then stowed it inside their ute cabin.

John thanked Charlie for showing them the machine. Charlie suggested that they meet at the Italian Club for a cheap meal and a couple of beers that night. John agreed.

They walked back to their ute. 'How did you feel in the machine when it was going?' asked John.

'I felt as if the belt was stopped and I was moving along the floor on my chair. The feeling went away after a while, but I felt really giddy at the time.' John was pleased that Tony had felt the same. He felt as if it might have been only him who had felt this way.

They had come to the end of the mine dumps, so they turned around and headed back towards town, past the working noodler. Just before town, John turned left along another track and headed for a huge area of blower dumps. They worked their way through the dumps, amazed at the amount of work which had been done over the years. There were still the occasional blowers standing like a big bird. The odd one was working, blowing the fine white dust from the pipe above the fan.   Occasionally, there were the remains of an old campsite, consisting of a concrete floor, one or two old kerosene refrigerators pulled to pieces, a few old car bodies, and the usual large bottle heap. There were usually a large assortment of different types of bottles in each heap, mainly the brown beer bottles, but with an assortment of clear whisky and green wine flagons. Finally, they drove out on to a well-graded dirt road. Ahead of them in between the dozer dumps, they could see the remains of a small cluster of wind-blown shacks.   The remains of an old service station with all the 1940 and 1950 car bodies heaped around. There were also the remains of, it seemed, anything which would dig a hole, dozers, old drills, and loaders. Some of the camps looked lived-in, most having some sort of wind generator, the blades twirling and whistling in the wind. The remains of a sign announced, 'Eight Mile Garage'.

There were a lot of bulldozer cuts around the Eight Mile area. The Eight Mile field had been a very rich field when it was first found. Lumps of good quality opal as big as house bricks were found in some of the claims, making the lucky claim holders wealthy men, wealthy beyond their wildest dreams in some cases.

The worked ground then stopped, only to start to appear again about a kilometer away on their left. From there, they travelled back towards the main road through blower dumps back to the main bitumen road and then headed towards the Fifteen Mile field where Bert and Harry were working.

Bert and Harry were out of the shaft and sorting through a bucket when they arrived. 'Have a good look around?' asked Harry. 'So did we.' He tipped the contents of the bucket on to an old wheat bag which had been spread out on the ground. The material looked like liquid fire running out of the bucket. Both John and Tony gasped and sighed when they saw the opal. 'Not bad for a couple of old codgers. Its a bit better than bloody farming at the present time.'

'What would this lot be worth?' asked Tony as he studied some of the opalised shells. 'I reckon about fifteen grand,' said Bert. 'we had a nice morning's work.' He was feeling pleased with himself. 'Here, look at this one.' He picked a solid perfect opal shell out of the pile on the ground. Half of the shell was still covered with dirt, but the part which wasn't shone as he turned it in the sunlight. The red, green, orange, and purple colours danced over the stone.

'It looks as if dinner at the club is on us tonight. At least, the bloody moonlighters didn't get all of our opal.'

John told them about the morning in the noodling machine with Charlie and Josh and how they were going to meet at the Italian Club for a few beers. 'They serve a good steak up there on a Friday night, so that's where we'll go. I've met the bloke and his son from Ceduna a few times before. Nice people.'

Bert and Harry had to be cajoled into the dreaded shower but finally gave up their protesting and had a short shower each. 'We don't even drink water unless we have to,' protested Bert as he entered the wash room. 'People have been known to drown and die in the water, plus fish crap in water.'

The Italian Cub commanded a prime position high on a hill, overlooking the town and the surrounding area. It was a long, low building with a car park along each side. An assortment of trucks, utes, and cars was parked outside. The building was also low inside as well and also full of cigarette smoke, which seemed to billow from the bar area, trying to find some means of exit.

A group of around fifty people stood around the bar, talking. 'Four beers OK?' asked Bert as he walked up to the bar. As with the hotel, there seemed to be a lot of different languages being spoken.

Charlie and Josh came in just as they were finishing the first beers. They already knew the Kelly's, so introductions were not needed.

Charlie and Josh joined them all for the meal. 'I told you the meals were all right up here. A bit better than the old dry boot we had for a steak on the way up, eh?' Bert recounted the tale of the tough steak to Charlie and Josh, embellishing the tale a bit as he went.

Following the meal, Josh asked Tony if he would like to come down to the local pub for a disco. Tony and Josh left to check the local girl's scene out.

The night's conversation centered on the prices and where most of the opal was coming from. A new find had produced some opal which had been sold for over thirty thousand dollars an ounce. 'Imagine one piece as big as your hand, probably ten to fifteen ounces. It would be three hundred thousand or more.' This conversation made John all the more determined to have a try for some opal. All other prospects to make some money legally to save the farm seemed to have been thought of and discarded.

That night when he went to sleep, John had vivid dreams of the colours of opal moving back and forth in front of his eyes. He woke a few times, but every time he went back to sleep, the dream returned.

John told Tony about the dreams of opal. Tony had experienced the same. Ha, you're hooked. That's the first sign of opal fever. The gold miners get a similar thing happen to them when they see a lot of gold for the first time. We had it. We still dream of the colours occasionally. The experts say if you dream of opal in the night, you will find it the next day. Keep on dreaming.' There was a lot of superstition surrounding the opal fields. Everyone, it seemed, had a different theory.

Tony walked out into the kitchen. John had let him sleep in because he had arrived home in the wee hours of the morning. 'Have a good time last night?' 'Yes, I met some of the locals. Gee, there are some different looking chicks up here. There were a lot of Greeks at the disco. A lot of the men had jewellery on, opal pendants and flashy rings so forth. Shit, I wouldn't be seen dead wearing some of the gear they had on. I met a couple of nice birds too. I was talking to one nice-looking Greek bird, and her brother came over and told me to shoot through. She wasn't allowed to hang around with Aussies. I nearly got into a fight with this arrogant prick.'

Evidently, Tony had enjoyed himself. It was a long time since he had a night out at Kimba because of the lack of money situation. 'We thought we might get a late start and go and pull a bit more dirt out of the hole. What are you blokes going to do?'

John thought for a while. 'I think we might do the tourist bit and have a look at the opal shops around town.'

The traffic was even worse. Cars and old utilities roared up and down the main street, swerving around each other instead of showing a bit of caution and slowing down a bit. The cars seemed to rev up. Small groups of people sat in the dust by the edges of the road.

A police van was stopped by one group. Two police were interviewing the rowdy mob. One of the women was swinging wildly at a man with a stick, trying to hit him. They parked the ute. They both got out and walked down the street.

They walked into the first opal store. A small dark man hurried out of the back and turned on the display lights above the opal display cases. 'You want to see special opal, very cheap price?' 'No, we're just looking, thank you.' The man looked disappointed and turned the lights off and went back inside.

The treatment in most stores was of a similar off-hand nature until they came to a store selling not only opals but cutting machines and art supplies. This was run by a happy plump Irishman. He had a lot of stories of yester years, some of the cons and crooked partners of best friends turning to enemies as soon as there was money involved. In between the interesting stories, the man served customers, asking the men not to go as he had more stories to tell.

They walked back to the ute and drove around the bottom of the Italian Club hill to an old mine which had been opened up for tourists. The Irish man had recommended this as one of the best tourists stops in town. The men walked into the shop and paid for a permit to go into the mine to look. The pretty blonde assistant gave them a hard hat to wear before they went down into the old mine. 'Wow, did you get a good look at the young bird?'. 'You should be ashamed of yourself. I'll tell mum when we get home.
She had a wedding ring on.' Tony had evidently noticed the pretty girl also.

John and Tony clambered through the narrow drives, marveling at the hardships which had been endured by the early miners. One main one was the lack of water in the town before the desalination plant was installed. 'Bert and Harry would have had an excuse for not washing a few years ago,' said Tony. John didn't' feel the claustrophobia that he felt when he had gone down the shaft out. In the field, it was possible because the drives were well lit and the air was not stale and clammy.

There was still opal in the walls of this mine, covered in glass, of course, to keep the tourists from digging it out.

The Kelly's were back at the camp when they arrived. They had put some shots in, had blasted the face of the drive, and then, after the fumes had settled, had bucketed out the dirt. A vacuum cleaner was rigged up with a long hose to blow fresh air into the drive after blasting. It was plugged into the alternator. The hose of the vacuum was joined to poly pipe this was nailed to the wall of the drive a suitable distance from the blast area. As soon as the shots were fired, they started the machine to blow fresh air into the drive. This was Bert's idea.

Going into a drive too soon after blasting could prove fatal if too many of the fumes from the gelignite were present. Men had died from this, whilst others who had survived had been sick for a long time.

John had bought some meat and fresh vegies and had offered to cook some tea for them. He certainly didn't want to go out for a meal again as it was too expensive on their limited budget.

Chapter seven

Landing in Australia

After carrying the bags off the ship, the impressions of Australia were very different from what Ali and Zeena had grown up with. Where were the people?

"G'day, Are you new to Australia" the cab driver asked as they got into the cab for the trip to the main part of town. "It is very different from the Philippines where we come from, where are all the people". "This is normal traffic for Cairns mate. Just watch out for the kangaroos though, they kick and bite".

Ali laughed "we got the kangaroo and emu treatment on the ship on the way to Australia". The cabbie went on to give a running tourist speech on all of the attractions of Cairns.

After paying the cab they booked two rooms in the nice small hotel, just off the main tourist area. Ali took some of the money out of the suitcase. He also had the silver and gold and some of the pieces of jewellery. Tourist towns all over the world had jeweler shops to manufacture and cater for the tourist trade, the case was carefully resealed.

The first jewelers looked at one of the pieces of jewellery. The only one Ali had taken from his pocket. After some haggling Ali sold the pendant for three hundred dollars.

While he was in the shop he noticed a rack of jewellery in a glass case. The stones in this case had a colour that moved all over the surface as the light shifted on them. He was fascinated by the beauty of these stones. "What are these beautiful stones "asked Ali. "These are Australian opals mate".

The jeweler opened the case and took out a green orange stone set in a pendant setting. The colours moved as if they were a liquid fire inside of the stone. "Where do these Opals come from". The jeweler went on to explain where all of the different stones had originated. Boulder opal from Queensland, black opal Lightning ridge stones, the green orange pendant stone came from Coober

Pedy in South Australia, The last stone was a beautiful blue green stone from Andamooka, also South Australia.

As they left the shop Ali could not stop talking about the opal. He had never seen anything so beautiful. The jeweler had said that there were a lot better quality stones than in his shop.
Three more jeweler shops, and more opals, Ali also sold another of the jewellery pieces. "Is there a manufacturing jeweler near to where we are". The lady pointed down toward the end of the long street, "The large shop down the end of the street makes a lot of the pieces we sell in our shop. We do make some jewellery but it is mainly for orders from our customers"

A nice café was found on the way to the large jewelers. It had a nice view through the palm trees to the ocean. A cool breeze from the sea wafted through the outside eating area. Ali still talked about the opals as they ate their lunch. "I would like to go and see where these stones come from." Zeena was thinking. We could get a car and go and see the opal fields in Queensland. It should only take a day."
The shops were an eye opener to the pair as they slowly walked and window shopped. "Look at those beautiful dresses, these shoes, that hat," Zeena was like a small girl in a lolly shop, all of the sweet things out on display to entice the customers, Ali was not commenting.
The manufacturing jeweler shop had a large array of opals on display. Zeena had never seen Ali so engrossed with anything like this before. "Look at this stone". The stone was a good black opal from the New South Wales town of Lightning Ridge. This stone had a very dark background and a blood red flash over the top of the underlying colours. The small stone had a price of two and a half thousand dollars. After some bartering Ali sold all of the gold and silver bars for three thousand five hundred dollars. "I could be interested in this stone. Do you buy diamonds; I have two large stones my father left to me when he died". The jeweler was interested. Ali looked at some men's rings set with opal; He purchased one for five hundred dollars.

As they left the shop Zeena chastised him for spending the money on the ring. "What are you going to do about the other opal you said you were going to buy? That's a lot of money". "You come with me tomorrow you will find out".

On the way back to the hotel Ali purchased some small plastic bags to hold the individual diamonds.

"I found some ads for trips to the reef in one of the tourist brochures in the foyer of the hotel, Would you like to have a trip to have a look at the coral and fish." Zeena thought this would be a good time to let go of all of the angst built up and act like a normal tourist. "why not, When? ".

"The day after tomorrow should be OK. I want to see if I can sell those two diamonds and then barter for that special piece of opal".

He went down the stairs and enquired about the trip at the hotel desk, the pretty girl at the desk took his details and the fee for the trip. "You will really enjoy the trip out to the reef; all of the tourists that have been have raved about the experience."

"Right the trip is 9.30 at the marlin wharf tomorrow morning. Let's go and sell the diamonds". Zeena was still chiding about the expensive black opal.

The two diamonds were weighed and classified for brightness. The classification was quite high, one stone was one point two carats and the other was one point four. The price finally offered was two thousand eight hundred dollars. "Now let me look at the black opal." The jeweler took the opal out of the special cabinet with the high priced stones. This stone had commanded the center of the case and had a special little stand to really show the rolling red flash.

"I want this stone for a ring for my mother. I will take it for your price if you set it in eighteen carat gold". The jeweler complained that there was no money in the sale as he had to buy the opal, "I am sure this is not the only good black opal in Australia. If you cannot do this, we will leave and look elsewhere." Zeena was pleased to have been offered the gift. She pored through ring designs in a book and selected a simple design which would highlight the opal.

Her finger was measured and all of the details noted down. "The ring will be finished in two days. Is that OK "Ali agreed to the deal.

Not far from the jewelers there was a tourist bus which travelled around the Cairns area. This trip through town filled up the afternoon.

The boat had a queue of twenty-three other people waiting to board when they arrived at the Marlin Wharf. They showed the tickets from the hotel then boarded the boat. The short trip to the reef was in glassy seas with a wisp of a breeze. It took a lot of talking to get Zeena to put the bathing costume on to swim with a mask and snorkel over the coral gardens. Ali had never been swimming before either. The thought of swimming bought back the memories of time he nearly had lessons in Manilla. This was a very different circumstance

Pushing effortlessly through the water over all of the different types of coral and the myriads of colorful fish was a very new experience; an occasional giant clam could be seen with its luminescent green lips slightly ajar to let the water and food flow through. Small crabs and shrimps scurried across the sand and coral. After an hour they boarded the boat, had a shower to remove the salt water the re dressed. The other people were from a lot of different countries.

A beautiful smorgasbord sea food lunch was served to all on board, Ali and Zeena found it very interesting speaking to so many different nationalities. The boat then moved off to a different location, with a different type of coral and fish. A few Black Tipped Reef Sharks swam in amongst the fish. They were evidently not hungry as they made no attempt to eat the fish.

The trip back in the late afternoon showed the spectacular scenery and beautiful city of Cairns to its best in the late afternoon sun.

The boat touched the Marlin Wharf; one of the crew jumped off and secured the mooring lines. A door was opened on the transom of the boat and the gangplank was pushed from the wharf in place. Ali and Zeena were asked to join two American couples for dinner at a restaurant.

The night was very interesting for Ali and Zeena. The two Americans and their wives had both run profitable export business. Both had been in the jewellery trade. Ali started to tell of his fascination for opal. "In the Philippines I had never seen an opal before. We have been looking in the jewellery stores in Cairns and have seen some extremely beautiful stones". The large blond American, Larry agreed about the beauty of opal. "This is the main reason we are in Australia. We are both on a buying trip for our companies. I prefer the Coober Pedy opal, Chuck here, is into Lightning Ridge". Chuck, a small dark-haired man with an acne scarred face stopped eating," The lightning Ridge opal is the most expensive in the world. We do a lot less business than Larry but still get about the same profit. It's either high volume and a lower profit margin, or low volume sales like me, and a higher profit margin. A lot of the stones I sell would net two hundred and fifty per cent by the time they are set into jewellery. Larry works on one hundred and fifty per cent markup. Now if we sell the jewellery in our stores, there is another eighty to one hundred per-cent mark up again." Ali's brain was calculating. The stone he had purchased had probably been bought for twenty-five per-cent of the asking price, about six hundred dollars.

The whole night conversation cantered around the opal trade. Ali was getting the most important lesson of his life from these two couples. Larry's wife Edith was explaining a lot of the business to Zeena.

What a chance meeting this had been for Ali. Nothing had been said about the opal trade on the boat during the day. It looked like Ali was getting a case of opal fever.

Breakfast was being served. "I had a weird dream last night I could see opals and the entire colour was filling my head flashing back and forth before my eyes ". "I had a similar dream "said Zeena.

The jeweler weighed the two diamonds and calculated the grade of stone. His calculation for quality and brightness was one point less than the manufacturing jeweler. "My offer is two thousand three hundred dollars firm". Ali knew what firm meant but still tried to talk up the price, the jeweler would not budge. Finally Ali agreed to sell.

As they walked to the manufacturing jewelers to pick up the ring Zeena was in deep thought, "I hope the dirty Indian who is swimming can see us sell his diamonds. I regret the life I had in the Philippines having to bear men like him beating me".

The deal was completed with the ring. Zeena could not wait so she placed the opal ring on her finger. The colours of the stone danced as she moved her finger. "When will we be leaving Cairns?" asked Zeena as they walked along the street looking for a café for lunch." I will go and see a car dealer and see about buying a car, I want to travel to the Quilpie opal fields, and then work our way down through the Queensland opal fields. Then go to Lightning Ridge and finally end up at Coober Pedy ".

In one of the shops there were a lot of different road maps of Australia. Ali bought a book of Australian road maps, plus some smaller maps to see how far it would be to travel from Cairns to Quilpie.

In the hotel at night Ali opened the book of maps. He found the Cairns map. Quilpie was nowhere to be found on that map. In the front of the book there were some graphs showing the distances from on point to another on the map. He looked up Cairns then found Quilpie. "This is one thousand four hundred kilometers. That is from Laoag in Luzon to Koronadal in Mindanao. This is a huge distance. We would still be in Queensland. How big is Australia?". He then studied the distance from there to Lightning Ridge, another seven hundred and fifty kilometers.

This changed Ali's thinking about buying a car. He was going to buy a small car. As he had studied the map he had noted the distances between the towns. It would have to be a good car to trust in the outback.

The cabbie was helpful when Ali told him where he wanted to go. He suggested buying a Toyota Land cruiser or a Nisan Patrol for the trip, He warned about buying a Land-rover because they always seemed to have mechanical problems.

The first dealer was a Datsun dealer. There was a new Nissan Patrol hard top in the show room. There were also some very nice sedan cars as well. Zeena was attracted to a Nissan Cedric sedan. This car had all of the bells and whistles and looked good. Ali explained to the salesman about where they wanted to go, "If you want to go exploring in the outback, I don't think the Cedric would handle the deep gutters in the dirt roads very well, as you would need a lot of ground clearance to clear the loose stones and other obstacles on the road".

After Ali finished having a drive of the Patrol, Zeena was still not convinced. Ali had some wheedling to do to finally convince her. The deal was finally made and the Nissan signed up, a deposit was paid. Ali was to come in the morning, as the dealer had to get all of the jobs like number plates and a final check done on the Patrol.

Next was the Queensland Automobile Association to find what they should take on their travels. "I have a list here for people travelling a long way outback." He handed Ali a list then went through the list explaining what they might need. First was twenty liters of water, two large jerry-cans of petrol, extra five liters of oil, small electric compressor, shovel, heavy tow rope, blankets, matches. "Have you ever changed a flat tyre before". "No I would not have any idea". "You should get the dealer to show you how". The Man suggested that Ali should sign up for QAA service as there was Australia wide assistance in case of breakdowns and other trouble. Ali paid and signed the papers.

The green Patrol was parked outside of the dealer's premises when they arrived. The payment was made; Ali and Zeena dove off to the accessories shop the dealer had given them directions to A large plastic box was purchased to put all of the gear needed to travel the out-back roads. The jerry cans had straps to tie them to the rear of the seats.

The Patrol was a lot different to drive than the Morris Minor or the Ford Consul. Being a lot higher was a different experience. After a short drive he started to get used to the extra height and width.

Cases and other bags of clothes were loaded in the rear. The water drum was filed and the jerry cans and Patrol fuel tank was filled. Ali was a bit apprehensive about the outback trip, but the lure of the opal and industry was the main drawcard. Like a carrot dangled in front of a donkeys nose.

They drove on bitumen roads, then some dirt roads in good order then some short sections of bitumen during the day. The occasional dead cow, kangaroo or large pig lay dead on the edge of the road. Ali realised that the car would have been a problem as in places there were ridges in the road created by the large trucks with two and three trailers of cattle.

They pulled in and stopped at a small bush hotel for the night at Hughenden. As they were waiting for dinner, Ali spoke to one of the obvious locals. This man had a bushies old hat, and spoke with a drawl. At the end of the sentences he always said Ay. He described the narrow bitumen roads and warned Ali to get off the road when a truck came in view. "There is two reasons for this Mate. Trucks are bigger than you and will not give you room, plus they toss stones off the tyres and might smash your windscreen ay". Ali had realised this early in the trip as he had found the truckies had no intention of moving for a smaller vehicle.

From Hughenden the road conditions were worse. There must have been rains a few weeks before and occasionally there were long trenches where a truck had been bogged. All vehicles had been using a detour past these ruts. A car would have been useless in these sections of the road.
The Patrol did not do too bad a job at keeping the dust out, but a fair amount still got inside. The temperature was in the forties, when they stopped to pour the contents of a jerry can of petrol into the tank, the small flies swarmed like bees around a honey pot. Zeena was getting a bit grumpy about the weather and flies. The Philippine weather was different to this searing heat. She would touch the windscreen and complain about it nearly burning her finger.

There was not very much traffic on the road. The occasional road train full of cattle could be seem by the dust cloud, long before the truck came into view.

The hotel in Windorah had an air conditioner rattling in the window of the bar. They walked past the exhaust side as they went to see about accommodation, the hot air would nearly have cooked eggs.

Ali booked in, they went to see the room, and there was a small air conditioner in the top of the window. The woman turned this on as they left the room.

The inside of the Patrol was covered with a fine red dust. A bag of clothes were taken into the hotel. Zeena had dusted as much of the dust as she could.

Ali went to fill up with fuel. The man at the service station asked if he would like a blowout. "What is a blowout "."This hose has a compressor on the end. I will put this nozzle on and blow the inside of your car out to get rid of the dust, ay". Ali opened the back door and both the side doors. The man blew the jet of air all through the Patrol sending a cloud of brown dust blowing in the wind.

"What is the road to Quilpie like". "Are you looking for some opal, ay?" "Yes, I met a man in Cairns who had been buying opals. I want to see where it comes from". "It's a big country here mate, and there are a few different opal areas in Queensland. The roads are bitumen, ok but there is a stretch of about ten kilometers which is a bit rough, there are holes in the bitumen. You will be OK in the Patrol though mate, ay."

The evening meal at the hotel was a large plate with a piece of thick steak covering the plate and another plate with vegetables on it. They looked at their plates. They had never seen a meal as large as this served up before. Ali finished his serve Zeena had to leave about half of hers. "No wonder they have such big men in this part of Australia", she said as they waddled back to the room.

The dust situation was much better with the thin strip of bitumen. The road was raised up on a high crown with the strip of tar on the top. When another truck or four-wheel drive approached one had to get off the side of the road to let them pass by.

A small section of stunted scrubby trees was on each side of the road. Ali had been driving for a long time and was getting tired. Suddenly a huge black pig lurched out of the bushes in front of them; it turned its ugly head with huge white tusks protruding from its mouth toward them and stopped. Ali braked hard, as he neared the pig it started to move toward the side of the road, Ali had been turning to try and pass this pig. The Nissan followed alongside the pig almost touching it as it now sped toward the scrub. The Nissan finally stopped just as the front bumper touched some leaves of the first tree. The black pig disappeared from sight in the bushes. Ali was shaken by this experience; he sat behind the wheel and waited for a short while, before reversing back onto the road. Zeena had now stopped yelling and was a rather pale colour. There was not much traffic travelling, they may have had a long wait for assistance if they had run down this large pig.

Some car doors and engine hoods were pinned upside down with star posts with hand painted signs advertising opal and meals just before Quilpie appeared.

There was a railway line through the town. This seemed out of place so far from habitation. Ali was keen to see some of the boulder opals in the shops.

The hotel had an opal shop in the ground floor. Ali sidled into the shop while Zeena booked into a room for the night. "Howryougoinmate", Said the grizzled looking man as Ali studied the opal. The opals had a backing of the ironstone coloured ribbon stone on the back of them. Ali settled into a conversation with the man about where the opal fields were. "There's one a few miles out that way "He pointed to a road leading out off the main road, "You should be able to see a couple of bulldozers working out there tomorrow if you want to have a look"

He rolled a cigarette, put it to his mouth and lit it. He had a bit of a cough. "One thing you have to look out for is not to get too close to where the men are working; they are a bit ticklish about this. There is a lot of crooks around in this game, especially when they are onto opal". Ali thanked the man then went to the Patrol and got the small bag of luggage out for the night.

The road had not seen a grader for years it seemed. Pot holes and corrugations in the road surface kept the speed down and nearly shook their top teeth out.

Dust was rising in the distance, Ali turned down a little used new track to where a bulldozer was ripping the hard stones up. Some checkers studied the rocks and gave the occasional rock a hit with the pick to break it open. Every few rocks which were broken were spat on and held up to catch the sun to check for colour in the thin band of potch. None of the checkers acknowledged their presence. Ali had at least seen the first opal being dug up by a bulldozer.

The trip back to town was another bone shaking journey. Before filling with water and petrol Ali wet to thank the old man. "We nearly had our heads shaken off on the bad road". The old man laughed. "The Shire Council did offer to grade the road a few times. The miners kicked up a stink about it. The rough road kept the tourists away; there was less chance of some coot coming back at night trying to steal their opal."

After a day and a half heavy driving, finally they were at the Imperial Hotel, Lightning Ridge. By this time Ali was beginning to realise what a huge country they were travelling in.

They booked into the hotel for a week. The case full of money was secreted into the room under clothes in the wardrobe. Ali took out ten thousand dollars from the stash. He was about to see if he could work out the intricate dealings of the opal buying business. He had the old kit bag with the money in it. A set of balance scales and weights were bought from the local store. Ali went out into the fields where miners were working and spread the word that he may be looking to purchase a small parcel of opal.

After the dirt with the opal traces were dug from the ground the whole lot was put through a large cement mixer for a few hours to clean the hard dirt off the opal. A lot of the opal was covered in this brown dirt and was impossible to see until the whole lot had been Puddled and then sieved to take the now brown silt off the hard stones. This idea had been devised many years before.

Old Charlie McKay sidled up to Ali as he finished dinner at night. "I hear you are looking for some opal". "Yes I could be if the price is right". Charlie had a small parcel of opal, about five ounces in weight. Ali was given the directions to Charlie's house. The house was sorely in need of a coat of paint as a lot of the wood around the window glass had begun to rot. The house seemed to be made of all of the bits and pieces Charlie could find cheap or obtain for free. Ali knocked on the rickety door; he had the trusty kit bag. He was apprehensive about making his first opal buy.

"You had better come inside then. Get out of the bloody road dog." A large red dog went and sat on an old miners couch covered in old blankets. The dog eyed Ali warily as he set himself down.

Charlie cleared a space on the kitchen table for Ali to set up the scales. He reached behind a chair and took a small desk light from a shelf on the wooden wall. The light shone brightly onto the table top. Charlie then lifted a plastic bag onto the table.

The table had a piece of black oil cloth as a cover. The small bags of stones were taken out of the bag and lined up; they each had a number and a weight on them. Ali was nervous, but was not going to show it. The contents of each bag were tipped into a pile and the bag placed ready to re bag them. The number one pile had seven stones the size of a thumb nail, almost round. He studied each stone under the light. There were three black opals with a dark red and green flash which stood apart from the rest. The next pile was studied, until the last which only had a small amount of colour on a potch base were looked at.

Ali looked into Charlies eyes. "What price do you have on the parcel". Charlie looked at a small piece of paper, which he held so Ali could not see. "I want six thousand an ounce for the tops, there is one ounce and eight twentieths of a penny weight. That would make the price about the eight thousand mark". Ali's trading in the markets had stood him well; he could read the man's eyes and knew he was asking an unreasonable price for the lot, as he fidgeted as he was talking. "What is the bottom line for the whole parcel". "I want thirteen and a half thousand dollars". "I can only see eight for the lot". "Jeeze you're trying to be tough",

A bargaining banter started. The end result was that Ali got the parcel for nine thousand five hundred dollars. He paid Charlie out of the money in the kit-bag. The opal was re-bagged, and then placed back into the large plastic bag.

Ali Showed Zeena the new purchase when he arrived back at the hotel room. 'You paid all of that money for those little stones." she thought that Ali had been robbed. Tomorrow I will look for a good opal cutter to cut the good stones out of this parcel and see what we have got. Ali asked around to see who was classed as a decent opal cutter.

The opal cutter was in a room of one of the better houses in lightning ridge. He had a small store front with display cases of set jewellery and cut stones for sale. Ali had the bag of opal with him.

He sat at a desk with black plastic to protect the top and also to high light the colour of the opal. In the room were all the tools of the gem cutters trade, grinding wheels and sanding discs plus a felt covered wheel for polishing. Rows of semi- finished stones glued to the end of a short piece of dowelling wood sat in pieces of wood with holes bored in them, the stones were glued to dowelling sticks which were poked into the holes in the wood.

"Let's see what we have got ". Ali tipped the first-grade stones out onto the black plastic Alex the opal cutter studied each stone under a desk light with a magnifying glass fitted to it. Three stones were separated from the first grade. These stones are very high so I will cut them in half so they make six. You may as well go and have some lunch while I get started". Ali did not like this idea too much. He did not know the man. He could substitute the stones. "No I would like to see the cutting work done"

Alex stood up then took the opal to a small diamond saw and sliced the three opals through the middle. Under the bright light the wet opals showed their true colour. The red and green flashed like fire across the black background. "These are bloody good opals mate. Where did you buy them"? I met a guy in the pub who was looking to sell some opal'.

After a few minutes the six opals were cut and polished. Alex weighed them and put each opal in a small plastic bag with the weight written on a small stick-on tag stuck to each bag. The average weight of the opals was five carats.

"What sort of price would you put on the opals ". "You should get at least eight hundred dollars a carat for these stones". "Is that a wholesale price or retail". "You should get the price from a Jeweler of some other dealer. He would be asking about twelve hundred a carat" Ali copied the suggested price down into a small note book. The cutter then sliced and cut the rest of the opal in the first-grade bag. These opals were not the same quality. "Ask about four hundred dollars a carat for these". Ali did a quick calculation in his head. This was forty thousand dollars' worth of cut stones. .

The next two bags of opal were cut. The lesser grade stones were worth fifteen thousand dollars. Ali asked the cutter what he owed him for cutting the opal. "That bag of potch and colour will do". Ali had noticed some of the opal Alex had for sale had some black spots in the opal when cut. " . "OK you have got a deal ".   As he left the shop, he noticed the girl at the counter was talking to three lots of tourists.

The cutting and appraisal had left Ali's brain in a spin. There was no need to commit a crime and do a stretch in jail if you were caught. This was all legal.

The bar at the hotel had some of the early drinkers starting to taste the brown ale. They had evidently been to work on first light to get away from the flies dust and heat. The hot sun shimmered off the galvanized iron roofs of the houses near the hotel.

The small Air-conditioner was buzzing away trying to dispel the heat from the room; Ali opened the door and entered. "How did you go with the opal cutter". Ali explained about the pricing of the cut opal. He showed Zeena the bags of cut opal. "Get the ring I bought you in Cairns." Zeena went to her hand-bag and retrieved the box with the opal ring inside. She took the ring out,   Ali had one of the top grade opals out of its bag, they compared the two stones. The loose stone was a far superior stone, plus it was a lot larger. Zeena's ring stone was similar to the second- grade opal from the first bag. This was the four hundred dollar a carat grade. Zeena's ring was one and a half carat.

Over the next week Ali spent fifty thousand dollars buying opal. The tricks of the market trade were a very good lesson, when buying in this business. Three of the miners told Ali to stick his deal where the sun doesn't shine. He was enjoying the challenges of the opal trade.

In the opal business most miners work hard for weeks without any income, just the expenses of explosives detonators fuse and diesel or petrol. If they do not find opal they have to sell the first parcel that they find to pay-off the store and other creditors. This is the time the opal buyers pounce. Just before Christmas is another time the prices drop for opal bought from an unsuccessful miner. They want to leave town to see their families.

Ali and Zeena said their goodbyes to the people they had got to know, The Patrol was loaded and a course plotted through the outback to Coober Pedy.

Chapter eight

Mining the opal

John and Tony drove through town and then turned right past the hotel and, after a short distance, called at the Mines Department office to see if the tags had arrived. The woman walked over to another counter and sorted through a pile of mail in a low cardboard container. 'Nickols, you said your name was?' she asked. John assured her that was right. She pulled two plastic bags from the pile and turned back to the main counter. As she walked over, she informed them that they had arrived. The men had to sign for their tags, after which the woman handed each of them a small plastic packet with the plastic tags in it.

The men left the Mines office, started the ute, and then turned back towards the main street. Then they drove to the hardware store behind the supermarket, where they bought eight wooden pegs. These were square pine posts about a meter long with one end sharpened to a point. John thought they were pretty dear, but as they had to have them, he paid the money. 'Hell, we've got hundreds of posts the same as these at home,' he remonstrated as he got into the ute.

They felt a sense of anticipation now, as all the red tape had been dealt with. They talked about what they would do if they were lucky enough to have a find like Bert and Harry as they drove out to where Bert and Harry were working. The thought of paying off the bank as Bert had done was foremost in their conversation. They knew this was pure fantasy, but at least, there was now some sort of hope of getting out of their financial quagmire.

When they arrived at the claim, Bert showed them how to put the pointers on to the corners of the pegs. These were pieces of steel packing tape from around boxes. They had been told to pick this up from the hardware store. Tony cut the thin steel for the pointers into eight pieces with a pair of tin snips. The pointers were nailed on to the top of the pegs to show the direction of the claim boundaries. The small plastic tags with their precious stones permit number were then nailed on under the pointers. John hit his finger with the hammer as he tried to hold and hit the small nails through the thin steel. He cursed the hammer roundly.

Bert and Harry helped them to measure out the claims with the fifty-meter-long tape. Each claim was a hundred meters long, making an area two hundred meters by fifty meters along the line in which the Kelly's were getting their opal. Harry had an old compass, which he had taken out of the ute glove compartment. They then walked around the boundaries of the claims and took the compass bearings from each corner and wrote these down on a piece of paper with a plan of the claims drawn on it. A compass bearing then had to be taken from a mines department survey peg, which was an iron dropper with a brass tag bolted to it. It was some distance away. A measurement had to be taken from the closest peg of each claim to the department peg, which also had a number on the tag. The number had to be recorded on the plan.

They helped pull some more dirt for the men and then headed back to town to register the claims before the Mines Department closed.

'What would you suggest our next move should be?' John asked Harry when they arrived home later that night. Harry thought for a while as he sipped on his beer. 'Well, there's two ways to go about that. You could drill a big shaft with a Caldwell drill like we have, or you could get a bloke with an investigator drill to sink a lot of smaller test holes to see if you can find any trace of opal. You will get a lot more holes done over your claims with the smaller drill. The big drill costs about ten times as much to drill a hole and also takes a heck of a lot longer to drill, plus it is a bloody dangerous machine.'
This was dangerous as it either entailed a trip to the pub or to the Italian Club to see if they could find a driller willing to do some cash holes.

John had a brilliant idea. He drove into town and called at the Irishman's opal shop and asked him where he could hire a driller for a day. 'Go up to the Italian Club any time after six o'clock. Ask for Luigi,' he was told. There was no getting away from the Italian Club or the pub. It seemed that most of the town's business was done in either. The man also told him to be careful of some of the drillers, as they would tell their mates if they cut any opal traces. The next thing was, the whole area would be pegged around them. This had happened to some people who had found that the blowers and tunneling machines working on their boundary had worked well into the neighbor's claim. This Luigi bloke was meant to be OK and kept his mouth shut about what he had drilled for other people.

John drove up to the Italian Club and asked for Luigi at the bar. A small man sitting at the bar a short distance away turned and asked, 'What you want with Luigi?' John explained about the drilling. 'Hey, that's OK. I think you might be from my ex-wife to look for more bloody money. She always chases me. Money, money, money. That is all she knows, how to say.

Here, have a beer. What kind you drink?, West End, Fosters? 'Make it a West End Draught.' Luigi ordered a can of beer from the barman and handed it to John. Luigi was a small, wizened-looking man with skin like dried-up leather, very similar to Bert and Harry's, a legacy of many hours' work in the sun. John explained what he wanted to do and arranged to meet Luigi at the start of the Fourteen Mile field road at nine the next morning. They had another beer each, and John excused himself. 'Hey, don't go yet. The night, she be young yet. Stop and have a few more of the beers. I like to have someone to talk to.' John was not going to let himself fall into that trap again, so he insisted that he had to go and help back at the camp. John walked out into the cool night air and drove back to the camp. He nearly got lost this time himself.

Luigi's drill could be seen driving down the Breakaways road and then turning left towards the men waiting in the ute. The drill slowed to nearly stop, next to John's ute. John waved out of the window. 'Follow me,' yelled John. The big drill followed behind them through the field to the freshly pegged claim.

Luigi gingerly climbed out of the six-wheel-drive yellow international army truck, nearly falling as his foot slipped off the step.

'Shit! I should have gone home when you did. A couple of mates they come in. We got bloody pissed. Oh, the bloody head she hurt. I think my eyes are going to drop out. Mama mia! Phew!' Luigi stood next to the drill. It towered over his small frame.

'What you think of my drill?' he motioned proudly towards the drill with his hand. 'She pretty good, hey.'

The drill consisted of a nine-meter auger, which was turned by a hydraulic motor on the top of a tower and was pulled down by strong steel cables. There were three, four-meter extension augers which could be joined on, which gave the unit a drilling depth, if needed of around twenty-five meters. The main auger was in a boom, which was laid down on top of the rig and protruded past the truck cab. The entire rig was driven by its own diesel motor coupled to a series of hydraulic pumps—a very impressive looking machine.

Luigi looked around. 'Why you come here? I don't think you do much good around here. Everyone piss off from here years ago. They say this is dead ground. I work over there with some mates ten years ago. We didn't do no bloody good.' John assured him that they would try the claims any way. 'OK, please yourself. It's your money. Where you want to try first?' asked Luigi sickly. Tony pointed to a small pile of rocks which Tony had built on the junction of one of the crossings he had wired with the divining rods. 'You guide me back so the back of the truck is about a half a meter from the rocks. That's where the drill points when she is lifted up in the air.' Luigi climbed back into the truck and started the motor. Tony guided him back to the rocks and waved for him to stop about a half meter from the rear of the truck.

The truck stopped, and Luigi slid out of the cab. The cab was so high and Luigi so short. It looked as if he would need a ladder to climb aboard, Luigi walked around the truck to the rear of the rig and started the diesel motor from a control panel situated in the left-hand corner of the drilling rig frame. He adjusted the throttle so the motor was revving at a fast idle. He then lowered the four hydraulic feet and levelled the drilling rig by looking at a level which was built into the rig near to where he stood, and then he raised the mast and auger. Watching the long tower and auger being lifted was an unusual experience. The tower looked as if it were going to fall as the clouds raced past it. The auger was then lowered down the short distance through the mast so it was resting on the ground, and then the hydraulic motor was started, turning the auger in the dry red dirt.

For the start, the auger pushed out dark red dirt, and then it started to grind as it hit a layer of hard stones at around the two- meter depth. There was a small, circular screen located at the rear of the auger. Luigi pulled a lever and started this turning. This screened the fine sand and dirt out of the material which the drill bored out of the ground, making it easier to see any of the traces of opal, if there were any.

Slowly, the drill bored its way down into the ground until it was to the full depth of the first long auger. 'Do you want to go any deeper?' asked Luigi.' 'No, Bert and Harry are only working at around seven meters.' Both John and Tony were disappointed at not finding any traces. Luigi slowly lifted the auger out of the hole, cleaning the dirt off it with his gloved hand as it rose so the dirt was funneled through the screen to be checked.

He then lowered the ten-meter mast. 'Where do you want to try next?' Tony showed him a new pile of stones nearby. The procedure was repeated. There were no traces of opal. The next four holes were the same—no opal. John was starting to count the dollars as each hole was costing thirty dollars. 'I tell you the opal, she not too easy to find, especially around here,' said Luigi as he noted the disappointment on the men's faces. Five holes dug and not a bit of trace of opal. One hundred and fifty dollars.

There was a small hollow in the ground in which some green grass grew. 'Try there,' Tony asked. He was running out of piles of stones. He had been so convinced that the opal would be easy to find. The depression in the soil was a departure from the divined areas as there was not even a trace of anything to keep them interested.

This hole was different. Right from the start, the dirt was wet. When the drill auger was about three quarters the way down, the auger crunched and shuddered slightly. Tony took no notice of this, but Luigi cocked his head slightly; he had heard this sound before. A half minute later, something glistened as it dropped out of the screen.

The man were worried and had started to think they were wasting their time and money. Some more pieces dropped out. Suddenly, Tony stopped daydreaming. 'Stop the drill,' he yelled to Luigi. Luigi had already seen some small pieces of trace in the sand being sieved out of the screen. He smiled as he stopped the auger and screen turning. John and Tony were sieving the material in the pile and building a small heap of opal in John's hat on the ground. Luigi put some of the small pieces he had picked out of the sieved fines into the hat. He reached in and took one of the brighter pieces out and licked it. 'By shit, you lucky buggers. I drill five hundred holes the last few weeks for myself and not find a bit of opal, only bloody potch (opal without colour). This bloody top red material. Look at the red rolling flash over it. About fifteen hundred dollars an ounce.'

The drill auger was started turning again, and a bit more opal came out and then only sandstone. The auger was nearly right in when it shuddered again. Luigi let the auger turn for a while and bring more material to the surface. He was just going to start to raise it when more opal started to come. This was shell material, mainly green.

'Shit, you lucky bastards! You got two bloody levels here, one seam, and the other shells.'

John turned to face Luigi. 'You think we're lucky? You should ask our prick of a bank manager. He was going to sell our farm and kick us out. He'll tell you otherwise,' said John.

Four more holes were drilled, each around two meters away from the first one, set out like the five pattern on a dice with the first hole in the center of the pattern. Each hole produced opal. Bert and Harry had just come out of the shaft. 'What do you look so happy for?' asked Harry with a wry smile. 'Find some bloody opal, did you?'

Bert and Harry inspected the different piles of opal, some in cut-down drink cans and a couple in handkerchiefs. 'Good luck to you. This looks as if you have got a pretty big pocket of good opal here.' 'What would you suggest we do now?' John asked Bert. 'Well, you could get a bloke with a Caldwell drill to dig a shaft for you, or you could bring the old dozer up from the farm and put a cut in. Personally, I would put a bulldozer cut in seeing you have got the dozer. With a dozer cut, you see all the ground from the top down, whereas we only see what is in front of us in the drive.'

Both John and Tony had the feeling that maybe their trials of the last few years might be about to resolve themselves. Hope at last.

Tony and John talked excitedly about the drilling to Bert and Harry. Luigi was paid for his work. He climbed back into the drilling rig. 'Good luck to you,' he shouted. He waved and then drove off towards town. 'Looks as if dinner's on us tonight. That's a bit of a turnaround. When they got arrived back in town, John stopped the ute at the phone box by the supermarket and rang Helen to tell her the good news. John and Tony took it in turns to tell her of their good fortune. Helen was thrilled to hear about the opal find but had some bad news from home.

Two days ago, Helen had gone out to feed the chickens and to collect the eggs from the 'girls' and had found a hole had been dug under the chicken yard gate. There were feathers everywhere; some of the 'girls' lay dead on the ground with their heads bitten off whilst the rest were standing hunched together in the far corner of the chicken run. They looked a sorry lot, far different from the usually beautiful Sussex hens they had been the day before. Helen was furious, how could anything do such a thing to these lovely birds. They were her friends. She used to talk about her problems to them as she collected the eggs and fed them. She had walked into the fowl run and looked into the hen house, only to see the fat fox asleep inside. She had stormed out and looked around for something to block the hole under the gate. She found a small sheet of roofing iron, which she pushed into the hole under the gate. She had then hurried back to the house and got the double-barreled, twelve-gauge shotgun and some shells.

By the time she had returned to the fowl run, the fox was running back and forth, trying to find a way out. The poor fowls, which were still alive, were also running, trying to keep out of its way. Helen loaded both barrels of the gun and sighted along the barrel, pointing it at the fox, who was in the far corner of the yard cowering. She pulled the trigger. There had been a loud bang and a cloud of smoke. Her last recollection before she had been pushed back to sit on her backside was of the fox disintegrating before her eyes. Helen had never shot out of a shotgun before and had pulled both triggers at once. Revenge may have been sweet, but she had a very sore shoulder and backside to remember this one by.

John recounted the sad story when he returned to the camp. 'By God, I would like to have seen that. You want to watch out when you get home. A woman with a shotgun can be a dangerous creature,' said Harry with a laugh. 'I think we will head back home tomorrow morning and get the dozer ready and bring it up to Coober Pedy.'

The excitement of the opal find was the main thing on their mind, the road rolled on and on in front of them. Travelling on the tarred road was not too bad, but when they turned off on to the Kingoonya to Wirrulla road, dodging the dusty holes and rocks, it made a long trip home. Both Tony and John felt tired from the excitement of the last few days' working and could hardly wait to get the dozer up to Coober Pedy and start working on the claim. They were in a hurry to get home.

As they neared the farm, some of the country started to look a little bit greener than when they had left. There were slight tinges of green on the pasture paddocks, and the wheat crops had changed from the sickly blue colour. They had been to a slightly darker shade of green.

Helen had spent the afternoon anxiously watching for the ute to drive off the Kimba road into the lane way. She was waiting at the gate in the house yard when they finally arrived. 'Have a good trip?' she asked as she gave both of the men a big hug. Helen recoiled back. 'Phew, watch out for my shoulder. It really hurts still. Here, look at the bruise.' Helen pulled back the sleeve of her jumper to show them the large bruise the shotgun butt had made on the shoulder. The outline of the gun's butt had left a dark blue outer bruise, grading to an orange angry-looking center. 'Revenge may be sweet, but I'll sure remember this lot.'

Helen recounted the fox story. John gave her an extra careful hug. 'I'm very proud of the way you defended the castle whilst we were away at our crusades.' They all laughed.

Tony helped carry the dirty clothes into the outside laundry. 'Gee, it's good to have you back home.' She cuddled up to John, and then she went back into the house and made three coffees.

The men recounted the story of drilling the opal up and how they had pattern-drilled to prove the size of the area. The excitement was carried through the conversation to Helen. John had the traces in a bag. He tipped each lot of opal into a dinner plate with a small amount of water in it on the kitchen table. 'Get the desk lamp from the office,' asked John. Tony hurried in and got the lamp and then plugged it in and put it on the table so the light shone down on the small pieces of opal. Helen marveled at the beauty of the coloured stones and the way the light changed the flashing colours. The thought of having some way to get out of the financial mess was at least something to hope for. The whole mood in the house had changed from one of doom and gloom to one of hope.

Helen put a frying pan on the stove and dropped some chops into it for tea. She then peeled and diced some spuds and carrots and put these on to boil.

The animated conversation centered on the chances of finding a big seam of opal in the claim. They all fantasized as to what they would do with their money. After the meal, John rang Tom Morgan, who lived at Kyancutta, and asked if he still owned the old low loader he had used when he had a dozer. Bert had said about the low loader. He was sure that Tom still had the machine. Tom assured them that he still had it on his farm but it would need a bit of work before it could be used on the road. He did not want to sell it but would hire it if they thought they could use it. John and Tony arranged to have a look at the loader in two days.

The next morning was spent feeding and checking the sheep and crops. The crops and the feed situation had improved slightly. At least, there were no more dead sheep to contend with. The crow trap's side had been lifted when they went away so any hapless crow who dared to go into it would not have had to stay in the trap and finally die. Even crows needed a little bit of compassion.

The next morning, they drove off in the utility. It was around forty kilometers to the Morgan farm. As they travelled, they noticed that the country was quite a bit greener as they neared Kyancutta. Evidently, they had received some rain lately.

They were not quite sure where Tom's farm was, as it was on one of the back roads which led from the small town. John was sure they were on the right road, but as most of the farmers had not painted their names on their mailboxes, it was hard to know which farm it was. Tom had described how to get to the farm, but as most things; it was different from the phone description when driving down a strange road. Finally, John drove into one of the unmarked gate ways and drove the short distance down the lane way to the house and shed complex and then pulled in to a shed near the house where they could see two men working. John climbed out of the ute, walked over, and asked the men for directions. They were close. Tom's farm was the next property.

The sheds and the house on the farm were almost new. Evidently, the Morgan's had been able to put some of the income from the farm back into improvements. The old timber and galvanized iron house stood forlornly some distance from the new one. It was very small and looked as if it would have been very hot in the extreme heat that this area was noted for. John turned into the circular driveway in front of the reasonably new house.   Tom Morgan walked out of the house to greet them. 'G'day! We've just come up from the shed for some smoko. Come inside, and have a cuppa before we go back down to the sheds,' invited Tom as they got out of the ute. They walked through a neat lawn and garden and then entered the large modern kitchen, which smelt of freshly baked cake. 'You've met Mary before, haven't you?' The plump, grey-haired woman turned, smiled, and then walked across the neat kitchen and shook their hands. 'Take a seat at the table.' She motioned towards the table with her hands.

The usual country commentary followed as was the normal manner, who was related to whom and where they had come from before moving to the district.

The men finished their tea, left the house, and walked over to the sheds to look at the old low loader. John noted that the machinery in Tom's implement sheds was of a pretty high standard and was reasonably new. A far cry from their old worn-out plant. John felt very envious of the shiny tractors and headers.

The loader trailer was used to keep the bulk grain bins off the semitrailer on, in the winter. It was parked under a lean-to next to the main implement shed. The tyres were fairly flat. John and Tony had a quick look around and under the loader. A couple of tyres would need replacing if it was to make the trip to Coober Pedy. 'We sold the dozer a few years ago. The bloke who bought it made us an offer on the loader, but it was so low that we decided to keep it. As you can see, it needs a fair bit of work. The tail lights have been broken. The bloody kids had some mates staying with them on the farm a few years ago, my sister's kids from the city. Real little hoons they were. They got into everything. I reckon you should be able to get a few second-hand tyres from the local council. They usually take them off when there's still plenty of tread on them.' Tom agreed to let them have the low loader for the trip up to Coober Pedy for two hundred dollars' hire as long as they fixed the few problems.

'There's one other problem. I think you may have problems registering the low loader, as it hasn't been registered for years. You know what a mob of mongrels the registration mob is to deal with.' John thought for a few seconds.

What if we change the rego and plates from our semi-trailer? If we don't have an accident, we should at least look registered. We don't want to hang around for another six months, going broke whilst some shiny-bottomed twerp in an office in the city finally makes his mind up if we can use the low loader or not.

'We'll be back tomorrow to pick it up, as long as this is OK with you.' Tom nodded. They shook hands on the deal. 'I'll take the bins off this afternoon ready for when you come to pick it up.'

They headed back home along the dry dusty roads. 'Well, that's the first problem over with. Now we had better do some work to the dozer and truck. Maybe our luck has finally changed for the better. John left the kitchen and walked across to join Tony who had just opened the door of the truck.

The sheepdogs were very keen to see the truck started as they were the dozer a few weeks before. It was another of their favourite machines for sport, catching the mice as they ran out from under the truck.

The mice had been particularly bad the last few months, even though they had tried to keep them down with rat poison. Tony had got an unpleasant surprise when he opened the door of the truck. The dirty mice had eaten the rubber grommet from around the steering column and got inside the cab. What a mess! Tony pulled out the nests from under the seats and threw them out on to the ground. The nests were made from old baling twine and some of the inner-seat cushion material.

There was mouse manure everywhere throughout the truck cabin.

The dogs made short work of the baby mice in the nest, one quick nip on the back of the neck to each one, whilst Tony accounted for a couple of the parents with his boot as they tried to escape out of the hole by the steering column. He tossed them out of the cab, where upon the dogs made doubly sure that they were dead.

Suddenly, Tony was out of the truck, clutching at his trousers and madly trying to take his trousers down at the same time. He was hopping around on one leg like a Scotsman doing a reel. John was worried that Tony had hurt himself in the truck cabin. Tony finally got his trousers off, whilst still holding the leg firmly. He ran out of the shed in his undies and then called loudly to the dogs. Laddie came over with an amused look on his face. John was still wondering what the trouble was.

Tony shook his trousers wildly until finally a huge mouse ran out of the trouser leg. Laddie true to his form ran in and dispatched the mouse with one bite. John by this time had realised what the trouble had been and was by now crouched down, laughing uncontrollably. Tony was not amused. 'That's all right by you, you old coot. If that bloody mouse had

latched on, you might never have been a grandfather to my kids.'

Finally, they tried to start the diesel motor. John was still chuckling from the recent pantomime. Nothing happened. Tony turned the key over and over, and the starter would not turn.   John got a piece of fencing wire and quickly shorted the battery terminals. 'There's plenty of juice in the batteries. Check under the dashboard.' Tony looked under the dash. The mice had eaten the insulation off the wiring loom and chewed some of the wires through.   'Would you get me some pliers, some insulation tape, and some wire joiners? The blooming mice have had a party under here.' Finally, the wires were re-joined. Tony turned the key again. The truck started, whereupon more mice ran out from under the motor. The dogs yelped with excitement as they chased their quarry. Tony slid out of the cab, walked over to the house, and mixed some disinfectant with hot water in a bucket. He walked back to the shed and splashed this through the cab and over the truck's motor.

'We'll draw straws to see who drives the truck over to the Morgan's.' John pulled a matchbox out of his pocket, then took two matches out of the box, and broke one in half. He held them out in front of himself, having them firmly held between two fingers. Tony pulled a match out. It was the short one.
'Bad luck, it looks like you can drive the truck,' offered John as he quickly put the other short match into his trouser pocket.
Unbeknown to Tony, John had broken two matches in half. He knew from past experience what the cab would smell like when the motor heated up.

John and Tony wound the jacks on the semi-trailer down and uncoupled the trailer. The trailer still had the bulk grain bins on it from earlier in the year when it had been used to cart the superphosphate for their crops. This was the truck's only use—carting grain into the silos and bringing superphosphate up to the farm from Port Lincoln. An old, seven-ton petrol engine Bedford truck did all the other work on the farm.

It took almost an hour to get to Kyancutta. Tony had all the windows open and had driven the first few K's with his head half out of the window. The disinfectant smell had not worked. It had only made the mouse smell sicklier. John chuckled to himself as he watched from behind. He had been in this position himself many times before.

The truck bounced through the potholes in the dirt road. It had never been a very comfortable truck to ride in. It was even worse without the weight of the trailer behind it.
Tony was pleased when he finally drove in to the Morgan's farm and reversed the truck back to the low loader. The loader trailer had been unloaded and pulled out of the shed ready. The tyres were pumped up ready. Tony reversed the old truck back and hooked the

two rigs together. They drove the truck to Tom's house for a cuppa, whilst Tony paid the two hundred dollars.

'When do you want the rig back?' asked Tony.

'Keep it as long as you like. But I do want it back home one day.'

'How about driving the rig home?' pleaded Tony. 'I nearly spewed when the engine got hot and the mouse poop started to cook. That bloody disinfectant I put in the cab made it smell worse. It's a lot better now,' John agreed. It was only fair to drive the truck on the trip home. The truck cabin still smelt strongly of mice. John also drove with the windows down. He would rather bear the cold air than the mouse smell. It was a long trip home. He was pleased when the truck finally drove up the drive to the sheds.

John parked the truck close to the workshop end of the implement shed so they were near to the welder and tools. The rear of the trailer was jacked up. John set about trying to take the wheels with the worn-out tyres off. Finally, they had to get the oxy welder and heat the wheel nuts before they could finally undo them.

They were hot and dirty. They went across to the house for a cuppa. John rose from the table and walked over to the phone, which was mounted on the wall, and then rang the local council workshop. The mechanic assured him that they had plenty of quite good tyres for the job.

After they had finished the cup of tea and jam scones, John drove off into Kimba with the wheels in the back of the ute to have the tyres changed, whilst Tony tried to get the tail and blinker lights working.

John arrived back home around dusk. The tyres had been just as hard to get off as the wheel nuts were. They had been rusted on to the rims. John was filthy and also had lost quite a bit of skin off his knuckles as he had helped to change the tyres at the local tyre repairer who was also not impressed having the job of helping change these tyres as it was a very hard work. John had also picked through the council scrap heap and had selected ten partially worn ripper boots to fit the dozer. The council also had a Cat D7 dozer. It was a lot later model.

Tony had changed his clothes and had a long shower but thought he could still smell the mouse poo on himself even through the strong aftershave he had doused himself with.

The truck was greased and the oil changed as was the dozer. John cut up some worn-down grader blades with the oxy and re-tipped the ripper boots with these pieces of grader blade by welding them on to the worn ripper boots, which, with a lot of effort, had been knocked off the ripper tines. Then he was hard-surfacing them with special rods, leaving them to cool down before replacing them on to the tines. The council scrap heap boots were brought from the ute. These were re-tipped and hard-faced as well.

Tony had the compressor and paint sprayer out and sprayed the low loader trailer frame with the leftover paint from the last truck spray job. At least, it would look registered. They were prepared to take a chance on the low-loader-looking part of the truck. Tony took the number plate off the semi-trailer, which was usually towed behind the truck, and screwed it to the freshly painted trailer. It looked legal even if it wasn't. The truck cabin was washed out and the motor squirted down again to try to get the mouse smell out. 'Right, Father, this is your big chance. You can drive the truck.'

Everything was filled with fuel, and a spare two-hundred-liter drum was filled with diesel on the back of the ute, plus all the heavy tools and a couple of jacks. The dozer pilot motor was started, and then the large diesel was started. Finally, the dozer blade and rippers were lifted, and the machine was slowly driven up on to the steep ramp at the rear of the loader trailer. The dozer pivoted in the center then tipped forward and then flattened out to follow the tray of the low loader.

John carefully lowered the blade and the rippers. Tony threw a heavy chain over the blade, whilst John secured the back. They pulled the chains tight with some chain dogs and then clipped them shut. The final thought was to paint two wide load signs on some flat iron, as the blade of the dozer was wider than the truck tray. These were attached to the front and rear of the truck. The procession was ready for the next morning.

As the men had their evening meal, they both talked of things they might have forgotten, but everything which they could think of was packed ready. Helen could feel the sense of the loss of her two men starting to creep up on her again, but she could also sense the glimmer of hope in their speech, which was something which had been lacking for quite a while on the farm. The excitement and enthusiasm the men felt was carried over to her.

The sun was just rising over the horizon. The sky was filled with the streaky red clouds of sunrise when they left the next morning. Helen felt quite alone again when the truck and ute finally disappeared from view.

After the men had left Buckleboo and had entered the real station country, Tony would have to drive ahead and open the gate next to the cattle grids and then drive through and wait for John, as there was no way the truck and dozer could cross the risen-up grids. It would have bottomed out and got the low loader stuck. Tony would then let the truck pass through and then close the gate behind the truck. He would then pass the truck and drive well ahead to stop the dust from being a problem, ready for the next gate.

It was a slow trip. The old truck was flat out at eighty kilometers an hour on good roads. The speed had to be cut back to between forty and fifty kilometer on these rough tracks.   Just before the procession drove out on to the bitumen highway, they stopped and had lunch. John jumped down from the truck and brushed the dust off his clothes. He blew his nose loudly. 'You must have had a good trip the other day. That bloody mouse' shit on the motor still stinks even with the new deodorant blocks we put in it and all the dust which has come into the cab.' Tony agreed to drive the truck the rest of the way.

After lunch, Tony pumped diesel into the ute and truck's fuel tanks from the drum on the ute, whilst John checked the oil in the old
Mercedes truck. 'Not bad, the old dear hasn't used much oil so far.'

Late afternoon, just as they got to the turn-off to the Coober Pedy Township off the main highway, John put his indicator on and turned left in towards the Black Flag field on the old dirt main road, which had been bypassed by the new bitumen highway. Tony followed for a short distance. John then drove off the road on to a track and parked the truck. 'I don't want to drive this through the town. It would just be our luck to have one of the maniac drivers run into us. Then the cops would find out the trailer isn't registered.'

Bert and Harry were nearly pickled when they arrived. 'We had a bit of fun whilst you were away. We found another twenty thousand bucks worth of opal. There's a nice pile of cash in the old safe now.' The cold beers were really appreciated first to wash the rotten mouse smell away and then just for no reason at all.

'What's that smell in here?' asked Harry. 'It smells just like mouse poop.' 'You don't smell too good either,' answered John.
Harry cackled. 'That's the smell of money, my boy.'

At half past eight in the morning, they drove out to the truck. John climbed into the cabin and started the old truck and then headed out north to the Fourteen Mile. Tony followed in the ute. So far, everything was going OK. Getting the dozer and the truck up to Coober Pedy without any large problems was a real bonus.

The truck and the dozer were parked on the Kelly's claim. John climbed out of the cab and then up on to the tray of the trailer. He put his foot on the blade arm, climbed on to the platform, and then sat in the seat. The dozer was started and left to idle, whilst the chains were removed by Tony. The blade and then the rippers were lifted, and then the tractor was reversed carefully back and unloaded. 'What do you think we should do with the truck?' asked Tony.

'I reckon you should leave it out here. There's less chance of anyone fiddling with it here than back in town,' said Bert. John and Tony walked over the claim and talked about where the bulldozer cut would be situated. They finally agreed on a spot. Tony fetched some rocks and marked out a rectangle, which had the five holes from which they had drilled the opal in the middle. 'OK, by you,' asked John. Tony then got some more rocks and made a line of rocks which pointed across the rectangle, which lined up with the area from which they had drilled the opal. Harry had told them to do this so they would be able to see where the area the opal traces were drilled from when they were getting close to the level with the dozer.

'Right then! Let's make a start.' John climbed up on to the old D7, which had been idling, revved the motor up, turned the machine, and drove it over until it was in line with the long edge of the rectangle they had marked out. He then pushed the full length of the marked area, pushing the rich red dirt as he went.

This man oeuvre was repeated over and over until around a half a meter of dirt was shifted off the marked area. By now, the ground was slightly moist and considerably harder, so John had to drop the rippers and rip back and forth. All of this time, Tony followed the tractor, carrying his miner's pick, checking the ground as it was ripped, or pushing dirt. Harry had told Tony to keep his eyes peeled as the Fifteen Mile area was known to have alluvial opal in the red dirt in some places.

Back and forth ripping, and then pushing the dirt, the dirt changed to very hard round stones, which made the old dozer's tracks squeal in protest. These were the stones which had made the drill protest when they were drilling the test holes. The hard round jasper rocks were in a level of about a half-meter thick. Then after the jasper, the ground started to change to a lighter coloured subsoil type with some areas slightly crunchy.

Tony followed the dozer, every rip and push, back and forth. What a boring thing to do, thought Tony as he walked. Around four o'clock, the ground started to change from the subsoil dirt to a more biscuit-like, crunchy light brown material. Tony's feet were beginning to get sore from all the walking on the uneven ground. The dozer was pushing a blade full of dirt in front of it and was making hard work of the job, spinning its tracks slightly. One track spat out a piece of rock which had been broken in half by the weight of the machine's tracks. It fell on to its side, and as it did so, the dying rays of sunlight caught it, causing it to flash. Suddenly, Tony's thoughts came back to reality, the reason why they were there. He reached down and picked up the piece of rock, and as he did so, he noticed the beautiful flashes of the opal fire dancing over the broken surface. He turned the piece of opal transfixed by the colours, almost forgetting the dozer. By this time, John was reversing the dozer back.

'Stop! Stop!' yelled Tony. John was evidently thinking of other things also, as he was nearly back to where Tony had found the opal. Tony bent down, picked up a handful of dirt, and threw it over the fuel tank of the dozer. As the small stones hit John, he decelerated the motor and then stopped the machine moving. He turned around, puzzled.

'What's up?' Tony waved the piece of opal around, too excited to talk. John throttled the big motor back, then climbed down off the machine, and walked back to where Tony was squatting, busily scratching at the ground.

'Here's some opal,' croaked Tony as he handed him the piece of opal which was about the size of a cigarette packet but half as thick. Bloody hell, look at that,' said John reverently. He was amazed to see the first piece of opal that they had found themselves with the dozer.

Tony walked back out of the shallow bulldozer cut to the ute and got the sieve, a shovel, and a small bucket. They then sieved the dirt from where the piece of opal had come from, being careful to remove and check any stones that were nearby. They found some other pieces of opal, and when the pieces were placed together, they could almost be arranged like a jigsaw to form one piece. The lump of opal, when roughly joined together, was about the size of a saucer, the thickest being over a centimeter thick. The outside of the stone was covered with a rusty iron-stone-coloured coating, so if it had not been cracked, Tony would not have noticed it. Only some small chips were missing from making the piece of opal back into one piece again.

Bert and Harry climbed out of the shaft. Harry walked over and shut the alternator motor down. Bert walked over to where John and Tony were still digging and sieving where they had found the opal. 'Found a bit of opal?' asked Bert nonchalantly. 'Yeah, have a look in the bucket.' 'Wow, this is nice opal. Shit, I reckon it would be worth around three thousand an ounce.' Bert put all the pieces into his hand and guessed the weight. 'Around five ounces. What do you think, Harry?' Harry, who had just walked over, had a good look at the stones and then weighed them in his hand. 'More like six ounces.' He did not want to agree with his brother. Harry licked the side of some of the stones. Tony noticed this and thought of how many people evidently licked the opal to see the colour highlighted by the moisture. Licking something after Harry had licked it was not on his menu. 'I reckon you might be right. Bloody nice colour.' They put the stones back into the bucket. 'I've heard the alluvial opal here was pretty good, but we had never seen any before. We've been working too deep. Found any more?' John and Tony both stood up. 'No, it looks like we've got the lot.' 'That will sure help with the fuel.
Looks like tea and beers are on us tonight.'

'How do we go about selling this opal? We sure need the money for fuel, plus I would like to send some home to Helen so she has some spare cash for a change. I'll make a call to her when we go to the pub.'

'There's a Pommy guy we have had classed ours. I can get him to have a look at it,' said Bert.

After they had showered, even Bert and Harry made the effort; they all went up to the pub for a few beers and a meal. The opal was secured in the old safe. Bert rang the opal classer from the phone box outside the pub as soon as they arrived. 'Well, it looks like you had better go and get the opal. He will have a look at it now. He's not a bad sort of a bloke. For a pom, that is,' added Bert. This was the usual Aussie banter about people from the mother country. No animosity was meant by it.

John took the safe keys offered by Bert, then left the men at the bar, and drove back to the dugout. He opened the old flimsy door, then went inside, and got the opal from the safe. The old safe door squealed in protest when it was opened and then shut again. John came back to the pub.

Bert drove in front of John to show the way to the classer's dugout. They all walked through the gate. John knocked on the door. The yard around the front of the dugout had the usual machinery and tools lying around. A large Rottweiler dog was locked in a cage at the back of the car shed, which was in front of the dugout. The dog barked loudly as they walked through the gate. It ran to the end of the cage and banged on the front mesh wall close to the men walking into the yard. Barking, baring its teeth, and growling as it did so. The dog was very intimidating, a very good watchdog. By the look of the dog tracks and chewed-up bones in the yard, the dog was usually let free to roam at night.

The bloke was evidently married and had kids, for a lot of toys were arranged on dirty and dusty roads which had been pushed by the children with their toy graders and bulldozers.

A skinny man with ginger hair opened the door. 'Are you the guys with the opal?' he asked. They nodded. 'Right, follow me.' They followed the man to another door way leading into a separate dugout. The man turned back towards them. 'The name's Leon,' he said. John and Tony introduced themselves. The classer shook hands all around, 'Come in. Let's have a look at the opal then.'

They followed Leon into the dugout. Leon reached past John and switched on the light. There was a large table and an assortment of chairs in the room. The top of the table was covered in black plastic, which had some large desk lamps, an assortment of containers, and numerous sets of different scales on top of it. Leon turned one of the table lights on.

The men sat down. John passed the ice cream container with the bag of opal in it. Leon opened the plastic shopping bag and tipped the contents under one of the bright lamps. He picked the first piece of opal up and studied it. 'This is pretty good opal, alluvial. Comes from the Fifteen Mile. Am I right?' They nodded. Leon turned the stones back and forth under the light and then weighed them. 'Just under five ounces, I reckon you should get twelve thousand for this lot.' He wrote the price down on to a piece of paper. One price was the top price they could expect; the other price was the lowest they should take. 'I'll ring one of the Chinese buyers if you like. There's one guy who likes this type of opal.' The men agreed as it saved them the trouble of chasing a buyer. Leon rang the buyer from a cordless phone which was on a shelf. He spoke to the buyer for a couple of minutes. 'He will see you at the dugout. You had better give me some instructions as to how to find it.' Tony explained where the dugout was. 'Will a quarter of an hour's time be OK?' Leon hung the phone back into its cradle.

'I charge 2 per cent to class opal, so if you sell the opal, just bring the cash around in the next few days.' The men thanked Leon and walked out to their utes and drove back to the dugout. John and Tony had no idea of what to expect with the Chinese buyer. It was just before dark when the Chinese buyer arrived. He drove an old brown Holden car. The small man got out of the car, locked the door, and then lit a cigarette.

Tony was waiting outside the dugout in case the man could not find them. He waddled up to Tony. 'You have opals for sale?' he asked in broken English. 'That's us,' said John. The man walked back to his car and opened the door with the key. He then reached into the car, got a battered bag, and then re-locked the car door. The man then rudely pushed past Tony and walked into the dugout.

The Chinaman sat himself down at the table. He put the battered bag out of the way of the light but within easy reach. 'Opals, I look.' Bert turned the desk lamp on. This was the first time they really took notice of the small man. He turned towards them, took the cigarette out of his mouth, and then smiled. The man had extremely rotten teeth, which were also brown with tobacco stains. When John handed the opal over to him, the man puffed on the cigarette. The smoke filled the room with a horrible smell. He butted the stub of the cigarette out on to a dirty plate on the table and then lit another straight away. The man puffed the cigarette, drawing deeply and exhaling the acrid-smelling smoke towards the men. He had an unusual way of holding the cigarette.
He held it backwards into his hand as if to keep the wind off it.

The buyer then tipped the opal out on to the black plastic sheet. He turned the stones over and over under the light, picking pieces up and studying them close to the light to see if there were any imperfections in them.

'How much you want for this opal?' he asked. 'Thirteen thousand dollars,' said John. The Chinaman sat back and laughed. 'Ho ho, I not pay that much. Much too dear. How much this classed for? What is real price?' The little man drew back on his cigarette and blew the smoke over towards the men. 'I give you nine, which top dollar for this opal. Some of the stones are clacky (cracked). See this one this have cotton in it (small filaments of gypsum).   'No, thirteen thousand,' said John. The bargaining went on and on. John was getting really angry.
'If we can't get twelve thousand, you had better piss off.' This tirade did not seem to faze the man at all. Finally, after three more rotten cigarettes, they agreed on eleven and a half thousand dollars. The little man reached forward and pulled the bag towards him, opened it up, withdrew a wad of cash, and then started to count the money out. John and Tony watched intently as the piles of cash grew. The little man stopped counting, then lit another cigarette, and blew acrid smoke over the men again. He looked up at John.

'You count again.' He motioned at John. John counted the money and agreed the figure was right. The man got up from the table and picked up the opal. 'If you have more opal, you ling me. I give you top dollar.' He then arose and handed a dirty printed card. 'See, Johnnie, That me. That my phone number at pub.' He turned and walked out of the door. When he got into his car, John let out a sigh.

'What a crook!' said Tony? Neither of the men was used to the bartering that the Chinese buyers were noted for.

'How do you like dealing with the Chinese?' asked Bert with a wry smile. 'I feel exhausted. That was as hard a work as pulling teeth,' said John. 'Well, at least I know what they make their Chinese cigarettes out of. It smells like burning horse poop in here,' said Bert. 'Right, put the money away. Let's go. I can't stand the smell in here.'

After the first few beers, John went outside to the phone box and rang Helen with the good news. Helen also had some good news. It was raining steadily, the first proper rain for the year.

Whilst John was away, phoning Helen, the Greek lad, who had warned Tony off his sister, walked over to the table with another older man. The lad had a grim look on his face. Tony was worried because both looked serious. I hope they don't want to fight, thought Tony as they stopped at the table.

'G'day, mate,' said Bert. 'What can we do you for?' The older Greek man turned to Tony and spoke, 'Ay, boy, my son he has an apology to make to you.' The young man looked down at the floor. He then slowly held his hand out to Tony and took his hand. 'Hey, man, I'm sorry about the other night, man.' 'That's OK, I'm prepared to forget it,' said Tony. The older man, evidently the lad's father, cut in. Bloody, boy, he came home and boasted about how he chased you away from his sister and was going to thump you. Stupid bugger, we in Australia now. We bloody Aussies like everyone else. If she want to talk to an Aussie, that's OK by me. Just to talk though is all right. You do anything else to her; I help my son to thump you.' The man turned and then walked off, followed by his son, back to the bar, where they re-joined their friends. ' I thought you were in trouble there. It might pay to keep your mind off some of the New Australian Sheila's up here. Some of the Italian or Greeks might be OK, but don't go chasing any of the Serb or Muslim women. You might have some trouble walking behind the dozer for quite a while and a change in your voice to a soprano.' Laughed Harry.

Chapter nine

Heading for Coober Pedy opal fields

They had three hot days on the road, passing through Port Augusta, then onto the road to Alice Springs. Some of the roads had been sealed. Broken Hill to Port Augusta was a good sealed road. From Port Augusta to Pimba the road was sealed but extremely rough in places, from Pimba was back to the dirt road.

The Patrol had performed well, but did not like headwinds. This cut the fuel economy down. The occasional stop for a meal, fuel, or a wee, did help break the trip a little bit.

The signs on the edge of the road heralded the entrance to Coober Pedy. Cheap fuel at Bulls, eat at the Acropolis, buy opal at Star Opal. All looked as if the sign writer had used a stick dipped in tar to write the signs.

A dust storm was blowing in front of the hot northerly wind. The sky was black and thundery. Ali learned that when one of the numerous willy willies (strong whirl winds) crossed the road it was not too clever to drive through one. He had tried this and the Patrol had been pushed off the other side of the road into the low shrubs when he had tried.

A long line of cars were each side of the road in front of the hotel. Small trucks and utilities, most with a winch on the back of the tray lined the road. They stopped in a service station and had an ice cream and drink. Ali then drove as close as he could to the hotel.

The reception area was a lot cooler than the searing heat outside. A loud din emanated from the bar area. The noise was of a lot of different nationalities trying to shout above the crowd in their own language. Ali booked a small unit to the side of the hotel. "You can bring your car and park in the area next to the unit", the lady said. Zeena sat in a comfortable lounge chair and waited.

There was a lot of yelling as two men were fighting outside the door of the hotel. Another group watched on and egged each of the fighters on. One man appeared to be taking bets on the outcome of the fight.

Ali walked across the street. A huge clap of thunder shook the ground and a lightning strike hit just out of town, heavy rain came tumbling down washing the dust in front of the water cascading down the road. As Ali ran for the Patrol he noticed that this rain had dampened the desire of the fighters. The crowd was heading inside of the hotel. A small mob of aborigines were trying to find shelter from the heavy rain.

He drove back to the unit at the hotel then ran inside to get Zeena. They then ran back to the unit and opened the door. Water poured off their clothes as they entered the kitchen area and made pools on the linoleum tiles on the floor. In one corner of the kitchen was a large modern safe.

The rain ceased in an hour. The parking area was like a shallow swimming pool as the water tried to find a way out to run down the street. The strong wind had stopped and the sun was just starting to appear.

The water level was almost to the doorstep. Ali waded through the water to carry the clothes and kit-bag into the room. He removed his shoes as they were filled with water. Zeena unpacked the bags and suitcase. The time was four o'clock in the afternoon. "Well that was a spectacular welcome to Coober Pedy" Zeena laughed as she mopped the water from the floor. "Four seasons in one day. I wonder if it's always like this".

Most of the water had drained away; the sun was really hot and created a steamy atmosphere outside, Similar to the climate in the Philippines.   Ali went to the counter of Reception and asked about the safe. The girl gave him a piece of paper with the combination and a set of keys to fit the lock. They went back to the room to put the kit-bag in the safe. The false bottom of the suit-case was carefully opened and the contents placed into the kit-bag .This was all locked into the safe, Ali put one key on the Patrol key ring and hid the other with the card with the combination., this was stuck with tape under the right-angle bed frame.

The traffic outside the hotel was chaotic to say the least, every vehicle seemed to be in a hurry to get somewhere else. Horns tooted to get the pedestrians out of the way as the people sped hell bent down the street. The opal shop proprietor turned the display lights on to show off the opals in the display cabinets as they entered into the shops. The opal was not the quality of the lightning Ridge black opal. The shop owners scowled as they left the store without making a purchase.

There was a shop with a talkative Irish-man behind the counter. He served some customers as he talked to Ali and Zeena. He had a lot of stories about good friends finding a large lot of opal and then trying to kill each other out of distrust and greed. People had disappeared down some of the many old mine shafts which dotted the surface of the ground as far as the eye could see. Some of the men who had been dropped down these shafts had deserved the fate which awaited them.
They were child molesters and pedophiles.

As they walked back to the hotel in the dusk Zeena commented on the Irish-man," I think that man could talk under water "Ali agreed.

A large rush was on in Coober Pedy some men had dug up good opals in a previously un-explored area fourteen miles along the road toward Alice Springs. There were three thousand miners jostling for a claim to dig for opal in this area. Many altercations had happened when one of the miners had been found to have moved the neighbors mining pegs during the night, so they could get closer to a claim which was producing a large amount of opal.

The opal was so prevalent that it was stored in 200-liter drums with the lid cut off. . The lid was altered to fit over the top of the drum, holes were drilled through so a rod with a washer welded across on end and a hole to take a padlock on the other. All partners had a padlock and key so the drum could not be opened if the partners in the claim were not all present. Ali and Zeena had been taught all of this in the hour and a half tutorial from Rob the Irishman.

There was a large crowd of people entering the Acropolis restaurant near the hotel. Ali and Zeena went to check what all of the people did at night. The town was a stir with activity. Ali wanted to check it out.

Most of the town's ethnic groups sat together in small groups Yugoslavian, Greek, Italian, German, and a lot of the world's other nationalities were in the club, Evidently not forgetting the ingrained hatred honed over centuries. They seemed to tolerate each other because of the potential for high returns if they had a good claim. Ali and Zeena sat in a corner and watched the nights reveling. Occasionally one of the groups would cross the imaginary line to talk to one of the other groups.

One would not want to make a rash statement about Croatia, Serbia or Greece and Turkey, or a lot of the other nationalities in the room.

"I can see a lot of opportunities in this town". "I can see a lot of trouble", said Zeena as she watched two men shaking their fists at each other across the room. "I am going to see about buying a house here". "Well I do not want to live here with all of these dirty men. Have a smell; most of them smell as if they have never had a wash. I put up with bad men in the Philippines and I am not going to do this here". Ali did not really blame Zeena for her loathing of the town; he did agree that some of the men were a lot worse than even the slimy Indian swimmer was.

Ali spent the day looking at some of the underground homes 'Dugouts'. Some were quite luxurious; others just a burrow in the ground with a dirt floor and just a door on a cliff showing that there was even a house hidden inside.

He also looked at some of the above ground houses. Ali asked Zeena if she would like a dugout to live in by herself, she relented and picked a nice three roomed dugout with a bathroom and kitchen on the outside of the hill. A deal was made with the Italian guy and the money paid, four thousand three hundred dollars. The papers were signed and given to the old man who was the agent.

Ali picked a small concrete block house a long way from the main street area. The huge yard had some old machinery in it left over from when the previous owner had left. This man had found a fortune in the last six months and was leaving to be with his family to enjoy his millions. One feature Ali liked about this house was a large modern safe which stood in the corner of the bedroom.

Zeena was reasonably happy in her furnished dugout, she was still worried about Ali, "you seem to have an uncanny gift in finding trouble.
This place is full of trouble for those who go looking. Just be careful. One of the women I have met said her cousin has gone missing and has probably been tossed down a deep shaft. He was up to no good with one of the Serbians." Ali assured her he would be careful of some nationalities.

Two German opal dealers arrived in Goober Pedy looking to buy either cut or rough opal. Ali had found this information while at the Italian club. He had been talking to some of the miners trying to get the word out about his opal buying and selling.

The two Germans were staying in one of the units at the hotel where the opal buyers usually worked from. Ali asked at reception about Helmut and Tomas, "Try room number five where the car park is" the girl said.

Ali knocked on the door of the room. "Ja commen in. The door opened to reveal a muscular tall blond man. Ali walked into the room. The table was covered with bags of opal some of which were opened and being sorted. Ali introduced himself. Another short plump man with a bald spot in his dark hair and steel rimmed glasses came from the bathroom wiping his hands. The tall man Helmut asked what he had in the bag "I have been to Lightning Ridge and have some black opal, some is cut and the rest is rough."

Tomas cleared a space on the table. "We supply some major jewelers in Germany and are looking for top quality opal.

A separate piece of black plastic was put on the top of the table to cover the opal being worked on. This was to make sure that the opals would not be able to be mixed. Ali put the bag on the top of the plastic.

He took the smaller bag with the cut stones in the separate bags, and then carefully laid the stones out in the order of quality.

The black opal shimmered in the bag. Tomas carefully took the first stone out of the bag. "My god, look at this stone Helmut". Each stone was studied.

"What do you want for the cut stones. " Ali made as if to think for a while. "I have to get sixty-five thousand "Helmut looked at him sternly. "We will not pay that much for this parcel. Fifty thousand is my top price. "Ali was studying his eyes, after a short banter the price was set at fifty- five thousand dollars. The rough opal was then careful studied. "What price do you want for these "Ali looked into his eyes?" I want one hundred and thirty thousand dollars." The usual bargaining took place the end price was one hundred and twenty thousand dollars.

The large safe was opened and a bag filled with cash taken out. As Helmut counted the opal, Ali also counted the already counted money. At the end of the counting, Ali took a hundred-dollar bill and handed it back to Helmut. "Two of the bills you handed across were stuck together". Thank you for being honest". Ali had stopped himself keeping the extra money, He liked the way these men did business and wanted to be able to sell to them again.

Ali talked to the two men for about half an hour after the sale about the opal trade, He did not want to show his ignorance, and was careful with the questions. "You are very interesting men to talk to, would you like to have dinner tonight at the Acropolis". The men evidently realised that Ali was also going to be good for their business as well so they agreed

Ali invited Zeena to come to dinner. He explained about the sale of the opal and how he had tripled the price paid for the opal. "You just keep your nose clean don't get too big for your boots".

Ali stopped at Zeena's dugout and tooted the Patrols horn. She had been waiting in the top outer part of the dugout and had seem him arrive. "You look nice tonight ", "Thank you; I thought I should dress up a bit" Ali noticed she had the opal ring on.

Helmut and Tomas were waiting at the bar and were talking to two other men. These men were German and had been lured into the opal game as miners. The men left the bar and joined Ali and Zeena. Ali noticed that Tomas did a bit of a double take when he was introduced to Zeena.

Helmut and Ali talked for a long time about the opal business and some of the stories about robbers and the consequences of being caught. "It is a pity the real law can't use some of the bush justice methods used in Coober Pedy, we would not have the crime in our countries like now ". Tomas seemed much more interested in Zeena. The two talked as if they had known each other for years, and had just met again.

Helmet nudged Ali and commented in undertones as to the two talkers. "Tomas's wife was killed in a bad accident on the Auto Bann three years ago. He has not looked at a woman since and is very lonely". Evidently Zeena had hit it off with Tomas.

As Zeena was walking in the door of the dugout she said. " Tomas is coming around to my house for dinner tomorrow night. He asked to take me to the club, but I said I would rather show him how to cook" "Do you want me to come", "No I think I am old enough to look after myself" Ali laughed and was still chuckling to himself as he drove off to his house.

"Have you heard the word Nick the Greek had his claim moonlighted?" Some enterprising person had gone out to the field in the moonlight and had walked a long distance to where the Greek was digging good opal.   The thief had lowered themselves down a rope and had dug the ceiling of the recently blasted drive, down on to the floor of the drive, to steal the opal. "I hear he would have dug a hundred thousand dollars out". Ali listened to the story with interest. A lot of the opal coming out of certain fields had some sort of signature as to the colour bars and flashes, plus the hue of the colour present in the stone.

If a certain person not associated with the field were to try to sell to some buyers, the buyer would contact the person who was robbed. The person selling the stolen opal may have an accident and somehow fall down a deep shaft.

This stolen opal could be a good source of income as some unscrupulous buyers would only offer a third of the price for this stolen opal. There was a notorious Greek who did this. He was very unpopular with the rest of the miners.

One reason why Ali had bought this house was that it did not have very close neighbors. He had thought of circumstances when he did not want the next-door people listening to his conversation through the thin walls of the next-door houses.

A few nights after the ruckus about the Nick robbery there was a knock-on Ali's door. Ali opened the door carefully. He had a baseball bat stuck to the back of the door with masking tape; His hand was on the handle.
A small ugly Hungarian man stood outside. I hear you are buying opals.
This guy Tom had a reputation for being a moonlighter. Ali opened the door and asked him to step in.

Tom had a bag filled with good opal, which had only partially been cleaned. Ali realised this must be the opal from Nick's claim. He carefully went through the opal and saw around sixty thousand dollars' worth of opal. "How much do you want". "I have to get forty thousand for it". Ali said,
"Is this the Greeks opal", the man nodded. Ali offered the man Twenty-five thousand dollars. The man accepted, "I do not like doing business with Johnnie the Greek, he is a bad man. "If I find more Greek or Serbian opals I will sell for you". "If I buy from you, you had better keep your mouth shut; I was known as the Dragon in Indonesia as I have burnt three men who have crossed me alive. Ali opened the safe and took a bag of money out, then paid Tom.

The news in town was out. One of the Croatian's had been caught down a man's shaft who had been using a Yorke Hoist. The hoist consisted of a steel pole set into the ground next to a shaft. A motorised hoist, which worked by friction wheels and handle was attached to the pole. When the handle was pulled up the wheels met with the pulley setup on the motor which lifted the heavy bucket out of the shaft. The claim holder had been to the railway line to get old discarded railway sleepers to put around the top of the shaft as the dirt had built up.   Rob and his mate had gone to work one morning and had found that someone had been digging in the face of the drive where they had finally found paying opal. Rob had worked for months with the mate without finding opal. They both were extremely short of money.

This claim was close to town. After the robbery Rob would go to check the claim every night. He would drive his old utility out toward the claim then walk to the shaft with a small flashlight. After six nights he looked down the shaft and saw a torch light being flashed around. Rob had carefully put four sleepers over the top of the shaft; he then had run back to the utility. He drove back to the claim and had driven the utility on top of the sleepers.

Rob had walked the mile home and had told his wife about the trapped man. Late the next day he went to the police station and told them about the man in the shaft. The officer said that they were going to be busy the next day. He would come out to the claim just before dark.

Two police officers waited as Rob took the utility off the sleepers. The cops had to help push it back. The sleepers were removed and a very worried looking man climbed out into the dying sunlight. He went with the police.

The man was told to leave town and not to come back, He knew what some of the other miners would do, so he left. The next morning Rob was leaving his home. As he undid the door he noticed a plug of gelignite stuck to the door with a short fuse and detonator in it. A note was written on a small piece of paper. 'next time we light fuse'. There was one less crook in town, who evidently had some mates.

One of the German buyers had gone back to Germany with the opal, Tomas had found a reason to stay in Coober Pedy, He had moved from the hotel to Zeena's house. He had been with her for three weeks. She was talking to Ali when they were alone. "Tomas has asked me to marry him, I have told him about how we had a tough time surviving in the Philippines. He understands and does not need to know details", "I am really happy that finally you will get a chance to be happy. I hope you will be happy with him. He seems to be a nice man" "After all of these years Ali, I am feeling love for a man".

Ali had a mixed sense of emotion he was really pleased that she had fallen in love, but for most of their life they had been together, with hardly any close friends.

Ali had been keeping his eye on a girl in town. She was working in reception at the hotel. Her parents were Austrian. Martha was not what one would call good looking but there was something different with her than other girls. She had an intelligent personality. In Ali's eyes, this stood her apart from all of the shallow so-called beauties.

As he drove past the hotel Ali somehow got enough courage to ask Martha out for a meal. The last almost encounter with a girl seemed like years ago, when he had asked the girl in Manilla for a date. What had happened after that had been a real turning point in his life. Thank god the Morris minor had a narrow wheel base and had fitted down the alley way.

Martha was taking a break and was having a cup of coffee in the lounge at the back of the hotel, Ali walked into the lounge, Martha's eyes lit up at the sight of him. "I was looking for someone to talk to, how did you know?" "My mother looks like getting married and I am feeling a bit lonely" "I know the feeling. All I seem to do is work all day and go home to mum and dad. The same old job, The same old time every day ". Ali thought carefully about the last time he tried to get a date, "would you like to come to the club for dinner tonight," "I was wondering if you would ever ask me". Ali was thrilled at the prospect of a date. Evidently Martha did not see the scar but the man. "What time do you finish up tonight" "About six o'clock. I will phone mum and tell her I won't be home for dinner".

Ali had just turned twenty-one years old. The worries of the last two years since the merchant robbery seemed to evaporate. He was very happy about the prospects of finally meeting a girl who seemed to genuinely like him.
On the way home to change he called to see Zeena and Tomas. "Good news at last. I have a date tonight with a girl from the Hotel." "You be careful about picking up some of the girls from the hotel, half of them are on drugs." "Don't worry this girl works as a receptionist" "Which one?"

"The skinny one called Martha." "I know her" said Tomas, "I have bought opal from her father. They are nice people, Austrian's."

Ali had a shower and selected some good clothes to try to make a special impression on Martha. The club was nearly full, the noise was deafening as each person tried to talk over the other. Ali found a table as far from the mob at the bar as possible. He asked Martha about her life in Coober Pedy.

Martha's parents had come to Coober Pedy after hearing of the opal rush in Australia. Peter had been working in a coal mine in Austria and had decided that the prospects of getting some disease from the coal dust. He was starting to get a cough which he could not shake off. The other worry was of being blown up in a mine fire, as some of his friends had been. These problems were working against him enjoying his old age, Heidi had worked in a baker shop, working long hours to try and make ends meet. They had migrated and had been in Australia nearly ten years. Since being in Coober Pedy for eight years Peter had lost the cough, thanks to the dry climate. Heidi worked in an opal shop.

"What about you Ali. It's your turn now. Ali was a bit flustered he did not want to lie to Martha. "My mother was not married and therefore we had a very hard life in the Philippines. Both of her parents were dead. We were alone; she had a sister living in the country.

I got into trouble stealing in the market to get food. The police were chasing me. I left town and went to live with my auntie Sasha who was a widow. I had never been so happy working with her on her small plot of land in the country. The village people were really nice. I was the happiest that I had ever been." Ali described the rebel attack on the village and how he had found Sasha and Missy the goat dead. "I was so angry when I found Sasha dead. I got a knife and stabbed the killer in the back." Ali had tears in his eyes as he recounted the murder of Sasha. Martha took Ali's hand and gently rubbed it. She looked very sad. " Then what happened to you?"

Ali regained his composure and carried on, "We left our island and went to Manilla. I think that was a big mistake, I met some people in the market and got tangled into the drug trade. We were poor and I was going to do anything to get a decent life for us.

One of the heads of the drug trade was going to take me to the wharf and tie concrete blocks to my feet and toss me in the water. I escaped, then I heard they were going to kill mother if I did not come back. I came back and was able to pick mum up and get out of Manilla. We went to another town as far from Manilla as we could. We got passage to Cairns on a timber carrying ship. I made some money in Cairns wheeling and dealing for a couple of months. "We went to lightning ridge where I bought a parcel of opal which was my first big deal."

Ali realised that he had omitted most of the really gory details from the story, he had told Martha a lot more than any other person in Coober Pedy knew. "Please do not tell any other person this story Martha". Martha patted Ali's hand and assured him that the past was safe with her.

Ali met up with Martha during her lunch break, and then met her at night after work. These meetings had been taking place over three weeks. "My mother want's to meet you she would like you to come to dinner on Saturday night".
Martha met Ali at the door of the large dugout. Ali was worried about meeting Peter and Heidi. He had seen them in the street, but had never met them.
The night and the meal went very well. Peter talked about the mining business and Ali spoke about the opportunities in Australia. How he had seen his first opal in Cairns and had fallen in love with it. "That is a bad disease we all seem to get when we first see opal, it is called opal fever. Some people in the gold mining see gold as they go to sleep at night. I would rather dream of the beautiful colours of opal.

Martha walked outside of the dugout as Ali left. They both looked at the clear night sky. The stars never seemed to shine as bright anywhere else than Coober Pedy. Martha put her arms around Ali and pulled him toward her.
They kissed a long enjoyable kiss. Ali could feel the mound of her woman-hood rub up against him through the thin cotton dress, she softly moaned. They kissed again, still almost joined as one; Martha took Ali's hand and guided it to her mound between her

legs. Ali felt as if he were going to explode. "Come and help with the dishes Martha." This broke the spell. They regretfully broke apart.

Ali was shaking with desire as he walked to the Patrol, his testicles felt as if they had been trodden on. "How the hell did Heidi know" thought Ali as he carefully slid in to the seat.

Ali had just arrived home and had not long before locked the door. Someone was knocking on the door. He opened the door, holding the handle of the baseball bat as he did.

A tall man stood at the doorway, he wore a leather cap. Ali did a quick study. The hooked nose and features were of a gypsy. He gripped the baseball bat handle harder. "What do you want" "my friend Tom, he sent me to see you, I have some opals. Ali reluctantly released the grip on the baseball bat handle and opened the door. In the light the man looked more like a gypsy. I am Silvio. He poked out his hand. Ali shook hands. He felt a sense of evil in this man.

I have found some opals I do not want any person to know about. Silvio lifted a large sugar bag onto the table. Ali did a quick class of the opals. There were some exceptional green orange crystal opal stones in this parcel. The whole lot of opal was weighed on some large scales. Ali did a quick calculation of the stones, He saw about seventy thousand dollars.   "What price are you asking "   "I would want forty five thousand "   "I will give you thirty five". The man looked as if he were going to argue. "Oh all right I take thirty five".

Ali had purchased a pistol from one of the miners. This was hidden in one of the money bags with the money. Ali had shut the safe, before letting the man come in. He went and opened the safe, making sure the man could not see the combination being turned. Only the cash and the unseen pistol were on the table. With care not to show the loaded pistol Ali took the wads of notes out of the bag. The money was counted and the opal handed across. "I will see you again, thank you." Silvio turned and walked out of the door.

Ali's loving feelings had been replaced with a feeling of evil as the man left the door of the house. Ali quickly locked the door, then put the opal and money with the pistol into the safe then locked it.

As he went to bed, he had the feeling that the devil had been in his house. A cold shiver ran down his spine. This man could be useful in the future he thought.

Martha finished work early, as the work roster at the hotel had changed She phoned Ali to see if he was home. "I will see you in ten minutes." "I will come and pick you up" "The walk will do me good". At least the ten minutes would give him time to tidy up and make his bed.   Ali had been getting slack at housekeeping since Zeena had told about her marriage proposal.

The ten minutes took a long time to go, at least the house and dishes had been cleaned up. Ali felt a warm glow of anticipation as to what might happen when Martha arrived. He saw her walking in through the gate in the fence of the allotment. He opened the door ready for her.

Martha had done something different to her hair it really suited her. As she walked to the door the sunlight behind her shone through her hair, giving her a warm glow. She stepped into the house, and then opened her arms for Ali to enter; Ali stepped forward and embraced Martha. His brain was buzzing with desire.

The kissing lasted about five minutes, Martha gently broke the embrace and led Ali to the bed. They sat on the edge of the bed embracing. Ali was feeling hot. He had only been with one woman before and was unsure of himself; the friendship in the Philippines at Sasha's village had been the only other one.

"I think I am falling in love with you Ali, I want to make love. Please be careful as I have never done this before.

After a lot of fumbling with clothes Martha lay on the bed with her legs slightly apart. Ali lay next to her caressing her raised nipples on her breasts. Nature took its course. Ali carefully climbed on top of Martha and started to try and make love.   This was the most profound loving feeling that either of them had experienced. They both lay in each other's arms and kissed. When the mood took, they made love again. Over the course of five hours they had made love six times. Martha was feeling quite sore by this time.

She extricated herself from Ali's arms and went to the bathroom to have a shower. Ali joined her in the shower. They cuddled together. After the shower they both took towels and dried each other.

Their sexual desires were spent for the day. "Have you got any food to cook? " "In the fridge ".Martha opened the fridge and found some eggs and meat patties. "Is this all you live on?" "I eat out a lot. This is the way I find people who want to sell opal". "If I am going to come to your house, I will stock your fridge for you." "Ok we will go shopping tomorrow".

When Ali drove Martha home, he felt the urge to make love again as they sat talking in the Patrol. Martha laughed. "It could be a bit uncomfortable in here with all of the gear levers and other things in the road. I am in love with you Ali you are my man." "I do not really know what to say about today Martha. I can think of no words good enough to describe it. I do know that I have fallen in love with you".

Ali did not accompany Martha into the dugout. He just gave her a long kiss as he reached across the gear levers. He had a bulge in his trousers and did not want to go in and meet Peter and Heidi in case it did not go away.

The supermarket was crowded, Thursday was the day the fresh fruit and veg came to Coober Pedy on the truck. Every person in town seemed to be trying to get the freshest and best fruit and veg. Women squeezed the fruit to see if it were ripe. The cabbages and lettuces were picked up, looked at the put back. Martha commented on the hygiene of the man, or woman handled fruit and vegetables. Martha diligently purchased a trolley half full of food. Ali and Martha went back to his house. When they arrived, Martha cleaned out the cupboards and refrigerator then packed both with the food. After she had finished, she turned to Ali and felt the bulge in the front of his trousers. "What have we got in here? I think this need putting away as well" she laughed then led Ali to the bed.

After they had made love numerous times Martha said "I have a feeling that mum and dad know what we have been up to, they asked a few funny questions when I walked in last night".
Ali felt alarm bells ringing in his head. "Don't look so alarmed." Martha laughed "It was going to happen sooner or later. Mum and

dad know that. He is not coming to chase you with a shot gun or something. You goose"

Martha cooked a tasty stir-fry for dinner. Ali drove her home after. "Come in for a while", Ali still felt guilty. He walked in the door Peter put his arm on his shoulder, Heidi gave him a kiss on the cheek. "Welcome Ali" said Peter.

The women were in the kitchen. Peter and Ali were in the lounge room out of hearing from the women. There was a slight titter as Martha and Heidi laughed together. "Martha told us that she has fallen in love with you Ali. I have no right to interfere. I would just want to know what you feel about the situation." "I can assure you Peter that the feeling is mutual". "I understand that you had a hard time in the Philippines. " " I think I should tell you the whole story. I love Martha very much and I do not want dirty secrets", Ali went on to recount the whole story .The robbery, the killing of the rebel. What Zeena had done in her previous life. How he and Zeena had moved to Manilla, and the greasy Indian incident. He then told about the drug trade and the contract which had been put on him, and also Zeena. He then described how he had killed Emilio Sanchez." Ali stopped talking and looked at Peter's face. Peter looked sad. " I have opened up to you Peter because I love Martha more than anything in my life, not that there was much to love before except Auntie Sasha". I always felt different with Zeena. He paused. "If you tell this story, Zeena's new love and life are finished, so am I."

" We all have our own stories Ali. I have never told any person here or elsewhere. I do not want this repeated or I will be sent to Germany and go to jail. During the war I was a diligent soldier. Hitler was the way out of the trouble Germany was in. The Jews in our eyes were the cause of our problems. I was a member of the SS, Hitler's elite killing squad. I have done a hell of a lot of things which I was ordered to do, which I am extremely ashamed of. Toward the end of the war most people in Germany began to realise what a mad man Hitler was. If I were to have disobeyed orders to kill some person, I would have been shot".

Peter went to the refrigerator and got a bottle of beer and two glasses. Ali did not drink beer, but did not feel right refusing the beer. The bitter taste was refreshing after both men had bared their souls. "The main thing Heidi and I worry about as being parent's, is Martha's happiness. She is our world now. Australia has been kind to us, and a lot of other people with bad pasts. As long as we can leave the hatred and dirty secrets behind, us and not keep the stupid wars going in this great country".

Peter went to get another Bottle of beer from the fridge. Martha came in to the lounge and sat on Ali's lap, Heidi was talking to Peter as he took the beer from the fridge. "Did you get the third-degree instructions from dad?" "Peter and I had a really good talk. I told him a lot of things about my life that I was too frightened to tell you. It appears a lot of us have secrets".

Tomas's son and daughter were going to come from Germany to be at his wedding. Helmut was bringing his large family of six children. The date was set for three weeks' time. They were to be married in the Catholic Church, and the reception would be at the Italian Club.

Ali had given Martha a nice engagement ring. The diamond had come out of the safe. Taking this stone to be set into a ring had flashed the memory of the night the Indian had met the fish. Ali wished he could drag all of these bad memories out of his head and leave them somewhere under a slab of concrete or a large rock.

Martha was thrilled when she had been offered the ring by a kneeling Ali. "Wow where did you get this huge diamond? ". "I have a bag full in the safe." "Stop telling such lies Ali" she laughed. "I really want to marry you Martha ", "I feel the same way". "Would you consider getting married with Tomas and Zeena", Martha thought for a while. "That would be really nice. I think I should ask mum and dad". "I have only just thought of the idea. I will have to ask Tomas and Zeena". Ali thought after he had said this, "Why could he not ever call Zeena mum". He knew she was his mother, but when talking about her he could not refer her as mum.

Weddings in Coober Pedy were a fairly rare occasion. Peter being a popular miner had a lot of friends. Tomas and Helmut also had a lot of friends in town. Ali in his opal dealings had met a lot of people. The double wedding was going to be a huge affair. This was going to be the number one event on the social calendar for Coober Pedy for the year.

Martha, with Peter and Heidi's blessing had moved into Ali's house. This was going to make buying the opal from Tom and the other moonlighters difficult. Ali did not want them in the house when Martha was there. The rules changed. These men would have to contact Ali. He would go and see them at their houses to buy the stolen opal.

The wedding plans were well under way. A large work force had offered their services for the decorating, cooking and other chores. Two of the miners had large American cars, which they had restored in their large sheds; these two vehicles were offered as the wedding cars.

The shops in Coober Pedy had bought in extra evening gowns for the ladies, plus food for the reception. They were not going to miss out cashing in on the town's premier social event.

Ali and Tomas walked down the aisle of the small crowded church. There were rows of chairs outside with shade cloth stretched on a frame above them. A PA system played music for the outside guests, Ali and Tomas joined their partners. Zeena looked radiant in her wedding dress, Ali looked at Martha. He felt a huge lump in his throat when he saw how beautiful she looked under the veil. The rituals and ceremony went by with a blur. Ali was so happy to be wedding this lovely young woman.

The ceremony and reception certainly kept up with their expectations. Beer and wine flowed easily as the guests ate the roast lamb and pig which were cooked over fire which had died down to a pit of glowing embers. The pig and lamb rotated on spits. The smell of the cooking meat had filled the hall with the delicious aroma.

As the night progressed a band struck up with some good music. The crowd became noisier as the feast progressed. During the night there was a hell of an explosion which shook the town. Ali found later that one of the Greeks had let off a full case of gelignite to celebrate the event. He evidently had a few windows to replace after.   Both couples left the proceedings to change into their going away clothes. They then returned for a brief stat then left for home   Outside the Italian Club were the two vehicles, Tomas's Holden and Ali's Patrol. These had been adorned with the usual slogan and had cans and old boots tied behind them.

Tomas and Zeena left first. They were driving to Adelaide, and then leaving for a honey moon in Queensland at Surfers Paradise. Ali and Martha were going to explore the lower part of South Australia.

The Patrol was parked outside the house. The couple walked from the car to the house. Ali unlocked the door and carried Martha over the threshold. They undressed and had just started to make love when all hell broke loose. Ali got a fright, so did Martha, they had no idea what the horrible noise was. Ali got up and pulled his trousers on and opened the rear door of the house. The large electric horn used at the oval to end the quarters at the football, was set up at the rear door. It was plugged in to an outside plug. He turned the switch off; his ears were ringing from the loud raucous noise. Ali could see the outline of a group of the town's kids in the dark. They were laughing loudly "Have a good one for us" one yelled before they ran away.

Chapter ten

No more money worries

John walked back into the bar. 'Looks like a double celebration tonight. Helen says it's raining. We've had a half an inch of rain already, and it's still raining.'

The beer flowed freely, a lot freer than John was used to, but the first opal sales had buoyed his confidence. The main level which they had drilled still beckoned to them.

'God, what time did we get home last night? My bloody head hurts,' said Tony as he pulled a chair out and sat at the table. The smell of the buyer's horrible cigarettes still wafted in the air. It was hard to get any ventilation down into the dugout. 'That's the trouble with you young blokes, no staying power. When I was your age...' Bert was interrupted by John.

'It's all right for you. I don't feel too good either. I've heard a lot of stories about your younger days. Most shouldn't be told with a young man like Tony's present.' They all laughed.

The strong black coffees had helped a bit. By the time the dozer started, both the men were feeling a bit more like work. The excitement of the previous day was still in their minds. Tony was full of enthusiasm at first, but as the day crawled on, he reverted to plodding behind the dozer, turning the stones over with his miners' pick and breaking the odd one with the side of the pick head. Towards the end of the day, they started to find hard rock. This material seemed to be a mixture of gypsum and jasper. It was a very tough material, if it had been the hard red and-white banded jasper, the rippers would have shattered it, making it relatively easy to get through. The rippers on the dozer would chatter and would not penetrate. Smoke was coming off the ripper boots. Every now and then, John was able to hook under one of the rocks and make a hole he could work from. He would have to drop the rippers into this hole and drag a few stones out and then come in from a different angle to get some more. It was a slow and tedious job as well as being hard on the old dozer. John was worried that the old dozer might not have held together in the rough ground.

'I thought you might have a bit of fun with that rock. The guy with the Caldwell drill who dug the shaft for us doesn't like drilling out here very much because of this rock. This field is noted for the hard rock on top. It is probably why this spot was left years ago. You guys are lucky you can prize the rocks out. Sometimes you have to use explosives. We have been told this this crap was hard to drill.' 'We had to dig three meters through this rock,' said Harry.

Bert had found a small pocket of skin shell material. It had a beautiful colour but was a very thin material. Skin shell was formed when the cockle shell, which was turned to opal, was opened at the time. If the cockle was tightly shut, this would form a solid shell, all solid opal. Some of the best of these commanded a lot of money—fifteen or twenty thousand dollars for one really good shell.

John was still worried about the dozer. It might not stand up to the rough work much longer. There were bolts coming loose and a lot more squealing from the tracks. John went to the opal miners store to get a new packet of hard-facing welding rods to face the boots as the tips were wearing off very quickly, and as soon as the cutting edge was rounded off, the boot just slid along the top of the tough rock. Whilst he was walking through the aisles, he noticed some tungsten-tipped cutting tools which were used in the large Caldwell drill buckets. The buckets were modified to take these tools by having the old tool holders removed and then new blocks welded on to take these tungsten-tipped picks. On a whim, John bought four of the picks and two blocks. 'Where can I get some welding and cutting done?' he asked the man at the counter. He was directed to a small street about three hundred meters behind the shop. John got out of the utility and walked into the yard. There was a huge pile of scrap steel at one end of the large block of land

and a dugout and large workshop on the other end. Near the workshop, there were a man and a woman working on a large blower. John walked over and stood watching the two working. The woman was working just as hard as the man, hammering a bent piece of steel with a sledge hammer. They stopped working, and the man introduced himself. He was Ivan; his wife was Anne.

'This is Anne's blower. She works it by herself when I am working in the workshop,' explained Ivan. 'What can I do for you?' John explained that they were working a dozer at the Fifteen Mile and were in the hard jasper. Ivan had worked this area and knew all about the tough material. What I want to do is to cut the ends off two worn ripper boots and weld these two
blocks on the nose of the boot to take these picks.'
Ivan thought for a while and said, 'I think you should cut the boots down enough to just be showing the end of the pocket where the boot fits over the ripper tine. This would allow you to remove the old pick with a hammer and long drift.' The design was worked out, and Ivan agreed to do the job the next day.

'That's a really good idea you have thought of. I have never seen this before. If it works, you should patent it.' A rough price was agreed on, and John left for the dugout.

John told the men about his new invention to try to stop the dozer from falling to pieces. He was also getting knocked around by all the severe jerking and twisting. He could not keep the dozer going in a straight-line as one of the rippers would hook in and pull the dozer off line all the time. This was extremely hard on the brakes and other parts on the dozer.

Tony's feet were getting really sore from all the walking over the rough stones. He still checked under these stones because there was a little bit of the brown opal-bearing level stuck to the bottom of some of these rocks. There was no opal to be found though. The only thing he found was a thin line of potch stuck to the bottom of one of these stones. He nearly gave himself a hernia, trying to turn this stone over, and was disappointed when he had finally achieved shifting it to find it barren.

He was really interested to see if John's new idea would work.

Friday night was pub night. The men cleaned themselves up and departed to the hotel. They had just had their second beer when Silvio, the ferrety mate of the dugout owner, walked past their table. 'Oi, good doy, mite. You finda the big opals yet.' He laughed.

'Nah, mate, we haven't found anything but potch yet,' lied Bert. Silvio had evidently been in the pub all the afternoon. He could hardly stand up.

'If you find the opals, you got no worries with the safe. She's a gooda one. You got the only keys.' Silvio staggered off to the table with his mates, a most unsavory-looking mob of crooks. 'Who is that prick?' asked Tony. 'Don't you remember? He's our landlord's best mate. That other crook with the grey beard is the landlord. It makes you wonder about the safe, doesn't it? Every one of them has probably got a key.' They look like a mob of bloody pirates to me. That other crook has even got a big gold earring,' said John. 'I wouldn't like to do business with any of them.'

'That's why I didn't tell them about the opal. The less you say, the better.'

What are you mob of bastards doing up here?' John turned around. It was a farmer neighbor Peter Murphy. Peter had his son, Joe, with him. Peter and Joe sat down at the table. 'Here, Joe, get a round of drinks.

Make yourself useful.' Peter handed Joe a fifty-dollar bill.

Peter was having the same problems as the rest of them. 'Bloody greedy banks', was his answer. Peter and Joe had built a small noodling machine to noodle the missed opal out of the old dumps and had brought it up behind the farm front-end loader. They were finding around a thousand dollars a week on an average. 'A lot better than the farming game,' he stated.

'Hey, did you hear about the rain?' asked Peter. 'Yes, I rang Helen the other night, and she said it was raining then. I don't know how much we finally got.' 'I rang Joan yesterday. We had just under an inch. Hell, that will sure help the crops along.'

Tony had teamed up with Joe. 'You old bludgers can talk about old times if you like. Joe has asked me to go around to one of his mate's places. There's a bit of a party. I just thought I would like to check out some of the local talent.' 'Well, don't talk to any Greek girls,' said Harry. 'If you find an extra one, bring her back for me,' said Bert, laughing. 'How do you think I should describe you?' asked Tony. 'Tall, young, and had some,' added Bert. 'Piss off, and don't do anything I wouldn't do. 'A couple of rough diamonds those two,' said Joe as they walked through the pub door.

The party was pretty rowdy as the two boys arrived. Joe had an Esky with some beer in it. He carried it inside the gate. There was loud music coming from inside the timber-framed house. The boys walked inside and were greeted by an Italian lad. It was his birthday party. Joe introduced Tony to most of the people he knew. The topic of the conversation was opal-based as most of the guys were mining or noodling. Tony did not let on to anyone about the opal that they were finding. Tony had a few dances with some of the girls, in between talking and drinking beer. Joe suggested that they leave. Tony asked why. Some of the guys here have got some grass and have started to smoke it. I don't want to get mixed up with the marijuana scene. My young brother got on to that shit and lost his marbles.' Tony agreed. There was too much relying on the mining venture to get tied up with the dope scene and shoot one's mouth off about the opal find.

Peter had asked John and Tony to come out and have a look at their noodling machine the next morning.

The sun was well up when John drove out into the Olympic Field. They had called into Ivan's workshop and picked up the finished tools. Tony was very impressed with the look of the tools as was Ivan. 'Let me know if they work OK. I can't see why these pointy tools should not work in the Tough jasper.' John agreed to let him know.

He tried to follow the directions he had been given the previous night, but they ended up getting lost. After driving around for about a half an hour and back-tracking their tracks, they could see a cloud of dust blowing off a machine in the distance. Tracks led everywhere. A lot of them ended in dead ends. They had to reverse out from between the white mounds of sandstone which had been left by the blowers quite a few times, being careful when they did so, not to drive down one of the many shafts which accompanied most of the mounds. Finally, they arrived at the machine.

The machine looked like something out of the Mad Max movie. It was built out of lots of things which came from the farm. The chassis was an old truck which had the motor, tray, and cab removed; only the chassis springs and wheels remained. On one end was a small bin with a coarse screen on top to remove the large stones. This was lifted occasionally with the loader bucket to tip off the accumulated large rocks. Under the bin was a conveyor belt. The belt led to a rotary trammel screen, which dropped the screened material on to another small conveyor, which, in turn, led through a small darkroom. The darkroom was made from an old van body. On the other side of the van, the material from the conveyor dropped on to another elevator which carried it up and away. The men could recognize most of the parts in this machine as coming from old farming plant, similar to what they had in the scrap heap on their farm.

There was a cone-shaped pile under the elevator, which Peter would pick up with the front-end loader and carry away to a dump.

The entire machine was driven by a diesel-powered alternator, which was situated some distance away to keep it out of the dust. Peter dropped the bucket full of material into the hopper and then stopped the tractor. 'You're late! Did you sleep in?' John explained how they had got lost. 'Bloody easy to do around here. I was talking to one of the miners one day who owned a drill. He went out drilling one day in this area and drilled up some opal. He got pretty excited. He put the mast of the drill down and went back to town in his ute. The next day, he could not find the drill amongst all the dumps. He had spent nearly all day looking and was almost going to the cops because he thought some crook had pinched it when he finally found it.'

Peter banged on the door of the darkroom. Joe shut the electric motors off, which drove the machine, and then opened the door. 'Come in and have a look.' There was only room for Tony and Joe in the confined area. 'Shut the door behind you. I'll show you how it works.' Tony pulled the sliding door shut. It was pitch-dark inside. Joe turned on the ultraviolet florescent lights, which shone an eerie purple. Tony looked down at his sneakers, which shone a bright yellow in the UV light. 'Wow, just like the lights at some discos,' said Tony. He had not noticed this in the noodling machine the other day.

Joe started the conveyor belt moving. The small rocks were carried by. They shone as a dark purple colour. Occasionally, there were some which shone orange. 'Alunite,' explained Joe. The small pieces of opal shone a brilliant white, similar to Tony's shoes. The men picked these up and put them into the small buckets which were next to the belt. Occasionally, a feather or a piece of greasy dirt would fluoresce. There was a brilliant green piece coming along the belt. Joe yelled as Tony was going to pick it up, "a scorpion." Tony pulled his hand back. Joe shut the belt off and turned the bright light on. It took Tony a while to be accustomed to the light. Joe speared the large scorpion, put it aside, and then carried on noodling in the purple darkness.

Suddenly, Tony got the funny feeling again that the belt had stopped moving and that the stool he was sitting on was moving instead, as it had done in the noodling machine before. After a while, he got used to the machine, and it all settled down again. Joe stopped the machine. 'Well, that's enough for today. It's about two o'clock.' He turned the light on inside the room and then shut the electric motors down in sequence, first, the bin, then the screen, then the conveyor through the room, and, finally, the elevator outside. The men walked out into the sunlight, squinting at its brightness as they did. Joe carried the small buckets filled with material out with him and the skewered scorpion.

'When we first came up here, we saw a noodling machine working. The bloke asked us if we wanted to have a look. They were from Ceduna. Cockies like us,' said John. 'That would have been Charlie and Josh. I know them,' said Joe. They all looked at the very large scorpion. 'I have been told that they are not deadly poisonous, but they hurt like hell if they get you.'

Joe poured some water into a tray and then tipped the contents of the buckets in. The material was mostly worthless potch, but hiding amongst this were a few good pieces of opal. The potch was discarded and the opal put back into one of the buckets. 'A lot of the opal they found in the fifties and the sixties was considered unsaleable, so it was tossed into the dumps. Now some of these are worth around four or five hundred bucks an ounce.' The days opal was probably worth around three hundred dollars. 'Not a bad pick up, considering the farming game at present. We get this nearly every day. Every now and then, we find a good piece which someone has missed. We got three thousand for a good shell one day.' The men agreed it was far better than any way of making money in the Kimba district at the present time.

Joe and Tony went for a drive around the field the next day. John was left with the washing. Even Bert and Harry had a washing session. Their clothes were so full of sweat and dirt that they would hardly bend. Monday morning. Working again. The dozer had to be filled with fuel from the two-hundred-liter drum every two days. Tony usually did this, whilst John checked the oil and greased the dozer.

John had picked up the new ripping tools he had got from Ivan's workshop. Ivan had still insisted that John should patent the idea if it were to work. 'This tool could save a lot of people a lot of money,' he had said.

The new tools were fitted to the ripper tines. Ivan had done an excellent job welding the tools together. The pointy tools looked a lot more aggressive than the normal spade-type ripping tools.

John drove the dozer into the cut and lined up along one wall for the first test of the tool. He lowered the tools into the tough rock and gunned the dozer motor. These new tools penetrated the rock and started to rip. The dozer was not pulled off line, and instead of skipping along the top of the tough rock, the tools ripped it up. John got off the dozer and walked back to Tony, Bert, and Harry. 'What do you think of this?' Tony was amazed at the difference these tools made to the job. The tough rock seemed to explode in front of the tools, throwing up the pieces from hard rock with a puff of smoke. Bert and Harry were also impressed.

'You should have done this in the start. Just think of all the hard work you would have saved.' John agreed. It was farmers' thinking which had designed the tool. John had modified a lot of machinery when they were developing the farm. A lot of the machinery did not like crashing over stumps and stones.

Tony's feet and legs felt a lot better, thanks to the weekend break from walking. Back and forth he walked, carrying the pick and turning the stones over as the rippers pulled them from the solid tough rock.

At the end of the day, the rippers started to break through the hard rock. The bottom of the cut was starting to settle down now, and the solid rough stones were almost gone. The old dozer now made light work of ripping the soft sandstone around thirty-centimeter deep, where the level of hard stone had been, the walls of the cut had started to slope in. If they lost some of the width of the cut from crooked walls, they were also losing a lot of the floor area. John set to work with the corner of the dozer blade at an angle to the wall and peeled as much of this rock off as he could. This was extremely hard work on the old dozer.

When work was finished, John got the camera out of the utility and took a lot of photos of the new tools from different angles. He called in and told Ivan all about the new experience on the way home. Ivan still insisted about the patent.

Some brown lines were beginning to appear in the floor of the cut. Bert told Tony to pay particular attention to the junctions where these lines met and also any changes in the colour of the sandstone, especially to a mustard colour as this usually meant that a level was not too far away.

The only things which Tony had seen in the last few days were a couple of thin pieces of potch. He did notice that when some of the sandstone was ripped, the shapes of shells were present, but only sandstone. 'Mud shells,' Bert had called them when Tony had shown some of them to him. Bloody boring, Tony thought to himself as he walked. He had convinced himself that the events of the first day when they found the opal would have continued every day.

The sandstone had appeared to be getting harder during the last couple of rips. Tony had noticed this but did not know what it meant. He was following the dozer closely when he noticed that the ground being ripped changed colour to a dark mustard brown. This must be the level which Bert had told him about. The cut was around four meters deep by now.

Tony had renewed his efforts in turning the stones over now and was following the dozer closely when he heard a sound like glass being cracked by the ripper tine as it was dragged through the solid rock. He looked hard at the place where this happened and noticed a very small reflection of the sunlight shining on the side of one of the larger rocks. Tony got his pick, and with an effort, he turned the large rock on to its back. The whole bottom of the rock was covered in opal. The fiery colours reflected off the opal as if the bottom of the rock was alight. John had just started to reverse the dozer back. Tony ran to the side of the tractor and waved for him to stop. John slowed the motor and then pushed the tractor's gears to neutral. He climbed down. 'Opal,' Tony croaked, not feeling the need for any other words.

The two men scratched at the rocks with their bare hands to turn as much of the opal-bearing rock over as they could, marveling at each stone they turned.

John walked out of the cut, got the tools and sieves out of the ute, and then walked back down, carrying the awkward load. Tony was squatting next to a large stone, picking the smaller stones out from around it and inspecting each one carefully. He had two piles of rocks next to him: one, the barren sandstone, and the other, the rock with the opal stuck to it.

John looked around for a comfortable spot to work. Finally, he sat on a large rock, whilst he chipped the opal off the stone with the chisel point of his pick on to an old piece of canvas which Tony had handed him. Tony used a hammer and screwdriver to chip the material from the sandstone. The opals went into the bucket whilst the stone was rechecked and then discarded on to the barren pile. They were working quite a large hole out from where the opal had first appeared.

Bert and Harry had come up from the shaft and had walked down into the cut. 'I think your bank problems are over, my boy,' he told John as he looked into the bucket. 'Where were the holes you found the opal in when you drilled?' 'Not here,' Tony said, 'I reckon it was more towards the front of the cut. In fact, I'm sure it was I who lined the holes up with those stones. I placed next to the cut so I would have some idea of where to look. They are further towards the dump.' The men all went to work, getting the opal off the sandstone and into the bucket, ready to be carried out of the cut.

The seam of opal still continued into the sandstone where the ground had not been ripped, so John got back on to the dozer and revved the motor. He reversed back and then ripped the area slowly and very carefully. It was quite late when they had finally cleaned the pocket of opal right out. There were close to two twenty-liter drums full of rough opal.

'You realise that this is not all good saleable opal,' said Bert as they loaded the drums into the ute. 'There's still a lot of sandstone stuck to the opal, plus there's a certain amount of potch, but there's a hell of a lot of money in these buckets. A couple of hundred thousand dollars, I reckon.' 'That much?' John croaked with amazement. 'I think you should go to the Opal Miners Co-op and buy a concrete mixer to tumble all of our opal. We will pay half.'

John and Tony called into the Opal Miners Co-op to see about the concrete mixer. The miners Co-op store had a concrete mixer for three hundred dollars. John bought it and also bought a nest of sieves to grade the opal into different sizes. The mixer was lifted with Tony's help, and he loaded it on to the ute tray amongst the tools.

John and Tony talked about what they would do to the farm with the money from the opal. The Lizard would be the first visit. They joked of all the different ways they would try to fix the Lizard when they paid the money.

When they got home to the dugout, the rough opal was tipped into the concrete mixer with some water and left to run to wear all the sandstone and grime off the opal. After running for an hour, the opal was tipped out through the nest of sieves. The sieves full of opal were then washed in a half two-hundred-litre drum full of water to get the grime off. The sieves were taken and taken inside where the opal was sorted out from the potch. About a quarter of the opal was either potch or potch with a bar of opal in it. The opal was then put into plastic bags and stored in the safe.

The next morning, an hour after they had started, two car loads of aborigines turned up. The occupants walked up and settled down on the dump and then started to noodle by hand. There were about ten adults and ten kids. They must have been stacked into the cars well, John thought as he watched them scratch at the sandstone with steel rods shaped like spears. The women seemed to do most of the work. The men would do a bit of sieving now and then. When they thought that one of the women had found something good, they would confront them and usually take it from them, under protest.

When John started to push the dirt from where they found the opal the previous day, the aborigines quickly settled on to the fresh piles of worked dirt which were pushed up on to the dump. John could see the people putting pieces into small shopping bags which they carried.

More opal came out of the next rip. A few others had turned up to noodle, including Silvio, Tom, and the part aborigine, Wombat, who seemed to be with them always.

How the hell did they find out, John wondered as they sat behind the dozer and dug the opal out? 'I thought I saw some aborigines watching us from over on the far dump yesterday. It doesn't seem as if you can keep too many secrets around here,' said Tony as he put some opal into the bucket. Bert and Harry came down to help them to gather up the opal. 'You blokes must be lucky. This is only the top level. You don't usually get too much opal in this level.'

Everything was cleaned up, so John reversed the dozer out of the cut and shut the motor off.

The aborigines had gone for quite some time, but Silvio and his mates had persisted, digging and watching intently. Finally, they walked over to their old ute and climbed in. The motor would not start; the battery was flat. The men tried to push the ute, but it was in the loosened, soft rough dirt the dozer had been driven over. Silvio walked over. 'Hey, boss, could you give us a push? The bloody basta she no go.' He tried to look into the bucket on the tray of the ute. Luckily, it had an old towel on top of it. 'You find some good opals today, hey.' 'Nah none, only a bit of potch and colour. Get in to your Ute. I'll give you a push with the bull bar on ours.' Tony had no intention of showing them the opal that they had just dug up. He got into the ute, started the motor, and drove around so he was lined up with Silvio's ute. He then pushed the bull bar up against their tray and gunned the motor, pushing the ute in front of him. Their old ute coughed into life and drove off. 'I don't like that bastard,' he said to himself as he drove back to pick John up. There was getting quite a pile of opal in the safe now. The bags were stacked one on top of the other.

The next morning, Tony filled the dozer with fuel, whilst John checked the oil and water. John climbed up on to the seat and turned the key to start the pilot motor. Nothing happened. 'Bloody flat battery', thought John. It must have shorted out, he thought. He lifted the battery cover to check the terminals. The battery was gone. Someone had stolen the battery after they had gone for the night.

John looked at the ground and noticed where someone had dragged something to get rid of any tracks. John was angry. He was sure he knew who the culprits were. But on thinking it over, people like these were known to have their revenge if they were dobbed in. 'Those crooks have pinched the battery out of the dozer. Get the ute close so we can use the jumper leads to start the pilot motor.' Tony got the ute and drove it next to the dozer.

'The bloody mongrels! I'll bloody have a piece out of them if they show up today,' growled Tony. 'No, we'll shut up about this. If we cause trouble, those types of men would just as likely fill the sump of the dozer up with sand or something else like wrecking the truck motor.'

Chapter Eleven

Finally married

Ali checked the house and safe before they left in the morning, Peter had promised to come and look at the house; he had a spare key to the gate. Ali locked the large gate with barbed wire across the top as they left for their honey moon adventure.

For ten days there was a period of sheer bliss. First they stayed in Adelaide in the Grand Hotel Glenelg for three days. They then worked their way around the south East South Australia. Finally visiting Port Lincoln, then back through Kingoonya to Coober Pedy.

First call at Coober Pedy was to see Peter and Heidi. Peter had a worried look on his face. "I did not want to spoil your honeymoon. Some crook had broken into your house and tried to cut the safe open with an angle grinder. They dug a hole through the rear wall of the house with a crowbar and hammer.
We had one very windy night. I found the damage the next day. A few small things seem to be missing, but the safe is OK.

Peter accompanied Ali to his house. A sheet of iron had been pulled off the side fence. The barbed wire on the top of the fence had not been much use. Peter unlocked the gate, Ali drove into the yard as Peter walked behind
The inside of the house had things strewn around from the cupboards and wardrobes. The paint on the wall next to the safe was covered in burn marks made from the heat and sparks from the grinder. There were plunge cuts where all of the thick rods were that secured the door of the safe. The hole in the wall had let a lot of dust into the house

Ali turned the combination and turned the handle to undo the door. He noticed the rods lifting through the angle grinder cuts. The door would not open.

Peter had a bit of a think. "I think the bottom rods have been cut and are not being lifted up" "how in hell are we going to get them to lift"
"It's got me beat, I will ask around town."

Heidi and Martha arrived in Peter's car. "I would like to find the crook who has messed our house up, I would wring his neck" Martha was really angry. Martha picked up a broom and started to sweep the dirt into a pile, she swept with angry motions as if she was sweeping the robber away. Heidi retrieved all of the clothes and other goods which had been scattered. "I would phone the cops" said Heidi. "What would they do? ", answered Ali. Peter agreed.

Peter was knocking on the door early in the morning. Martha was just getting breakfast. I went to the Club and asked about someone being able to fix a broken safe. One of the most notorious safe crackers in Australia is mining opal here. He has not been in business since he got out of jail five years ago. He is married now and has got a couple of kids". Peter had contacted the guy and he would have a look lunch time.

Ivan knocked on the door of the house. Peter introduced him. Ali already knew him; he had bought a small parcel of opal from him. "I got sick of the life in jail. Every time some crook cracked a safe the cops would come and see me. That's why I moved up here. They know where I am and I do not have the problems any more", Ivan turned his attention to the safe. "Bloody idiot he could have cut here with the angle grinder and have been able to open the door." Ivan went to get a bag of tools from his utility.

He had a large electric drill with a diamond tipped drill bit; He drilled five, inch wide holes into the door adjacent to the rods which held the door shut. He then had a hammer and punch, then tapped each rod back into the door, When each rod was lifted he tapped a very thin wedge of steel in next to the rod to stop it from dropping again.

The work with the hardened steel of the door was time consuming as the drill could only grind very slowly. When all of the rods were finally held tight with the wedges, Ivan took a long lever out of the bag and carefully inserted the sharp end into the crack between the door and safe.   The safe door would not budge. He then took the hammer and gave each of the top rods position a sharp crack with the hammer Ali heard the offending rod drop down with a click. The safe was now opened.

"Would a thousand bucks be OK " "Shit yes thanks mate" The money was counted out. Ivan picked up the tools and walked out to the utility. The money and opal was transferred to Peter s safe in his office at his home.

A few days later, one of the Hungarian miners had a bad accident. He had a steel rope break on the winch. The winch bucket filled with rocks and dirt had dropped down a seventy foot shaft and landed on his legs this caused him to have both legs amputated at the hospital. His mining and walking days were over.

Ali knew that Silvio was going to be handy at tidying some messes up.
Silvio was two thousand dollars richer. Silvio was always short of money. He was a good picker of slow race horses in the TAB at the hotel. The word was spread around to a select few as to why the man had the leg problems. This was linked to name The Dragon.

Miners were just starting to use a vacuum sucking machine to suck the dirt out of the tunnels and drives when mining. An old truck had a large diesel motor mounted on the tray, a large suction fan was mounted and driven by belts from the motor to a small pulley to increase the speed of this fan. The fan sucked the dirt up from below ground to a large drum. This drum had a door on the bottom which was held shut by the powerful vacuum. A length of rope was taken from the speed mechanism of the motor. When this rope was pulled the motor would slow down to idle and the vacuum would lessen, allowing the weight of the dirt and rocks to fall out of the counter balanced door. These machines really saved miners a lot of work hauling drums and manually stacking the rocks in worked out areas.

Some people had started to use a tunneling machine which dug a tunnel with a rotary cutting head which could be lowered and raised to cut a neat rectangular drive two meters by one meter wide. The suction pipe was connected to the end of the machine. When opal was found it was dug out by a jack hammer or a hand pick.

A new comer to the field pegged a claim well away from where any mining was taking place. The man, Hugo drove to where some men were working one of the large Caldwell bucket drills which was drilling a meter-wide shaft for exploration. These holes, if they found opal allowed the person to work down them. First the area where the opal was opened up by blasting under the opal, then the opal carefully dug out.

The drill operator was hired to drill one hole on the claim to look for opal. As the drill bored down through the ground, then pulled the heavy bucket out of the hole the swung to the side of the hole to empty the bucket, the dirt from the bucket was checked for opal.

The heavy bucket as it rotated crunched through something solid. When the bucket was emptied the mound of dirt was covered with beautiful opal. The operator and the claim owner Hugo sat and sieved the dirt to collect the opal. Hugo was then lowered down the hole to check the opal with an electric lead light. The hole was surrounded by the good seam of opal. Hugo thought he was going to be rich.

This claim was about two hundred meters from the nearest claim. Hugo had found from a friend that the opal was possibly worth fifteen thousand dollars. The friend had agreed to come and work with Hugo on a twenty percent agreement.

Upon arriving at the claim the next morning there were mining pegs all around the claim. The guy with the drill was drilling next to Hugo's border. The Mines Department warden was also at the claim with a suspension of work notice. This meant that Hugo was not able to work until the matter was resolved in the Opal Miner's court in three months. One of the miners had measured his claim and had put the non-work order on the claim.

Hugo and his mate were not happy. His utility was loaded with a Yorke Hoist and alternator ready to start to dig the opal out. An altercation took place with the drill operator. The Mines Warden stepped in and told Hugo to go home and wait. He was sure the problem would be resolved in his favor.

As Hugo and his mate were leaving another large Caldwell drill arrived and started to drill on the other side of his claim. "You know what those bastards are going to do. They are going to clean this opal out".   In court the matter of the dispute was resolved in Hugo's favor. He went to the claim with his mate and was lowered down the shaft by an electric winch. There was a huge hole dug out with a tunnel coming from both sides which led to where both of the Caldwell drills had drilled their shafts. Both of the drill operators were a part of a large ethnic team. One was Croatian and one Italian. Neither were ones which a single person would have a dispute with.

Ali and Martha were at Peter and Heidi's waiting for dinner to finish cooking.' I think we should buy some better mining gear so we can compete with some of the bigger mining companies". Peter thought for a while. "This is a good idea, I am tired of having to drill and blast, then drag drums to the Yorke Hoist. I feel I am getting a bit too old for this ". I have heard that one of the Greeks, Little George is trying to sell up and leave town. This is one of the few Greeks who is very fussy with his machinery '. "You mean the one with the late model white truck and the late model Caldwell drill on its back." "That's the guy. He also has a truck with an alternator and good tunneling machine". Ali and Peter would look George up the next day

George was out in the field working. His partner was using the tunneling machine. The truck with the alternator and motor on the back was sitting near the mine-shaft, A truck mounted blower was blowing dust from the outlet for the air. Both motors of these machines were working hard. Peter and Ali walked onto Georges claim and waited. George noticed them and called them over. George met them half way from the noisy machines, "She is no bloody good to talk with them making the noise", he pointed his thumb at the two machines.

"I have been told you want to sell your machinery and get out" . "Yeah I have a woman from my home town in Greece going to marry me. I bring her up here, she don't like the place. She tell me to go to hell, she go home. I have a plenty money from the opals, I think I get out. This woman she's a bloody good looker. I think I not working up here and have her in Adelaide. I might find some bastard in her bed. " "What do you want for the machinery "asked Peter. "I think the drill at ninety thousand and the blower tunneling machine and alternator about the same. Say the one hundred and eighty thousand. I tell you what. I sell the drill now and in three weeks I sell all the rest. I have a partner in the mining and he wants to keep the tunneling machine going for a bit longer, we are finding opal here" . "That sounds like a reasonable deal. We would like to see the drill working before we buy" the men walked to the truck mounted drill to check it over . The drill was a fair distance from the noisy motors. .

The large drill rig appeared to be in very good order. Ali looked at George. "I will go looking for a spot to drill. If we find something wrong and do not want the drill. We will pay for drilling the hole. That sound ok" George agreed to the terms. . "We will see you tomorrow afternoon" said Ali. They walked to their Ute. 'Hell that drill looks in bloody good order' "Yes it does .But I want to see it running" said Ali.

Peter and Ali had been prospecting in a new area just past the opal rush that was still happening in the Fifteen Mile Opal Field. They had both pegged claims together. Peter had walked over the ground with two bronze welding rods to look for the faults and slides which are likely to carry opal.

The edges of these faults seem to carry some moisture; this can be picked up when using divining rods. The method is similar to divining for water. Peter thought that he had picked up two crossing slides, if this was true there were usually a lot of cracked levels in the ground caused by the pressure of two moving rock masses meeting.

The next day they net up with George at lunch time "I tell my mate that he could have the day off. He was in the pub when I left town. George climbed into the large truck with some effort as his legs hardly reached the step to the cab. "Follow us "Yelled Peter. The convoy moved off along the track.

Peter directed George to the spot where he thought the two rock slides should be crossing. He waved his arm for George to stop. George stopped the motor then half slid and fell from the cab. "Why you silly buggers come here. The opal is getting hard to find behind you where the claims are. I think this is the end of the run of opal'." Ah well we really just want to see the drill work. We thought that this place should be as good as any to do the test" said Peter." George climbed onto the drill platform, and then started the diesel motor. The jacks were lowered with the hydraulics to level the drill. The long drilling mast was lifted with a large hydraulic ram. The Kelly Bar was lowered into the large drilling bucket and the pin knocked through, a Lynch Pin was fitted to retain the thick pin. The bucket was started turning. The full bucket was lifted from the hole A rope with a loop was fitted to a lever on top of the bucket as well as a hook to swing the bucket and Kelly bar away from the machine. Peter pulled the rope which let the bottom of the bucket swing clear and drop the freshly dug dirt. This was repeated over and over, A conical pile of white sandstone rose from the red soil.

At ten meters the drill shuddered and crunched its way through a level of opal. When the bucket came out of the ground and was emptied, the top of the heap to the bottom was covered with blue green crystal opal. There were some pieces as big as match boxes. George jumped down from the drill rig and started to help fill the bucket. "Hey I tell you what, I swap the drill rig for the bucket of opal, which by now was nearly filled.
Ali winked at Peter, "Not much chance of that George" George laughed
"Well I thought you might not know how much it was worth."
"One thing we do not want George is for you to tell anyone about this." "She's right mate I know what happens when that shit goes on. You have all of the crooks pegging you out and digging under your boundaries. I have had this shit happen to me."

This was Coober Pedy Black opal. "I hope no one comes past here while we are sieving this "Peter said. "I think they are all working a mile back. There are no roads around." The hole was dug three meters deeper so the dirt and rocks blasted out when opening the hole up could be dropped down the bottom of the hole. There was another advantage the dirt that was dug from the hole covered the brown level material in which the opal had formed.

This claim only had the pegs in the ground with the date on them. This claim would have to be registered. The mining pegs had to be the right distance apart fifty by fifty meters. Coordinates had to be taken with a compass from each peg to another, then a measurement had to be taken to a survey post which had a number on it. Finally this measurement on the drawing for the Mines Department had to have the direction in degrees off the compass reading to show exactly where the claim was situated.

"Why don't you go back to town and register this claim and pick up Heidi and Martha and all of their pegs. I will just sit and wait." Ali drove the Patrol back to town and loaded the mining pegs and the two women, and his cheque book. On the way out of town he registered the claim.

"There are some bloody nosy Parkers around here. I have had two different lots of visitors here asking why we dug the hole so far away from the other field. I told them that we had hit hard jasper and had broken some parts. You had gone to town to get the parts. Peter showed Heidi and Martha the black opal, before they started to put all of the pegs in.

While Ali had been in town Peter had walked around the area with the bronze welding rods with one end bent to hold. These were divining rods. They did not divine opal but did find the faults and slides along which opal usually formed. He had found a very strong slide and had traced this for two hundred meters, one hundred each end of where the hole was.

The pegs were put into the ground along this line. All of the coordinates were taken. The girls left for town to register their own claims. Before leaving Peter lowered the drill of the Caldwell drill into the hole to keep any nosy people out.

Peter and Ali agreed to buy the drill and arranged to go to George's dugout to pay him for the drill, after they had dropped him back at his claim to pick his ute up.

George had a nice dugout on North West Ridge. He was waiting outside. "I have a good bottle of Ouzo to celebrate your find and me selling the drill. You come inside." Ali had a bag of money with him to pay for the drill. The inside of the dugout was nicely furnished, George had the table covered with nibbles Almonds, Greek biscuits, Cheese and dry biscuits. The top was taken off the bottle of Ouzo and tossed in the bin. The Ouzo was poured into small glasses. As they sipped the first of the Ouzo and counted out the money George plied them with nibbles.

George then counted the money. "Yes this is ok it is all there "said George. He took the money and went to the bedroom to evidently put it into the safe.

Ali had never tried Ouzo before and did not mind the taste. "You be careful, this shit is rocket fuel." George came out of the bedroom. You guys have found a good patch of ground. There must be two or three hundred thousand in that bucket.
That is bloody top black opal." When the bottle was empty George offered to get another "No, sorry mate, Ali usually does not drink, I think another bottle would really stich him up". Ali was feeling a bit glassy eyed already.

When Peter and Ali returned to the drill the next morning there was a pegging frenzy of miners around their claims. No one knew that they had drilled on to opal; they had only assumed that they had. Some fifty claims had been pegged after they had left for the day. Some of this information may have come from one of the girls working in the Mines Department. Most of these girls were either married to miners or had mining parents. When a family came in to peg a group of claims, there was a reason to wonder why.

The two women had accompanied the men to work. Peter had taken his utility with the electric winch on the back. This would make the drilling and blasting in the hole a lot easier. Peter had a special platform which he could lower down the hole to work on, for safety.

The drill rig was started and the bucket and Kelly bar was lifted from the hole. The retaining pin was taken from the Kelly bar, and then the mast was lowered. The jacks were lifted and Peter climbed down to start the main motor of the truck, the truck was moved five meters forward.   Peter moved his ute in place and swung the electric winch out from the tray The small alternator was started. The winch, drill and light lowered him down the hole. The holes were drilled with an auger with tungsten tips.

This was driven by a large Sher drill.

Peter first lowered himself to the bottom of the hole and picked up any pieces of opal which had fallen down the hole when the drill had been pulled out.

The explosives were placed into the holes and tamped with a short length of broom handle. The fuses were lit. Peter came up out of the ground. He unhooked the platform then drove the utility away from the top of the hole. The time spent waiting for the explosives seemed to take forever. Finally, a WHOOMPH. Dust and small rocks shot out of the top of the hole.

Peter Reversed the drill truck back to the hole. Ali guided him as he stood just off line of the truck so Peter could see him in the mirror, Ali waved his arm Peter stopped the truck the turned the motor off. The drill was lowered down the shaft. There was no room for any person to be able to climb down next to the heavy Kelly bar of the drill.

Without a blower hooked up to the shaft to suck the fumes out, it was very dangerous to attempt entering the shaft that had the fumes of explosives in it. Some miners had died in their hurry to see what treasures they had uncovered, others had been ill for months after entering a shaft or drive.

Heidi made some sandwiches for lunch. Peter took the black opal out of the safe; he then spread it out onto the black oilcloth of the table in the opal room. The opal was soaked in water to get some of the gunk off. Each piece had been studied under a bright light. The black opal had a dark green colour which had a spectacular flash of light green appear as the stones were turned in the light.

On the way home the subject of Martha being able have a baby reared its head. They had not been using any protection since being married six months before. "This is getting to be hard work. Toiling all day trying to make money, then having to make love all night trying to make a baby." Martha laughed and dragged Ali to the bedroom of their house.

"You are not toiling to make money now, are you. How about seeing if you can make some babies" "Some "said Ali with a feigned look of outrage "I would like a baby not a litter like puppies".

Three large drill rigs had started to drill on the adjoining claims to Ali and Peter. More claims had been pegged in the area. The gibber plain with the stunted shrubs looked like it had grown small square trees over quite a large area. The Fifteen Mile field was still going strong. It made one wonder where all of the extra miners had been found to claim all of the extra ground.

One of the Greeks had been notorious for bringing up a busload of people from the city to tie up large areas of ground by having them peg vast numbers of claims. He was to give them a share if anything was found. "There would be a fat chance of that," Ali said to Peter when he had heard the story "knowing Nicky, he would just toss their pegs away and put his own pegs in their place."

The large truck engine rumbled to life. Then the smaller motor on the drill rig was started then the drill bucket was raised from down in the shaft. The tall mast of the rig was lowered to allow the truck to drive forward ten meters to allow access to the winch on the utility.

When the winch had been swung over the top of the hole, Ali slipped into the old steel tractor seat which had been adapted to fit to the hook on the Winch cable, he pressed the button on the winch control and lowered himself down. The lead light was already lowered to the floor of the shaft.

The shaft was now almost full of dirt from the blasting of the walls of the hole under the opal. Large chunks of opal were almost falling from the edge of the shaft. Ali laid some thick material of an old bed spread onto the floor of the hole. He carefully prized these pieces out with a sharp small pick. The pieces were tossed into a small bucket. As the opal was being prised out smaller pieces dropped down onto the bedspread on the floor. Ali continued doing this until all of the loose pieces were taken out.

The bedspread was carefully lifted to put all of the extra opal in the bucket. The walls of the hole were then picked back until there was only a thin width of sandstone under the seam of opal. This extra dirt and rock bought the level of dirt to where the explosives had been set the night before. Ali placed the bedspread back and carefully removed the chunks of opal. Any dropped pieces were removed from the bedspread. It was then emptied of the dirt again.

The small twenty liter bucket was filled buy now. Ali winched himself and the bucket up to the surface. Peter took the bucket from Ali before he climbed out of the seat frame.

After lunch Peter took a small electric jack hammer down with him to dig further under the opal seam. The system was repeated, but as the dirt was being jack picked down it started to fill the hole more so it was more difficult to dig.

The winch started to pull Peter up to the surface; he had all of the tools with him, plus the bucket filled with opal.

The drill truck was started and reversed back until the wheels were exactly where they had been in the morning. The mast of the drill was raised again and the bucket let down the hole. Peter started the drill turning and after lifting two buckets full and tipping the dirt he came up and lowered the mast again and shifted the truck.

The main reason for this ruse was, because the opal was very valuable, the men did not want to leave the shaft open for some moonlighter to help himself.

Peter then lowered himself down, Ali lowered the large electric drill and tungsten tipped auger bit to the bottom of the now cleaned shaft. Peter started to drill ten holes to take the explosives. He now drilled under the floor of the original blasting to give more head room. The drill was bought up and the bucket filled with the fuse, detonators and explosives was lowered down. Peter lit the fuses and returned to the surface. The explosives went off one after the other. They both counted to see if they had all fire. Ten bangs, this was good as unfired charges were very dangerous especially if the detonator was to be accidently drilled into at a later date.

The drill was returned to the shaft position and the bucket dropped once more. All gear was packed and the men returned to Coober Pedy. " I think we have a large pocket of opal there Ali. The width of the opal stones are the same still, even on the other side of the Shaft. We must have drilled through the middle of the pocket." "This must be about ten thousand an ounce material. It could be what Helmut is looking for instead of Lightning Ridge opal".

Peter drove on toward town. "This sure beat working in a dirty coal mine in Austria and dying of the dreaded lung disease. I have never felt so healthy since I came to Australia. Bloody cold got to me as well, I was coughing from the coal dust and the cold weather."
The first lot of the opal was tumbled for one and a half hours in a small concrete mixer. The stones were tipped into a nest of sieves to grade the size of the opal. Most of the stones were in the top large sieve. The colour was spectacular.
  The next morning the drill was lifted and the truck shifted. Peter lowered himself down the shaft. He had a pelican pick and the jack hammer. When Peter had dragged the dirt from under the blasted area he started to dig the roof of the drive carefully to not damage the opal. The colour of the opal was changing to a washed out potch and colour material. Then the opal seam stopped all together. A black line ran from the roof of the drive to the floor. This had been the fault which had made the opal.   Peter then dug out from the drive. After a short distance he hit another black line which stopped the opal.
  It was lunch time, Peter came to the top of the hole, thin after handing Ali the bucket climbed out of the seat on to the ground, "I have found out why this was such a good lot of opal, The two slides are crossing. I hope we have pegged in the right direction to be on the slide which carried the opal".
  It was Ali's turn to work; the other side of the drive was dug down. The seam of black opal was diminishing in width. He followed the seam until the trace of opal pinched out. The thick material was still carrying from the shaft in the other direction. So far he estimated that they should have about three hundred ounces of the top quality black opal. At ten thousand dollars that was a huge find. Ali came up out of the hole. The tools were pulled up with the rope. He was still puffing from the effort of picking and

moving dirt." It looks like I have found the other side of the seam too. The seam still runs back from the shaft,

The drill rig was positioned to drill out the dirt again. Peter then went down to drill and blast in the other direction, the shots were fired. The big drill was lowered into the hole again.

"I have been thinking Peter, how would I become an Australian Citizen"." I think you would need some records of where you came from. The Australian consul would contact the Philippines and check up on you". Ali thought for a while. "I have a friend who would probably know how to bribe an official to get the papers forged."

Ali was worried about travelling overseas on business. The short time he had been in Australia had been very kind to him. He did not want this to be ended if some person were to find that he was using a forged passport. After being poor most of his life Ali had a burning desire to accumulate wealth.

The phone call to Enrico was very interesting. "You should know Ali, if you have enough money you can bribe almost anyone in the Philippines. Ali went on to tell Enrico about the opal business, and the money they had found. As you can see Enrico money is no object. I would not like all of this business to come crashing down. I am married now and we are trying to start a family." "What you really want is to have a record of birth, school, and the other records for Zeena, as your mother. This would not be impossible but I think it would probably cost about ten thousand dollars. There would be a lot of work to do, leave it with me for a few days and phone back, I think I know a man who could do this for you. ".

At least the process was going to be investigated. Ali trusted Enrico, he could not think of another person to talk about this problem to.

The new safe had finally arrived. Ali and Peter installed an alarm system into both his and house and Peters dugout. The system had back up batteries in case someone was to disconnect the power. A vivid flashing light, plus an intermittent siren, similar to the one used after the wedding, was connected. The system was programmed to run for half an hour then set back to a short beep and flash of the light every thirty seconds.

Martha and Heidi had made lunch for the men while they had been slogging to get the large heavy safe into place in the house.

After lunch the contents of the old safe were bought back and replaced.

While travelling to work the next morning they found large pieces of jagged metal strewn across the road. Peter stopped the utility. Ali got out and removed the jagged steel from the road; these pieces of metal could easily have punctured a tyre. A crowd could be seen some thirty meters away. A truck with a blower on it was lying on its side. Ali and peter walked across to the truck.

The truck was a mess. Some person had evidently loaded the truck with explosives and had blown the truck up during the night. A lot of the claims around this truck had been systematically robbed over the last few weeks.

Some of the miners had suspected one of the men and had left one man hidden in a blower truck when they had all gone home for the night. The man had seen the claim holder and his mate climb down three of the adjoining claims shafts just before dark the previous night.

The hidden man's mate had driven out to pick him up. When he had found the details they had put half a case of gelignite into the truck and had lit the fuse before going home. Of course no one knew which person had done the job.

The day's work had finally worked the rest of the pocket of opal out. The colour started to fade as it had along the other direction of the drive; it then pinched out to a black line in the brown level material.

The pocket of quality opal was a very rare find. Usually such quality opal was only in very small pockets.

After carefully investigating the identity problem with Ali and Zeena, Enrico had found some officials who would help establish the new papers and identities for both him and Zeena. It was going to cost fifteen thousand US dollars. "I have told them that they are too expensive. Their answer was to go and get someone else. The identity is going to be created in my area as there is not the bull shit to go through. In Manilla or one of the other big areas, there would be more problems. I know most of the officials in the town and region. They also know what I would do if they tried to cheat me". Ali told Enrico to start the proceedings.

Tomas and Zeena arrived back in Coober Pedy. Ali had let Tomas know about the black opal find.

Peter had classed the opal after all f the bulk material had been cleaned. There was just less than four hundred ounces of opal in the parcel. The pieces were laid on the table and inspected under a bright light. A plastic spray filled with water was used to spray water on the opal to show the colour better when the opal had dried out under the glare of the bright light.

The job took all day. One piece was shifted from one pile to another. The end result was that the large one-hundred-ounce heap would be worth about ten thousand dollars an ounce, the next eight thousand dollars, and running down to about one thousand dollars for fifty ounces where the colour had started to fade, before the opal had finished.

The end price would be well over two million dollars. "Well that was a good week's work" said Peter as he packed the scales and light away. He then placed the bags of opal into the safe. "What say we take the women out to celebrate"? Ali agreed to this as he had been neglecting Martha a bit lately, due to trying to work out his new identity, plus the opal find.

At the club a large Serbian man walked over to Peter. "Hey Peter I hear you and your mate find the big opals past the Fifteen Mile fields last week." Peter shook his head. " Hey Milan I wish that we had I would be in the city with the normal people chasing the race horses, like you do" "Why you put the drill down the hole every night for", "We have just put some different new teeth on the drill and don't want you guys pinching them". " I think you tell me bullshit, I don't pinch the drill teeth I pinch the whole bucket ha ha".

The night was enjoyed, the late hour did not agree with Peter and Ali, they started to yawn. Heidi suggested they go back to their dugout and have a coffee on the way home. Ali knew that Heidi had just created one of her Bavarian chocolate cakes for desert. He was not going to miss out on this. He had tried the cake once before.

Martha and Ali waddled out to the Patrol. "Your father should be as fat as a whale from Heidi's good cooking." "I think he would be if he didn't work so hard."

The pressure of mining was lessened for a short while. Ali felt a little more relaxed. "Come along baby maker have another try". As they started to nod off Ali asked if there was a baby being made. "Not tonight I think tomorrow night it will happen. "said Martha as she kissed Ali goodnight.

Zeena and Tomas arrived at Coober Pedy. They had flown from Germany to Adelaide then driven the car he had left with a friend in Adelaide to Coober Pedy. Zeena looked very healthy and attractive in the designer clothes she wore; she has a pack of photos, which she showed around to Peter and Heidi when they came for dinner. Ali had already seen these as Martha had looked through the box. Zeena had a new Mercedes coupe to drive.

Tomas was keen to inspect the black opal find. After dinner Ali removed it from the new safe and displayed it onto the black top table, where he graded the opal he bought. Tomas undid each bag and laid each piece under the bright light to inspect the opal. "You two have certainly had a good find of opal, this is good quality black opal." As he sorted through the pieces and started a new pile he wrote some prices into his small book.

Tomas was adding up the price he put on the opal and the ounces of material in each bag. " This is a large lot for black opal; usually it is in very small pockets with other material. I am looking at nine thousand dollars an ounce for the top grade. The price for the lot would be two million two hundred thousand dollars. Peter and Ali agreed to this price.   "Now I will take you out to celebrate your find tomorrow night" They sat up until late that night talking of what had been happening in Coober Pedy and Europe.

The Italian club was filled with noisy people; they all seemed to be speaking another language. Each person tried to talk louder to be heard.

Peter and Ali were asked about the big find they had just had in the new part of the field. They both laughed and said. You mean the ten-thousand-dollar parcel?" said Peter. "You have the German opal dealer here; you must have some good opal". "He is married to my mother; He has come on a buying trip" Ali laughed.

"I drill next to you I do no bloody good" said the Greek. "We must have got all of the opal there is in this spot Nick". "I buy you all a round of drinks" . "Ok we'll have beer and the three women will have a white wine". Nick disappeared toward the bar.

Nick made two trips through the crowd with the drinks. He sat at the table. "Did I ever tell you about the first shaft I dug at Coober Pedy in nineteen fifty-six. I pegged a claim and dug down by hand. I climbed up and fished for the buckets of dirt which I stacked three high in the shaft. These were twenty-liter buckets with handles; I climbed past the buckets out of the shaft then used the hook on the steel cable on the windlass to fish for each bucket handle to pull it out. I have had plenty fishing experience at Port Kenny when I was a kid." Nick emptied his glass of beer.

"I get you another round. Nick waddled through the crowd again and returned with the glasses" the women had only started to drink the white wine. I hit the bottom of the shaft and cannot dig any more it is like I am trying to dig through glass. I have only a candle for light. I get the candle and sweep the loose dirt off the floor of the shaft with my hand. Bloody hell it is thick opal. I have to go back to town and buy a heavy hammer and chisel to dig a hole in the opal so I can start to prize it out."

Nick took a long drink of beer. "I get the opal out then I dig and find a full opal tortoise more than two feet long. I dig him out. He will not fit in the bucket.

I leave him there and go to town and ask a mate of mine. He tells me that the government will take this from you as it is a fossil. I went back then broke the tortoise up with the hammer. I find two more tortoises' and break them too. I would like to find that mate now. I find out later that these tortoises would have been worth five hundred thousand pounds each. I did find two hundred and eighty thousand pounds the first year. A car was four hundred pounds, and a reasonable house was a thousand pounds. I turned one and a half million into fifteen thousand. Bloody bastard cost me all of that money". Nick left to see another man about doing some work for him.

"Was that a true story" Asked Ali. "I have heard that from other people. He also found another two hundred thousand Pounds the next year, that was four hundred and eighty thousand pounds, nine hundred and sixty thousand dollars. About ten million in today's money." "I have heard the story about the tortoises as well, they were meant to have been solid opal, and good quality. They would have gone to museums like the Smithsonian in America. They were almost priceless objects". Said Tomas.

"I have heard a story of some people going out into the field one Sunday trying to shoot a rabbit or a Bush Turkey, and then getting bogged in the soft dirt.

The father and kids were trying to push the car out. The father had a shovel in the boot. He started to dig the car out, one of the kids rushed in to the pile of dirt and retrieved a large piece of good opal, the car was a minor concern then. They loaded the boot of the car with good opal then drove back to town. The car had plenty of room to drive out of the boggy sand by then. The next day the father and mother went and pegged claims on the spot. That is how the Seventeen Mile field was found." Peter suggested that they go back to their dugout and have a feed of Heidi's new Chocolate Bavarian cake. The noise in the club was almost unbearable by now.

Chapter twelve

Black opal dinosaur eggs

The aborigines were back just after they started to work, not long after Silvio and his rotten mates showed up.

The day produced another small pocket of opal, not of a very good quality this time.

When John had shut the dozer off for the day, he noticed that when Silvio and the pirates got into the ute, the motor started with no trouble at all. There are some real thieves around here. They're probably the mongrels who moon-lighted our claim when we were away, was Bert's thoughts on the day's activities.

That night when they filled the fuel drum up with diesel at the Opal Miners Co-op, John had to buy another battery for the dozer. He bought some latches and a padlock as well.

The next morning, John put the new battery into the dozer and then fitted the latches with pop rivets. He locked the battery box with a new padlock he had bought. 'Padlocks only keep out honest people,' warned Harry. Tony noticed that during the next rip, they did not find any opal. The sandstone had mostly changed back to what it had been like before they had found the opal. A different type of material started to show. It was a soft moist dirt like grey ashes.

John pushed the dirt and then started to rip again. When he ripped through the ashy ground, Tony noticed the shape of shells on the edges of the soft sandstone. No flashes of colour could be seen. John looked around as he started to back up. Tony motioned for him to back nearly right back to where he was, out of sight of the noodlers. Tony carefully picked out one of the shells and tapped it on the pick head. A brown skin fell off to reveal the beautiful colours of opal. All of the shells were covered in a brown coating of iron stone.

Tony showed the shell to John. John turned the shell so it caught the sunlight. 'Wow, this is pretty good opal. We'll try to get it out in large lumps, and then we'll clean it up at the dugout when we get home. The dozer hid them from the prying eyes of Silvio and the pirates, as they had become referred to by the men.

It did not take long to extricate the opalised shells from their nest, as the ashy ground was very soft. John took the bucket back to the side of the cut where they had been keeping it. By this time, Silvio had crept around from the rest of the noodlers to try and see what they were up to. He walked back when he saw that they had taken the bucket back to the side of the cut. Tony sat his hat on the top of the bucket and then put a stone on top of it to stop any prying eyes.

John got back on the dozer and continued ripping the floor of the cut. Bert and Harry came down into the cut when they finished work. They had also found some opal. Harry had put the bucket inside their ute and locked the door.

'We found some really good shells today, but don't look in the bucket whilst the pirates are watching. I don't think they know. We picked them up pretty quickly and tossed them into the bucket whilst we were behind the dozer, I don't think we missed any. They were really easy to get out of the soft ground. That bloody Silvio crept down and tried to see what we were up to.'

John drove the dozer out of the cut past the noodlers and then turned back to the ute. 'Let's get back to town and have a couple of beers to wash the dust out of my throat.'

Whilst the first batch of opal was being tumbled in the concrete mixer, they had a good look at some of the shells which John and Tony had found. Bert scratched the outer coating off, some with his pocket knife. 'Look at this one, Harry.' The outer shell was only a cheap grey type of opal. There was a small piece chipped off the end of the shell, which revealed a totally different quality of opal underneath. 'Shit, I would not have known this. I thought the shell was only rubbish,' he said in awe as he passed it over to his brother. John took this shell from Harry. He got his pocket knife out of his pocket and prized the cracked end of the shell. One complete side of the solid shell came off, to reveal a completely different quality of opal underneath. The new opal shell was worth nearly ten times much as the poor one which they had seen for a start. The others had separated the shells by this time. There were eighty-five full colour shells in the pile, plus a small amount of skin shell as well. 'This is a real top find, you lucky buggers. Beats the shit out of farming, don't it? Each lot of opal was left turning slowly in the tumbler for about an hour. John was amazed to see the difference when it was finally pulled out and then tipped on to a black polythene sheet on the kitchen table. The colours danced in the bright light as if they had a life of their own. It looked as if someone had poured Metho on the stones and had set it on fire. The flames were dancing over the top of them. There were two mixers full of opals to clean, so it was a late night by the time they had finished. They had a job to concentrate from looking at the vivid colours. 'I think we'll have a day off from the field tomorrow and try to get this opal graded,' said Bert as he yawned. The opal must have had an effect on both Bert and Harry as they had forgotten to have their usual dozen cans of beer each that night.

The next day was spent cleaning the dead pieces of potch from the good opal. This was done with a pair of tile cutters. The pieces of opal were studied, and the dead pieces were cut off. Some of these pieces still had a small amount of colour. These were to be sold as potch and colour for a lesser amount. The shell material, which John and Tony had found the previous day, did not need much cleaning at all. The tumbler had cleaned all the rubbish off them, taking the coated grey opal as well.
They were top crystal opal shells.

Bert looked at the shells and the other seam opal that John and Tony had dug up in the last two weeks. 'I reckon, there's about five or six hundred thousand dollars sitting just here. And you still haven't got to the main level where you dug the material up with the drill.'

Bert and Harry had over one hundred thousand dollars' worth in their stash. 'I think we should see about selling some of this opal soon. I am getting a bit paranoid about this safe and how many people who might have keys for it,' said John.

Both John and Tony were surprised at how much the opal, which had filled all the buckets, had shrunk in volume by about a half when it was cleaned.

Bert went down to the town and phoned the opal classer to have a look at the opal, class it, and put a final price on the material. Then an opal buyer with enough resources to be able to pay what it was worth had to be found. This amount of opal was usually out of the small-time Chinese buyer's league. They would sometimes buy a large parcel, only if they could con the owners.

Two o'clock up at north-west ridge. 'We'll see the Pommy guy who classed our last lot of opal. He doesn't seem to be as big a crook as some we have tried before. There was a Greek, John, who looked at and classed our last lot and offered to buy it for fifteen thousand. We got fifty thousand instead.

They loaded the opal into the ute after lunch and headed out to the opal classer's house. Leon met them at the door of his house. 'Come on down to my classing room. The men entered the dugout room, which had the long table covered in black plastic and the assortment of chairs around the side. 'Take a pew,' offered Leon, the classer.

'Would you mind getting a round of beers out of the fridge?' he asked Tony. Tony obliged. 'Now let's see what you have got in the bags.'

'You guys have been busy.' Leon opened each bag of John and Tony's opal and carefully tipped it out on to the table-top. 'This is Fifteen Mile opal again, am I right?' They agreed. 'You've got some bloody good material here. Cripes, those shells are good.' Leon started to build little piles out of the opal, sometimes shifting a piece from one to another. It took a couple of hours to finish. He then weighed each pile, then put it into a new, clear plastic bag, and wrote the weight and a number on each bag. So many ounces, and so many penny weights. Leon then studied each bag over and over, finally writing a price per ounce and then a price for each bag number on to a sheet of paper.

'If my reckoning is right, the grand total should be six hundred and twenty five thousand dollars. You're lucky. There's a guy in town at the present time who would be very interested in this parcel. His name is Achmed Farrah. I'll give you his mobile number if you like, or would you like me to try and phone him.' Leon wrote the number down on to the piece of paper with the prices on it. 'It might be easier if you would phone him, we have to use the pay phone' added John. Leon then proceeded to class the Kelly's opal. This came to one hundred and forty thousand dollars.

'OK, I'll ring this guy for you, if you like, and tell him about the opal.' The men sat, whilst Leon rang the buyer and described the parcel of opal to him. He then asked again how to get to the dugout they were renting. Leon told the buyer the relayed directions and then hung the phone back on to its hook. 'He reckons he knows where you are. He'll see you in an hour's time.'

The men left with the opal, all bagged up into its new bags ready for the buyer. To John, this seemed like a dream. It was only a few weeks ago that the bank was going to foreclose on them and they were going to be kicked off their farm. Now if all of this came off, there would be no more worries.

The hour wait seemed to take a hell of a long time. Finally, there was a knock on the door. Harry opened it up.

He then ushered a plump very well-dressed man with a short dark beard and dark olive skin. He carried a large briefcase into the room. Achmed politely introduced himself, then sat at the table, and talked of the opal business for a few minutes. 'Now I understand you have got some special opals to show me.'

Harry turned on the large desk lamp, whilst John passed the large bag with the opal in it. Achmed opened each bag and studied each lot. 'Hmm... ah... hmm,' Achmed said as he turned some of the better opals over in his hand. John and Tony were feeling a bit ill at the time from the tension. They had heard of the stories how the Chinese buyers wanted to get everything for half its value. Achmed put the opal back in the bags. Oh shit, John thought, he's not interested. Achmed smiled, showing a large gold tooth. 'What price have you got on your opal?' asked Achmed.

'It's six hundred and twenty-five thousand dollars. That's what the classer classed it at.' John answered in a croaky voice. Achmed sat back in his chair.

'I see no point in beating around the bush, gentlemen. I will agree to that. Now there was another parcel, I understand.' Bert showed him their opal, which he agreed to buy also.

Achmed took the large briefcase he had brought with him. He opened it up on the table. On the top was a very large handgun, a large Colt 45 automatic. Under this, the case was full of money. There were packs after packs of hundred-dollar bills pulled out. 'Now, gentlemen, I would like you to count and check all of this money. I have a reputation for fair dealing in the opal business, and I do not want anyone to say that I short-changed them.'

By the time both lots of money were counted out, the bag was nearly empty.

Achmed picked up the opal in the shopping bags and bid them farewell. 'If you ever find anything special again, I will be very interested. Have you got a piece of paper and a pen? I'll write down my Adelaide phone number.' Bert found a sheet of paper and a biro. Achmed wrote the number and his name on to it. He shook all of their hands. He then walked out the door. The men followed and watched as he got into the large Mercedes and drove off.

'Holy shit, I thought I was going to faint,' said John as he walked in through the door. 'Now what will we do with all of that money. I don't really feel like leaving it in this old safe. I don't trust that mob of pirates who watch us every day.' John agreed with Tony. The size of the bundle of cash was a problem. It was about two large shoe boxes in volume.

'What if I go and get the small toolbox out of the ute? I'll put the tools in the other toolbox.' Tony went out and got the toolbox. John and Tony jammed the money into the box and then shut its lid. They then went outside and dug a hole at the back of the old laundry and buried the cash. They kept out one of the bundles of notes for fuel and expenses. It was dark, so no one could have seen the twosome secreting the cash. They rolled an old drum back over the hole and flattened the dirt out. 'We'll just jamb ours up under the dash of our ute. Ours isn't as big a stash as yours. No one comes near our ute with our dogs sitting on the back, They would eat them if they tried to open the door.'

John had a job to sleep that night. Every time he shut his eyes, he could see the flashing colours of the opal that they had been working with all day. In the morning, he grizzled to Tony about the bad sleep he had. Tony had experienced the same problem.

When they left for work, John walked past the drum which they had shifted the night before. It looked no different from the day before. There were no signs of the hole being dug.

The noodlers were still at the claim when they arrived. They had slept in; even Bert and Harry had not risen until nine o'clock.

John started the dozer, drove into the cut, and started the first rip for the day. Tony followed. The cut was about six meters deep by now. John spent a long time trying to square the walls of the cutup again. He had a devil of a job, trying to keep the walls square when they were still in the hard material higher up. Now they were in the softer sandstone material, it was a lot easier.

Back and forth again he travelled with the dozer. The cash was on Tony's mind all day to think about.

Their problems with the bank were finally over. Tony's one thought was to see the look on the manager's face when they went in and paid the mortgage off. The day was fairly uneventful with only a small amount of potch being found.

The next day, the noodlers' numbers had dwindled; the aborigines had evidently found somewhere else more profitable to noodle. Silvio and the pirate mates still remained, though. John was hoping that they would have left too. John drove the dozer down the steep ramp into the cut.

Tony followed with the bucket and tools.

During the first rip, Tony noticed that the ashy ground was starting to appear again. He scratched at it with his pick, but there was no sign of any shells. John had finished pushing the dirt and was ripping through the ashy ground for the second rip, when Tony noticed a large, round piece of material roll out of the ash. John was looking over the back of the dozer. Tony motioned for him to stop.

John climbed down off the dozer and walked back. Tony was on the ground, carefully scratching the ripped ashy ground. He had two oval objects, each nearly as big as an emu egg, lying on the ground next to him. He was just carefully prizing another out of its nest of the last hundred million years. John picked up the egg, got his pocket knife out, and scratched at the coating on the egg. Finally, he made a small hole in the coating. He then turned the knife and prized the coating. A quarter of the coating came off in one piece, to reveal beautiful black opal underneath.

John was taken aback. He nearly dropped the opal. 'Holy Christ, these must be dinosaur eggs. And black opal. What would they be worth?' John handed the egg to Tony. Tony thought that no one could have seen them behind the dozer. He held the egg up to the light to get a better look at the colours. All the colours of the rainbow flashed back and forth across the dark curved surface. Tony carefully laid the egg into the bucket.

Both of the men were engrossed with the work extricating the eggs from their nest, John looked up and noticed that Silvio had walked along the top of the cut again and was watching them with great interest. There were four eggs. All had been heavily coated so the colour could not be seen. Tony took the bucket back to the opposite wall of the cut from Silvio. He put a couple of pieces of the ashy stone on top of the eggs so Silvio could not see into the bucket.

They finished the rip and then pushed the dirt out. It was home time by now.

'We think we may have got something pretty special today,' John told Bert as they loaded the ute. 'We'll have a look when we get back home.' He motioned with his thumb to the band of pirates who were still watching. 'I reckon that the crooked little bugger saw the opal when you held it up to the sunlight.'

John carried the bucket into the dugout. He sat at the table and carefully took the first egg out of the bucket. He took a kitchen knife from near him on the table-top and scratched the rough coating on another egg. It resisted his efforts for a while until John was able to make a crack in its surface. He got the point of the knife under it and twisted the blade. About a quarter of the coating fell off in one piece, the same as the first egg had done. All of the men were dumbfounded by what they saw. 'Christ, it's solid black opal. The same as the last one,' croaked Harry. 'If the others are the same, these are worth millions.' John repeated the exercise with the other two eggs with the same result.

The men sat around the table, admiring the opalised eggs. They turned them over and over under the desk lamp. They were almost hypnotized by the array of changing colours, which flashed brilliantly across the surfaces of the eggs. There were scattered beer bottles on the table from the celebratory drinks which had accompanied their meal. John was deep in thought. 'I've got a funny feeling about that old safe. I don't trust those bloody pirates who have been watching us every day. I reckon that we should head off out of town back to the farm with the opal and money. I would feel a lot happier if I was at home with all of this large find. We can easily come back later and finish the cut.'

'We will still keep our cash up under the dash of our ute. No one would know,' said Bert.

'I wouldn't worry about the bags of potch and colour.' These had not been sold to Achmed with the parcel of opal. He was not interested in buying potch and colour. 'Any-way half of that is yours,' said John.

Tony went outside and looked around to see if there was anyone nearby. The coast was clear. He shifted the drum and then dug the cash out of its hiding place. Tony then dusted the toolbox off and brought it inside to the table.

It was just getting dark when John and Tony had finally loaded the ute.
The two-hundred litre drum on the back was still half full. This would mean that they could get home without having to fill at a service station in the middle of the night.

Tony put the toolbox full of money on the seat of the ute next to where he sat. The bag of opal eggs was put under the passenger seat. They both shook hands and thanked Bert and Harry for their change of fortune. Both men then slid into the ute, and drove off. 'Well, good luck. We'll see you when you have your millions,' chuckled Harry as they left the dugout. The men waved goodbye.

The ute was filled with fuel at the service center. 'Hell, look at the price of their fuel. It's nearly ten cents dearer than we are paying. It must be good to be a tourist not knowing the difference.' The ute was finally filled and the fuel paid for. The men drove off out of town into the dusk. It was hard driving at night because of the kangaroo problem on the roadside. The large driving light mounted in the middle of the bull bar made it a lot easier to see off the side of the road. There were a few newly run-down kangaroos on and next to the road. Occasionally, John had to swerve to miss one of the hapless animals which had been recently run over. The occasional road train with its ultra-bright lights was the only traffic on the road.

The longer that John drove, the more the shrubby bushes on the roadside looked like kangaroos. Tony had drifted off to sleep by this time. It was very tiring, trying to concentrate by now. So many things were on John's mind at the present time. The thought of seeing Helen, the farm, and especially the opal they had to sell. This did help to keep him awake.

The men reached the Kingoonya turn-off. John drove down the dirt road for a couple of kilometers and stopped. 'Right, now, sleepy head, it's your turn to drive.' Tony woke groggily, got out of the ute, and walked a short distance off the road to have a pee. The desert air was like ice, which helped to wake him properly. 'How about starting to fill the diesel tank whilst you are out there? It will wake you up.' Tony started to fill the ute from the drum, pushing the pump handle back and forth.

Driving on the dirt road was worse than the bitumen. The shadows cast by the lights were really tiring. Even with the large spotlight on, the shadows still seemed to move as the ute neared. Tony had to concentrate when he came to a cross road so he did not get lost. The road looked completely different in the dark. John had long since gone to sleep. Tony was close to sleep as he drove on. He had two frightening experiences: one with a few sheep which had camped on the road and the next was a kangaroo which had hopped across in front of him, but thankfully, it had not stopped or turned back and had kept going.

Tony was trying to keep himself awake by thinking of the opal and the farm. His mind kept wandering off. Suddenly, the whole of the road in front of the ute seemed to be filled with a huge roo. The roo had come from behind a small bush and was hopping across the road and had stopped, evidently dazzled by the bright lights of the ute. It squatted down and turned to face the bright lights coming towards it.

Tony hit the brakes and swerved, trying to miss the kangaroo, but it was too late. The kangaroo hopped the same way as Tony swerved. The ute slammed into the huge kangaroo. By this time, Tony was well off the dirt track and into the small shrubby bushes. The ute bounced wildly as it careered across the grader ridge left on the side of the dirt track. The ute then swerved madly, leaning sickeningly, almost tipping over. John sat bolt upright. 'What the hell has happened? Where the hell are we?' He slurred sleepily. The ute finally stopped.

'We've hit a bloody huge roo,' Tony informed him. He put the ute in reverse and reversed slowly back on to the road. The ute was making a grinding noise in the front as it went backwards to the road.

'Well, that's great. I think we must have busted something. Cripes, what a place to be marooned. We're a hundred kilometers from nowhere.   John and Tony both got out to inspect the damage with the torch, which lived under the seat of the ute for emergencies. John got down on his haunches and shone the torch under the ute. 'Well, thank god for that. We've still got our lights, and the radiator seems OK. No water dripping. There's no oil dripping out either. Just drive on slowly, whilst I see if I can pinpoint the noise.' John shone the torch towards where the noise was coming from and found that the front mudguard had been bent against the tyre. He was able to pull it off by hand. 'Bloody hell, that was lucky. If the diesel tank had been full, I reckon I may have rolled the ute.'   The heavy farm-built bull bar had taken the brunt of the impact on the passenger side of the vehicle. Even the driving light was still in place. The impact with the roo had bent back the bull bar almost to the bonnet. One side indicator light had been torn off in the collision.

Tony then reversed back to check the roo. It was very dead. John got out of the ute and pulled it off the road so no one else would run over it and smash their vehicle.

'Hell that was a big roo. I had a job to pull it off the road. Oh shit, smell my hands.' John was covered with the musty smell, which only a buck kangaroo can smell like. 'The old bastard must have been chasing the does around lately.' Roo's, like a lot of other animals, they always smelt a lot worse when they were in season. 'Oh double shit!' John started to scratch and squirm.   'That old buck must have had kangaroo ticks. I can feel them running around under my clothes.' Tony looked over at John. 'Just make sure you stay over your side of the seat. I got those on me one night when I was out spotlighting with a couple of mates. They nearly drove me mad.'

Tony took a lot more care, watching for the rest of the journey. Having a bad accident on these barely used roads could be very dangerous, as there may not be any cars along for a long time.

John still wriggled and scratched. It'll keep him alert at least, Tony thought. The sun was just showing the first streaks of red on the horizon as he drove up the drive to the house. They could hear the dogs barking as they pulled into the rear of the house. Helen opened the door and walked out through the back gate in her nightie and dressing gown just as the men got out of the utility. Helen yawned. 'What are you doing home?' she asked sleepily. 'I knew it was you from the way the dogs barked.'

The morning air was very crisp. A light frost lay on the ground. After the warmer climate of Coober Pedy, the men felt frozen. They hurried into the house. Helen stoked the fire back into life, tossed some more sawn wood through the grate door, and then filled the old blackened cast-iron kettle with water. Tony had brought the old toolbox into the kitchen. 'Have a look in there, Mum.' Helen lifted the lid and then carefully tipped the contents of the box out on to the table. She gasped.
How much money is there? There must be hundreds of thousands of dollars!' John sat the other bag on the table next to the money. 'That's not all. Look at these.' He carefully lifted one of the eggs which was wrapped in layers of newspaper out of the bag and undid the wrapping, leaving the egg sitting in the middle of the newsprint nest. The colours rolled over the dark base of the egg. It was spectacular even in the dull light of the kitchen. Helen's eyes widened as she looked at the black opal. Helen, as a lot of people, had never seen any really good opal before. She was fascinated with its dancing colours over the egg.

'What would that be worth?' she asked in awe 'somewhere around a million dollars, we think. There are three others.'

John had warned Helen not to touch him because of the kangaroo tick problem. He went outside and stripped down to his undies, tossing his clothes into the wash trough. John turned the hot tap on and then rummaged in the laundry cupboard for a bottle of dog shampoo which was used when the dogs had fleas. Drastic measures for drastic problems, he thought. No wonder the roo was not worried about being run over. John poured a liberal amount of shampoo on the infected clothes. Then after turning the tap off, he adjourned to the shower in the laundry, with the bottle of dog shampoo. John threw his undies in the shower cubicle and then proceeded to soap himself down with the shampoo, starting with his hair, which felt as if it was the local tick race track. He pushed his feet up and down, making sure the undies got a fair coating of the shampoo.

Tony went on to explain to Helen about the doubts they had in the old safe and also the men whom they rented the dugout from. John had another shower when he finally woke just after midday. 'I know why those bloody dogs go so crazy after we give them the flea treatment. Hell, the shampoo gets really hot on your skin.'

The men went for an inspection of the farm after lunch. Things had changed dramatically since they had left. The crops no longer looked grey; they were now a dark shade of green and had started to stool out well. Even the pasture paddocks had changed to green; the sheep now sat contentedly in the corner of the paddock, feeding every now and then. There had not been much rain but just enough to change the farm's fortune.

John rummaged through his case and found the piece of paper which
Achmed had written his Adelaide phone number down on. John phoned Achmed that evening and told him of the eggs. Achmed was amazed. He had never heard of any eggs ever being found before. There had been the occasional opal bones of some sea creatures, plus, very rarely, a few turtles had been found. He sounded amazed by the description and weight. They had been weighed on the kitchen scales. He was very interested in

purchasing such rarities. John arranged to meet him in Adelaide in two days' time at his home, where he had his office.

Helen rang the bank and made an appointment to see the manager. It was made for the next day after lunch. John was eagerly looking forward to this meeting.

The trip to town was a more joyous occasion than the last visit to the bank. How different they felt! Even the old car didn't seem to rattle as much. No more having to grovel to unpleasant people.

They entered the small bank building and told the teller that they were present. She buzzed the manager and informed him that they were waiting.

The manager evidently had another farmer in his office. The sounds of a heated argument emanated from behind the door. Finally, a red-faced man emerged from the office. 'I hope you have more luck in there,' he said, pointing his thumb in an obscene gesture towards the manager's office, knowing that the manager could still hear him. He stormed out of the door.

The manager met them with his superior smile, more like a smirk, the look of a lizard as it was about to pounce on a small beetle and gobble it up, Tony thought. He ushered them into his office and bade for them to sit down. The Lizard sat down at his desk and shuffled the wad of papers with their name on them in front of him. He leaned back in his chair and then looked up at them, over the top of his steel-rimmed glasses; the smirk seemed more obvious. The Lizard knew what John's opinion of him was. 'We still seem to have this major problem of your overdraft. You have not made any attempt to change this situation in the last four weeks. You had better start to make arrangements to sell some of your farm to recover some moneys to rectify this problem in the next week, or the bank will have no option but to place you in receivership and sell it ourselves to try to recoup the moneys you owe us.' He looked up at them with his superior sneer.

John reached over to the folder of papers in front of the Lizard and pulled them towards him. The Lizard jumped up and tried to get the papers back. 'These are the property of the bank,' he squeaked.

John started to tear the papers up. There were too many papers in this sheaf to rip through them in one go. 'I'll get the police on to you. You'll go to jail,' squeaked the Lizard once again. John reached down to the floor and picked all the papers which had dropped. He then put the torn papers back on to the desk. He stood and then leaned towards the Lizard, towering over his small frame. You know that things have not been any good on the farm for the last few years. We have been trying our hardest to get the money. We do not appreciate being bullied by a sanctimonious little arsehole like you. You should be ashamed of yourself for treating all the good people in this area the way you have. It's small wonder that someone has not thumped you for your insulting remarks that you have been making to everyone.'

The manager had not had this treatment before. The smirk disappeared from his face, to be replaced by a vicious sneer. 'I see that I cannot reason with you,' he said icily. 'The only recourse the bank has is to put your farm on the market forthwith.' 'I don't think you will do that,' said John in a matter of-fact voice. 'How much do we owe you?' John already knew this to the cent but wanted the Lizard to still think he had the upper hand. The Lizard shuffled through the torn papers. 'The sum is 74,522 dollars.' He smirked again. John pushed the torn papers aside on the desk and then lifted the bulging shopping bag on to the desktop. The Lizard cowered back in fright, evidently thinking that there must have been a gun or something else very unpleasant in the bag. John picked the bag up by one corner and tipped the contents on to the desktop. The Lizard's mouth fell open in surprise at the sight of the money. His prominent Adam's apple poked further out of his scrawny neck and moved up and down as he gulped. John had left three hundred thousand in the bag just for the effect. 'Now if you would count out what we owe you, we will get out of your office so you can have your nasty way with the next poor victim who has the misfortune to have to see you.'

The Lizard's superior attitude vanished as he set about counting the money. He had to go out and get the change for the amount owing. 'I would like a receipt now. Thank you.' The Lizard fumbled in his desk and finally produced a receipt book and hand-wrote a receipt for the amount of the debt which had just been paid. 'I think that will be all.' John bundled the rest of the money back into the bag and then led the family out into the sunshine. 'What was that they said about revenge being sweet? I feel as if I have just had a sugar cube dipped in honey in my
mouth. Wow, what a feeling!'

The rest of the day was spent paying some of the other outstanding accounts in the town. Finally, after paying another twenty-five thousand dollars, mainly to the stock firm for the stock mortgage, their slate was all square.
John took the camera into the chemist shop to have the photos put in a bag to be sent away to be printed off. Helen was very interested in seeing the design of the new tools.

'I'll never forget the look on the Lizard's face when I dropped the bag on to his desk. He must have thought it was a bomb. 'Well, I feel as if we have had a weight lifted from our shoulders,' said Helen as they drove back to the farm.

Tony got the cash and counted out fifty thousand dollars out of it. He then wrapped the remainder in plastic and then sealed it into a five-gallon paint drum, which had a tight-fitting lid. Tony picked up the drum by the steel handle and carried it over to the workshop where he found a posthole shovel. He then walked around to the machinery graveyard behind the shed and buried the drum under an old wrecked harvester right behind the workshop. When he returned to the house, he explained exactly where he had buried the drum.

Chapter thirteen

Ali's disaster

Ali was smart enough not to have employed Tom or Silvio. He would have not ever seen any opal with these two crooks mining. He would never see his share of the opal he had grubstaked them for. Zeena and Tomas had gone to Germany to live. Tomas had a beautiful home near to Cologne. Zeena sent a lot of photographs and tourist trinkets from the area. Zeena was extremely happy for the first time in her life. She would be coming back to Coober Pedy on a regular basis to visit when Tomas returned to purchase opal.

Life was good. Opal was coming out of the ground. He had a direct link to the European market with Tomas and Zeena. Martha and Ali were extremely happy. He felt as if he were very close to Peter and Heidi.

Ali received a telegram from Tomas in Germany. Evidently Zeena had been ill for the last two weeks. She could not keep her food down. Tomas had taken her to hospital where they were doing a lot of tests to try to find the cause of her problem.
He was extremely worried.

Ali told Martha when she came home from visiting Heidi. He was very worried as he and Zeena had been together through a lot of different circumstances together. Ali had never really thought her of being his mother; Gentle Sasha had been the closest thing to a mother in their short life together. Ali often had bad flashbacks to the killing of his aunt. This had bought a wave of rage whenever these happened.

When Ali and Martha retired to bed Martha very gently started to make love to Ali, This always helped to relieve him of the problems with his stress. Ali responded quickly, the lovemaking took quite a while before each of them climaxed together. In the morning Ali spoke of travelling to Germany to see Zeena. He was extremely worried for her, but was also worried about the forged passport.

The passport had been OK when getting into Australia at a small port like Cairns. But to have to leave from a large international airport like Melbourne or Sydney would be dangerous. He definitely did not want to be deported back to the Philippines. This could be disastrous in many different ways. Ali had never asked too many questions about the passport in Australia. He did not want the wrong people to find out that he had a forged passport. Did the fact that he was married to Martha who was now Australian make any difference?

He had not contacted Enrico to further the deal on the new passport.

He had been too busy making money and trying to make babies. The next day Ali visited the post office and found the time zone for where Tomas lived in Germany. He was going to phone to try and catch Tomas before he went to see Zeena at the hospital.

He sent a telegram to Tomas to ask if he would phone him in the morning Australian time. Ali sat around near to the phone. It finally rang, he got a fright. "Zeena is very ill Ali she has a cancerous tumor which will need operating on. I have been at her bedside for the last week. They doctors are going to operate tomorrow to try and remove it. The operation is going to be very dangerous as the tumor is in a bad place. I will phone you again at this time tomorrow. Ali spoke some small talk about Zeena and her affliction.

He was shocked and really did not know what to say to Tomas. Ali told Martha about the serious operation that Zeena was about to have. Ali did not leave the house that whole day, he just sat and looked out of the window, In Ali's eyes Zeena had been bulletproof because of all of the bad things that had happened to her in the last ten years.

During the day he muttered to himself. Asking himself why had this happened just when Zeena had a new happy life with Tomas. Martha tried her hardest to console him to no avail. Ali would just say why her, why not some other person.

The phone rang the next morning it was Tomas. Tomas was crying. In between sobs he told Ali that the doctors who were the best he could find had not been able to help Zeena and she had died on the operating table.   The tumor had taken over some of her vital organs and had been far larger than they thought when they had operated. Zeena had died.

Martha was standing next to Ali as he heard the news. She could vaguely hear Tomas's conversation. Ali had tears running down his face and a look of rage about him when he replaced the telephone receiver. 'Why have I tried to get ahead when some shitty thing like this happens?   I May as well have been stuck in the bloody market wheeling push carts for the stalls '. Ali left the house and went to the rear of the house block and sat in the cabin of an old wrecked truck. After a half hour Martha went to see if he was OK. Ali had tears streaming down his face.

He saw her standing with a worried look. "Go and leave me alone please." Martha returned to the house and phoned Peter and Heidi.

After a short while Peter drove to the front of the house and followed Heidi into the kitchen. Martha had tears in her eyes. Peter went to talk to Ali in the old truck. He came back with a worried look on his face. "He does not want to talk to anyone".

Martha boiled the Kettle and made some coffee for all of them. She took a cup out to Ali and left it on the off- side seat of the truck. He was staring ahead out of the old cracked window. He did not acknowledge her presence. As she left she noticed that he was drinking the coffee.

Ali did not return to the house. Before going to bed Martha walked over to the truck with a heavy blanket. Ali took it from her and mumbled 'thanks '.

Ali stayed in the truck all day and would not eat any of the food which Martha offered. Heidi had walked from her home early in the morning to be with Martha. She was worried as to what Ali may do.

He came back to the house that evening and sat at the table.

Martha offered to cook him a meal, he said he was not hungry. Later that evening Ali went to the refrigerator and got some crusty bread and some cheese. Martha went to bed later in the night. There had been no dialogue about Zeena. She felt she should not broach the subject. Ali went to the spare bedroom and slept alone.

The week passed with Ali barely eating and hardly muttering a word. Martha had missed her period and had thought that this was to do with the trauma that Ali was going through. The house had returned to some sort of normality. Ali had moved back into the bed with Martha, but there had been no suggestion of the usual love making.

For the next three weeks Ali stayed around the house. He had started to speak about the death of Zeena. He lamented the fact that he had not had the chance to be with her to comfort her during her sickness.

Martha missed another menstrual period and decided to go to the doctor just in case there was some sort of problem. She walked to the hospital to meet up with the doctor for a check-up.

Martha had a brief examination. She then had a good talk about the situation with Ali. The doctor did not think this situation had stopped her having her periods. He suggested a test for pregnancy, the test was carried out, and she had to wait for two days before the results of the test would be available.

"What happened at the doctors"." I was just feeling off colour and thought I should have a check-up". "What did he say ""he thought it was just stress from what happened to Zeena." Martha did not want to build Ali's hopes up about the fact she may be pregnant.

Ali had a phone call from one of the crooks, who evidently had just found some opal that the claim holder did not know he had lost. Ali was going to tell him he was not interested, but the greed got the better of him.

As he drove to the rough shack he resolved to make the guy pay for his loss. He knocked hard on the door. A dirty man opened the door and motioned for Ali to enter. The inside of the house smelled like dirty dogs and the aborigines who hang around the streets. He nearly gagged at the smell. Hargo went to the other room and rustled around. He returned with a dirty bag. He pulled a seat out from the table and sat. He pushed the dirty plates and mugs to the other end of the table. Ali sat down. Hargo reached behind himself and took a desk lamp from the old kitchen dresser.

The opal that he tipped on to the table top was only partially cleaned. Ali picked up pieces and studied them under the light. The opal was top quality material from the Eight Mile field. It was predominately red in colour and big chunky pieces. Ali did not weigh the parcel but estimated that there was about twenty ounces. This in the claim holder's hands would be worth seventy to eighty thousand dollars.

"What do you want Hargo". I have to get forty thousand. This is bloody good opal ". "I will give you twenty." "Shit Ali I could get better for it from Johnny the Greek crook. "Do you want to deal with Johnny ". "Stuff that rotten bastard he has robbed too many people around the town". Ok I have the cash with me" . "No I think I will keep the opal and see if I can sell it somewhere else."

"I know where you got this Hargo, this was from the Serbian mob at the Eight Mile, what if they find out it was you who moon-lighted the claim". "If you chuck another five grand in I will sell" Ali's anger had started to subside. He would have normally given thirty thousand for this parcel. "Oh, Ok Twenty Five it is" Ali took a roll of money out of his case, he then counted the money out slowly so Hargo could see the notes. Hargo was illiterate but knew enough to know if he was being cheated.   Ali packed the rest of the money and the opal into the case. "You are getting a bit tough Ali. Just as well I hate the bloody Greek".

Ali dusted himself down when he left Harjo's dirty house. The dog and other smells clung to his clothes. He did not even like having to get into the Patrol with the stench on him. He certainly did not want to go into the house smelling like he did

When he arrived home Martha opened the front door to greet him. "I will go around to the back and get undressed and have a shower in the laundry, I really stink from being in the guy's house. The smell is a mixture of dirty dogs and the street aborigines". Ali walked around the house and showered. He put his clothes into a wash trough filled with hot water and disinfectant.

Martha took a new set of clothes for him to the laundry, Ali thanked her. When he came into the kitchen Ali sidled up to Martha and gave her a hug. "I am sorry for the last few weeks; it was a hell of a shock to me, Zeena had I had not what you would call close. But we had always been together, except for the time I was in the mountains with Sasha. I always felt I was not wanted and in the way. But the time I got in trouble I realised that she did love me in her own way. We always looked out for each other. Not as a normal family".

Martha was so pleased that Ali Had finally opened up about the death of his mother." I have some news that might cheer you up. The doctor's surgery rang this morning and confirmed that I am finally pregnant". Ali stepped back and looked adoringly at Martha.' Well that is a turn up. Finally we have some good news for a change.

Have you told Peter and Heidi? " "No I just got the call while you were in the shower". Come with me we will go and visit them with the good news. I want to see their faces when you tell them" They walked out to the Patrol Martha opened the door "What have you had in here .It smells like something dead ' . 'I forgot about Hargo. You should have smelled his house." Ali went to the laundry and returned with a bucket and sponges, plus a towel, He sponged down the seats with the strong disinfectant, then wiped the steering wheel, some of the disinfectant was slopped in the rear as well. After drying the seats they set off for Peter and Heidi's house.

Heidi put her arms around Ali when she opened the door. "I am so pleased that you have finally come to see the people who care for you" Peter even hugged Ali. After they had sat and started to talk, Heidi walked to the kitchen and started to make coffee. She soon returned with a plate of her famous cake. Then turned back and then carried the coffee to the family.

"I have some news "Peter and Heidi looked worried, but noticed that Martha was smiling broadly. " Come on what is the news"..
"Do you really want to know" Martha had a mischievous smile on her face. "Of course, we do ". "You had better start knitting baby clothes. I have just found out that I am pregnant". "Wow that deserves a celebratory drink Ali What do you think" Peter went and got a half full bottle of Bergermeister, German rocket fuel from the freezer, he had two very small glasses , "Just sip this Ali it is nectar from the god's. "Ali sipped the liquor and felt a hot flush hit his

face. "Here is to the start of my new grandchild" .Peter tipped the contents of his glass down his throat, Ali did the same and nearly choked.

The next morning Ali opened his eyes. The room started to spin, he closed them and went back to sleep. When Ali woke Martha looked at him with a look of reproof. "For a man who does not drink you sure made up for it last night" Ali looked up from the bed. "I think I am going to die 'he rasped in a weak gruff voice. Martha laughed and bent down and gave him a kiss on the tip of his nose.

Ali rose at lunch time "I am never going to do that again" he said as he sat and ate a slice of bread and cheese. Martha laughed and said "we shall see".

Life slowly returned to normal. Ali was able to talk to Martha about the loss of Zeena. The growing bump in Martha's tummy was a hot subject, with both Ali and Martha's parents.

Ali found a guy who had to sell his almost new Ford Escort car to pay his mining bills before he left town. As in his usual business dealings Ali cut him back with the price wanted. He paid the man and then got the registration and other papers signed to transfer ownership. He drove the car home and tooted the horn as he drove into the yard. Martha came outside. "Here is a new baby carriage to take the baby in when it comes.' Martha was so pleased to have her own small car to drive around town in.

Peter and Ali were having a really bad run as far as the mining was concerned. They had break down after break down on the drill. They had drilled over two hundred shafts in the last three months for no opal.   The moonlighters had evidently found some new source to sell their stolen opals to. The only customers Ali had was Silvio Tom and Wombat. Evidently Hargo had put the word out about Ali ripping him off and being so grumpy.

Martha was getting used to driving the Ford escort around town shopping and visiting friends and Heidi. She was now eight months pregnant and feeling really healthy.

She had just been to the shop to do the main weekly shopping and had just reversed out into the traffic and was turning at the cross road near the Opal Inn when she had a hefty kick from the baby. Martha was distracted by this and did not see the old car with a mob of drunken lads from The Lands coming. The old car ploughed into the door of the escort pushing it into a large Stobie power pole. The escort was crushed on both sides. All of the lads in the rear of the old car jumped out then ran away.   The driver and front seat passenger had hit their heads on the front windscreen and had blood running out of their noses and ears. Martha was slumped forward, her lower body was crushed in the car from the two sided impact. The old car had been speeding at almost one hundred kilometers an hour. Martha had no chance of avoiding it. A crowd formed around the car. The ambulance arrived. All three people had been killed in the accident.

Peter and Ali had finished work and were just entering town when they came across the terrible accident. Ali recognised the car and tried to force his way through the crowd to where the CES were starting to cut the car to pieces to get Martha out. As he fought to get through a tourist who was watching said "You are too late mate they are all dead". Ali felt an icy pain in his chest, just like he had been stabbed with a frozen dagger. He screamed and fought the crowd. Peter came and gently pulled Ali Back. "She is dead Peter "Peter had not fully realised who the car had belonged to as the crowd impeded his view "Who is dead". "Martha was in the car" Peter's mouth opened to speak, His eyes rolled back into this head, he then grabbed at his chest then screamed. He screamed again then arched his back and fell to the ground. His body was convulsing then he lay still. People in the crowd noticed this and made way for a ambulance officer to come to Peter's aid. The man checked Peters pulse then looked into his eyes. He turned to Ali "I really do not know what to say Ali but Peter has evidently had a massive heart attack and has died. Ali felt the world spinning around him. He fell over backwards and blacked out.

Ali woke in the hospital. The room was in semi darkness, he shut his eyes and thought of how he was where he was. He felt as if he had just had the worst nightmare he had ever experienced. He closed his eyes. He then tried to wake himself to prove it was not real. He fell back into I fitful sleep. He could see in his dreams a loving Martha and his friend Peter looking down at him and smiling.

The rattle and crash of the morning shift of the hospital finally woke him. A tearful Heidi was sitting next to the bed and holding his hand. Ali looked at her and realised the nightmare was reality. His beautiful mother to be Martha and Peter had indeed died the day before. "Oh Ali what has happened to us. Our whole world has gone away and left us alone" She started to sob convulsively.

Ali squeezed her hand. His thoughts were on who, or what had caused fate to do this to him and Heidi. His
life had returned to some sort of normality as it had done in the Philippines with his loving Aunt Sasha. He felt a wave of extreme anger at the losses he had incurred over the last five years

Ali Left the hospital the next day He was going to make the world pay for his loss.

The funeral was to be five days later. Ali had moved into Heidi's house since he had left the hospital. he could not face the house where he and Martha used to have the baby making competitions and all of the loving   times they had.

The funeral was a large affair with a lot of the local people attending. Even the crooks and moonlighters which Ali had his clandestine deals with were in attendance. Most of them had at least had a wash and wore clean clothes. After the funeral there was a wake held in the town hall. Ali asked Heidi to come and help clean out Martha's clothes and trinkets, especially the baby clothes and crib.

They spoke about Peter and Martha as they worked. Both had tears running down their faces as they worked to fill the boxes. The clothes and baby goods were taken to St Vincent De Paul's to be given to the needy.

Silvio and Tom came to the house. Al had moved back the day after he and Heidi had done the cleaning out. Tom had been to a bulldozer cut during the night and had climbed under the bulldozer which had been parked on the half dug out seam of opal. He had worked by lamplight until early morning and had a large parcel of good opal. Silvio and Tom discussed a new prospect for getting some good opal. Some farmers from Kimba had just started to find good opal with a bulldozer next to where he and Tom had moon-lighted the good opal a few months before. They had been noodling the bulldozer dump.

Chapter fourteen

Selling the Eggs

John rang a man he knew at Cleve who owned and chartered a light aircraft. John chartered him to fly them to Adelaide the next day.

They drove the old car from the farm to the Kimba airfield and sat in the car, waiting for the plane to appear. Soon after they arrived, the small plane could be seen circling ready to land. The pilot Peter Schubert got out and helped pack their luggage into the rear of the plane. 'I hear that you had a run-in with your friendly bank manager,' he said with a laugh.
News travels fast in the bush. This news had travelled to the next town.

'Yes, revenge is sure sweet. We had a lucky find at Coober Pedy and were able to pay the little twerp what we owed the bank.' John put the bag of opal on the wing of the plane and opened it. 'Have a look at these.' Peter looked into the bag as John unwrapped one of the eggs. The colour flooded out of the bag as the egg caught the sunshine. 'Shit, what would that be worth?' asked Peter in a reverent voice. ''We are about to find out from a guy in Adelaide.

The three got into the light aircraft with the pilot for the trip to Adelaide. The pilot got into his seat. John sat next to him. 'I wish you luck in the city with the opal,' he said just before he started the plane's motor. The opal had been wrapped up again in the tissue paper and then a newspaper and put back into the sports bag. Helen had packed a few clothes for the trip. 'Just think, girl, no more money worries. You can have a shopping day in the city for the next week.'

Helen was uncomfortable about flying in the small aircraft. She had never flown before. Both John and Tony had flown with Peter,

who owned the plane, which they were travelling in now.   The
plane taxied across the bumpy airstrip prior to take-off. Helen had a
large lump in her throat. She was not happy about this flying racket
at all. Finally, she settled down and even started to enjoy the trip,
looking out of the window and marvelling at the scene which was
passing underneath them.
The plane landed bumpily at the Parafield light aircraft airport.
Even though she had started to enjoy the flight, Helen's knuckles
were still white from having her hands clasped tightly around the
edge of the seat all the way over.

   This was only Helen's second time in the city. The last time was
when she was a teenager with her parents. She had come over to
see an eye specialist then, for treatment for a lazy eye. The trip then
was only from the bus station to North Adelaide for the specialist
visit and then straight back on to the bus for Kimba. Helen was
amazed at the mansions they passed in the cab on the way out to
Achmed's home. The leafy tree-lined streets were also different to
what Helen had imagined the city to be like. Achmed's house really
impressed her,the high wrought-iron fence and gates and then the
beautiful bungalow-styled home inside them. The roses and lawn
were neatly manicured.

   Tony had told the cab driver to toot the horn three times to have
the gate opened. These had been the instructions which Achmed
had given them. The heavy gates opened slowly to allow them
entry to the circular driveway, which led to the front of the home.
The edge of the circular drive was bordered with lovely rose
bushes; all the roses had beautiful pastel-coloured blooms.

   When they had alighted from the cab, the back gates shut, whilst
the ones in front of the cab opened. Achmed walked out of the
house. 'Welcome, good people, to my home. Would you please
follow me inside?' They walked on to the tiled veranda and then
through the heavy oak doors in the doorway, which had multi-
colored lead light windows on each side. The lead light threw a
scatter of colour through the inside of the large lounge room. This
reminded John of the recent opal finds. They entered the room.
Helen was amazed at the inside of the house. The expensive

furnishings were only something that she had seen in magazines. Such opulence was beyond her wildest dreams.

Achmed's wife, a pretty, small, olive-skinned woman walked out of the large kitchen. 'This is my wife, Fatima.' John introduced himself, Helen, and Tony. Fatima asked if they would like some coffee before they got down to business. They spent around twenty minutes making small talk, whilst Fatima served the coffee. The coffee was served in tiny cups and was extremely strong, and the home-made sweet biscuits were so delicate in flavor. Helen was almost too afraid to sit on the furniture.

'Would you like to stay and talk to Fatima whilst we men look at the opal?' offered Achmed. Helen would have rather watched the opal being sold but felt that good manners dictated that she stay and talk to Achmed's wife.

The men followed Achmed through the house to the rear. They were confronted by a large steel door, which had a heavy lock on it. Achmed opened the door with the keys from a key chain, which was attached to his belt, and then entered the room. John and Tony followed. There was some opal-cutting machinery next to one wall, whilst almost all the other wall consisted of a huge safe. This safe was a far cry from the one in the old dugout at Coober Pedy. This one looked almost new. There was a huge desk. A window on the other wall was covered by thick steel bars.
Achmed walked around the desk and sat in the heavily padded chair.

'I am so excited. I want to see this opal to see if it is as good as you say.' John put the bag on to the desk and opened the top. He carefully lifted one of the eggs out of the bag. John then proceeded to remove the wrapping. Achmed turned on the desk lamp. John placed the first egg in front of Achmed. Achmed's eyebrows arched. 'My god, this is even better than I thought it may be.' He turned the egg in the light, fascinated by the colour changes which took place. 'Are all the others the same?' he croaked, his voice full of emotion. John proceeded to undo the rest from their wrapping. Achmed was amazed.

Achmed pulled out a drawer on the desk, took out a set of opal scales, and then set them up on the desk. He put one of the four eggs into the dish of the scales and weighed it. Achmed repeated this gesture with the other three eggs and then added the total weight of the eggs together. 'Those kitchen scales are not too bad. The weights are almost the same.' Achmed was deep in thought. He picked up each egg and turned it over and over. 'This is very unusual to have so much opal almost the same. They are almost identical.' Achmed leaned back in the chair, deep in thought. 'I am willing to offer you $800,000 each for these eggs. That is 3.2 million dollars for all of them. Are you interested?' John felt a little faint at the thought of all the money. 'Yes, we are definitely keen to sell,' he finally said when his wits had returned.

Achmed got up from his chair and walked around the desk to John and
Tony. He shook them both by the hand. Achmed put the eggs back into the paper and then the bag and then walked over to the large safe. With his back to the men, he proceeded to punch the combination into the door. Achmed then turned the lock and opened the large safe door. It opened with a hiss of rushing air.

Achmed removed a large leather case from the safe. The large leather case was placed on to the desk. Then Achmed put the eggs into the safe, leaving its door open. John had noticed that there had appeared to be drawers and more drawers full of material in the safe.

The case was opened, and the neatly packed money lifted out and counted by both parties. When the figure was finally reached, Achmed tipped the remaining money from the case and then replaced it with the counted notes. 'I think that completes our deal, gentlemen. I hope you are satisfied. Would you like me to phone a cab for you?' John agreed. 'What about accommodation? Are you staying in the city?' John had not thought of this as his mind had only been on selling the opal.

Achmed rang the Sheraton Hotel and booked a room for Helen, John, and Tony. 'You must have a bit of luxury for you and your wife.' Then he called the cab.

During the trip back to the city, Helen recounted the tour of the garden that Fatima had taken her on. The beautiful roses, shrubs, and lawns had really impressed her. 'Well, darling, after all of your hard work and going without, it looks as if it's finally your turn to enjoy life.
You will be able to have a proper garden too.'

The cab pulled into the hotel driveway, and as in the movies, a doorman opened the cab door for them. John felt as if the hotel staff would look down on the dilapidated luggage and their clothes. Being waited on at the hotel in the elegant surrounds was a change from their normal frugal lifestyle. The next morning, John gave Tony some cash from the bag of money they had brought from the farm. Tony was going off to buy himself a new utility, a thing he had only dreamt of a few weeks ago.

After a hearty breakfast in their room, John and Helen went down to the hotel office and retrieved the suitcase full of money and booked a cab to pick them up. They waited for the cab in the foyer of the hotel, worrying about the suitcase full of money at their feet. They told the cab driver to take them to the nearest large bank.

The cab pulled in, and John paid, as Helen alighted with the heavy suitcase. John walked over to information counter and asked the woman where they could see about leaving something in a safety deposit box. The only times they had seen this done before was in the movies on the television. The whole routine was similar to what they had seen. They had been directed to a teller who had them sign and pay for the box. Then they were ushered into the bowels of the bank through security doors to the deposit area. John had obtained some bags from the teller. They unlocked the large steel door of the box and withdrew the drawer. Helen opened the case and started to transfer the money from the case into the bags. John neatly stacked these into the drawer of the deposit box.

Finally, he closed the heavy drawer and locked it with the key which had been provided. They walked from the bank with the now-empty case and hailed a cab to take them back to the hotel.

John looked through the phone book in the room and found a list of patent attorneys. He rang one of the numbers and spoke to the attorney for about ten minutes regarding the new tool they had designed. A time was made to visit the firm the next day. The attorney's office was not far from the hotel. So they had a map drawn by one of the counter staff to show the way. They were ushered into a large office and met two men. They explained a lot about the patenting process, where to file patents, and what countries they should file in. The main point was a search to find if there was a similar type of tool already patented. Dargo, the main attorney, looked at the photographs, sent them to be copied, and then started an account for the cost of the patent search. He commented that he had never seen a tool patent like this before. The meeting was over, and the pair walked back to the hotel .

Chapter fifteen

The opal robbery

Silvio Tom and Wombat walked down on to the floor of the cut where Tony had found the opal eggs earlier in the day. Silvio had seen a brilliant flash of colour over a black background— the unmistakable colours of top black opal. The men had a scratch around but could not find any opal. 'Hey, look at this.' Wombat held up a piece of skin, the poor-quality grey opal filled with sand, which Tony had prized off the first egg he had found.   'It looks as if it had an egg in it,' said Tom as he carefully turned the skin over in his hand. 'Have you ever heard of an opal egg? He asked the other two. They both shook their heads. 'Must have come off a big shell.' 'No, I haven't seen any shells this shape before. It looks more like a big eggshell,' said Silvio.

The men walked out of the cut and drove back to town from noodling. They drove along the main street through the town past the Council Depot and then stopped outside a small, Besser brick house, which was set well back on a large fenced block, which was on the outskirts of the town. There was a sign 'Opal Buyer' nailed to the door by one nail; the sign swung in the wind. The house was surrounded by the usual old, wrecked mining machinery.

Silvio got out of the ute, walked up, and banged on the door. The door opened slightly, and a man peeped out through the crack. The young man who looked out would really have qualified for the title of a pirate. The thin man of Philippine appearance had a large scar on his left cheek, which caused his left eye to be permanently half closed. This was the result of a fight he had before coming to Australia. He did not fight his own fights now. He was too wise for that now. He had other people do his dirty work for him.
The man opened the door further and waved for them to enter. 'Come on, hurry up,' he said grumpily. The man scratched at the large scar on his face. He usually did this when he was annoyed at something or someone. It was as if scratching the scar reminded

him of the time he had acquired it.. He was known as the Dragon. Over the last three years, the Dragon had been the mastermind behind a lot of the robberies and murders in the town. He was smart enough not to be directly involved in the crimes. He usually had other people do his dirty work whilst he always reaped the lion's share of the reward. The Dragon usually bought the opal which had been moonlighted or stolen by any other means.

Belying the image of the small brick house, this man was extremely wealthy.

'Hey, boss, you know those farmers we told you about the other day at the Fifteen Mile. I saw them dig a big bit of black opal out about an hour ago. There may have been more. They put a lot of stuff in the bucket. Here have a look at this.' Silvio handed the outer piece from the egg to the Dragon. 'Hmm, where did this come from?' Silvio explained about the opal again. 'I think this came off the opal they found.' 'What do you want me to do about it?' said the Dragon in a high, raspy voice. He scratched at the scar on his face again. 'We reckon they go out nearly every night to the pub with the old cockies they are staying with in your dugout. Let us have the keys to the safe. We'll pinch the opal and any money they have got tonight.'

The Dragon agreed to this simple plan. It sounded very easy. He left and went into the bedroom of the shack and came out with two keys joined together. 'Don't open the front door with this one. Kick the door in. It's not very strong. Then use the safe key and get the opal. Make it look like a proper robbery. I know of at least two other people in town who have got keys for the safe, so it would be hard to prove who broke in, unless you are stupid and leave your fingerprints all over the place or get caught in the act. Wear the gloves like I have told you before. Here take these.' The Dragon reached into one of the kitchen drawers and got some thin surgical gloves out of a packet. He handed these to Silvio.

The men drove off from the Dragon's house and went to the hotel to wait until it was properly dark.

The trio drove the old ute from the pub and then the Italian Club looking for the farmers. Bert and Harry were at the Italian Club. Their ute was parked outside. John and Tony's ute was nowhere to be seen.

'Where are those other bastards? They always go to drink together.

Bloody bastards.'

They then drove up through the old water reserve, then around the back of the hill above, and behind where the dugout was and then with an effort in the half dark, climbed to the top in the moonlight. The top of the hill was very rocky, covered in round stones, which, if a person was not careful, would shoot out from under his feet. 'You see them fellers anywhere?' asked Wombat. 'No. You had better climb down and have a look,' said Silvio. 'Bugger you, it's bloody dark. I'll fall down the cliff and break my neck.' 'What about you Tom?' 'Get stuffed.' Tom was no surer of making the descent unharmed as was Wombat. Amongst the rocks, there were small shrubby plants, every one of them having prickles, some were very nasty, having thin spines about a centimeter long, which, when got into the skin, usually broke off and took a lot of getting out.

"I can't see the ute there. Why don't we drive around to the front of the dugout?' 'What and leave our tracks, you dopey prick, and probably get caught if someone comes back. There is no other way out?' The men walked back to the ute. 'All right, get the tyre levers out of the ute. We'll all go down and have a look.'

The first couple of steps over the side of the steep cliff face caused Tom to slip. He clutched madly for something to stop himself from sliding to the bottom. He managed to grab one of the shrubs. It was one of the worst prickly ones he could have chosen. 'Bugger,' he mumbled and then let go. Then he rolled into Wombat, knocking him over also. They both rolled to the bottom.

'Clumsy bastards. Have you still got the tyre levers?' 'Yes, of course, I have.' Silvio had a hessian potato bag with him so they could carry the spoils. 'You two stay out of sight.' Tom and Wombat waited in the shadows cast by the half moonlight, whilst Silvio knocked lightly on the door. He knocked again. No one answered. The nearest dugout was around the corner of the cliff some fifty meters away, out of sight. 'Come on, down here, and give me a hand.' The men quietly sidled up next to him. 'These pricks must be out visiting someone. Here put these gloves on.' Tom and Silvio rolled the rubber gloves on to their hands. Tom had some extra trouble getting the gloves over the ends of the spines stuck into his fingers. 'Dopey bugger,' mumbled Silvio. 'Hurry up. If anyone had answered the door, I was going to tell that we had

broken down. Right prize the door opened. You stay out here and keep watch,
Wombat. Let me know if you see any lights coming and looked down on to the dugout's small yard, which was just visible.   The old door was easily prized open. The dry, rotten door jamb splintered easily, allowing the door to be opened. The two men slipped inside. Silvio handed a small torch to Tom. 'Don't shine it towards the door. One of the neighbors may see you.
Everything OK out there?' he called softly to Wombat.   'No one coming yet,' called back Wombat. Tom shone the torch, whilst Silvio opened the old safe. It squealed as it usually did as the door was opened. Tom had the thin surgical gloves on. 'Here shine the light on these bags. Let's have a look.'   'There are lights coming along the road,' called Wombat softly through the doorway. 'Bugger! Here, you hold the bag open, whilst I put all these bags into it.'

The job was soon finished. Silvio shut the safe again. They ran out of the door. The lights were getting closer. 'Quick, let's hurry up.' They ran around the side of the hill so the ute lights wouldn't pick them up. They then scrabbled up the side of the steep hill, losing a lot of skin as they went.

They watched the Kelly's old ute pull in front of the dugout. The two dogs, which seemed to live on the tray, barked as they stopped. Bert and Harry got out. Harry was just going to open the door, when he saw the broken door jamb. 'Hey Bert, some prick's been here and broken in.' The two men rushed inside. The dogs followed behind them.   The three men stood puffing at the side of the ute. 'Jesus, that was close. We had better drive away without the lights.' By this time, their eyes had become accustomed to the dark. They drove off slowly in the dark.   'Lucky the bloody moon was up a bit,' said Wombat as the ute crawled slowly along the road. 'Bloody lucky the old coots didn't catch us,' added Silvio.

The men drove back through the town and stopped outside the Dragon's house.   Silvio banged on the Dragon's door. 'Oi, open up. It's us.' The Dragon opened the door slowly and peered out through the crack.   'Don't make so much noise,' he hissed. 'I thought it might have been the cops looking for you,' he said as he opened the door fully to let them in. 'Hurry up. I don't want the neighbors seeing you here.'

The men entered the house, blinking at the bright light. 'Those old bloody cockies came home early. We nearly got caught inside the dugout. We couldn't see the others anywhere. Well, let's see what you have got,' hissed the Dragon. Silvio carefully took the bags out of the sugar bag and laid them on the table. The Dragon opened the first bag. 'Well, you didn't do any good with this bag, you useless turds. It's only potch and colour.' The rest of the bags were opened on to the table. 'Well, that was a good night's haul, you useless bludgers, about three thousand dollars' worth. Not three million,' said the Dragon sarcastically.
Silvio was angry.

'The rotten bastards, I have seen them take a lot of opal out of the claim in the last three weeks. That's right, isn't it, you blokes?' The other men nodded their heads in assent. 'There's not even any blasted money. We heard they sold some good opal to the Arab for a lot of money.' 'Useless pricks!' The Dragon shook his head. 'Them old buggers were even getting
opal. We saw them sort through the bucket when they came out of the shaft.'

'Well, you had better tick off home and let me think about this. I just hope for your sakes the cops don't come around,' said the Dragon sarcastically.

'Those crooked bastards must have hidden the opals somewhere else.
Christ, don't anyone trust anyone around here anymore?' grumbled Silvio.

They drove home to the grotty dugout they shared. 'You may not have seen the opal they dug out yesterday, but you saw what they were getting on the other days. What about what we and the abos noodled in their dump? There was some pretty good opal there.'

The next morning, they went out to the claim to noodle again, mainly to check if John and Tony were working. The dozer was not working. The men kept on noodling until finally Bert and Harry emerged from the shaft. Wombat sidled over to them. 'Where the dozer driver and the boy is, boss?' he asked. 'They had to go home to shear the sheep,' lied Harry.

'They get some pretty good opal?' angled Wombat. 'Nah, only a little bit,' said Bert. 'Why?' Wombat just shook his head and then walked back to the pirates.

'Them cunts have gone home. That's what them old buggers said he pirates got into their ute and drove off. 'I reckon they're the arseholes who broke in last night. I'd bet my balls on it. I bet they were happy to find our potch and colour instead of the opal and cash.'

'Hey, boss, what you find out about the opal?' Silvio had told him about the farmers going back home. 'I ask around today. That Achmed, he was up here the other day. The rumor was that he bought a lot of opals from some broken-down farmers.' 'Hey, maybe you're not such a dumb prick after all, Silvio. You heard the story right.' Silvio felt privileged. This was as close to a compliment that he had ever got from the Dragon. 'I told you we noodled some bloody good opal from the dump. That's the stuff we showed you the other day. The stuff you bought off us.' The Dragon scratched at the large scar on his cheek and thought for a while. 'I reckon those pricks may have found something pretty good like you said. I have been thinking all day. There may be a way we get plenty of money if this is true.' The Dragon sat down at the table. He motioned for the others to sit. The Dragon thought for a while. 'I want you guys to go down to Adelaide and pinch a car each. One of you is to keep watch on the Parafield airport, the one the little planes use out by Gawler. There are only two opal buyers who would be able to buy a big parcel if it is as big as you say, in Adelaide. All the others in South Australia wouldn't have enough money. The farmers have already dealt with Achmed. I think they would deal with him again. I want you to watch both houses. I'll find the addresses of both of them.' The Dragon rummaged around in a large roll-top desk, which sat next to the rusty safe. He finally found the address of both of the buyers. The Dragon took a small cash box out of the desk and put it on to the table. The Dragon then pulled the top of the desk down and locked it with one of the keys on a chain looped to his belt. He then got an old Adelaide street directory and found the right page for each address and circled each one with a marker pen. He then counted out seven hundred dollars from the cash box and then handed the money to Silvio.   The Dragon went to the fridge and got three beers for the men. He was evidently planning as he did so. 'If those farmers take the opal to the city as I think they will and sell it to the buyer, I bet he doesn't keep it long. If he sells it soon, he would probably double his money. That's the time to hit him. Pinch the opal and the buyer's money. That would be a lot more than the cockies get. It would be a lot better and easier than trying to rob those miserable farmers.

The Dragon let the men have one of his cars to take to the city, a ten-year-old Holden Commodore station sedan. 'Park this one out of town. Hide it if possible, and pinch three others to do the work with. I don't want my car used in this robbery. Understand?' All three nodded in assent. 'I don't want the cops chasing after me. Understand? If you involve me in any way in this, I will stitch you up. You won't want to chase the women any more. I'll have your nuts. I will feed them to Dog' They each nodded their heads again.

As the men walked out the door of the house, the Dragon followed and handed Silvio the keys to the Commodore wagon. He then added,
'Take your old ute with you. I don't want it left around my place.'

The men took the Dragon's car back to their camp as well as their ute. The Dragon certainly didn't want the ute left at his place to incriminate him if the men were caught conducting the robbery.

Silvio felt very cocky as he drove the late-model station wagon down the road towards their dugout. 'Hey, what do you think of this car? She a bit better than the old ute, hey. If we do a good job on this one, we will all be able to have a good car. The boss said he would look after us if we did OK. Hey, and maybe we can get some mining gear of our own. Money would buy us anything, maybe even a woman each.' The three were not classified, even by Coober Pedy standards as very eligible bachelors. The only women who would have anything at all to do with them were a couple of the really down-and-out old women. This was usually paid for with a couple of casks of wine.

The men had been warned by the Dragon to keep off the booze. As they had left and the Dragon had handed them the seven hundred dollars, he told them again, 'If you bastards stuff this job, or my car, I will have your nuts off and feed them to my dog.' The Dragon had given them three sets of number plates from wrecks around town. When they had stolen the cars, they would have to change the plates.

The men stopped at the local hotel and bought a carton of beer with some of the Dragon's money to see them out on the trip down south. It was around dusk when the men neared Adelaide. They stopped at a small pub at Lower Light, a small hamlet just before Port Wakefield. There were only a half dozen houses scattered around the pub and very little street lighting. Wombat was sent to check the cars over. There was a battered fifteen-year-old Holden parked in an inconspicuous spot, not far from the hotel. It had its keys left in the ignition with the window down. Wombat looked around carefully, then undid the door quietly and slid into the seat, started the motor, and drove off.
No one noticed the car leaving.
It was dark by now with a half-moon just rising. Silvio stole another car at Port Wakefield, a Valiant ute. Now where to hide the Dragon's car ?. Silvio remembered that closer to the city around Virginia, there was a lot of tall artichoke thistles growing on some of the side roads near the market gardening areas. They checked two roads out in the headlights before they finally found a good hiding place.

They drove about a kilometer from the main road and then turned down a disused track. The track was ideal as the artichoke thistles were taller than the car. The Dragon's car was left in the thistles. 'Why do I get all the shitty jobs?' moaned Wombat as he walked back to the stolen car from the Dragon's vehicle. 'I've got these bloody thistle spines stuck into my legs and hands.'
'Stop grizzling and get in. Just think how rich you'll be if this plan works,' growled Silvio.
The third car, another Holden was stolen from the car park of another hotel in the outskirts of the city. The men then found a deserted area near the Wingfield rubbish dump and changed the

plates, using the headlights of one of the other cars to work by. They sure knew they were near to the dump because of the strong smell. The men then drove off and found a cheap motel to stay the night.

They each booked a separate room at the run-down motel. They carried their clothes into their room and then went to Silvio's room for a conference.

The men studied the street directory maps the Dragon had given them with the homes of the two opal buyers clearly marked on the pages the Dragon had copied out of the street directory book. 'Walk down and get us a pizza.' Silvio tossed a fifty dollar bill from their stash to Tom. Tom walked out to walk the short distance down the street to the pizza parlour.   Next morning, they met again in Silvio's room. Wombat was given a map and sent out to Toorak Gardens to keep watch on the Aussie opal buyer's house, whilst Silvio went to Urrbrae to watch Achmed's home. Tom was to watch the terminal where the small planes land at the Parafield airport. Each man had the phone numbers of the other two written down on to a piece of paper.

The men had taken some food with them so they didn't have to leave their positions. The plan was to change cars every day so the people in the streets would not get suspicious.

John Tony and Helen had arrived at Parafield airport on a light plane and had transferred their bags to a waiting taxi. The taxi roared off from the airport, heading for the city. Tom followed a couple of car lengths behind. The taxi was only halfway along Main North road, heading towards the city when Tom got caught behind a red light and sat and watched the taxi speed off. Tom rang Silvio with the news. Silvio realised that keeping up with a taxi in the city would have been almost impossible. Most taxi drivers drove like racing drivers.

Silvio was parked a few doors down the tree-lined street from Achmed's beautiful bungalow-styled home.
He took note. The house was set back from the road behind a manicured garden of roses and shrubs. There was a high fence along the roadway, which had a tall ornate wrought-iron gate at each end, which led on to the road from the half circular driveway,

which led to the front veranda of the house. Silvio was very envious of the house.

The taxi pulled up in front of the gate and tooted its horn three times. The gate opened by remote control and let the taxi inside. Silvio noticed that the gate took around three minutes to finally close after the taxi had entered.

Achmed came out of the house and met the Nickols as they alighted from the taxi. They followed him inside the house. After the people had got out of the taxi and had just gone inside, the gate at the other end of the driveway opened so the taxi could leave. The taxi duly drove out. After an hour and a half, another taxi tooted at the gate, which opened to admit it. The gate took a similar time to close. The Nickols family emerged, carrying a small suitcase instead of the sport bag they had entered with. The taxi left through the other gate, which was evidently operated by a remote control in the house.

The Dragon was informed of the day's events from a call from a pay phone near the motel. His only concern was to have thought the Nichole's had got away with all the money they had. To have tried anything with them would have jeopardized the rest of the operation.
The Dragon did not like missing out on anything.

Silvio had noted the next day that Achmed's wife left in the morning with three children to evidently take them to school. He was working on the fact that she also picked them up every evening, as she also went out around school leaving time and returned with three children Right. Let's have a night out on the town. I would like to see if I can find a woman for a bit of company,' said Wombat. They all agreed as there was not much likelihood of the buyer turning up for a few days.

The men caught a taxi into the city and were dropped off in Hindley Street. They went into the first rough-looking night club they could see. The night club was filled with patrons of a similar ilk to the pirates. There were also a group of bikies was at one end of the bar. A tired-looking stripper gyrated on a small stage near the bar, waggling her floppy boobs at the patrons. Silvio was looking around and checking the women out. He liked the look of one of the bikies women sitting next to the bar. She would give him the eye every now and then. Silvio thought his luck had changed. He stood up and walked over, then sidled up to this woman, and made a lewd remark softly in her ear. The woman ran her hand up Silvio's leg. 'Come on, big boy,' she said, 'let's see what you have got.' Silvio stood up in front of the woman. The next thing he knew was that someone had reached from behind between his legs and had him by the testicles. Silvio craned his neck around. A huge bearded man had him in his grip.

'I'll show you what he has got, Mavis.' The bikie squeezed harder. Silvio thought his testicles were going to burst. He tried to stand higher to get away from the man. All this he did made things hurt even more. 'Right, mate, I am going to let you go.' The bikie squeezed harder. 'If I look like I'm going to have any more trouble from you or your mates, my buddies and I will thump all three of you. We enjoy thumping people, especially arseholes like you.' Silvio felt the pressure on his testicles released. He dropped to the floor with pain.

The men hurriedly left the club and walked further down the street to another strip joint. Silvio was treading very lightly and was not making any sudden movements. This place was a real dive, tailored just right for the trio. They, finally, with the help of some of the Dragon's money, found three women who would talk to them. Silvio still sat very tenderly on his bar stool. He kept buying the women drinks. Finally, they caught three cabs to take them back to the motel.

Silvio held his head in his hands. 'Shit, my head hurts. You bloody rotten cows, why didn't you leave?' He sat down heavily. Then because of his sore testicles, he rose quickly and then adjusted himself carefully back on the chair. 'Shit, that woman you brought back, Wombat, I've never seen one uglier in my life.' Wombat scowled at Silvio through his bloodshot eyes.

'She was bloody good in bed. They say the ugly ones are always the best ones. They may not get another bloke for a long time, so it's worth trying harder with the one you have got.' Wombat sat down at the table and held his head in his hands. 'You weren't too bloody proud anyway, Silvio. The one you had was pretty ugly too. She looked pretty good last night when I was pissed. I got a shock when I woke up and found her in my bed. I asked her where she had come from. She said I asked her to marry her last night. Shush, I must have been full of booze. Fancy waking up and finding her next to you for the rest of your life, yuk.' This was real boys talk as any of the women at the motel last night were better than the women the men were usually used to entertaining. Tom wandered in from his room. 'Where are the girls?' They started to bay at the moon, so we sent them home.'

'It's funny how ugly women look good when you're pissed,' said Tom. 'What about the bikie bird. She looked pretty good, hey, Silvio.' The two men laughed. 'Not as good as her bloody man, though. I thought he was a big hairy gorilla from the zoo.' The recollection of the large bearded bikie made Silvio's problems seem to hurt even more.

They left the ute and one car at the motel, and all travelled out to Urrbrae and watched Achmed's house. After a short while, they drove off and came into the street from the other end and parked the car so it didn't look so obvious. The car had dark tinted windows, which was an advantage, because unless you were to look closely, they were not easily seen sitting in the car. They got used to the normal visitors and the children being delivered to and from school each day.

On the third day, a taxi pulled up outside the house and tooted three times. It was half past three in the afternoon. The gate opened, and the taxi pulled in front of the house. A fat, well-dressed man was met by Achmed. He was carrying a large suitcase. He ushered him inside. 'The woman has just left to pick the kids up. We'll follow her in when she comes back. Here put these ski masks and gloves on.' Silvio handed the masks to each of the men. The masks had been bought at a nearby supermarket two days before. They had bought the gloves with them.

After a half an hour, the large silve- grey Mercedes drove up to the gate and then waited until it opened. The car, driven by Fatima, slowly drove into the driveway.

Silvio started the car, roared the motor up on the old Holden, sped down the road, and then turned through the gateway just before the gates shut. Fatima was still in the Mercedes talking to the three children, when the old Holden swerved on the driveway, then drove over the rose bushes on to the lawn, and then slid to a

stop next to the Mercedes. Silvio leapt out of the car, ran to the Mercedes, and pointed a revolver at
Fatima through the glass of the closed window.

'Open the bloody door, or I'll shoot,' he said quietly but menacingly. He waved the revolver towards the children in the rear of the car. Fatima, fearing for her and the children's life, obliged. Silvio reached into the car and grabbed the keys from the dash. Then having second thoughts, he poked the key back in the ignition and broke it off in the off position. This would save being chased by the Mercedes. 'Right, you kids stay here or mum might get shot. Climb over the back with the kids.'

Fatima awkwardly climbed through the car and sat with the children, trying to be ladylike with her dress even in these circumstances. The children now were very scared and were whimpering. 'You,' Silvio pointed to Wombat, 'you sit in the front of the car and keep an eye on the woman and the kids. If the woman gives you any trouble, shoot one of the kids.' Wombat climbed into the front of the car and sat facing the rear. He waved the small automatic pistol menacingly at the family in the rear of the car. He did not say a word.

Silvio and Tom headed for the front door of the house and ran inside. They ran quietly down the hallway to the rear of the house, checking visually in each room with an open door for other people. The opal room door was different from the rest as it was heavily reinforced. Silvio could hear low voices coming from this room.

Silvio and Tom then burst through the partly opened door of the opal room. The two men sitting at the desk were startled. Achmed made a move to reach under his desk. 'I wouldn't do that if I were you,' snarled Silvio. 'Shift your chair back from the desk, we have your wife and kids outside, and if anything happens to us, our mate will shoot them.' Achmed immediately put his hands up on the desk. The other man, a very plump man with a red florid face, was nearly having a heart attack. On the desk in front of them were the four eggs laying on a nest of newspaper and tissue. Shit, Silvio thought, we've hit the jackpot, as he saw what good opal the eggs were. 'Right put those back into the bag.' He waved the gun towards the four eggs. Achmed leaned forward and reluctantly replaced the eggs into the bag.

Silvio handed the bag to Tom who held it in his other hand to the sawn-off shotgun he carried.

'Right, put the suitcase on the desk.' The florid man was trying to push the case under the desk slowly with his foot. 'Hurry up, or I'll blow your nuts off.' Silvio pointed the revolver down towards the man's crotch. This had the desired effect. The man reached down and lifted the heavy case with difficulty on to the desktop. 'Open it,' snarled Silvio. The man slowly reached into his pocket and produced some keys. He undid the case and opened the lid. The case was brim-full of hundred-dollar bills, all neat in their banded bundles. 'Right, shut the case.' The man shut the case and locked it again.

Silvio turned to Achmed. He pointed the revolver at his head. 'Right now, open the bloody safe, Arab. Open it, or you will never see your wife and kids again.' Achmed was very shaken at this remark.

I cannot open the safe unless I phone the security company,' he lied. 'Then I have to wait an hour before the lock will open. If there is a change from my regular habits, they send a security van around straight away to check.'

Silvio thought for a second. He did not know if this was true or not, but he did not want to waste time or take any extra chances. He pulled the phone cord from the wall. 'Get your mobile phones' He held his hand out and waved the gun menacingly at the two. Both men reached into their pockets and deposited their mobiles on to the desk. Silvio put the phones on the floor and stamped on them with the heel of his shoe.

Finally, he was satisfied with the job.

Silvio and Tom backed out of the door with the opal and cash.

As he shut the door, Silvio said loudly to Tom, 'You wait for ten minutes. If that door opens, blast whoever comes out with the twelve-gauge shotgun.'

'Right, let's get the hell out of here,' Silvio whispered to Tom as they crept down the hallway.

'How do you open the gate?' snarled Silvio to Fatima as she and the children cowered in the rear seat of the car. 'That button on top of the dash,' she said. She was so frightened that she had trouble speaking.

Silvio pushed the button, and the large gate slid slowly open.

The bags were tossed into the old Holden, closely followed by the men. The car was started, and Silvio spun its wheels madly on the green lawn, burning a track into the green grass, and then swerved past the Mercedes, mowing down some more of Fatima's roses as it sped off the lawn and then spinning its wheels in the gravel of the driveway. It tossed loose stones back all over the Mercedes. The car then careered off through the gates and then on to the road.

Silvio slowed when they were around two hundred meters past the house, then turned, and merged with the traffic on the main road, heading back to the city

Silvio was carefully driving through the city. They had their seat belts on, trying to at least look legal. After driving in the bush for so long, driving in the city was a real chore. The Coober Pedy traffic was bad, but the two—and three-lane highways were totally different. The weaving impatient drivers were a real worry. Silvio was getting really rattled, driving through the city. There were at least four times they nearly sideswiped a car in the lane next to them. Silvio was yelling and making obscene gestures to the opposing drivers.

Finally, the heavy city traffic started to thin out as they neared the outskirts of the city. The car was dumped in a side street in Gepps Cross, next to where the other Holden and Valiant ute had been left. The area where they dumped the cars was a pretty rough area with run-down houses, some with wrecked cars or rubbish in their yards. Silvio left the windows of the cars down and the keys in the ignition of the cars, hoping that they would soon disappear from the scene. The men transferred the bags and the case from the getaway vehicle. Then they searched to see if there was anything which could associate them to the car left inside.

The other Holden was exchanged for it. The whole robbery operation had only taken about ten minutes, but time had seemed to almost stand still and felt like hours in real terms.

'Did you see that red-faced old turd? I reckon he nearly crapped himself when we went into the office,' said Tom. Silvio laughed. 'The other Arab wasn't much better. I wonder if they are still waiting for us to leave the outside of his office.' They slowly drove off towards Virginia where the Dragon's car was hidden.
'How much do you think this lot is worth?' asked Wombat?
'That suitcase is full of hundred-dollar bills,' said Silvio. 'Must be millions. No doubt about that young Dragon. The little prick knows where to get a dollar.'

They turned off the main road and then drove off down the weed-infested road to where the Dragon's station wagon was hidden in the thistle patch. Wombat again had the job of climbing through the tall thistles to reverse the Dragon's vehicle out of the road where it had been hidden. The Holden was then driven down the track by Tom to replace the Dragon's car. Tom also didn't like wading back through the tall thistles either. The men were now able to take their sweaty gloves off and drive away.

'What about getting some booze to celebrate?' said Wombat? 'Bloody good idea,' said Tom. They drove into the drive-in bottle shop at the Virginia hotel.
'What will it be, blokes?' asked the burly barman in the bottle shop. 'A couple of cartons of Vic Bitter stubbies and a bottle of brandy,' yelled Tom. 'I'll have a bottle of Bundaberg rum,' said Wombat.
'And a bottle of Scotch whisky, too, mates. Make it a good one,' added Silvio. They paid for the booze and drove to the petrol station and filled with petrol ready for the long trip home.

There was a phone box, outside of the Post office, not far from the petrol station. Silvio stopped the car and went inside he got a stout mailing box and some bubble wrap. Wombat and Tom had headed for a small scrubby tree not far from the Post office and were having a pee. He went outside to the car and took one of the black opal eggs and placed it inside the wrap then carefully put it into the box. He took it back into the Post office and wrote his name on the box and mailed to himself at Coober Pedy. He then went outside and phoned the Dragon with the news of the successful robbery. By this time Tom and Wombat had returned to the car.

'I think the little bastard even sounded a bit pleased with us. That's a bit of a change.'

The men headed back on to the main road towards Coober Pedy. 'Well, here's mud in yer eye.' Silvio opened the first stubby of beer and passed it on to Tom and then one to Wombat and then opened one for himself.

They all joined him in a toast to the successful heist.

It was dark when they arrived at Port Augusta. The beer supply was fairly depleted by now. The car was refilled with petrol, which would be enough for the rest of the journey.

Get another beer?' asked Tom as they sat waiting for the car to be filled with fuel. Wombat shuffled around, rattling through the empties. 'I think they have all gone.' "Well, what do we want first, rum, brandy, or Scotch?'

'Let's start on the Scotch first. Here, Silvio, you have your first drink.'

The bottle was passed over the back of the seat to the men in the front. The cork was dropped on to the floor of the car started to drive out of the service station towards the bridge over the top of Spencer Gulf. 'Let's call into the pub over the bridge and get another couple of cartons of beer,' asked Wombat. They drove across the bridge, then turned left into the bottle shop of the hotel, and bought two more cartons of VB cans.

The beer and the odd Scotch were starting to take an effect on the men. They had just passed Pimba and were heading towards Glendambo. The men had made a lot of plans as to what they would do with their share of the loot.

'What the hell are we taking this back to the bloody Dragon for?' Tom said with a slurred bravado.

'Why don't we keep it all for ourselves?' Wombat chipped in. 'Yair, bugger, the Dragon.'

'You remember little Jimmy, the Greek, who was blown up last year. Everyone thought he had an accident. That wasn't an accident like everyone said. That was one of the Dragon's paybacks.' 'How do you know?' Silvio answered, 'Well, who did you think set the charges down his mine? I did, you silly bugger.' A few minutes later, Silvio said, 'you remember that Serbian George who got shot up in Queensland. That guy who pinched the opals off the Dragon. That was one of the Dragon's jobs too. He pinched some opal off the Dragon and got killed for his trouble. There's been quite a few. The little bugger is worse than the Mafia. He never does the jobs himself. I certainly wouldn't want to cross him. There are a lot of people who have been dropped down old mineshafts with a bit of dirt thrown on top of them at the Dragon's orders. We'll do all right out of this
lot. Just take my word for it. The
Dragon said he would give us 20 per cent.'

The car sped on through the night. They were past Glendambo. Both Tom and Wombat were fast asleep, snoring loudly. Silvio was having a real problem staying awake. The car was travelling from one side of the road to the other. When the car swerved, the bottles strewn through the car would clang together and wake Silvio for a short while.

When the wheels hit the dirt next to the bitumen, Silvio would wake and continue driving. He knew it would be no sense asking one of the others to drive as they were a lot drunker than he was.

Silvio was about halfway between Glendambo and Coober Pedy. He had just had a fright. He had gone to sleep and had woken up when the car was well off the road. Luckily there was a flat area alongside of the road, so the only damage was a few stones rattling under the car

.

Silvio got out into the cool night air to try and wake him up. He had a pee and then got back into the car. Both Tom and Wombat were snoring loudly. Silvio thought very seriously of sleeping in the car but knew the Dragon would be waiting for them. He restarted the car and drove off down the road again.   There was a slight turn in the road. Silvio had finally succumbed and was fast asleep. The car drove straight on. There was an embankment around two meters high, where the road had been cut into the earth to keep it levelled. The car drove up the bank at 130 kilometers an hour. Silvio woke up with a start, but there was nothing he could do. The car was airborne, about three meters in the air.

The car travelled around twenty meters before it hit the sandy dirt. This caused the front of the car to dig into the ground. This made it roll end for end. The car finally came to rest on its wheels, after tumbling at least six times. Wombat had been thrown out of the back window and was lying on the ground with his head cocked to the side at an odd angle. The suitcase full of money was also thrown out and lay on the ground with the lid torn open. There was a trail of packages of money leading back towards the car.

Meanwhile, the bag of eggs had tumbled around in the car and had also come open. One of the eggs had broken and was lying on the floor of the car. Both Silvio and Tom were still alive but unconscious. They had been wearing their seat belts.

The middle of the broken egg had been full of some slimy, moist goo. There was also something else. A skinny segmented worm was beginning to stir on the floor of the car. This worm was nearly a meter long but very thin. The creature thrashed back and forth on the floor, trying to extricate itself from the bottles and other rubbish on the floor of the car.

The creature's skin was beginning to harden and dry out, very much the same as a butterfly as it dried its wings. It opened its ghastly mouth and convulsed as it took its first breath of air. The creature lay and breathed for a short while. It exercised its mouth, which was surrounded by rows of sharp serrated teeth. Almost like shark teeth.

Silvio, by this time, had regained consciousness and was beginning to moan softly. He tried to move but was pinned by the car seat, which was wedged forward from the bend in the middle of the car. The car was bent like a banana from the accident. The roof was crinkled like an accordion. He tried a little harder to shift himself, but it was impossible. He scraped his foot on the floor, trying to get some purchase to move himself. He was firmly pinned by the seat and the steering wheel. The creature wriggled along the floor of the car towards the faint movement and waited for it to start again.

Silvio again shifted his leg slightly. The creature moved up to Silvio's foot and prized itself off the floor, entering his blood-soaked trouser leg. Silvio felt the movement and tried to shake his leg but was too constricted to do so. His first thought was of a snake, but snakes did not usually slither around at night. The creature moved purposefully towards Silvio's warm crotch. It stopped moving for a few seconds and then struck. The animal's row of needle-like teeth with sharp serrated edges grabbed a mouthful of Silvio's testicles and bit. Silvio screamed in terror at the pain. He tried harder to move away. The creature kept eating, finally devouring Silvio's testicles, and then it worked its way inside his body, pulsating and chewing as it went.

For a while, Silvio's loud screams could be heard, but these slowly abated as the creature chewed further into his body. The skinny worm was getting fatter with every mouthful of Silvio it took. Finally, it started to pass castings out of its rear end, which was not inside Silvio's body yet, and was leaving a sticky trail of droppings in its wake.

Tom had regained consciousness by now. He had been roused by Silvio's loud screaming. Tom tried to move also, but like Silvio, he was also pinned to his seat.

Silvio's cries had long since died down. He was past caring what happened to his lifeless body. The creature kept eating and moving forward. Finally, the creature emerged from Silvio's lifeless body under his ribs. The creature was caught for a while in Silvio's clothes. Its razor-sharp teeth gnawed their way through the layers of clothing, allowing it once more to emerge into the cool night air in the car. The hood light of the car had come on when the doors were buckled. The creature lay on the floor of the car bathed in the dim light. It was a ghastly sight with the clotted blood and dirt from the floor of the car stuck to its wet body. Tom sat pinned to the dash of the car, softly moaning from the pain of a broken leg and arm. He could hear a slurping sound and had the feeling that something was in the car and moving around. He thought it might have been a lizard or some other small animal.

Suddenly there was a thrashing of something large in the car cabin. Tom was a bit frightened. There was an unusual smell in the car. He wondered what it was. Tom tried to squirm around to see what was in the car but could not see the floor of the car as he was pinned hard against the dash. He felt something brush against his leg. He wriggled his leg to get it to go away, but the creature was determined to moved further up his leg. Suddenly, the creature struck at his groin and bit into his trousers. It thrashed about and then got another mouthful. This one was latched on to Tom's penis. It bit hard. Tom found out why Silvio had been screaming. He let out a blood-curdling scream and tried to writhe out of the creature's way. The creature was far stronger now and was not going to be denied its feast by Tom's feeble moving. It bit in further and kept eating.

Tom was dead and getting cold when the first rays of dawn were just starting to appear. The creature extricated itself from his lifeless body, having satisfied itself with its gory feast.

The creature was two meters long now and as thick as a man's arm. It finally cleared itself from Tom's trousers and then slithered out of the open door of the wrecked car. When it fell on to the ground, it lay and purged itself of some of its gory feast and then burrowed down under the car, swinging its head to move the earth so it could get under the car, which was half buried in the warm sand. The creature then went to sleep.

A light breeze heralded the first rays of dawn. As the sky lit up with more light, a wedge-tailed eagle and some crows circled well above the scene of the accident.

After some time, two of the gamer crows landed next to Wombat and strutted warily around his body. They would come closer, take a furtive peck at his clothes, and then scuttle back away. Then they strutted for a few seconds to see if everything was safe and then move back. The crows were not too sure of a human lying on the ground. Finally, the greediest of the pair fluttered on to Wombat's chest and waited to see if there was any reaction. The crow was getting gamer. Finally, it pecked at his sightless eye. As there was no sign of movement, the other crow joined in, pecking with their sharp beaks at the eyes. The wedge-tailed eagle landed and tried to hunt the crows away from their feast. They cawed loudly in defiance at the intrusion and flapped their wings. Finally, some more crows and three more eagles landed and squabbled over the carcass. The Wedge Tailed eagles had torn the skin off Wombat's bare body, which was not covered by his clothes.

Chapter sixteen

A lucky find

Some trucks were starting to move along the main road by now—heavy transports and road trains, who had obviously been camped in the parking bays off the side of the road for the night. The signs of the car travelling up the embankment were quite visible. There were also quite a few other such signs along the road, usually left by city people in four-wheel drives, who were trying to impress their passengers with their ability to drive up a steep incline in the outback, or someone who ran off the road, trying to dodge a kangaroo.

An old, hand-painted Volkswagen Kombi was kangarooing along the road, its engine revving up and then cutting out. It stopped alongside of the embankment, and then a young bearded man got out and proceeded to open the rear engine compartment.

A girl got out of the passenger side and joined him. 'What do you think the problem is?' she asked. 'I think the drum of fuel we put in this morning may have had water in it.' He pointed to the glass filter bowl on the fuel pump. 'There it is. The water was visible in the glass inspection bowl under the fuel pump. I'll have to drain the tank and carburetor.' The filter bowl was taken off and then cleaned out with a piece of rag, and then the carburetor was drained.

Droplets of water balled up and ran off the petrol from the carburetor. The man then got an ice cream container and slid under the bus and, with a small shifting spanner, undid the drain plug on the fuel tank and drained some petrol out of the tank into the container. He put the bung back in the bottom of the tank, having some petrol run down his arm as he did so.

He looked into the container. This also had a small amount of water in it, balled up under the petrol. The petrol was carefully tipped off the top of the water back into a plastic funnel into the fuel tank.

Charlie and Karen had met at university and had decided to travel north, chasing the warmer weather, trying to get some work as they travelled. They had bought the old Kombi from some friends, not realising that the motor was not too sound. This was typical. Charlie always believed the hard-luck stories people told him. He had been told that the motor on the Kombi had just been done up.

Charlie got in the Kombi, started the motor, and then revved it up. 'Right, let's go,' he called to Karen ''Wait a second. I think I'll go and squat behind a bush,' said the girl. 'OK, but don't take all day.' Karen walked up the embankment to have some privacy from the passing traffic. She called to Charlie, 'Quick, come up here and have a look.' 'What do you want now? We should keep going,' yelled back Charlie. Karen was annoyed. 'Just bloody hell, come here.' Charlie knew from the tone of her voice that she meant what she said. He got out of the van and followed her tracks up the bank.

'Bloody hell! What a mess!' Charlie surveyed the accident scene. The crows and eagles were still arguing over Wombat's body. Charlie did not realise what the crows and eagles were fighting about until they had hopped away and then flown off before alighting a short distance away. Charlie felt a hot wave of nausea envelop him. He crouched down and spewed on the ground. 'Don't come over here,' he warned Karen. 'There's a dead body here. It's not too good. The birds have been at it.' Karen backed off and watched from the sidelines.

Charlie peered through the car window from a distance and checked to see if anyone was breathing. Both Silvio and Tom were obviously dead.

They were a horrible blue grey colour. 'There are two guys in here too. Both are dead.'

Charlie was starting to walk back to Karen when he spotted the suitcase. He could not believe what he saw. 'Hey, Karen, come over here, quickly. I want a hand.' Karen had no intention of coming anywhere near the station wagon.

'I'm not coming near the car. Let's go and flag a car down on the road and let them cope with this mess.' Charlie was starting to pick the wads of money up and toss them into the case.

'Hey, have a look at this then.' He tossed one of the bundles of hundred-dollar bills the twenty meters over to where Karen stood. She walked to where it had landed and picked it up. Karen lost her fear of the dead and quickly came over. She started to help Charlie stack the money back into the case, occasionally glancing towards the remains of Wombat's body.

'There must be hundreds of thousands here,' she said. 'I wonder what these blokes were doing with all of this money.' Charlie thought for a second. 'it's probably drug money. Anyhow I don't think they will need it anymore.'

They finished stacking the cash into the case and were lucky enough to be able to do the catches up again. 'Right, let's get the hell out of here.' Charlie swung the heavy case on to his shoulder and walked to the edge of the embankment to make sure no one was coming along the roads. The coast was clear.

They stumbled down the steep embankment and walked over to the van. Karen slid the side door of the Kombi open, and then Charlie tossed the heavy suitcase inside.

They both climbed in. Charlie turned the key. The old Kombi spluttered to life. Charlie turned back on to the road. Pebbles shot out from the rear tyres as he gunned the sick old motor to try and leave the scene in a hurry. They headed back on the road towards Coober Pedy. 'What do you think we should do with the money?' asked Karen. 'Well, I don't think those blokes will need it any more. No one went past whilst we were stopped, did they? ''No, I didn't hear anyone.' 'So I think it's finders keepers,' said Charlie.

'How much do you think might be in the case?' asked Karen? Charlie thought for a while. 'There must be hundreds of thousands of dollars there.'

The old car bonnet signs on the highway proclaimed that they were getting closer to town. Karen did not know what to think about the money. She had heard all the stories about the drug dealers and had seen a lot of films about the Mafia. 'Do you think we should hand the money into the police. 'Do you really think they would hand it on?' Charlie was a cynic when it came to honesty and all things good, especially the police. He had been involved in a few arguments with the police over having some marijuana a few years back. 'I reckon we should keep the money and get as far away from here as we can.'

The old Kombi was at its best speed at eighty kilometers an hour. Anything over this caused the motor to rattle in protest. It was hard keeping the speed down to this, especially with the suitcase of cash on board, but one thing was for sure. Charlie didn't want the motor to give up on them at this time.

Above the furthest hill on the horizon, there appeared a large cross. Both Charlie and Karen were mystified by this until they finally got closer and saw the tower of the wind generator, which helped augment the power supply for the town. Charlie drove down through the town, then turned in to a BP service station, and filled with fuel and filled the old motor with oil, plus bought two more five-liter tins for the trip to Alice. Then they drove off to the supermarket to get some supplies. 'I really think we should ring the cops and tell them about the accident,' said Karen. 'Just don't tell them who you are. I'll get the groceries whilst you do the phone call.' Charlie reluctantly agreed. Karen walked along the wall of the supermarket to a group of phone boxes and then rang the police. She described the accident and the position of the vehicle in relation to the road, stating that they would be able to see the skid marks from the road. Karen declined the police man's request for her name. She just said that she did not want to be involved and hung up.

Charlie had bought some cooked chicken as well as the groceries.
'Right, let's get out of town.' He got into the van. Karen slid her bottom into the van and shut the door. The old van trundled back through the town, followed by a cloud of white smoke, and then back on to the main Alice Springs road.
Charlie worked out that they had enough fuel to get to Kulgera, which was over the border. They passed Cadney Park and then Marla. The van was protesting loudly. If he exceeded seventy kilometers an hour speed limit, it had placed on itself the motor would start to rattle. They camped the night just over the border in a deserted parking bay.

Chapter seventeen

Egg and money hunt

Three police officers left the Coober Pedy police station for the thirty-kilometer trip down to the accident site. The Toyota Land Cruiser troop carrier was equipped for most emergencies that they were likely to encounter in their travels through the rough bush country in the outback.

The trip only took half an hour. The scars on the roadside embankment were easily seen. Officer Sean Murphy drove well past the scene of the accident, then put the vehicle in four-wheel drive, and drove up the embankment to check whether this was the right place.

Upon seeing the wrecked car half buried in the sand, Sean then turned back towards the wrecked car and then parked about thirty meters away.

It was now one thirty in the afternoon.

The flock of crows and eagles reluctantly flew off Wombat's body and alighted nearby, crowing their disapproval at being once more disturbed. One greedy wedge-tailed eagle was loath to leave. Finally, as Sean neared the bird, it reluctantly hopped off and flapped its wings across the sandy ground, finally becoming air borne.

It did not matter how many times constable Tony Arbon had seen the results of these accidents; it always turned his stomach. Some people, such as Sergeant Sean Murphy, did not ever seem to be affected by the gore of the roadside carnage. Vince Jones was a little like Tony at these accidents; he did not like having to pick and scrape up the pieces of someone's misfortune and have to put it into a body bag.

Vince bent down, picked a branch of a tree up, and tossed it at the greedy eagle who was trying to sneak back for another mouthful of the hapless Wombat's body. He was almost tempted to take his pistol out and open up on the greedy birds.   'You blokes work around the edges from around here and see if you can find any tracks. Be careful where you step,' said Sean. 'I'll go down to the road and have a look.'

Vince and Tony worked their way around the edges of the accident, taking notice of the tracks which seemed to lead to one central place about twenty meters from the rear of the station wagon. They then studied the drag marks where the suitcase had been picked up. Sean walked back up the embankment. 'There are some tracks down there. I'll get the camera. I think the vehicle tracks look like old Kombi van tyre marks. They are the only vehicles on the road now with the old-fashioned skinny tyres with the wiggly tread pattern, unless it was a very old car.' Sean thought for a while. 'It looks as if it was broken down from the look of the scuff marks. Someone was lying down under the vehicle.' Sean went back and took some photos of the roadside, noting that most of the footprints and scuff marks were at the rear of the vehicle.

This substantiated his theory of a rear engine Kombi van. He then climbed back up the bank and re-joined the other two officers. 'I am pretty sure it was a Kombi. Someone has been lying under the rear of the vehicle working on it.' Tony and Vince pointed out the shoe marks in the soft red sand, near the wrecked car. 'Looks like a bloke and a girl by the size of the shoe prints,' he surmised.

The trio then approached the wreck and looked inside. Oh shit, thought Tony. He walked back and nearly spewed. Sean was a lot more interested. 'Hey, come back and have a look. I reckon that's that bloody crooked Silvio bastard. That means the other one is probably Tom, and the other poor bastard the birds have eaten would most likely be that Wombat cove.' Sean walked over to Wombat's body and pulled the shirt down from where the birds had feasted.

'His skin is a bit dark like Wombat's.' Sean thought for a while. Then he walked back to the wrecked station wagon. 'I wonder what those crooked buggers were doing this far out of town. It's not their car. Why were they coming from down south?'

Sean noticed the bloodied sport bag lying on the floor. He bent to pick it up by its corner. One of the remaining eggs rolled out on to the floor of the car. 'Jesus Christ, have a look at this.' He reached into his pocket and got out a pair of rubber gloves which he put on, and then he picked the egg up. The other two looked reverently in awe at the black opal. 'What the hell would this be worth?' asked

Tony as he studied the opal egg. ' I think a hell of a lot of money. More than you'll earn in the next few years.'

Tony went back to the four-wheel drive and called the station. He described the egg to the police radio operator, who informed him that they had just got a memo on these from Adelaide. The eggs had been stolen the day before. There were four. There was meant to be a large case full of money too.

A tow truck and car trailer would be sent down to move the wreck and would be dispatched straight away to the scene of the accident

The other egg and some of the broken one was recovered. The men looked for the other egg. They could not find it. It was not lying near the car. Maybe it was underneath the car. The two solid eggs and the broken pieces were put back into the bag, then carried, and placed in the rear of the police wagon. There was no sign of the case full of money.
They deduced that this might have been the scuff marks and all the tracks near the wreck.

The inside of the station wagon really smelled bad. The officers could not work out what the round bloody balls were on the floor of the vehicle were. These had a particular bad odour. Sean pushed one of these with a short twig he had picked up off the ground. He was puzzled. These things looked like minced meat.
Skinless sausages crossed his mind.

Sean studied Silvio and Tom's bodies. 'I don't think these two were killed straight away in the accident. Look at all the blood coming out of their crotch areas. Plus the scuff marks in the blood on the floor. It looks as if someone or something has pulled their nuts out whilst they were stuck in the car, and they bled to death.' Even Sean shuddered at the thought of what might have happened.

'There weren't any tracks we could see really close to the car that we noticed,' said Tony. 'Yes, you're right about that, unless they brushed them out with something.'

The men walked away from the scene and sat, waiting under a small scrubby tree for the tow truck to arrive. Tony would still have liked to have had a shot at some of the eagles which were still perched in another small shrubby tree twenty meters away, as well as the crows, which were squatting on the ground some distance away, still cawing in protest, wanting to get back to their feast of Wombat.

Sean was puzzled about the accident. Things did not seem to add up. The three crooks pinching the opal were plausible but definitely out of the threesome's league. They were well-known night shifters and claim robbers, cunning and sneaky, certainly not intelligent. Plus the tracks up the embankment meant that they had come from down south. It was plain to see. There were no skid marks prior to the car mounting the embankment, so another vehicle being involved was unlikely. The main reason for the accident was plain to see. Empty bottles and beer cans littered the ground around the station wagon, as well as some still being inside the car. They were mainly VB beer bottles and cans.

What happened to the men in the car, causing them to be killed so violently? And what happened to the case full of money? Where was the other egg? Also why did the people who reported the accident not want to be known?

After a half an hour, the Ford F250 four-wheel drive ute and a car trailer drove up the bank on the same tracks the police had used. Harry Francis, a part-time miner, tow truck owner, and a bit shifty on the side, got out of the big four-wheel drive. 'Everything OK for me to pick the car up?'

'Yes, I don't think we are going to learn any more around here,' said Sean. His off-sider,

Willie Brooks, got out to guide him back to the wreck. Willie was one of the town barflies. Willie was noted for his assignations with the young aboriginal girls in town, usually much to their parents' disgust. Willie was also one of the main suspected marijuana suppliers in town. He was a rough-looking character with a host of tattoos and a greasy black ponytail.

Willie guided Harry as he reversed the car trailer into the front of the car, and then Harry got out, undid the bolt on the front of the trailer, and then tipped the trailer so the rear dropped down under the half-buried front wheels of the wreck. He then walked over to the car to have a quick look. When he saw the bodies, he turned back and bent over to tie his shoelace up. He did not really care who was in the station wagon.

He had seen plenty of accidents on this road before. Willie ran the cable out from the winch on the front of the trailer near the drawbar and then hooked the cable on to the front of the wreck. He had to scratch under the half-buried car to find the towing hook.

'What's that inside?' Willie asked Sean. 'That's a couple of mates of yours. I don't think they mind you shifting the car too much.' Wombat, by this time, had been slipped into a body bag, and the bag was zipped up.

'Wait a bout; we'll put the other guy in the back.' The three police manhandled Wombat's corpse over and slid it into the rear of the station wagon through the broken rear window. Everything had now been photographed for evidence.

Willie was a bit reticent about getting too close to the bodies in the car. Harry put the winch in gear and tightened the steel cable. The winch squealed in protest because the station wagon was half buried. 'Come on,' Harry chided to Willie. 'Give it a bloody push, you lazy cow. They won't hurt you now.' Willie half-heartedly pushed the station wagon to get it to move.

Harry started the electric winch going again. The car's body finally started to move. 'Give it another push to get it straight.' Willie was still not too keen to get too close to the dead men in the car but went over and pushed the side of the car so the front mudguard would not catch on the side of the trailer.

Under the car, the sleeping creature was rudely awakened from its sleep by the moving car. It was not happy. It coiled back, then sprang out from under the car, and struck up at the poor hapless Willie's crotch. The razor-sharp teeth dug in through the material of Willie's jeans, taking most of Willie's penis and the front of his trousers in one bite. It was wrapped around his leg, trying to get more purchase so it could bury its head deeper inside Willie.

Willie dropped to the ground, screaming. Sean, who was the closest to Willie, thought he must have got his hand caught. He ran around the side of the car to get a better look at what had happened. Sean noticed the writhing creature and thought Willie may have been attacked by a snake. He grabbed the writhing creature by the tail end and pulled it from Willie's leg. The creature spun quickly back, curling back over itself, latched on to Sean's other hand, and bit.

Sean reeled back and shook the creature off. Blood streamed from his hand from where the two middle fingers had been. The creature spun on the ground and tried to return under the slowly moving car. Tony had pulled his gun by now. He fired at the creature, hitting its flaccid body. He fired again and again, until the gun was empty, and the creature finally stopped writhing. It lay limp on the ground.

Harry had not seen the start of the action as the slowly rising car had partly obscured the scene from him. He stopped the winch when he heard the shots. Harry stood back. Then upon seeing the creature on the ground, he leaped nimbly on to the ute tray. 'What in the blazes is that thing?' he yelled over the noise of the idling ute.

Sean had pulled his handkerchief out of his pocket and had wrapped his hand in it. He was evidently in shock. He had started to shake uncontrollably. Willie lay moaning next to the car. 'What the hell has happened?' yelled Harry from the safety of the tray of the ute. He had been concentrating on getting the vehicle into the trailer and was more intent in watching the mangled front wheels so they didn't get caught on the trailer frame. 'What the hell is that?' he yelled again, pointing to the creature on the ground.

Tony and Vince were reluctant to even come near the creature on the ground in case it was not dead. Tony got the tree branch, which he had thrown at the eagle earlier, and prodded the creature with it.

Vince called the station on the radio and requested an ambulance for Willie and Sean. Vince, in the meantime, had removed the first-aid box from the police car and had started to treat Sean's hand with disinfectant and then applied a new bandage. The men then cut away Willie's trousers and inspected the damage. Most of Willie's penis had been bitten off and was bleeding profusely. His testicles were also a bloody mess. Vince wound a bandage around the remains of Willie's testicles and the remains of his penis and stuck it the best he could with sticky tape. Both Willie and Sean were given a dose of morphine for the pain.

'What do you think we should do with this?' He pointed at the creature lying still on the ground and shuddered at the thought of what it had just done. The men looked around. 'What if we tip all the tools out of the big toolbox in the back of Harry's ute and we put it in there? Yuk, I can hardly bear to look at the horrible thing. I certainly don't want it in the police van on the way back home.' Harry agreed to let them put the creature in the toolbox. They stacked the tools in the front of the ute tray behind the cab.

Tony laid the toolbox on its side, next to the creature, then pushed the creature with the stick, and started to push it into the now-empty toolbox, which was laid on its side. He quickly tipped the toolbox back, then shut the lid, and put the padlock through the catch. The toolbox was carried on to the tray of the Ford tow truck.

The ambulance arrived twenty minutes later. The ambulance attendants looked at Willie's bitten-off privates after they had removed the temporary bandage. They applied some more disinfectant and gave him a tetanus needle. The whole area of the wound was re-bandaged, ready for the trip back to Coober Pedy. Willie was carefully put on to a stretcher. He had been given more morphine but was still moaning loudly. 'What in the world did that?' asked the female ambulance officer. 'It looks as if he was caught in some sort of mincing machine.' Vince tried to explain about the giant worm to the lady and finally reluctantly showed her and her assistant the creature in the toolbox on the ute. A discussion ensued as to what this creature was. Afterwards no one was any wiser. Vince could hardly bear to look at the creature. He was pleased to finally shut the toolbox again.

The bandage on Sean's hand was undone and rechecked, and more disinfectant applied and then bound up again. Sean, who was still able to walk, climbed shakily up into the rear of the ambulance, next to Willie. The rear door of the ambulance was pulled shut by the St John's officer. The ambulance drove back down the embankment and then headed back towards Coober Pedy with its light's flashing and siren wailing.

'How about giving me a hand to finish loading the car?' asked Harry. 'I'm not standing anywhere near the bloody car. There might be another one of those bloody things under it.' said Vince, keeping his distance. It was late afternoon now, and the light was just starting to fade. The shadows were lengthening Harry climbed on to the ute tray, then leaned over, and started the winch, sitting on the tray of the ute whilst he worked the controls. The car slowly pulled straight; then with an effort, it was towed up the tray of the trailer, the buckled wheels with their flat tyres grinding in protest on the steel floor of the trailer, finally causing the pivoted trailer to overbalance and drop down so the catch could be bolted shut. Harry still didn't climb down. He had the bolt in his pocket. He reached in, got the bolt, put the bolt through the hole, and then screwed the nut on with his fingers.

Harry still didn't climb right down on to the ground. He slid around the side of the ute tray, opened the door, and then lowered himself into the seat. The creature had brought out the sensation of fear in Harry. This was a sensation Harry was not used to. He always prided himself that he was afraid of very few things. Evidently, the creature had gone to the top of his list.

The men were anxious to leave the accident site. Neither of them wanted to be around the area after the sun went down. In case, the creature had not been alone. Having seen what its sharp teeth could do and its favourite method of attack made the men's crotch feel very itchy.

Harry unhooked the trailer at the police station, then helped lift the toolbox down on to the ground, and then headed for his home. He was more than happy to leave the car, toolbox, and bodies for the police and hospital staff to deal with. What else might have been lurking in the wrecked car?

Harry went straight home, which was unusual for him. Harry usually detoured into the pub on the way home each night unless he could not afford it. Harry walked through the door of his shack. His wife saw the look on his face. 'What happened to you?' she asked, knowing something strange had happened.

He recounted the story of the attack of the creature on Willie and the police officer. 'I don't think poor Willie will be chasing the young aboriginal girls around anymore. The bloody thing bit his dick off,' he shuddered as he thought about the afternoon's events. This was unusual as Harry thought he had seen just about everything, everywhere; it took a lot to move him.

'Here, have a look at this.' Harry reached into his pocket and pulled an oval piece of opal, about five centimeters long and three across; it was a centimeter thick. The opal was curved slightly, obviously a piece of the egg which had been broken. The brilliant colours flashed over the black background even in the dull light of the dugout. This was obviously the missing piece of the egg. Harry's wife picked the opal up. 'I've never seen such good opal before. This must be as good as the best Lightning Ridge black opal. What would this be worth?' Fifteen or twenty thousand dollars, I reckon,' said Harry. He picked up the piece of opal, then walked over to the kitchen dresser, and picked up an old-fashioned square tea tin, which sat on top of the kitchen dresser. Harry prized the top off and put the piece of opal in it.

'If it had not been for the opal, today's fiasco would just about drive a man to give up the demon drink,' he said as he walked over to the refrigerator and got a long neck of beer out of it. He then lifted its lid with a dirty knife which was sitting on the sink amongst the array of unwashed dishes. Harry had no use for a glass. He tipped his head back and poured the beer straight from the large bottle down his throat.

The three bodies of the accident victims were carefully removed from the wrecked station wagon, Silvio and Tom's bodies were put into body bags then, with Wombat's body loaded into the ambulance, then taken to the Coober Pedy hospital, and put into the morgue.

Willie Brooks had been operated on the next morning, and the mess the creature had left was sewn together the best the doctor and staff could.

Willie's willy was well known around town before the accident; it was more talked about than it ever was before.

Willie didn't have enough penis left to even hold to pee. The other genital parts, the testicles, were so chewed around that the doctor had to remove them also.

Sean Murphy had his hand stitched up as well, where the two middle fingers had been was neatly trimmed and repaired and be monitored by the hospital

The Coober Pedy airport had never been so busy. Two chartered planes had flown in from Adelaide, carrying staff from the Adelaide Museum and the CSIRO to study the dead, now frozen creature. Two of the scientists went to the hospital to concur with Dr Canopoulis

The robbery and the attack by the creature had made world news. Everyone wanted to be in on the discoveries which were about to be made.

The creature in its steel toolbox had been taken off the ute when the car trailer had been unhitched. The police were still reticent about opening the box, in case the creature was not really dead. Finally, the box was opened, and the creature was tipped on to a large piece of plastic. The large worm lay on the plastic with its mouth with the rows of needle-sharp teeth open.

A red liquid oozed from the open maw. The smell was revolting. The other end of the worm had purged out two stools, the gory remains of its last feast, which explained the sausage-like material on the floor of the wrecked car. The skin of the worm was a sickly grey green colour. It looked revolting as it lay on the black plastic sheet. The police took some photographs of the creature. The plastic sheeting was then folded and then the worm rolled up in the sheeting. Then the creature was taken on a stretcher and tipped off into a large freezer for the night. No one wanted to touch the plastic or get too close to the body of the now-dead worm.

Achmed and Aaron Goldstein, the American buyer who had been in Achmed's office at the time of the robbery, had chartered a light aircraft from Adelaide for the journey to Coober Pedy to reclaim the remains of the eggs and to try and find what had happened to the lost money and the other egg. All of the commercial flights had been booked out for the next few days.

The trip to Coober Pedy seemed to take forever. The men wanted to be on the scene to try and find out what happened to the money and to regain the eggs.

The plane finally descended through the light cloud to reveal the almost alien-looking landscape of the Coober Pedy opal field, which was pockmarked with the thousands of white dumps, which were mainly in tight clusters, denoting one or other of the named fields.

The scene of the opal workings never failed to fascinate Achmed as he flew in to the area. It was as if this was another planet that they were going to land on. A world which was pockmarked with meteor craters. Achmed and Aaron were met at the airport by one of Achmed's friends who had been phoned before leaving Adelaide. He drove them to Achmed's dugout. The dugout was a far cry from the one the Kelly's rented from the Dragon and his ex-mates. The front of this dugout had a room with windows. The walls of this long room were sheathed in the brown baked rocks, which had been gathered from the Moon Plain, which was situated just out of Coober Pedy towards Oodnadatta. There was a wall in front of the dugout which was sheathed and topped with these rocks. These had some of the hardy trees, which would grow in the harsh climate, growing behind the wall. Two peppercorn trees grew near the doorway. The men took their clothes inside the dugout. Aaron went and freshened himself up by having a wash in the bathroom, whilst Achmed got the keys for the old four-wheel drive out of the kitchen dresser and then walked outside into the bright sunlight. He blinked at the glare of the sun and then opened the roller door next to the dugout where the ute was kept. He walked into the shed and then started the old ute, which was always kept at Coober Pedy. He then reversed it out of the shed and drove it to the front of the dugout. Achmed stopped the ute and then returned inside the dugout.

Aaron had a large natural history museum in Chicago in the USA and was always looking for unique items to display in the gem section of the establishment. Rare gems and fossils were one of the main attractions of the museum. Aaron had spent most of his life travelling the world to acquire such materials. The eggs were to have been the jewel in the crown of a lifetime of collecting. Finding and purchasing such rare objects was a once-in-a-life-time experience. Such rare objects were a draw card for the public. Aaron had hoped that the eggs would have paid for themselves from the extra attendance at the museum.

Achmed thought for a while and then spoke, 'We were in a business deal involving these eggs. In simple terms, if you were to buy a basket of eggs and one hatched into a chicken, you would still be the owner of the newborn chicken. Wouldn't you? So I think you should also claim that you own that monster worm. If, heaven help you, it had hatched whilst you had it in your possession; there would be no dispute at all about your rights.' Aaron had not thought of this new angle. He brightened up considerably at the thought that he may also be the proud owner of the now-dead prehistoric worm. The publicity that this creature had kindled in the last two days in the imagination of a lot of people worldwide could be worth millions.

The men drove to the police station to claim the eggs and to formally put in a claim for the now-dead monster. When the eggs were presented, Achmed was livid. There were four eggs stolen from Aaron and I in Adelaide not three. Where is the other one? Sean Murphy walked to the counter he could hear the conversation from inside of the station. "We only found two solid eggs and the pieces of the broken one. "Are you sure "asked Achmed with a look of skepticism ". Sean was not happy about the tone of Achmed's voice. There were three of us at the accident scene. I can assure you that none of us picked up another egg." Achmed let the matter rest.

There could be no doubt about the ownership, be it either Achmed or Aaron, to the opalised eggs. John Nickols had been contacted by the police and had said that he had sold the eggs to Achmed. John had described the eggs and had told what they had weighed.

Luckily John had said to the police that the eggs had been sold for an undisclosed price. There would be problems with the Taxation Department at a later date as both parties had not intended to declare the dealings. A story would have to be cooked up between John and Achmed. This would make things difficult for both parties.

The case of money, which was now missing, was another matter. The dealings with the cash in the suitcase were well documented. Achmed had told the police of the amount of cash which had been in the suitcase. Having the eggs returned was not a major problem. They were handed over without a fuss. The two eggs and the pieces of the broken one were bought out. Achmed opened the bag and checked the eggs. He replaced all the pieces of the broken egg, trying to rebuild it. The result of this was to reveal that there was a large piece missing. The police had not tried to recreate the egg. 'There is a piece of this egg missing,' stated Achmed to the police officer.

'What about the car? Have you searched the car?' The officer informed him that the car had indeed been very well searched by the boffin brigade from the museum. They had taken samples of the stools and the now-dried fluid from the floor of the car. The car interior was being completely dismantled inside a shed at this present time. The seats had been removed, as well as the carpet and center console.

Aaron thought for a while. 'What about the crash site? What work is being done down there?'

The crash site was also well searched by the museum staff to see if there was anything extra to be learnt about this mysterious creature. They were sieving the ground from around where the car had come to rest following the accident at the present time. This was a setback. Aaron had thought that the missing piece of egg may have fallen out of the car during the accident. If the museum staff had been looking, they may have already have sieved it from the ground around the accident site. Where had the other egg disappeared to? Achmed and Aaron left the police station. 'We'll drive down south to the accident site and ask the men working down there if the piece of opal and the other egg have been found.' Achmed was keen to try and find out what had happened to the missing egg and the piece of egg as soon as possible. If the matter was not dealt with straight away, the missing piece of egg would probably be sold and on its way to China or another country. There was also the slight chance that the piece of egg may have fallen from the car on its trip back to Coober Pedy.

Four men were working at the accident site. The site had a circle of star fence droppers around it to keep the sightseers out. A circle of orange twine was tied to the droppers. A few curious people stood around, watching the men work.

Achmed called one of the workers over. The man reluctantly left his sieving job and walked over, obviously thinking that Achmed and Aaron were just two more tourists. Achmed explained that they were the owners of the opal eggs. One egg and a piece of the broken egg were missing. The man's attitude changed from one of indifference to a more helpful nature. Achmed asked the man if they had found the piece of opal. 'We have sieved all the ground around where the car was wrecked. The only thing which we have found is some pieces of broken beer bottles and some of the worm's castings.' Achmed thanked the man very much for his trouble. The two men walked back down the embankment, got into the four-wheel drive, and started back to Coober Pedy. Achmed and Aaron returned to the police station and started to speak to the officer at the counter. 'Someone must have stolen this missing piece of opal,' Achmed bluntly stated to the police officer. 'Could it have been one of your men?' Achmed was noted for his lack of diplomacy when dealing with public servants. The officer was taken aback. He assured him that the three officers who were at the scene of the accident were beyond reproach. By his manner, he was evidently not pleased by Achmed questioning the honesty of his work mates. "You have already spoken about this before you went to the accident site".

Achmed was still deep in thought. 'Who else was at the site?' asked Achmed. ' There was only the tow truck driver and his assistant.' 'Who was the tow truck driver?' asked Aaron. 'Harry the Horse,'

volunteered the officer. 'Willie Brooks was his helper. Willie
certainly didn't have any opal. He was stripped off at the hospital,
and his clothes were checked over by the museum mob for clues.'
The officer thought of the misfortune which had involved Willie's
willie. It made him shudder at the thought.

'Willie was the bloke who had his dick bitten off by this monster,'
added the officer. Achmed signed for the eggs, and then the men
left the police station.

They drove back through the town to Achmed's dugout. The
men got out of the ute. Aaron and Achmed went inside. Achmed
put the eggs into the large modern safe, which dominated one wall
of his bedroom. 'Right, I think we should go and put a bit of
pressure on this Harry the Horse character. I have heard he is a bit
shonky,' said Achmed. Achmed phoned his mate again and asked
where this Harry the Horse lived. The Ford ute was parked outside
of the small iron house, which was set well back on the large
block. There was an assortment of old mining machines in various
stages of disrepair littered across the block. Most of these
machines looked as if they had not been moved for years.
Achmed knew Harry slightly. He had bought a few good shells
from him a few years before. Harry had the reputation of being a
bit light-fingered.

The driveway was a circular gap between the wrecks. Achmed
drove through to the house and parked next to the Ford ute. He got
out of the vehicle. Aaron stayed in the ute. He did not want to be
involved in these transactions. He thought he might frighten the
guy off if the two of them were to be involved.   A small mousy
woman answered the door. 'Yes. What do you want?' She said
curtly, unsure of what Achmed was doing at their house.

'Is Harry at home?' asked Achmed. The woman looked at
Achmed. 'What would you want him for?' 'I understand he has got
a good piece of opal he wants to sell.' Harry had evidently
overheard this conversation.
He appeared at the doorway.

'Who told you that?' asked Harry, displaying a guilty look.' We
have just been to the police station and picked the opal eggs up
which were stolen from us. One of the eggs is missing and another

of the eggs has a piece missing. The museum crowd have been down at the accident site. If the opal piece had been there, they would have found it. Now the only other person we could think might have this opal was you.'

Harry spluttered and hotly denied having any opal. Achmed still kept very calm. 'Look, we are not trying to get you in any trouble with the cops. But we can get them involved if you like. The thing is that I have sold those opal eggs, and it's more in the new buyer's interest to get the other piece of the egg than anyone else. Right, here's the deal. You can sell us the opal at a more than fair price with no questions asked. Or we can do this the hard way. I will report this to the police, and the cops will become involved.'

Harry's shoulders dropped in resignation. He thought about this for a short while. 'You had better come in then.' Achmed followed them into the untidy house. Harry walked over to the dresser and got the tea tin down. He opened it up, took the opal out, and handed it to Achmed. 'Aha, yes, it surely is,' said Achmed as he turned it to catch the light's rays so the colour flashed.

Harry had an excuse. 'It was just lying on the ground next to the car when I was looking for an easy place to hook on to the wreck before I was going to load it. I didn't even know about any opal eggs. I certainly have not seen another egg.'

Achmed studied the piece of opal. 'What would you think this is worth?' Harry became cagey. 'What about thirty thousand?' he said hesitantly, not too sure what Achmed had in mind. 'I thought more like twenty thousand, seeing it's not yours for a start.' Harry dropped the bravado; his shoulders slumped in resignation. Harry's wife was about to say something. She looked as if she was going to start to argue. Harry waved his hand at her.

'Keep out of this woman.' He then turned back to Achmed. 'Oh, all right then, take the bloody opal then.'

'I will be back with the cash in fifteen minutes.' Achmed turned, walked out, and then got into the ute. As he left, he could hear the woman bickering in a high nasal voice; an argument was about to ensue. 'I've found your opal' was all he said to Aaron, and then he drove off back to his dugout to get the cash.

The dead monster was a different matter. Most of the boffins from down south seemed to think they had some sort of claim over this creature. There was even talk of the eggs being reclassed as fossils and thereby not being able to be sold to be shipped out of Australia. Another compounding factor was the ownership of the eggs. Had Aaron just lost his money, or was Achmed responsible and should he be made to hand the eggs over?

The price that Achmed and Aaron had agreed upon just before the men had broken into the room was for five million dollars. This was the amount which Aaron had in the suitcase and had been stolen from the office.

Had the eggs been sold to Aaron and therefore Achmed had lost the five million dollars? Or if the deal was not finalized, then Achmed had got the eggs back and Aaron had lost the five million dollars? This was very confusing, especially when dealing with a good client who had bought some very expensive items from Achmed in the past. Achmed drove Aaron back to the dugout after paying Harry for the piece of egg. He made a coffee and put it on to the table, then sat down, picked up his mug, and sipped his coffee. Achmed was deep in thought. Aaron sat opposite, sipping his hot coffee.

Both ourselves,' said Achmed. 'If we bring lawyers into the matter, they will make a lot of money from each of us, and they will eventually be the ones to win. Also the ownership of the eggs would be in limbo for years. I certainly don't want to be bogged down in court cases for the next five years and have the eggs held by the court, possibly to be forfeited to the crown as fossils. What would you suggest?'

'There is the matter of the museum people trying to make it so the eggs have to stay in Australia. If the eggs are held here in Australia for too long, they might get their way,' added Aaron. Aaron was deep in thought for quite a while. 'I really want these eggs for my museum. As far as a draw card is concerned, they have received a lot of worldwide publicity, so I can see no sense in losing all of this with the eggs locked in a vault for years. I will pay you Two million dollars for the eggs, on the understanding that if the money is found, I shall receive the other three million back.'

Achmed thought this was a fair way of resolving the problem. The case of the claim against the different groups of experts from the various museums for the return of the monster worm was a different matter. This was Aaron's sole responsibility. If he could swing such a deal this way, this would be worth millions in extra attendance fees for his museum.

The men started talking about the ownership of the eggs. 'I think this matter should be able to be worked out between Achmed and Aaron. "I wonder if that crook Silvio or one of the other thugs stole the other egg. From what I hear about them, I would not put it past them".

Chapter eighteen

Ali's quandary

Ali was worried there had been no news from Silvio regarding the robbery since the call the night before. Where were they, had they taken off with the opal and money? These questions were bouncing around in Ali's head. "The men should have arrived before seven am. Ali decided to drive to the dugout looking for them. There was no car when he arrived. Just the old rundown ute outside. Ali got out of the Patrol and walked to the door and knocked loudly. There was no answer. He took the key ring from the Patrol and selected the door key fort the dugout. The inside was really smelly and, in a mess, this was the usual state it was in when he had been to buy opal off the men.

On the way back to his house Ali drove past the hotel, just in case they were celebrating the successful robbery, No sign of his station wagon there He was confused. He knew that Silvio was extremely frightened of him. They were not the only crooks who Ali used to do his dirty work.

In the months since Martha and Peter had died Ali had been involved in some very shady deals with some of the town's worst crooks. There were plenty to choose from. Money was pouring out of the ground in a new opal find. This sort of money always attracted people ready to relieve the worker of it. There was a young Croatian lad called Jargo who Ali bought a lot of opal which had been moonlighted from claims. This lad was small, but very strong. He would climb down into people's claims at about three in the morning when the fumes from the previous days blasting had settled. He would use a small pick to bring the opal level down onto the floor of the dive which was under where the explosives had been used the previous day, then with a powerful torch he would sort the best of the opal and fill his kit bag which he had tied to the window sash cord he used to climb down the shaft   Jargo had a girl friend whose family were tied up with the Mafia in

Queensland. She was Sicilian. Ali bought a lot of opal off him as well. Jargo was known to have helped a few people fall down deep shafts head first. He was about the same age as Ali. Ali and Jargo had a bit of a friendship going. He was a lot brainier than any of Silvio's gang.

Jargo had been involved with a verger in one of the town churches who preyed on young girls and married women. This man had an accident which caused him to have his testicles and penis cut off. Ali's sort of person   Ali was back at his house in the afternoon when the police called and told him that his car had been involved in an accident. Ali listened to all of the details and was asked to come to the police station,

When he was travelling to the police station he was thinking of all of the excuses that he could use to get around the fact that the men had been using his car. He had too much going for him at this time to be caught up in a robbery investigation

Chapter nineteen

Trying to hide

Charlie and Karen wanted to put as much distance in between them and the accident as possible. They left Coober Pedy and drove as fast as they were game, towards the Northern Territory border. The Kombi was definitely on its last legs. Their speed was down to sixty-five kilometers an hour now as the rattling of the engine was getting worse.

They stopped in the first parking bay just over the border. This had taken all day at the Kombi's snail's pace. The suitcase full of money was still untouched since leaving town. Their main concern was to put as much distance between them and the accident site. The sick motor in the old Kombi van was certainly not helping their nerves.

Lunch was eaten on the way in a deserted parking bay, when they stopped to see if the oil level in the motor was OK. Charlie had to refill the motor with oil to the full level on the dipstick. The motor had used two liters in the short distance from Coober Pedy. The Kombi was billowing a cloud of blue smoke from the exhaust as it travelled slowly along the road.

The sun was just setting when they finally did stop. The case full of money had to be shifted so they could sleep. This was put into the front seat with much effort, as it was awkward and very heavy. Even though they were very worried about the case full of cash, they were too tired from the strenuous day to check the contents to see just how much money was inside the case. They laid the table down, rearranged the cushions to make the bed, then undressed to their underclothes, and then went to sleep.   The tweeting birds woke the pair in the morning. The dawn sky was just starting to redden; the beautiful red and gold sunbeams preceding the sunrise radiated from the horizon and then shone through the windows of the van. The inside was covered with the golden light.

Karen had a bad night's sleep. She was evidently having nightmares. She had thrashed around in her sleep all night, moaning and jumping occasionally. This had also kept Charlie awake.

Charlie walked into the scrub for a short distance and had a pee. He noted that they were the only ones in this parking bay. Charlie returned. He then filled a small plastic bowl with water from the large plastic water drum they carried, and then set it up on the concrete table which they had parked next to. He washed his face and hands, whilst Karen went for her morning walk to the scrub, carrying a small spade and some toilet paper; the spade was to dig a hole. Charlie then cooked some toast on the small gas stove in the camper van, then set it on some plates, which he carried out to the concrete table, and then placed the plates on the table.

The sun was just peeping over the horizon now. The clouds in the east were coloured with the beautiful reds and gold colours which were even more brilliant. This was a spectacle that only the outback can produce. The bed was put back down and the suitcase was stood on its side on the seat whilst they had breakfast outside. The breakfast dishes were put in the wash-up bowl and shifted on top of the stove.

Charlie lifted the suitcase up on to the table-top in the van, then opened the lid, and then set about taking the money out, putting it on the table and counting it in the half-morning light, being mindful of any traffic which might be slowing down to enter the parking bay.

Karen's dreams had involved the Mafia chasing them, and they were in the Kombi going slower and slower. The Mafia were getting closer all night, nearly catching them. The dream had seemed so real.

First one of the bundles of hundred-dollar bills was opened and counted. There was five thousand dollars in each bundle. Then the bundles of notes were individually counted. They were put into heaps of fifty, and then each heap returned to the empty suitcase. Karen wrote down a mark on a piece of paper for each ten bundles, which were returned to the case. They finally finished the job. They were jumpy every time a car slowed down. There had been one hundred bundles of notes put into the case. 'Wow,' Karen said, 'five hundred thousand dollars.' Charlie thought for a second.

'No, you didn't carry enough zeros when you worked it out. Here look at this.' Charlie took the pen from her and showed her the error. Karen was very quiet for a while.

'Bloody heck, there's five million in here.' She looked around, fully expecting a bevy of Mafia troops in their black suits to jump out of the bushes.

Charlie packed the large suitcase back on the floor of the van, walked around to the rear, and lifted the motor hood and checked the oil. 'Bring the oil tin out, please Karen. The old girl has started to use a lot more oil than usual.' Karen walked around the side with the oil tin. Charlie filled the motor through the oil filler intake to the mark on the dipstick, then walked around, and slid into the driver's seat and started the motor. A cloud of blue smoke poured out from the rear of the old van. Karen got into the passenger seat. 'That old engine is rattling a lot worse than yesterday,' she said as they drove off on to the main road 'Right, let's go, Gertie,' Charlie said to the old Kombi. 'I only hope this old bomb holds together for the rest of the trip to the Alice.'

It had taken all day to finally coax the old Kombi to Alice Springs. They had stopped at Kulgera and filled up with fuel. They were about a hundred kilometers from Earldunda, when they stopped for a wee break. Charlie stopped the old protesting motor, checked the oil, and then topped it up again.

He was very pleased to drive in through the Gap to the city of Alice Springs. He felt extremely exhausted, almost as if he had carried the van there himself.

They drove around the outskirts of the city and finally found a place to stay. They booked in at a small inconspicuous van park on the edge of the town for a couple of days. They were looking for a decent shower and a place to wash their smelly clothes. Charlie had kept out thirty thousand dollars from the suitcase. Karen paid a two-day fee for the site. Charlie was not too sure what the future was going to bring. His brain felt as if it were in overdrive.

Karen was the one who came up with the brilliant suggestion. 'Let's buy a van privately if there's one for sale around town. We can ditch the Kombi. We could just keep the old registration on the other van in the previous owner's name if there is enough time left on the registration to get well away from here.'

Karen minded the fort, so to speak as Charlie went over to the kiosk and bought an Alice Springs newspaper. They studied the for-sale adds in the newspaper. 'There's four Winnebago's and three camper vans in here that I can find.' They ringed the address of each add and the name of the owners. Charlie went back to the kiosk and got a street map for the Alice Springs area. They drove off to look at the dearest van advertised, which was a late-model Mitsubishi canter truck with a beautiful, near new, professionally built van body on its back. This was what the ad stated.

The usual cloud of blue smoke followed the Kombi out of the van park as they set off to look at the vans for sale.
The van belonged to an old couple, who, by the look of their house, were not short of a dollar. The unit looked as if it was in a new condition. It was parked in the front yard of the house, facing the street with a 'for sale' sign on it. Charlie drove off from the house so the old Kombi was out of sight. He left Karen in the van, minding the cash, whilst he walked back to the house. Charlie had the thirty thousand out of the suitcase ready to offer for a good van. The price of the dearest one the list was twenty-five thousand dollars. The van at the old people's house—the canter truck and van.

Karen sat in the Kombi, whilst Charlie went for a drive with the old owner. Charlie had talked for a while to the owner of the van and his wife. They were selling the van because the man had suffered a mild stroke a few months before and did not think he could travel any more. Charlie really liked the van and had agreed to buy it off the man. 'I hope you don't have any aversion to cash,' he asked the man. 'This is nearly all the money we had saved for our trip,' Charlie lied. The man agreed and was more than pleased to get the cash.

Charlie counted the cash out for the man, who, in turn, checked the amount. Charlie was handed the registration papers, which the other couple had signed. He promised to take these to the Alice Springs registration office to transfer the registration as soon as they had left with the new van. There was still nine months' registration on the new van.

Charlie drove the new van around the corner to where Karen had been waiting and showed her through the new vehicle. Karen was very impressed with the fittings inside and the extra space. To be able to lie down without building the awkward bed every time was a real bonus.

Charlie drove out of town, heading north. Karen followed in the new Canter van. Ten kilometers along the road he turned into a parking-bay .

Karen followed.

The Kombi was cleaned out thoroughly, and then Charlie removed the number plates and also scraped the registration disc off the windscreen, making sure to pick up the pieces. They had spoken of burning the van, but they thought this would only draw attention to them and the burning vehicle. A last check under the seats for forgotten papers, which might have had their names on it, was carefully conducted.

The money in the case was well stashed in the bottom of the wardrobe in new camper. At least, they had some room to move about now.   The new van was driven back to Alice Springs and filled with diesel whilst Karen bought some food. Charlie started the van. He stopped at a hardware store and bought some wood glue, saw, hammer, and nails, and some plywood and battens. They returned to the caravan park where Charlie made a false bottom for the wardrobe. There was already a place under, where the clothes hung to do this. The battens were cut and glued just under the floor level; each had small brads hammered in to hold it in place. Then the lid was fitted to the top; the money was shifted into this hidden recess. Charlie had kept out three bundles of notes. He then nailed the lid in place with four nails. This looked as it were part of the wardrobe. It was dusk by the time they had finished. They stayed the night in the caravan park.

Karen studied the road map the next morning before they left Alice

Springs. The road to Darwin forked some distance up, just passed Tennant Creek. Their options then were either Darwin, Western Australia, or Queensland. She was hoping to vanish into obscurity. North Queensland in a commune, somewhere near the beach sounded pretty good, Karen thought.

Chapter twenty

The lost egg

Two detectives flew up from Adelaide in a chartered, light aircraft. They were to help the local police to investigate the robbery. They were met at the Coober Pedy airport by Tony Arbon, one of the local officers who had been at the scene of the road accident, in a police car and taken to the police station. The detectives had a meeting with all the officers involved and were given a thorough briefing about the accident and the robbery.

After lunch, the detectives were taken down to the scene of the accident on the highway to start with their investigations. They got there just before the scientific staff from the museum. They arrived in a large van. The detectives had thoroughly scoured the scene by this time and left the scene for the museum people to start their work, looking for clues about the worm.

The car was traced to being registered in the Dragon's name. This certainly didn't surprise the police as the threesome of dead crooks usually associated with the Dragon. This type of robbery was more to the Dragon's planning than the three dead men. The finding of the car's owner tied him in with the robbery. This was as close as the police had got many of the crimes in town, which might have been associated with the Dragon. Usually, he was far more careful to not be able to be traced or have any distinct evidence which could be traced back to him. The huge amount of money and opals in this robbery must have clouded his judgement.

Two police officers were sent around to the Dragon's house. They parked their four-wheel drive, alighted, walked to the door, and knocked. One of the officers stepped back so he could get a good view of the rear of the shack.

After numerous knocks, finally, the Dragon slowly opened the door slightly and peered out at the officers. 'What do you want?' asked the Dragon warily, as he stood in the half-opened doorway of the house, trying to block the officers' view of the inside.

The news of the accident had not had time to travel all the way around town yet. No one had called to see him. He was more interested in finding out where Silvio and the others were and why they had not contacted him.

Not knowing about the accident was what the officers were hoping for. For if the Dragon had heard that his car had been wrecked and dragged into town on a trailer complete with the three dead men, he would have probably left town.

'We want you to come around to the police station to help us with some inquiries.' 'What sort of inquiries?' asked the Dragon warily. 'We will talk about that when you get there,' said one of the officers, not wanting to give the game away before the Dragon was at the police station. 'I will drive around to see you in a minute,' offered the Dragon.

'No, I think you had better come with us in our four-wheel drive. The matter is very serious,' said the officer. 'Just wait a minute.' The Dragon shut the door of his house. One of the officers went around the rear to check that the Dragon didn't leave by the rear door.

Inside the house, the Dragon gathered up the spoils of a good night's work by one of the local night workers. This man had gone down a shaft in the middle of the night and had robbed the claim's owner. The Dragon put the opal he had bought for less than half of its value, in his safe and locked the door.

The Dragon's mind was racing, trying to figure out what had happened. Which one, he thought, and who? He had a couple of dirty deals going at the present time. The robbery was he thought, the least of his worries. The men had rang and told him they were on their way up to Coober Pedy. They had the opal and the money. The Dragon was worried that they were late. He had thought they may have stopped and had a sleep on the side of the road or picked a couple of women up in Adelaide. The men never were very reliable. The thought that the men had double-crossed him and had shot through with the money and opals had also crossed his mind. He knew that Silvio was extremely frightened of him. The Dragon reluctantly came out of the house and joined the officer at his door. He locked the door with a large padlock. The other officer walked from the rear of the shack and joined his mate. One of the men opened the rear door of the troop carrier for the Dragon to get in.

The Dragon was still thinking. He was trying to think of ways as to not incriminate himself with the robbery. The Dragon was grilled for about two hours. He genuinely did not know of the accident. His face had dropped markedly when he had heard the news, but true to his form, he had recovered quickly. The Dragon was, of course, the prime suspect.

The men were in his station wagon.

The Dragon sat impassively through the lengthy interrogation, sometimes scratching the scar on his face when he became annoyed with the questioning. 'I knew nothing of the men taking my car to Adelaide. If I had known they were going to do this, do you think I would have lent my car to them? They told me that their ute had broken down and was being fixed, and they had no way of getting around. They wanted my car to go noodling.'

The police hated interviewing the Dragon. They had done it before on many occasions and never looked like making any charges stick, even for more incriminating evidence than this. The Dragon was an expert liar, and, as a lot of Asians, he could sit and not show any emotions when he was being questioned. The Dragon would just stare at a fixed point on the wall when the questions got too hard for him to lie about.

The police were sure the Dragon was involved in this crime, but through the normal lack of substantial evidence, they had to let him go. The dead trio would not have had the brains or resources to work out a job like the opal heist in Adelaide.

The two officers drove the Dragon back to his house. 'I should ring my lawyer and charge you with harassment of an innocent person,' threatened the Dragon. 'I wouldn't push my luck too far if I was you, mate,' said one of the officers as the Dragon departed through the door of his house.

All of the caravan parks and other accommodation venues were phoned and asked about a Kombi van. The Volkswagen Kombi van travelers were getting less every year. This was mainly because of the age of the vans and the lack of highway speed in the old vans. They were usually driven by some of the younger people because the old Volkswagens could be bought very cheaply.

Two Kombis were found to have been staying in the Coober Pedy area on the day of the robbery. Both of these were checked out to prove they were not the van which had stopped at the scene of the accident.

The police had obtained the names and addresses of both of the Kombi owners from the caravan park proprietors and had phoned the owners who both had just returned to Adelaide. Both of these people in the vans had been heading down south and could prove that they were not near the scene of the accident at the time. The next aspect of the inquiry was to canvass the service stations and the supermarkets to ask if anyone had seen a strange Kombi in town. One of the proprietors of the BP service station could remember a Kombi van filling up with fuel. It was driven by a young man, with a girl with him. The time the van filled up corresponded to the phone call which the police had received about the accident. The man from the service station could remember that the old van was hand-painted with some flower motifs painted on it. The attendant could also remember the man being very edgy when filling up with fuel. He also explained about the pool of oil on the driveway and the cloud of blue smoke from its exhaust as it had driven off. The Kombi and driver had been filmed on the CTV camera which watched over the remote fuel bowser which was to the side of the service station. The Police copied the section of the video and noted down the registration.
'With a bit of luck, the van may be broken down on the side of the road,' the station owner added.
The registration number was checked and the owner contacted. He was in a Adelaide and said that he had sold the van to Charlie. He had forgotten to take the transfer papers to be verified.

The Marla Bore police station was contacted to check Cadney Park and Kulgera to see if the old van had passed through. The

Glendambo roadhouses and the fuel stop at Pimba were also contacted. Staff could remember the two other vans at the Pimba fuel stop going south. There had been one travelling north. This had stopped, and the young couple had bought some takeaway food the day before the accident. This sounded like the one they were looking for. This van had flowers painted on its body.   Later in the afternoon, the Marla police rang. The van had been seen filling with fuel at Kulgera, just over the Northern Territory border. The service station owner could remember the van sounding very sick at the time. He was not sure that it could make Alice Springs.

The police were convinced by now that this was the van that they were looking for; the time factors seemed to coincide with the crash. The next step was to ask all the van parks in Alice Springs to check if the van had been staying the night before.

The Alice Springs police rang back. There had been a van of this description staying at a small park in town. The people had paid cash for the two days they had booked for. The park operator remembered that they had left after the first day. The park attendant had not taken the registration number and driver's license details as they should have. The van was not entered into the books. This was usual practice with some park operators when a cash payment was made. This was to save paying tax by down-stating the amount of people who stayed in the park.

This dead end was a blow. The only recourse now was to send a facsimile of the van from the photos from the BP service station man and fax this to the Alice Springs police station to be circulated through the town and in the local newspaper. A large reward was offered for information leading to the van or its owners being found.

Before he left Adelaide, Aaron was going to engage the best law firm in Adelaide to try and claim the monster back from the boffin brigade who were studying it. If he could do this, he would more than recoup the cost of the trip.

Newspapers all over the world were carrying the story on their front pages. The robbery, the prehistoric creature which had hatched from the broken egg, and the subsequent killing by the creature of the two crooks were definitely front-page news worldwide. The flaccid dead monster was an instant celebrity.

The day after Charlie and Karen had left the town; there were some news from the Alice Springs police. The Kombi van had been found driving around the town. There were a large group of aborigines driving it, and when questioned, they said that they had found the van about ten kilometers out of the town, in a parking bay. They must have found the van the day that Charley and Karen had left the town.

The aborigines had been walking along the road and had seen the deserted van. They had managed to start the van by crossing. The ignition wires and had been able to start the van and drive it back to Alice Springs.

The police did a thorough search through the van and took fingerprints from it. The fingerprints did not have any matches on the computer. The registration plates were not on the vehicle or the stick on tag, but there was an engine number which was checked. This was a breakthrough, thought the officers.

The Alice Springs police did a check on all the car sales, both commercial and private, for the period of the van travelling to Alice Springs. There had been five cars sold, as well as the private sale of the Mitsubishi canter van. The car sales were all OK as there had been trade in vehicles; the names were all checked and found to be local people.

The canter truck was a different case. The old owner had the registration number and the name of the purchaser. He had taken the papers to the registration office to do his half of the transfer, but there was no record of Charlie having done his side of the paperwork. The police showed the man a photo of Charlie taken at the BP service Station in Coober Pedy. "That is the guy who bought my van; I am one hundred per-cent sure".

The old man described the van and said about the names on the back with the Citizen Band radio frequency call sign. The names were Bert and Amy, and the call sign number fifteen. Bert had been a spray painter in his younger days and had customized the side and rear of the van with some stripes and some other marks to make the van more attractive. Bert had some photos of the van which he loaned to the police. At least, the police had the registration and the owner's name now. But when the check was made on the owner of the Kombi van, the name was fictitious. Charlie had used a bogus name. At least, the plates could be picked up on the Canter truck.

The canter camper van did have some different markings on the side, two names, and a radio call sign on the back. The police sent photos of the van, with the registration numbers to all the police stations further along the highway.

Chapter twenty-three

Nabbed with the money

What a delight it was to drive a decent vehicle instead of the clapped-out old Kombi! Having some room to move was another bonus.

The new van could easily travel at one hundred kilometers an hour, with plenty of extra in reserve if needed.

Charlie and Karen were not in a hurry. Now they were convinced that no one would find the old Kombi hidden in the bushes, and as their names were not on the old man's registration papers, the need for stealth and speed were not their main concern. Charley was convinced that they were home free.

He stopped the van at a service station at Tenant Creek to fill up with fuel. When they had finished, they drove to the local shops to have a meal and buy some much-needed groceries.

When they came out of the shops and got into the van to continue their journey, a police car pulled in behind the van, cutting their exit off. Two officers got out and walked to the door of the van. Charlie's face dropped. There was nothing that they could do. The officer told them to follow the police car to the station.   'Well, that's a nice mess. I wonder what is going to happen now,' said Karen. Charlie was in deep thought. 'I'm glad I didn't change the plates for the old vans. We could be in a lot more poo if I had done that.' Charley turned into the police station driveway after one of the officers directed them to do so.

The officer asked Charlie about the money. Both Charlie and Karen could see no use in lying to the police as this could only make matters worse. Charley showed the officers where the money was and helped take it out of the false bottom of the wardrobe. He was now resigned to the fact that there was nothing to do. The money was put into secure plastic bags. Charley and Karen followed the officers into the police station. One of the officers rang the Coober Pedy station and gave them the good news about the recovery of the money. The Coober Pedy police sent an officer around to Achmed's dugout with the good news.

Achmed and Aaron were having lunch when there was a knock on the door of the dugout. Achmed looked out of the corner of the window to see who the person knocking was. He then opened the door and let the officer inside. 'I have some good news. The van with your money has been found at Tennant Creek.' Both Achmed and Aaron were extremely pleased and thanked he officer. 'It appears that the two people in the old Kombi van had broken down and had got out to fix the van, when they had found the accident. They were the ones that reported the wreck to us, but as they had the suitcase full of money, they did not want to give their names.' 'Could I go and get the money? I have a friend with a small plane here which I could hire.' Achmed was worried that the longer this amount of money was lying in someone else's care, there might be some more of the cash disappear. The office gave Achmed the number of the Tennant Creek police station. Achmed thanked the office profusely, reached into a cupboard, pulled out a bottle of expensive Scotch whisky, and gave it to the officer.   'I don't know whether I should take this,' said the officer. 'Just share it with your mates to thank them all from me.' The officer took the bottle and then walked out the door and drove off.   'Well, Aaron, this must be our lucky day. Aren't we lucky we didn't leave the town yesterday as we had planned? Would you like a trip up to Tennant Creek if Tony is around the town with the plane?' Aaron agreed as he wanted to get out of Australia as soon as he could with the eggs. Achmed rang the Tennant Creek police station and said he was going to fly up and pick the money up. He also added that he would like to meet the couple who found the money.

Tony Lang was around the town. He had taken some tourists flying around the Coober Pedy area in the morning. There was a good business with the tourist trade as there was probably nowhere on earth with the scenery that this part of Australia offered. Tony was going to fill the plane with fuel ready for the next trip, when Achmed phoned and asked about flying him and another man to Tennant Creek. The plane would be able to get to Alice Springs in the late afternoon and then finish the trip in midmorning.

'G'day, Achmed. It sounds as if you have been having a bit of fun.' Tony Lang was a weather-beaten, lanky guy of an age which could have been between forty and sixty. He was very well versed with inland Australia as he had flown nearly anywhere there was to go. He did a fair amount of work to Mimili, Indulkina, and Freegan, which were aboriginal settlements, ferrying the administration staff and their ilk for inspections. Tony finished filling the Cessna with fuel and then started to do the normal check of the plane. 'OK, guys, get aboard.' The trio settled into the seats of the plane. Tony started the motor, then taxied out on to the runway, and then gunned the motor, and after a short run, the plane was airborne. Tony liked this sort of job. There was a lot more money in the long charters than just carrying tourists for an hour at a time.

Achmed started to discuss the trip and recovering the cash. He drew Tony into the conversation I would not like to think that this young couple would be prosecuted over finding the money. It was only a coincidence that they had broken down at the spot where the thieves had run off the road. I wonder what most other people would have done about the suitcase full of cash. Would they have kept it?' Both Aaron and Tony agreed with this. 'I have had a bit of a run-around regarding the money. But I think I will give this young couple a reward.' The rest of the long run to Alice Springs centered on the eggs and the Dragon and his mates. Tony had the same opinion of the Dragon as most others in the town. He had been robbed of opal from a claim he was working part time with a mate. Silvio and crew were the prime suspects.

Tony landed at the Alice Springs Airport just as the sky was starting to turn red. He taxied the plane off the runway and shut it down in a parking area. Achmed called a taxi and phoned for some accommodation. All men had each small bag with a change of undies and pajamas.

After an interesting night at dinner and some good discussions about the problems in the world, although they did not fix any, the men retired to bed ready for an early start.

The sun was just about up when they left. The sky was a golden colour in the east. Finally, they arrived at the small Tennant Creek airport just before lunch. Achmed phoned for a taxi. Tony was going to have a look around the town for an hour.

Achmed and Aaron walked into the police station and asked at the counter about the stolen cash. Achmed also wanted to see Charlie and Karen. Achmed was asked for proof of identity, which he produced to be photocopied. He then proceeded to an office, with Aaron following. The bags of money were produced. Aaron and Achmed set about counting all the money. This took quite a while. Just as they finished counting the money, Charlie and Karen were ushered into the office by one of the young police women. The count on the money was just forty thousand dollars short.

Charlie and Karen did not know what to expect from the man who owned the money that they had picked up at the accident scene. Both were quite worried as to the profession of the two men in the room; a couple of heavies from a drug cartel came to mind. Achmed stood up and shook both Charlie and Karen's hands and then thanked them for finding his money. They both felt a lot of relief. 'You have led us on a bit of a chase to get this money back. Do you know how this money got to be where you found it?' Charlie and Karen then heard the details of the robbery and the demise of the trio in the getaway car.

Both were extremely thankful that they had not ventured near the car at the accident scene when they heard about Willie and the police officer being attacked by the worm, as well as the thieves. Achmed went on talking, 'I had offered a reward for the return of this money so, even though you picked the money up and drove off with it, I am prepared to let you keep the vehicle you bought and give you another seventy thousand dollars and ask the police to drop all charges related to this matter. Both Charlie and Karen were so pleased that they did not have to face any charges relating to the picking up the cash. They thanked Achmed very much. Achmed counted seventy thousand dollars out of the bag of money and handed it to Karen. 'I think you should keep this, my dear. Most women have a lot more idea about money than men.

This is my gift.' Karen took the money.

The police officer said, 'Ok guys you are free to go now if you wish. Just pick up all of your belongings at the counter'. Charlie and Karen walked to the counter and got the keys of the canter van.

The young police officer said, 'I think you should fill in the registration forms with your right names before you go and pay the stamp duty on the van.' Charlie picked the forms he had got out of the pile of papers he had picked up, sat down, and filled the form out in both his and Karen's names. He paid the stamp duty and the transfer fee. Then both walked out of the police station free to travel in the near-new Canter van. After they had left, Achmed said to the police officers, 'What should I have done? I do not want to see young people like that getting into trouble for doing what half of the people in the world would have done. I am more than happy to get my money back. I consider myself to be lucky to ever see it again. If there had been another car other than the old Kombi van, I do not think we would have found it.' The officers agreed. One of the officers offered to drive the men back to the airport ready for the trip back to Coober Pedy.

Chapter twenty- two

Slippery business

Ali was thinking how he could try to get out of having been
involved with Silvio, Tom and Wombat in the robbery of the opal
dealer in Adelaide. Two days had passed since he had been taken to
the Coober Pedy Police station and had been grilled by the officers.
Ali had contacted a criminal Lawyer in Adelaide called David, who
did a lot of work for some of the les honest members of the local
community. David was known in town as the criminal , criminal
lawyer as he had been struck off the register a few years before
when one of his cases had gotten a bit too close to home for the
authorities to tolerate. He had been dis-barred for four years.
David had a list of charges. He would get an acquittal for murder
for five thousand dollars; any second murder by the person would
cost double the amount. He was coming to Coober Pedy in two
weeks on one of these cases, involving a very nasty Italian called
Emilio. He had evidently dropped a partner down a mine shaft after
they had just found a huge seam of opal.

Ali was wary of the police. They were an unknown equation in his
opal buying and other activities around town. Some officers could
be bribed to look the other way and also be able to argue the point
with others to also look in their way of seeing a situation. There
were others who, if a bribe were offered would go out of their way
to make a person's life hell. Sometimes it was really hard to tell
one from the other.

Ali still had flash backs to the times in his life where all things
had seemed to be almost normal. His child hood stealing in the
marketplace and pimping for Zeena had definitely not been a
normal situation. Gentle Sasha and the girl in the mountains had
been the first taste of goodness he had experienced. The large scar
was a reminder of these first times. The scar would start to ache on
the frosty early mornings in winter. This bought the flash back
sensations of Sasha and Missy. His happy memories were of
sunny days when they were catching the tasty silver fish in the

river. And walking to town, and then selling the produce in the market.

Other good memories were of the love he and Martha had and the loving association with her parents. Little things caused these sensations to appear, almost real, tears would form in Ali's eyes, and then the reality would hit with a hard thump.   Ali had purchased a large dog from one of the town's crooks wives. The man had had the misfortune to step backwards when he had been caught coming out of one of the miners shafts that he had been robbing at the time. The guy he was robbing was one of the heads of a Serbian mining syndicate. The Serbian had shown the police the edge of the shaft which had been undermined from having the soft Kopi like dirt seep out from under the crust of top soil. The man had meant to have trodden on this and then toppled down the shaft, possibly with the help of the claim owner.

The dog was not what one would call pretty, or even slightly so. It was a bad tempered ugly dog. Ali had been bitten by this new member of the house on numerous occasions before there had been gained a mutual respect with the help of a piece of knotted rope. Ali had thought of numerous names for his grumpy watchdog, and had ended up just calling him Dog. His previous name was an almost unpronounceable name of Hungarian descent.

Ali caught up with David the Criminal lawyer. There was a long discussion about the police and the business with Silvio and the other thieves. David was a drinking man and downed a bottle of good Scotch which had been left over from better times when Peter would visit. This had been missed in the cleanout. Ali had noticed this but had left it as some sort of reminder of Peter. The evidence that the cops were talking about should only be classed as a bluff as Ali had not known what the three crooks were going to do. He had not even known where the thieves were going in his car. He had been lied to by Silvio about this. The police had made reference to the street directory with the circled opal dealer's names. Any person could have done this. There were no references to Ali or his phone number in any of the books. David was going to see the police and mention all of this to them and tell them that if they tried to harass Ali any more there would be trouble.

Two days after David left town Ali was in the Post Office getting his mail when the man behind the counter asked Ali if he knew whether Silvio had any family such as a wife or kids. They got talking about the robbery. Ali finally asked why the concern about whether Silvio had any family. Ali did not know, "Why "he asked, "A Couple of weeks ago we got a heavy box sent up from Adelaide from the Virginia Post Office. The box was sent to Silvio," Ali had a flash of an idea. "That cunning bastard", he thought "This would be the other egg". "Wait a bit I know what that is. That is a new filter to put on my tank which Silvio said he would buy for me. He knew someone down in Virginia who deals with these things. He got it a lot cheaper than the price here", "Well it is only cluttering up the shelves her you may as well take the bloody thing home with you ". Ali took the box from the counter and slowly walked out of the Post Office. He felt like running.

The box was carefully placed on the seat next to him on the passenger seat. Ali carefully drove home to his house. Dog was locked in the yard as usual. He wagged his tail as Ali opened the gate, and then drove in. He shut the gate then parked the Patrol next to the door of the house. The box was carefully retrieved then taken inside. Ali found a sharp knife then cut the packing tape and finally opened the box The protective packing was removed. The top of the egg was revealed. "Holy mother of God", Ali muttered as the colour started to flash over the black background." I nearly missed out on seeing you". He carefully removed the egg and stood reverently admiring it as he turned it over to reveal all of magnificent colour patterns. The egg was returned to the box, then placed into the large safe

Chapter Twenty- three

Life changing events

After two days in the city, Tony had driven back to the farm.
Typical of most country people, he could not wait to leave the mad
pace of the city. He, especially, hated driving in the crowded
highways. This was totally different from the snail pace of Kimba.
Most of the time when driving, Tony was lost, having been caught
on the wrong lane when he wanted to change roads. He then had to
stop and study the new Adelaide street directory he had brought
when he had filled up with petrol. Tony wanted to get home so he
could keep an eye on the sheep. He felt so proud, driving the new
Ford utility, but had the horrible feeling that if he didn't get out of
the city soon, he would end up in a car accident with it. City
driving certainly was not Tony's forte. He hated it.   His only hope
of getting a ute prior to the opal find was to have bought an old,
clapped-out one and do some work on it himself. He had no
intention, as a lot of young people did, of tying himself down with
hire purchase, especially, when the finance situation had been so
bad. ,Tony had kissed Helen and then given John a big hug before
he left for home. He insisted that they stay at the hotel for a few
more days. It did not take a lot of convincing to get Helen to stay.
The change of fortune and circumstances was most welcome.

  John had read with great interest of the robbery and then the
grizzly demise of the three pirates by the worm. The police had
contacted John at the hotel to ask if he had sold the eggs to
Achmed. He had to describe the eggs' colour and weight to try and
verify Achmed's ownership.

  'I reckon that if we hadn't left Coober Pedy when we did, those
bloody pirates would have stolen our opal and money which was in
the safe. I would bet that they were the ones who broke in to the
dugout. Bert said the safe must have been opened with a key, as it
had not been forced in any way. It would have been those three
blokes who were killed in the accident that were involved.' Helen
was so pleased that John's hunch about the eggs and cash had been
right. To have been so close to getting rid of the bank debt and then

to have the chance of the opal and cash stolen from them by a mob of thieves would have really broken her heart.

'Well, what do you want to do?' asked John as they sat in the small restaurant and had their lunch. It was still hard to let the purse strings open, as they had such a battle for the last three drought years. Helen thought for a while,

Why don't we buy a new car and then drive up through the Barossa Valley for a couple of days on the way home? I would like to go and see where my grandparents were born. My parents always used to talk of the place they grew up and where both of their parents were finally buried when they died.

It was still hard to bring himself to finally agree to buy the new Holden. The change of fortune was still like a dream to John. He did not want to wake and find the bank was still hounding him for the money. If it is a dream, he thought, at least I've had the dream of beating the Lizard at his game. His mind came back to the reality of the moment. He had been daydreaming as the salesman got the registration papers ready for him to sign in the Holden dealer's office. John wrote a cheque to pay for the car.

The new car was left at the dealers. John had no intention of trying to drive in the city for the first time, especially in the new car, which he was not used to.

John hailed a cab, went to the bank, and redeemed the suitcase full of money. They were not sure what to do with the cash. They were going to make an appointment to see their accountant when they got back to Kimba.

What a change to be able to take their time and finally begin to relax after the ordeals of the last few years!

When John and Helen arrived back at the Holden dealers, they made arrangements for the salesman to drive the new car out of the city for them. John gave the man fifty dollars for his trouble. He felt that this was better than smashing the new car in the first day they owned it. It was a pleasure to finally leave the city and drive up through Gawler and finally to the Barossa Valley.

The green fields of the Barossa Valley rolled before them as the leisurely drove from one small town to the next. What a pretty country after the dismal Kimba of the last few years! Green paddocks, with fat sheep and cattle. The wheat and barley were almost up to the top of the fences. In the lower valleys, there were the lines of grapevines all neatly trellised, with their bare black limbs pruned back, waiting for the kiss of the warm autumn sunshine to bring forth the first green buds.

Helen had never been to the Barossa before but had heard a lot of stories about her German ancestors who were amongst the early settlers in the valley.

She studied the road map and finally found the small hamlet where her great grandparents had settled. John followed the back roads to the ruined church. This was a very emotional time for Helen as she got out of the car and walked into the church yard. She was holding John's hand tightly as they both walked through the graveyard, looking for the family plots, which were the final resting place of three generations of her ancestors.

Two lots of the graves of the first German emigrant great grandparents and one of her grandparents' graves as well. 'This has been one of my dreams to visit this spot and do this.' She hugged John. They then left for the car as a misty shower of rain came over the hills. As they walked back to the car, Helen looked back towards the graves and noticed that a ray of sunlight had shone through the clouds and was shining on the small graveyard, illuminating the tombstones of her ancestors. It was as though they were saying how they were watching over them.

John and Helen were quiet as they drove back to find a motel for their last night's break before going back to the farm. The visit to the ruined church had been a very moving experience, especially for Helen.

The smell of the new car, and the lack of rattles, which had inhabited the old one, and were getting more and more as the years passed on the rough dirt roads, was a strange feeling. They had never bought a new car or tractor before in their lives. They had not been able to afford such luxuries.

Just past Port Augusta, John bought up the subject of the opal claims and the dozer. 'We had better go back to Coober Pedy and finish the cut and bring the low loader back home. We still haven't got down to where we drilled the opal from. I think we will leave the dozer at Coober Pedy. There is still a lot of work to do with the rest of the claims. We don't need the dozer on the farm now.'

The Kelly's paid them a visit the day after they returned from Adelaide. 'Come in and have a look at the new suitcase we got in Adelaide.' The men followed John and Helen into the lounge room of the house. John reached behind the old lounge suite and pulled out the case full of money. He lifted it up on to the small coffee table, then undid the clasps, and then lifted the lid. 'Christ,' croaked Bert 'is that all money in the case or have you got the bottom padded just to make it look good?' 'All solid cash,' said John. 'We don't want the news to get around that we have got it here. It's just that at present, we don't know what we are going to do with it. ''Spend it,' joked Harry.
'When are you going back to finish the cut?' asked Bert. 'When do you think you might go back'? Asked John. ' We will go in about a fortnight's time. That should give us enough time to get a bit more work done at Coober Pedy before harvest time.' They went to the kitchen and sat at the table.
'We bought a better dugout on the North West Ridge,' said Harry. 'What's it like?' asked Tony as he got some stubbies of beer out of the fridge. 'It's a hell of a lot better than the Dragon's. We have a front section with a lot of windows with tables and chairs. This leads into the main dugout. There is an opal room with a steel door and even a proper bathroom. The main bedroom has a big safe with a combination and key lock.' This sounded a lot better than the Kelly's home at Kimba.

This time, the evening meal with the Kelly's was not the usual skinny mutton chops but good fat steaks instead. Buying meat was a new experience for Helen as they had always killed their own sheep and the occasional pig,

The sheep on the farm had improved in condition. Tony had fed a couple of bins of oats to them, mainly to empty the silo of the old musty oats so the silo could be cleaned out ready for the new season's crop, which, by now, was showing some promise of some sort of yield. A far different prospect then a month ago, when everything looked as if it was going to die.

The wheat crops were just showing the first signs of running up to head. By the look of the crops, the yield would not be fantastic— a little below average but far more heartening than the wipe-out the season looked like a few weeks before.

Helen had been in contact with the patent attorney. He had done a search on the new ripping tool and had found only one patent, which looked slightly similar to the tool they were using. He suggested to Helen that they should think of starting a provisional patent to cover the product. John phoned him back and then authorized the provisional patent to be drawn up.   John and Helen drove into the town. John felt embarrassed about driving the new car into the town. He felt as if he was trying to show his friends up. Another thing which John felt guilty about was not buying the car through the local dealer, who also had experienced the hard times with the demise of the farmers.

Buying the car in the city had saved them freight on the new car and the air fares home. Old habits were hard to break.

John drove up to the bank. They walked in and deposited thirty thousand dollars into their working account. Whilst they were talking to
Debbie, the Lizard peered around the corner of his office and sneered at John and Helen but made no attempt to greet them.

After doing a few days' work on the farm, John and Tony were ready to go back and finish digging the cut.

John and Tony followed the Kelly's up to Coober Pedy. This trip did not have the desperate feel of the gamble they were taking in the last two trips. They were both looking forward to getting back to work again.

'I wonder how many people know the bloody combination and have a key to this safe,' said Bert as he showed John and Tony around through the new house. 'See it's even got a proper inside toilet and bathroom,' which was a far cry from the primitive setup in the small outside iron room on the farm.

There was a spectacular view from the front of the dugout over the plain towards the blue mesa-type hills towards the Breakaways, which poked up off the Moon Plain like a mirage, in the far distance. The front room had a table and chairs set up so the people sitting at the table could really enjoy this scene. 'A bloody good place to have a few beers,' pointed out Harry as they looked around the new acquisition. John and Tony complemented the men on their recent purchase.

The next morning, the men drove out to the claims to check the machinery before starting to work. The truck was the first thing which John noticed. Its windscreen and lights were broken. When the dozer was checked, all the glasses of the engine gauges were also broken. There were the small footprints of bare-footed children around the machines, even a disposable soiled nappy was tossed in on the front seat of the truck. Evidently, a large mob of people had been noodling on the claim and had bought all of their children out with them.   John was extremely worried that the dozer and truck's oil might have been tampered with. Tony went over to the dozer and checked the oil filler of the motors and transmission, whilst John checked the truck. Both of the motors still had a heavy film of greasy dirt stuck to the oil-filling plugs, as did the transmission filler with no tell-tale marks of any tampering. Both radiators were still full of water. 'Just bloody kids whose parents couldn't care less,' growled Tony.

Bert and Harry had splashed out with some more of their cash before they had left and had bought an old truck with a blower on it. The poor truck had suffered a similar fate as the other vehicles. 'I'll stuff the bloody rocks up the little sods' bums if I see them around here again,' threatened Harry as he cleared some rocks, which had evidently been thrown at the windows of the truck, out of the cab. 'Those bloody kids toss rocks through the windows in town. The rotten little sods can stay back there in town and do it to their own houses.'

Bert had another shaft drilled with a Caldwell drilling rig so the new blower could be sited near to the old shaft and have its pipe lowered down through it to the drive below. There was not enough room to have the pipe and be able to climb down underground through the old shaft past the thick suction pipe of the blower. 'Well, at least this lot haven't stolen any batteries.' The alleged previous battery thieves were well past taking any more batteries.

John stayed and helped Bert and Harry finish installing the blower pipes, whilst Tony removed the old gauges from the dozer and drove back to town to try and buy some replacements. The main worry was the oil pressure gauges for the transmission and the motor. These had been gouged at with some kind of tool, and the insides were hanging out. This would have let the oil leak out of the broken pipe if the motor had been started.

Finding parts in Coober Pedy was usually a headache. One firm would have one piece, and then you had to go to another business to look for another. Tony was able to get the engine oil pressure and ampere meter gauges at the Opal Miners co-op store where they usually bought their fuel. The transmission gauge was harder to find. The firm he was sent to still had the gate shut at ten o'clock in the morning. Tony had to wait for half an hour until the sleepy-looking man finally opened his gate. There was a queue of people waiting to get into the shop. Finally, it was his turn to be served. At least, he was able to get the part for the dozer.

The Kelly's new blower was belching a plume of dust out of the outlet. John was waiting next to the dozer. He had seen Tony turn off the road and head towards the claim.
'Why didn't you go down and have a look at the way they worked with the blower?' asked Tony with a wry grin. John didn't bother to answer. They went on working and finally got the dozer going around 2 p.m.

It seemed as if they had been away for months, not just the few weeks. The men soon settled back into the familiar routine of ripping, checking, and then pushing the old, worked sandstone out of the cut. Only a small patch of potch was found for the afternoon's work.

Bert emerged from the shaft, carrying a bucket. He had a beaming smile on his wrinkled face. John had just shut the dozer motor down for the day. He and Tony walked over to the Kelly's utility. Bert had just tipped the contents of the bucket on to a piece of black plastic. Harry, who had just come out of the shaft, joined them. 'Have a look at these beauties,' offered Bert.
There were ten full shells and a small amount of skin shell. Two shells amongst them stood out. These were black opal. 'You're not the only smart arses who can find black opal, are you?' joked Bert. 'Have a good look at these beauties!'

It was back to the routine of a trip to the pub again to celebrate. Bert started in a serious mood, 'I don't know why we didn't get a blower when we got our first lot of money. Crikey, it's a hell of a lot easier than dragging those bloody heavy buckets back and forth along the floor of the drive. The more work we did, the longer the drive was, and the further we had to drag those damned buckets.' He went off and bought the first round of beers. 'What do you think the opal would be worth that we got today?' asked Harry in a low voice when Bert got back and had finished handing the beers around.

'I reckon those good shells may be worth around twenty or thirty thousand each,' he answered quietly so the men at the next table could not hear him.' As much as that?' Well, do you remember the shell that Black Mick was showing off. He got twenty-five thousand for it. I reckon ours are as good as that was.'

After the meal, Tony went off with a couple of lads he had met up with when they had been up working before. 'That boy of yours has made us a bit worried. He wants to get himself a couple of Sheila's to relieve the pressure.' 'That's probably what he is going to do right now,' said John with a wink and a smile.   The next three days were walk and check. There were no signs of any opal.

Walking and checking by one's self soon became boring to anyone when there was no sign of opal. The sandstone was the same. The brown line of the slide showed in the floor of the cut. This was about two centimeters wide in places. There were thinner lines crossing the main fault. These were the usual places that opal or potch was found.

Tony still turned the sandstone blocks, which the ripper pulled from the solid floor of the cut, occasionally scratching at the bottom of the rock to try and hear the tell-tale sound of cracking glass on the sharp point of the pick.

The men had estimated that the cut was now about seven meters deep. This was approximately the depth that the second level of opal had been drilled from before they had bought the dozer up from Kimba.   The first rip of the new day, the sandstone showed signs of changing. Small darker brown patches began to show in the floor. The old dozer was finding the sandstone harder to rip. This was the sign that the main level should be showing up soon.

Because of the harder stone, John was only able to complete one rip and push instead of the usual extra rip. The new design ripping tools were working very well, although changing the picks was difficult. The boot had to be removed from the tine, and then the broken tool then belted out with a sledge hammer and long drift. John found a place on the dozer where the boot could be wedged between the track frame and the long blade arms to set the boot so it could be worked on. The picks were cooked into the hole on the nose of the boot and took a lot of work to remove. The job was dangerous, for if the drift was hit at an angle, the person holding the drift could get badly hurt.

Bert and Harry had come out of their shaft at lunch time and had looked down the wall to notice that the floor of the cut was beginning to change colour. At the end of the work, the four men had walked the floor of the cut, chipping at the darker patches of sandstone to see if they could see any traces of opal.

Bert scratched his wiry grey hair. 'I reckon that you should cut the level tomorrow by the look of this. This light brown is what we have got about six inches above the main level. What say we give you a hand to check tomorrow as well,' he offered.

John thanked him but didn't want to impose.

'You silly coot. We wouldn't offer if we didn't want to help. When the level comes up, it's bloody hard for one man to check. Hell, you don't want to push the bloody opal out on to the dump. Plenty of people have,' Bert motioned towards the small group of people who had arrived and started to noodle that day. 'They're probably the same bludgers whose kids smashed all of our windows. Do you want to give them the opal?'

'Don't be so bloody pig-headed. I could sure do with a hand,' said Tony. John agreed. He always felt uncomfortable imposing on someone else to help.

John and Tony called in to Ivan's workshop on the way home to discuss some modifications to the new ripper boot design. John wanted to have a tapered shank on the pick to make removal a lot easier. The boot could be left on the tine when removing the tool.

They sat at a table in the workshop and drew some plans. Ivan had some very good ideas as to the retaining pin and removal tool design. Tony got two worn ripper boots from the tray of the ute for Ivan to modify to build the new tools. Ivan was very interested in helping and said that the tools should be ready in a day.

Bert and Harry had only been shifting dirt for the last few days. They were looking forward to the change of scenery. It was always exciting to see opal dug up by a bulldozer. The dozer scrabbled down the steep ramp of the cut. John lowered the blade and then cleaned all the loose dirt from the floor of the cut. This was to make it easier to spot any opal traces if they showed up. All of the men were keyed up with anticipation of what might happen with the first rip. They wished that John would back up and start ripping. He pushed the blade over the floor to remove some small, long mounds of sandstone which had escaped the ends of the blade in the previous rip. Finally, John reversed back along the straight wall of the cut and dropped the rippers and then started forward. The dozer tracks spun slowly and fought to get traction on the stone. The harder stone now made a cracking sound as it was reluctantly freed from the hard parent rock. The thin brown cross slips in the cut had now thickened and turned to hard shiny black ironstone in places.

As the stone was turned, there were plates of the dark hard ironstone on the bottom of some of the rocks. 'Bloody good level,' muttered Harry as he turned over a stone to check for opal.

The dozer was halfway across the cut, nearly to the main fault line, which ran from one end of the cut to the other. There was a sound of breaking glass, like glass being trodden under foot. Crunch, crunch it went as the ripper tore through it. Bert turned a stone over with the point of his pick. 'Bloody hell,' he said in awe, 'opal. Look at that.' John had felt the dozer shudder and had heard the opal cracking, even over the noise of the rowdy old dozer. He was looking over the rear of the machine and had seen the shine of the opal in the bright sunlight. He throttled the dozer off and took it out of gear, leaving it with the motor idling slowly, he tossed his earmuffs onto the throttle lever, and then he climbed down and joined the three men who were squatting by now and separating the opal from the dirt. Tony finally took his leave and went back up the steep ramp to get the buckets and sieves.

The noodlers were trying to get a better look to see what was taking place behind the dozer.

John had a hammer and screwdriver from the tractor toolbox and was chipping the thick pieces of opal from the virgin rock. He had flattened out a piece of ground next to himself, on to which he had laid the piece of old tarpaulin to catch any pieces which fell to the ground. He was putting the large pieces of opal into a large round sieve as he took them off the virgin rock.   The sun's rays caught the pile of opal, making it look as if the heap was alight. The fire colours of the stone flashed in the sunlight. Tony transferred the opal to the bucket, which he left next to John.

The rocks were carefully checked and then discarded if there was no sign of opal. Occasionally, a particular piece of opal was shown around to the other men. A pile of rock was building up next to John, waiting for him to remove the opal. A similar pile of rock was building up in the dead area.

The light breeze wafted the not unpleasant fumes of the idling motor of the dozer over the working men. It helped to keep the small sticky bush flies away. Tony took over from John on the cleaning side of the operations, whilst he climbed up on to the dozer, reversed slowly back, and did a short rip where the opal had disappeared into the solid rock.   One of the rocks which had been pulled out had the unmistakable sign of the drill hole through the middle of it. This was where they had drilled up the opal three months previously. John did another short rip as the opal seam was still carrying into the rock.

The ripper had now ripped the line which was showing in the floor and running through the cut from end to end. This was now the hard black -stone and appeared to be the edge of the opal find. The drill hole must have been one of the outer holes they had drilled. Tony had to walk up and get another bucket from Bert's ute as theirs were full. A lot of the opal still had stone on it, but there was still going to be a lot of material when it was cleaned.

No one had thought about lunch, only the digging out of the opal.

Finally, the men were convinced that they had picked up all the opal. The heavy buckets were loaded on to the floor of the dozer. John carefully drove out up the dump, past the noodlers, who were watching the other men intently, as they had their last scratch at the ground before leaving for the day.

The buckets were off loaded on to the ute, and then the dozer motor was idled to cool the turbocharger for a short while and then shut off for the day. Then they headed off towards the dying sun to the main road back to town.

The opal was tipped from the buckets into a two-hundred-liter drum to wait for a chance to clean and class it ready for sale. The drum had a series of holes on the rim around the top, which allowed a bar to be put through, which had a padlock fitted. This was not for Bert and Harry's sake but to be a bit of a deterrent if someone else should try to help themselves. The bulk of the material was too large to fit in the safe.   Some of the pieces of opal were studied under a bright light before the opal was finally tipped in the drum. Bert thought the best of the opal might bring as high as four thousand dollars an ounce. There were a lot of ounces in the three buckets which had been tipped into the drum. 'Money attracts money,' said Bert as he helped John fit the top to the drum and lock the padlock.

The room the opal drum was in had a very solid sheet-steel-covered door with a deadlock fitted to it and steel door surrounds, so the men felt reasonably comfortable about going to the Italian Club for a meal. Secrets were hard to keep at Coober Pedy. The minute they walked through the door, the men sensed that the conversation had begun to include them. A lot of faces turned towards them. One of the local men, who had got to know Bert and Harry, came over and asked, 'I hear you guys have found a lot of opal again?' 'Nah, only just some potch and colour.' Bullshit, one of the abos told me that you dug some opal out today. He was noodling your dump.'

'What were you doing chasing the abos? Chasing their women, I suppose?' asked Bert. The man laughed and walked back to his mates at the bar. 'I think we had better clean the opal soon and sell it.' John walked over to the bar and got four more beers. 'Bloody farmers, coming up and pinching our opal,' said one of the men with a wry smile. John couldn't really work out if the man was joking or having a shot at them.

'I reckon that we should get busy and clean the opal tomorrow. Everyone seems to know we have had a find,' said John as he came back to the table with the four beers. They didn't stay at the club for very long after their meal. The fact that most of the people in the club knew about the opal meant that most of the crooks about the town would know also.

The door of the dugout was open when they returned from the club.

There were marks where someone had forced the door with a round bar. 'Bloody hell, some prick has broken in.' The furniture inside of the dugout had been shifted around. Cupboard drawers were pulled out, and clothes had been tipped out of the suitcases on to the beds. Someone had scratched the paint on the safe room door but had not been able to open it. The fridge was open, and all the beer was missing, as well as a new unopened carton plus some food. 'God, what is that horrible smell?' said Bert sniffing, trying to determine from where the odour was coming. He looked behind the lounge chairs. ' Poo, some dirty bugger has crapped on the floor.'

The door of the opal room had been hit and prized at also. Something that the thieves did not realise was that the heavy door of the opal room was covered in a sheet of steel. It was a very unprofessional burglary job. 'I think we had better ring the cops.' The new dugout had the advantage of having a telephone. Bert rang the police.

The men made sure they didn't touch anything that had been moved. The police arrived within half an hour and checked the outside of the dugout for footprints with their torches. There were a few sets of bare-feet marks in the dusty dirt outside the dugout. Evidently who had broken in had not driven in to the dugout but had walked. 'They may have only walked up from the road,' the young officer said. When they checked the opal room door, the officers looked closely at the marks on the door, I reckon this was done by some young blokes who have just come to town. They use round reinforcing bar when they are noodling. See the round dents. The crap on the floor is one of their trademarks too.' He pointed to where the door had been interfered with. The men could see where the reinforcing bar had been bent. 'You're lucky they didn't have a proper jemmy bar. They would probably have got the door open.'

Tony went out, got a shovel out of their ute, gingerly picked up the smelly mess left by the burglars, then took it outside, and then dug a hole to bury it. He had thought about the Kelly's dogs rolling in it so he dragged a large piece of stone over the filled-in hole. He got some disinfectant from the laundry and then scrubbed the floor. The other men tidied the dugout up after the police had left and then went to bed.

The police rang the next morning just before Bert and Harry left for work to inform them that they were not the only dugout to be broken into in the area. There was a mob of young men who were in town. They had come down to Coober Pedy from past the Mintabie opal fields. The police said they were known troublemakers in their own community and had been kicked out by the elders of the community.

Bert and Harry went to work. They had offered to help to clean the opal, but John, in his normal pig-headed way, did not want to impose on their working time.

The opal was taken out of the drum, put into the concrete mixer drum in small lots, and then tumbled. When the opal was cleaned, they noticed that there was quite a bit more potch in the cleaned material than they thought there was. There was still a lot of good quality opal.   As the mixer turned and cleaned the next lot of opal, John and Tony sat and classed the potch from the opal, cutting the dead pieces of potch from the good opal with the tile cutters. The job took all day. They were still working on the opal when the Kelly's returned from work.   Bert looked at the opal under the bright lamp. 'It's a pity about all the potch, but the rest of the opal is still pretty good. Probably up to three thousand an ounce for the tops.' He shuffled through it with his horny old hands, turning the material over and over under the light. He would pick a particular piece out and hand it to Harry, who would hand it on. This was almost like a ritual amongst opal miners. No two pieces were ever the same.

John went to the supermarket to get some more beer and some groceries. He met a man who spent some time at the Italian Club. John asked if he knew of any halfway honest opal buyers in town. 'Hmm. There is one man from near Streaky Bay, who is in town at present. He makes a lot of triplets for the tourist-type trade,' Guy explained where the man lived. John offered to buy Guy a carton of beer if this man was OK.

John called into the man's house, which was quite easy to find. He knocked on the door. A woman answered the door and gave John the once-over. 'Yes, what are you looking for?'   'I was talking to a man called Guy. He said your husband is looking to buy some opal.' The woman walked out of the door, pulling it shut behind her. 'Follow me. Bob is down in the opal shed.' The shed behind the house had a steel door and bars on the window. There was a light coming from the window. The woman yelled out, 'Bob, there is someone who wants to sell a parcel of opal.' The door opened slightly, and then Bob took the security chain off and then opened the door. John introduced himself. The three

shook hands. Bob asked if John would like to see some triplets
being made.

Inside the shed, there were three large tables and an assortment of
opal saws and polishing machines. The tables had thin pieces of
black potch lined up on to which Bob was sticking thin slices of
opal with a clear epoxy glue. He then stuck a domed, clear glass
cap on top of the opal. The end result was a lot brighter stone as the
black enhanced the colour of the thin opal and the dome magnified
the material and scattered the colour. 'Do you mind if I finish this
job? I have all the glue mixed and don't want to waste it.' As he
worked, he explained the process of the triplet making. John was
very interested. John described the opal that they had found and
approximately what value they thought it would be.
Bob asked if they could bring the opal the next night.

Before leaving for work the next morning, they drove to Ivan's
workshop. Ivan proudly showed the two new ripping tools and the
four extra picks. The concept looked as if the picks would be a lot
easier to remove. The retaining pins and the removal tool were very
well built. John and Tony fitted the new tools which Ivan had
fabricated to the bulldozer. The performance in the hard sandstone
of the opal level was similar to the other pointed tipped tools. They
were hoping that changing tools was going to be far easier and
safer. John had nearly been hit by the heavy sledge hammer on one
occasion when the drift had shot out from the hammer head.

The Kelly's were still walking with Tony. There was the usual
good-natured banter as they turned the rocks and scratched. After
the dozer had ripped back and forth four times, the glass-breaking
noise was heard again. One part of the large rock was kicked up by
the ripper to reveal an edge of opal approximately two centimeters
thick. A brilliant green orange colour flashed as the sunlight hit it.
John had heard the noise through his earmuffs and stopped moving
and then turned on the seat. Just looking from the seat of the dozer,
he could see that this opal quality was superior to any other seam
opal that they had found. Tony had already set off to get the
buckets and sieves.

The rocks were being checked for opal and the barren rock discarded. There were two rocks close to a meter across, one which had been turned on its side and its adjoining mate. Tony came down the steep ramp and slid on a loose rock. He landed heavily on his behind. He very gingerly got up and walked over to the men and the new opal seam. 'Hell, my bum landed on a small round rock. It hurts like hell.' He squatted, got comfortable, and started to chip the opal off the rocks which Bert and Harry were tossing to him.

'Now you know why some of those TV wrestlers walk about on tiptoe after they have been lifted and jammed down on the other guy's knee.

You've hurt your coxic bone. It'll be sore for quite a while.' A large hole over two meters across had been excavated. This opal did not have the potch pieces in it that the other find had. It was a very clean material. 'Well, you have outdone yourselves today. This is the best yet other than the eggs.'

Finally, after three hours' chipping and sieving, the opal had all been removed from the rock and put into the buckets. I think I would like to go home now. My bum really hurts now.' Tony started to hobble carefully up the ramp of the cut, looking where he put his foot, in case he had another slide. Very carefully, he slid into the utility and slowly wriggled his bottom until he found a comfortable spot to sit. John had received a few of these bumps in the rear region when he had played football in his younger days. These were usually a payback for a black eye or some other sore wound he had given his opponent.

The opal was started to be tumbled in the concrete mixer. Bert and Harry were doing the work. Tony had had a very hot shower and was sitting in a padded chair with his pillow under his bum. It still hurt like hell, but the pain had abated a little after the shower.

John picked up the opal from the previous find and headed off to see Bob. Bob's wife opened the door. Bob yelled, 'Come in if you are good looking.' John walked in with the bag of opal. 'Sit down and have a cuppa coffee.' White with one,' said John as Bob's wife set three mugs on the table. Bob rose and picked up a desk

lamp from a box on the floor. He put it on the table and then turned
it on.

'Let's have a look at the opal.' John slipped the large plastic bag
over to Bob. The buyer sorted the opal into different grades and
then reached over and picked a set of balance scales from the box
where the light had been. The heaps of opal were weighed, and the
weights and numbers of each heap were noted on the pad. After
some more considering and adding on a calculator, Bob started to
write down the prices. 'What doe's $260,000 sound like?' This
was about the price they had been working on. So John agreed. The
men shook hands on the deal.
'Do you want more coffee?' asked Bob's wife. 'No thanks.' 'As
you probably realise, I haven't got that much money here at this
time. Would you take a bank cheque or do you want cash?' 'I can
have
the bank cheque tomorrow, or the cash will be here in three days.'

  John said he would wait for the three days. The opal heaps were
bagged up, and the numbers, weight, and price were written on
each bag. John took the opal and left for the dugout.

  Tony was feeling a bit better. He was walking slowly to try and
get some exercise to the affected part. 'How did you go? 'We have
got two hundred and sixty thousand dollars.' 'Shit, that's not a bad
price. I reckon we should see this guy, Harry,' said Bert.
  'I have been thinking about the dugout security. We don't want
any more unwelcome visitors in here. Seeing Tony has a sore bum
and would not be too good walking, we should clean our opal. I
will go and get a strong bolt and padlock for the door, as well as
some sheets of steel to cover it with, plus some builders reinforcing
mesh so we can make some guards to fit over the windows. We
could have a building day whilst the opal is tumbled.
  Bert and Harry returned with a sheet of builders mesh tied over
the top of the ute. There were new tools and fittings to complete the
job, plus
the sheet of steel for the door. He had also bought two other heavy
bolts to fix to the top and bottom of the opal room door. The
outside door was removed and planed down to allow the iron to be
bent around the edges of the door. Wood glue was smeared all over

the door, the iron fitted, and the edges of the iron carefully bent over the edges of the door, leaving the hinges and lock cut out. 'What about some paint to make it look better?' 'No, I like the look of the silver finish,' said Harry. The door was refitted, and then the bolt was screwed in place. It shone in the sunlight like a dull mirror. 'See I told you it would look OK.' The opal room was then fitted with the new bolts on the top and bottom of the door. The two like keyed padlocks left in the bolts without the bolts pushed in place.

The next project was to cut the mesh with an angle grinder to fit the windows. The edges were bent to make a box for each window; the box sections were screwed into place with some tabs which had been drilled.   The door and window protectors made the dugout entrance look a lot more secure. Bert had at least bought some galvanized paint which they had used before fitting the boxes.

The opal had been cleaned by the time they had finished. Tony had tried to help but had to admit that the sore bum was still giving him some serious problems. John rang Bob and asked if he would come and class the opal the next day. He agreed to come after lunch.

Tony did not want to come to the Italian Club because of his rear end problem. John called in to the bottle shop and bought a carton of beer for Guy on the way to the club. He was standing at the bar of the club, ordering a round of beers, when Guy walked over. 'How did you get on with the deal with Bob?' ' We did really well. I have a carton of beer in the ute for you.'
'You didn't have to do that.' Guy said showing embarrassment. 'Do you know how hard it is to find out about opal buyers? I think a carton of beer is very cheap.' Both men walked out as the beer was transferred from John's ute to Guy's car.   'I often wondered about that spot where you and the Kelly's found the opal. It's funny how everyone shoots through to a new find and leaves more money back where they came from. It's happened lots of times.'

When they arrived home Tony said that one of the Greek opal buyers had called. He was snooping around where the mixer was. Tony had walked out and asked what he was doing.   ' I have heard that the tumbler has been going a lot today. You must have found a lot of opal.' 'No, we have used it to do a bit of concrete work inside the dugout,' Tony lied. He had met this man before and did not like him. 'I think you have a big parcel of opal for sale. Let me have a look. I will give you top dollar for it.' 'We have not got any opal for sale.' 'Are you sure?' 'I'm sure, mate, and if you do not leave, I will let the dog out that lives inside. You would not want to meet him.' 'Ha, I don't hear no dog.' 'This dog does not bark. He bites. Now piss off.' The pushy Greek walked down to his car and drove off. 'I reckon that if you shot that crook, he would push his fingers into the bullet holes and keep talking.'

Bert and Harry had gone to work. Tony's affliction was improving, but he did not think he could walk behind the dozer yet. John had made some sandwiches, which they were eating when Bob knocked on the door.

Bob was studying the new additions to the security. 'Have you had some unwelcome visitors?' John explained about the break-in a few days before. That's why I have such a strong door and bars on my windows. I was broken in a few years ago and had sixty thousand dollars stolen. That was a bit more professional than the job you had done.' Bob walked into the dugout. He was carrying a parcel with him. 'I have been able to get your cash for you.' He handed the money over. Tony walked out with the opal from the recent find. John introduced the men. 'You had better go and get the other lot of opal from the safe as well. Bob has got the money.' John started to count the money as Bob had a quick look in one of the large bags of opal. John finished counting. 'Is all of the opal in these bags the same?' 'Yes, we have just randomly bagged it up, straight out of the tumbler.' John explained about the visitor that had been sneaking around the concrete mixer the night before.
'That man is a real con merchant. Never sell any opal to him. He would a be worse crook than the Dragon.'

It took Bob three hours to finally get the opal sorted out ready for sale. The bagging, weighing, and pricing were all finished. 'This is exceptionally good opal. There is not much difference between the top grade and the lower grade. The final price was totaled up on the calculator.

'Six hundred and eighty thousand dollars,' said Bob. 'Bert and Harry said it should be worth over a half a million,' said Tony. 'I cannot afford to buy a parcel like this,' said Bob. 'There is a Greek, Manuel who visits during the year, or two buyers in Adelaide I would recommend.' 'We have sold two lots to Achmed Farrah.' 'I would stick with him'. 'Yes, we are going to give him a call,' said John.

Bert and Harry arrived home. They were introduced to Bob. The men talked for about two hours on the state of the opal field, some of the crooked deals that had happened and also about a few men who had disappeared down some of the deep exploration mineshafts over the years. There was no need for lawyers and courts in this multicultural community. Some of the nationalities had their own way of dealing with thieves and pedophiles. Bob was very interesting to listen to. 'Hell, I had better go home. My missus will kill me. We are going out tonight.' Bob left with the opal he had bought. John phoned home and told Helen about the new sale and the valuation of the new find. She was very excited.

John phoned Achmed and also the patent attorney and made some appointments to see them on Monday. He was going to fly down to Adelaide on the Commercial Airline flight. Helen was flying to Adelaide to meet up with him.

Chapter twenty- four

Getting out of Australia

The black opal egg had been kept in the safe for two months. Ali had the habit of taking it out and admiring it every two or three days. The thought of phoning Achmed and asking him if he would buy the opal egg had crossed his mind, but there was the chance that Achmed would bring the police into the act worried Ali.

Business was very slow. Some Indian and Chinese buyers had moved into town and were not too worried where the opal they bought had come from
Even the lower echelon of the moonlighters like dirty Hargo had deserted Ali for the Chinese buyers. It was as if Ali had the mark of the devil on him. Ali was obsessed with making money. He had more than he would ever need, but the upbringing in poverty in the Philippines had tempered his resolve to get money at almost any price.

Ali spent a lot of time eating out at the Acropolis and Tom and Mary's restaurants trying to meet up with the potential sellers of cheap opal. Nick the Greek and a few others would come and talk to him during the night. Ali's claim to being popular in Coober Pedy had been his association with the popular Peter and Heidi when he had been married to Martha.

Ali had a lot of flash back memories of far better times when his life had been almost normal. The bitterness of the situation welled up in his chest on some occasions, almost taking his breath away.

By now Ali had acquired fifteen dugouts and houses in the town and would travel round on every Friday evening to collect the rent. Most of the tenants in the properties were of the Hargo and Silvio type of people. Ali occasionally bought small parcels of opal from these unprofessional thieves. He would take his dog on a choker collar as he visited the properties for protection.

The Acropolis was full of people, the noise of all of the nationalities trying to talk over each other was almost deafening. Nick came to Ali's table 'and sat down." Hey Ali I have some news for you". He leant over and started to whisper. "I heard a guy called Yargo and his mate talking about knocking your safe off. They had been selling you moonlighted opal and were not happy with the last deal that you did with them a few weeks ago. Do not tell anyone I told you. This is in confidence. Normally I would think this was bloody pub talk, but theses pair of bastards are really bad news. Yargo was responsible for the young Serbian guy falling down the shaft a month ago. The police did not do much of an investigation. They said it was an accident. His mate Nicola is in Coober Pedy for a reason. The cops down south would toss him in jail if he were there doing his usual monkey business. He was in jail for a long time over a home invasion where he pinched a lot of opal and money from a safe in a house in Adelaide. He had beaten up the man in the house and had threatened to kill one of his children.

Ali left the Acropolis and returned home. This was not good news. He sat thinking for quite a while as he patted Dogs head. "What would you do Dog. I think I should sell up and pack up and get out of Australia and go back to the Philippines". Ali started to empty the safe. There was nearly three million dollars in it. He rang Heidi and asked if he could put the money in her safe while he worked a few things out.

Heidi was in her nightie and dressing gown. She welcomed Ali and gave him a hug as he entered the door. She went off to make some coffee while Ali transferred the money to their now nearly empty safe. Heidi had been worried about the cash in her safe and had taken it to Adelaide and put it into a safe deposit box in a major bank.

Heidi and Ali talked long into the night about his plan to leave Australia. She felt sorry as Ali was the last link to Martha and Peter. "Why don't you go on a cruise to Europe and see the people you knew before you came to Australia. Get out of Coober Pedy and enjoy the rest of your life travelling". Heidi had not thought of this, she was just in a rut of doing her everyday chores. "You are right Ali, The only real thing to hold me here is that Peter is buried here" She poured the coffee and added the milk, "I have a feeling that this is what Peter would want. I have a lot of money which you both earned with the mining". Ali sipped the hot coffee. "I am going to sell up and return to the Philippines and work with a friend, if he will have me. I will phone him tomorrow and ask."

The only remaining things in the safe were the Black opal egg and fifty thousand dollars of capital to work with in case any deals with the moonlighters came about.

In the morning Ali phoned Enrico in the Philippines. Enrico was pleased to hear from Ali and was more than keen to have Ali back in his town to start to work with him. Business was good. Ali was thinking while he was talking to Enrico and came up with a plan. He did not want to be anywhere near Manilla.

People in the drug trade have long memories. He was not going back to be caught by one of the cartels and taken for a swim at the wharf. Too many people knew him in that city. If he could get to Cairns and catch another timber boat to Enrico's town, this might be the way around a lot of problems. Customs were not so vigilant in the smaller ports. There was no need to be anywhere near Manilla.

There was a lot of thinking to do regarding as to how to get the cash and black opal egg into the Philippines. Some sort of box or other object to hide the cash in which looked legitimate. A brainwave came to him; he would paint the egg grey and have it classed as a fossilized dinosaur egg. He would put the money in a strong suitcase with some clothes on the top of the money. The money weight was around thirty kilograms. The suitcase had a distinctive logo painted on for personal identification, also to make it less likely to be taken by mistake.

The dugouts were a minor concern. He would not try to sell these as the total price for all of the dugouts would be about twenty thousand dollars. He definitely did not want to advertise that he was leaving Coober Pedy; this would alert the local crooks that he was going to be moving with a large stash of cash. There was the matter of Dog. Ali was sure that Heidi would take him. Dog was well behaved in Heidi's company and would be a deterrent for unwanted visitors.

After two days of organization Ali took Dog to Heidi's house in the evening the packed the suitcase with the money. They had dinner together. Ali offered to let Heidi find some person to collect the money from the dugouts. Heidi was saddened by Ali's decision but as there was the threat of problems with him staying in Coober Pedy, she could see his reasoning.

Ali stayed at Heidi's dugout that night. He was in Martha's room, there were still a lot of Martha's clothes and the trinkets from when she and Ali were first married. Ali had trouble sleeping. He had a real tightness in his chest when he looked at the pieces of jewellery and ornaments. How different life had been those few months before. He felt Martha's presence with him all of the night.

The patrol had been packed and filled with fuel. Three jerry cans of extra petrol were in the back.

Ali left at dawn after loading the suitcase and carry bag with the now "fossil "egg which had now been painted grey and other small items. He had booked and paid for the flights to Cairns.

Ali called at a car dealership in Adelaide and after some bickering about price finally sold the Patrol to the used car dealer. The Patrol held a lot of memories of the good times when he and Zeena had travelled through Australia. There were also the trips with Martha around Coober Pedy and out in the bush having a picnic lunch, them making love on the rug trying to make babies.

Ali had the dealer call a taxi to take him to the airport to catch the flight up to Cairns.

During the flight to Cairns Ali fully realised what a vast country Australia was.

The plane finally landed in Cairns. Ali collected the suitcase. He then found a cab to take him to one of the better class hotels. He took the suitcase to his room, the removed some of the clothes, then placed the well wrapped egg into the case, he returned to the lobby and asked if the case could be put into the safe. He had important documents inside he told the person on the desk.

There were freighters at the wharf as Ali walked along he noticed the shape of the Wandana. It had the cranes swinging logs onto the waiting trucks. Ali walked up the gang plank. Peter Fitzgerald was overseeing some work to a broken winch. He looked up, a hint of recognition showed in his eyes. "You came over from the Philippines with us a few years ago? You had your mother with you". "Yes, I would like to book a passage back to the Philippines. "Yair I can arrange that, just come to my office in about an hour when I finally get this mess cleaned up." Ali wandered off down the wharf to a small café and ordered a cup of coffee. When he returned to the ship he went to Peter's cabin. Peter was just scrubbing the grease from the winch off his hands.

"Well how did you get on in Australia" I worked opal mining at Coober Pedy". "Geez that would have been interesting. " Ali recounted some of the story about finding opal ,Zeena getting married then having died of cancer . He told of the accident where Martha was killed and his friend and partner had died of the heart attack. He left out the main part of the story. "I just feel that there are too many bad memories in Coober Pedy and Australia. I have sent some cash to a friend in the Philippines. I should be able to live comfortably the rest of my life there. The boat would be leaving in four days, if all went well with the unloading of the timber. He paid the fare.

Ali spent some time on the ship helping get the timber unloaded. He reacquainted himself with Pedro and the rest of the crew. Two of the crew from four years ago had left and two more had taken their place. Ali bought his luggage onto the ship and moved into the cabin, two days before leaving.

The customs guy came around to check Ali's papers and to inspect the luggage. Ali had cunningly secreted to cash under the mattress of the bed. "You should not really have come aboard mate, before I checked your luggage". "I was only sitting around doing nothing so I thought I would give the guys an extra hand." The man searched Ali's case and found the now grey opal egg. "What is this". "A mate gave me this at Coober Pedy, they found a nest of fossil dinosaur eggs", "What would that be worth "the man raised his eyebrows. "Not as much as you would think. He got five hundred bucks for the other two". "She's right mate.   You have been here a long time" "Yes I was married to an Aussie girl at Coober Pedy". Ali searched and found the marriage certificate in his papers. The guy just glanced at the paper." My wife was killed in a car accident in Coober Pedy", the man signed the papers then stamped them. "Sorry to hear about that mate'. He shook Ali's hand then left.

The routine of the trip and the seemingly endless work on the rust and other jobs made the days pass easily. Ali and the first mate talked into the night each night, Ali told some of the stories of the shonky business at Coober Pedy and what some of the characters had gotten up to.

Five days out in to the journey Peter talked to the mate and Ali about a cyclone which was brewing up not far from their course. "Looks as if we will have to batten down the hatches and secure all of the loose objects. We are going to be in for some really shit weather. He tapped the barometer on the wall of his cabin, the needle moved alarmingly toward the storm written on the dial. "Have you ever been in a storm at sea", asked Peter. Ali was very worried about the prospects of the impending cyclone. "No I haven't.". " Well Ali, this is where men are made into sailors".

The ship was heaving from end to end. then rolling frantically as if trying to squirm its way from the crashing waves. Ali was trying to lie in the bunk with the lee sheets tied up to stop him from falling out he had already been sick into a bucket. This had since shot across the cabin floor and had upended and now was rolling crazily across the floor in tune to the heaving of the ship   He had sat the egg in the top of the wash basin wrapped in newspaper to stop it rolling. He undid a corner of the lee sheet on the bunk to get out enough to spew in the basin. At this time the ship hit a huge wave and slid sideways down it tossing Ali out of the bunk. He flew across the cabin and hit his head on a bulkhead, knocking him senseless. The egg rolled out of its paper wrapping and dropped onto the cantered steel floor and skidded into the wall near Ali. The now painted shell cracked in half, some slimy goo seeped out, and a long thin slimy creature slid out and shuddered as it took its first breath of air.

The end